Xavier Wallace

SHAW CONFRONTATION

Xavier Wallace

Xavier Wallace was born and raised in regional New South Wales, Australia. He attended public primary and high schools, before studying business at the University of Newcastle. He worked in Canberra for the Australian Government in both the public service and politics for over a decade. He has a Master of Politics and Public Policy from Deakin University. Xavier's interests include politics, government, national security, media and communications, philosophy, ancient history and mythology. He is an advocate for equality and human rights, including LGBTI+ rights. Live music, thriller novels and action movies occupy his time outside writing and work. He loves spending time with his family and friends, and his groodle, Atlas.

Xavier Wallace is the author of the Max Shaw spy thriller series.

Dedication

For Nikki.

Acknowledgements

Every once in a while, you meet someone who just makes you smile. No matter how bad your day is or how long you go between catch ups. No matter the time or place you find yourself in life. This person will always be there to laugh with you, cry with you or just share life with you.

About twenty years ago, while at university, I met my best friend and true soulmate – Nikki.

Never has the world known a truer free spirit or fun-loving woman. Nikki is living her best life, chasing an (almost) endless summer and following her dreams. She managed to escape the grip of the dreary office with its seemingly endless cycle of nine-to-five under the flickering neon lights. Nikki has explored the world far and wide as a freelance journalist and small businesswoman, and she serves as both a mentor and a constant inspiration to me.

Nikki is helping people find themselves, shake off any pre-set notions of how they should act and live, and take a path towards aligned living. It's a journey I'm currently on and have been on since I met her, and it's a path which has led me to chase my dreams, including writing these novels – and I'm forever grateful.

Since the first publication, Nikki has married the wonderful, Chase, and the pair have two gorgeous kids.

This novel is dedicated to you, Nikki, to say thank you for your unwavering love, friendship and support. We may be on opposite sides of the world, but I know you are always there for me – as I am for you.

I love you.

Miss your face x

The Max Shaw Spy Thriller Series

Shaw Vengeance
Shaw Initiation
Shaw Confrontation
Shaw Intervention
Shaw Reclamation
Shaw Salvation

SHAW CONFRONTATION

By Xavier Wallace

Third Novel of the Max Shaw Spy Thriller Series.

Prelude

The large heavy steel door slid to the right with a soft metallic scrap as she pulled her hand back from the biometric palm reader which sat next to the door. She walked into the cavernous space, her heals clicking on the gleaming white tiles with each step. The walls were covered in the same white tiles and the roof was painted in a fresh white. The harsh neon lights bounced off the white surfaces giving the space a stark, bright and sterile feel.

Two men were waiting in the centre of the room next to three stainless steel tables. A third man was walking toward the woman. All three men were wearing white lab coats over white business shirts and black trousers. Their polished black boots shined under the neon lights.

"Ma'am," the man said stopping in front of the woman and standing at attention.

"At ease," she said dismissively, focusing on her surroundings, rather than the man himself.

"Ma'am, the devices are ready. Would you like to see them?"

"That is why I am here."

"Please follow me," he said leading her down the sterile room.

The lead scientist led the short woman towards the stainless-steel tables. She was wearing an expensive navy suit, more blue than black. Her yellow blouse matched her yellow broch and high heal shoes. She was a bigger woman, but quite beautiful, and she commanded an air of respect and strength which drew people to her. Power she had found was alluring and she used that to her advantage every day.

"The three devices are ready to be deployed at your command, ma'am," the scientist said with an enthusiastic grin which almost begged for praise. "You will see here they have been completely overhauled. New steel suitcases with a fine leather wrap to ensure they blend into their surroundings. The internal mechanisms have all been replaced with new stainless-steel gears and state-of-the-art electronics."

"The triggers, how do they work?" she questioned as she ran a hand along the top of the steel briefcase.

"There are three ways to set off the devices, a timer, a remote app from the matching mobile devices currently sitting in the briefcases or by trying to disarm the device in the wrong sequence."

"And the material?"

"The cylinder holding the fusion material is from the original Soviet devices that The Sixteen provided us. How did you come across them?"

"Our reach is far and our hands never idle, but it's not important. What is important is where it leads. What I need to know is if these devices will lead any investigations back to the Russians?" she said finally looking him in the eyes.

"Yes, ma'am," he said in a reassuring tone. "All of the components, everything from the fusion material to the new gears, have been sourced from Russia. The evidence will point to Soviet era weapons which have fallen into the hands of terrorists. The Arabs will take the blame for the attacks or the Russians will, whoever you and The Sixteen decide to pin this on. It will never come back to us."

"Excellent work gentlemen," she said retrieving her mobile phone from her bag. "I am pleased with your work, and I look forward to sharing you progress and success with The Sixteen."

"Thank you, ma'am," the scientist said excitedly, turning to nod congratulations to his peers. "To have your acknowledgement is a real honour to us."

"Yes, I am sure it is," she said dismissively before raising her phone. "It is me, please send them in."

The heavy steel door slid to the side again and three man dressed in black suits walked into the room. They were members of her security team. Each man was tall, fit and muscular. They looked like former soldiers who traded their camouflaged uniforms for black suits, but kept the gruff and dominating physiques.

"Ma'am," the lead agent said standing straight like he had so many times to indicate respect for a commanding officer.

"Retrieve the devices and clean up, will you?" she said turning back towards the door still looking at her phone.

"Yes, ma'am," the agent said focusing his attention on the scientists.

The three agents drew their pistols and each shot a scientist at point blank range. Their bodies crumpled to the floor, their blood spilling down and staining the white tiles as the security men walked over to the stainless-steel tables. Each man shut a briefcase, handcuffed it to their wrists and followed the woman out of the laboratory-style bunker, leaving the dead scientists in pools of their own blood.

As she climbed into the back of her waiting Rolls Royce, the short woman retrieved her phone and dialled a stored number.

"Robert, it's me," she said.

"Ma'am," Robert said. *"What can I do for you?"*

"I have the devices, they will be shipped this afternoon."

"Excellent. I have made the arrangements for the diplomatic cartons to be delivered this morning."

"Good, we need two of those boxes to get the devices out of the country and into to the target locations. The diplomatic tags will ensure they are not searched at the airports. They are crucial."

"They will be on site within the hour. Your team have been given instructions for their handovers. Will you bring the third device with you?"

"Yes. Thank you, Robert. You have exceeded my expectations and I know The Sixteen will be pleased to hear our plans are coming together."

"Yes, ma'am, our reach is far and our hands never idle."

"Our reach is far and our hands never idle."

"Is there anything else I can help you with?"

"Yes, we need to start the process for electing a new Knight. After Shadow's death we are one member down and now we are moving into the final stage, we need a full table."

"I agree. I will make the arrangements."

"Good. I would very much like to meet the candidates. As you know, we have significant work to do in these final phases, but more importantly, when this is all done our workload will dramatically increase. Within the week we will change the world and the course of history, and it will be up to us to shape it."

"Yes, ma'am," Robert said with excitement in his voice. *"Your leadership has been without comparison or rival. You will change the world and be forever written into history."*

"I appreciate you saying that. I could not take these horrific, but necessary, steps without your support and the support of The Sixteen. I thank you all, but I do not need to tell you of the importance of our mission. You all need to continue to take whatever steps you feel are necessary to ensure we are not interrupted or stopped from achieving our dreams."

"Yes, ma'am, I have already taken some steps to ensure our success. I have put all our teams on high-alert and I have given our friends in Rome the evidence they need to cause some disruptions for the Australian Intelligence Service. They seem to be the only ones really focused on us at this stage. Our plans should be carried out before they get any closers, but I have taken some action to slow down their progress."

"Good. Greg Lloyd, the Shadow, underestimated them," she said with pure distain for his failure. "We will not make the same mistake."

"No, ma'am. Prince and his team will be taken care of."

"Good. Thank you, Robert," she said ending the call.

She smiled as her big luxury sedan pulled out of the driveway. She had waited a lifetime for this moment. No one would take it from her. No one.

Chapter One

He walked up the small, narrow staircase leading to the deck of the private yacht they had rented for the week. It had an immaculate, shining white roof which doubled as the deck. The hull was solid wood which had been painstakingly sanded and smoothed with precision and lacquered with a dark stain. The maroon and white sails were rolled in tight after being stored for the night. It was gently rocking on the swell and there were soft splashing sounds as the little boat rose and fell on the water. A light breeze was rattling the stainless steel and chrome rigging, and the ropes were pulling slightly and slapping gently against the deck. It was a large yacht with a full kitchen, four bedrooms with ensuites and a small entertaining area below deck. A second dining and entertainment area was available for guests on the deck itself. It was normally booked out by room, but they had rented the whole yacht for privacy. Just the two couples and three crew who mostly kept to themselves.

The morning sun embraced him warmly as it moved its way down his bearded face to his pecks and chiselled abs as he climbed the steps and walked out onto the deck. He flexed and stretched his back and rolled his shoulders bringing his six foot three frame to life after sleeping awkwardly in their little bed downstairs. He had a small scar on his left arm near his shoulder from a bullet wound and a couple of fading scars from previous injuries running on an angle above his ribs on his righthand side. He was wearing a pair of pink boardshorts and his favourite Oakley sunglasses as he padded silently across the deck barefooted.

Max "Prince" Shaw was an agent with the Australian Intelligence Service, known as AIS. He was fit, handsome and intelligent, and a highly trained spy. After months hunting down leads, assassinating and arresting targets, and suffering the effects of a reopened emotional trauma, his superiors had decided to send him on a break to recuperate. He had let his beard grow and his hair was getting longer too. He did not look like the polished professional he used to be, instead he looked a bit unkept and scruffy. More hipster, than office worker. More spartan, than public servant.

He took a moment to look around at the beautiful view of the coastline. The water was aqua-blue and although they were anchored hundreds of metres offshore the crystal-clear water let Max see right to the ocean floor. He saw fish of various shapes and sizes dancing in and out of the seaweed, and the white pebbly sand of the seabed. Sea-cucumbers and other marine life danced on the seabed. He traced the sunlight shimmying on the water's surface to the white sandy beaches off in the distance where he could just make out the tourists and locals alike moving in to enjoy the warm summer's day. It would not be long before the narrow beach was packed with tourists all vying for position to enjoy their European summer holidays.

Max reached the bow and found his blond companion sunbaking in a small light blue boyleg swimsuit. He dropped down into a push-up position placing his hands either side of the blond's handsome face, lowered himself down slowly and kissed him gently, upside down.

"Good morning," Sam said smiling broadly without opening his eyes. "You know, I think this is the first morning I can remember where you haven't woken at five."

"I think you're right," Max said. "First time I can remember in a long time."

"Good. It means you are relaxing and unwinding. You need the break. I'm so glad we did this."

"Yeah you might be right. I'm glad too."

Max did a push up and swung his big frame athletically around to lay next to Sam. Sam Walker was five feet eleven inches tall and had a perfect v-shaped torso from hours of surfing the break at Bondi Beach. His shoulder length surfer blond hair was tied in a loose bun behind his head and his strong chin and defined cheek bones were covered in several days' worth of sandy beard. They had met several months earlier at a bar in Sydney and had been through a great deal together. After a difficult period where Max was away for great lengths of time for work, he and Sam tried to work out what their relationship would look like into the future. They knew they both cared for each other, but things just were not clicking, they could not find their rhythm. They had decided to head overseas for a holiday to get away from it all and see what could happen when Max was not rushing off on some new mission.

"Where are the others, they haven't surfaced yet?" Max asked looking around the deck.

"No, I haven't seen anyone this morning," Sam said rolling onto his side to face Max. "But I'm not surprised, you all drank a fair bit last night. What time did you end up coming to bed?"

"Oh God, I'm not sure. Flash just kept turning up with more drinks," Max said rubbing his stomach as if it would cure his handover.

"Well, I think you both needed to unload and talk the night away, and after everything that has been happening, it's good you can get a break. You both need it, you've had permanent bags under your eyes for months and Flash isn't much better."

"I'll tell him you said that," Max laughed. "But, you're right, it's been a crazy few months. I'm sorry I haven't been able to spend much time with you."

"It's okay, Max. I get it. You have a lot on your plate and I don't have to imagine what you have to do in your line of work, I experienced some of it firsthand. That's why I want to be there for you, to support you, to show you that no matter what happens out there, you always have someone to come home to. I know your job will always be competing hard for your attention, but I also know how important it is for you to do what you do and I don't think you could ever walk away from it, even if that's what I wanted."

"Thanks, Sam," Max said rolling on his side to look Sam in the eyes. "I'm glad you understand, but I'm still sorry I can't be the boyfriend you deserve."

"Max," Sam said resting his hand on Max's arm. "You are an amazing guy and I have fallen for you. I love you exactly the way you are. I want to spend more time with you, but you wouldn't be you, if you weren't out saving the world. But, maybe every now and then, you can let someone else handle it, so we can be together. I love you and I want to be with you."

Max was about to reply, but Sam pulled him closer and they kissed passionately and made love in the morning sunlight on the bow of the yacht, before jumping into the Mediterranean for an early morning swim.

As the couple climbed back onboard, Flash and his wife, Jane, emerged from below deck followed by a crew member carrying a tray of fruit, croissants, juice and coffee. Jacob "Flash" Gordon was Max's best friend and his partner at AIS. They had trained together at the secret AIS base in Western New South Wales, known as the Wool Shed, where they had first met. They had been partners and conducted hundreds of missions side-by-side since. Max had in fact saved Flash's life after he was shot in the neck on their very first mission. Ignoring his orders, Max tendered to his friend's wounds instead of chasing a target, which had upset his superiors. He did not care, his friend's life mattered more than the rules.

Max and Flash had each other's back in work and in life. They were the same age and similar in many ways, including similar builds, although Flash was not as solid as Max, he was leaner. Even though Flash was lefthanded, they had similar fighting styles and techniques which came from training and fighting together, and they were fairly-evenly matched in combat and weapons skills. Flash had started losing his hair a few years ago, so shaved it close giving him a rugged, tough guy look, but he was a gentle giant, unless you pissed him off. Max was best man when Flash married Jane after the two were introduced by Lachlan, Max's fiancé.

"Morning boys," Jane said watching them climb back onto the yacht. "Up early, how's the water?"

"Morning," Sam said reaching for a towel. "It's beautiful. You should jump in."

"I think I might need to, to wake up and wash away my hangover."

Max took the coffee plunger and two mugs from the crewmember who had stopped to offer him the tray as Sam and Jane headed to a little table towards the back of the yacht with the waiter in tow, chatting full speed, like long-lost friends. Max handed Flash a mug and proceeded to fill both to the top before resting the plunger on roof of the yacht above the stairs. They both took a sip of the strong black coffee and grimaced as the bitter brew went to work waking them from a red wine and beer haze.

"How are you feeling?" Max asked turning to Flash.

"I've been better," Flash said massaging his forehead. "But, I'm sure this coffee will help."

"It should, it's strong enough. Bloody hell."

"Yeah, it is," Flash said taking another sip and grimacing.

"Thanks for the chat last night," Max said looking over towards the beach.

"It was good to talk, Max. It's been a while since we've been able to just hangout away from work."

"Yeah, we've had a big run hunting down Shadow's associates. There can't be too many more surely?" Max questioned turning back to Flash.

Greg "Shadow" Lloyd had been one of their superiors at the Australia Intelligence Service. He was a traitor hiding in plain sight, at the top of Australia's chief spy agency, working as part of a group they were coming to know as The Sixteen. Lloyd was the mastermind of a series of terrorist attacks which six months earlier had claimed the lives of almost one thousand innocent Australians. The attacks did irreparable damage to the Commonwealth Government Building in the Sydney central business district which was due to be finally demolished in the coming weeks. The attacks also did millions of dollars damage to the iconic Melbourne Cricket Ground and Rod Laver Arena which were only now starting to be repaired following months of investigation and political squabbling. They also left a permanent scar on Australia's normally unwavering psyche as the nation recalled the assassinations of a number of high-profile politicians when the Australian Parliament was overrun by a group of terrorists. The country had retreated into itself.

The Prime Minister Edward Kirby and his Government had spent six months ramming tougher intelligence, police, military and counter-terrorism legislation through the hastily refurbished and upgraded Parliament. The legislation removed some liberties and freedoms previously taken for granted by the Australian people, but they felt safer, so they did not seem to mind the new impositions. The Government had also purchased significant new and second-hand military equipment in the largest peacetime expansion of the country's defences in history, and they were rolling out new surveillance equipment and tools across the country. All in the name of protection and security. The Australian Prime Minister was in London for a series of meetings including the Commonwealth Heads of Government Meeting or CHOGM, as it is known, where he intended to share Australia's recent terrorism laws and experiences with the other heads of Commonwealth nations. He planned to encourage the Commonwealth leaders to adopt similar laws to increase their safety and the strength of the Commonwealth.

Max knew the new laws and tools helped him achieve results, but he was worried about the path the country was taking. In moments of reflection, he wondered if they had gone too far, but the truth was he was operating in a daze of semi-consciousness. Lloyd had not only terrorised the people of Australia, he had also ripped open an emotional wound in Max that had not healed when he was forced to relive the brutal murder of his fiancé, Lachlan. Lloyd had captured Sam taking him to the same warehouse where Lachlan had died in Max's arms only a few years earlier. Max, Flash and their team eventually rescued Sam, and Max killed Lloyd when he learned he had been responsible for Lachlan's murder. Ironically, Lloyd had killed Lachlan in an attempt to break Max, but instead it gave him an unwavering drive for vengeance and an unshakeable desire to put The Sixteen and all terrorists out of business. The saga had taken a toll on Max, but Sam had been there to help him through it. For the past six months, Max and his team had been hunting Lloyd's co-conspirators in a network which had spread across the globe.

"I think the Irish guy we captured last month brought the tally up to twelve we have arrested or killed since you took out Lloyd," Flash said. "But, every time we take one out, we seem to find more."

"Yeah, you're right," Max said. "I wonder how far The Sixteen's reach spreads, I mean we've taken down twelve, but I'm not sure they were big players, other than Lloyd?"

"We don't have to worry about it now, let's just enjoy our time with Sam and Jane. God knows we've earnt a break," Flash said patting Max on the shoulder.

"He told me he loved me this morning," Max said taking a sip of his coffee.

"Oh right and what did you say?"

"I didn't get the chance. He kissed me then we got a bit carried away up the front of the boat before we went for a swim."

"Well I'm glad we didn't venture up here before we did," Flash said laughing and patting Max a couple of times on the shoulder. "Do you love him?"

"I do, Flash, but," Max said trailing off in his thoughts.

"He's not Lachlan?"

"That's part of it, but I honestly just don't know. We have been fighting a lot, because I haven't been there. I feel guilty."

"You have been through so much Max, more than most people could handle. Lachlan would want you to find happiness, but as I said last night, you don't have to rush anything. If it's meant to be, it will be."

"Thanks, Flash," Max said looking down at the deck lost in thought.

"Come on," Flash said putting his arm around Max. "Let's go have some breakfast, we don't need to solve all our problems in twenty-four hours."

They walked over to join Sam and Jane who were talking about heading over to the city for the day to go shopping and enjoying their breakfast.

"Ah, here they are," Jane said. "We were just figuring out what to do for the day. We thought we might go shopping. Any thoughts?"

"That could be fun," Flash said as he cut open his croissant. "We could go find a couple of new Italian suits for work, Max, never know when you'll need to look the part. Maybe even get a haircut and trim that beard."

Max raised an eyebrow, but dismissed the comment without a word. He knew he had let his looks go a bit over the previous months, but he hadn't felt the need to tidy it up for some reason. As for the suits, a large number of AIS agents were embedded in regular jobs around the world covertly gathering intelligence and undertaking missions for AIS. Max's former cover role had been working for the Defence Minister James Johnston who had turned out to be helping Lloyd. He was now in a maximum-security prison awaiting trial for treason, mass murder, and planning and conducting terrorist attacks on Australian soil. Max had not taken on a new cover role, instead he and Flash had moved into AIS as full-time agents.

"Well, now I don't work at Parliament I don't get to wear suits that often," Max said slicing some fruit. "But, I could always use a new suit for special occasions."

"You should buy a couple," Sam said. "You wrecked the last one when you were in Adelaide."

"Oh, that's right," Max said taking a mouthful of fresh mango.

"We were talking about capturing the Irish guy a minute ago, he was an arsehole that bloke!" Flash exclaimed.

Flash was interrupted by a crew member who walked up to their table holding out a satellite phone.

"Agent Shaw, it's General Scott," the crew member said passing Max the phone.

"Good morning, Hulk," Max said looking around his table at the various faces each of his companions were pulling on hearing their boss's name.

Patrick "Hulk" Scott was Max's boss and the Head of the Australian Intelligence Service. He was a hard-line former Special Air Service General who had risen through the ranks because of his mastery of intelligence collection and counter-intelligence techniques. He got his nickname for obvious reasons, given his often-angry disposition and the fact he was built like a mountain and tough as stone. According to his former Army mates, he was also allegedly impossible to kill. Hulk had recruited Max when he was studying at university, trained him at the Wool Shed and he had mentored him throughout his career. Max had also saved Hulk's life when he had been captured and tortured by terrorists several years ago. Since then their bond had been unshakable.

Sam and Jane looked unimpressed that their long overdue holiday was being interrupted so early in the trip by AIS, while Flash looked inquisitively at Max wondering what the phone call was about.

"Prince," Hulk said in a soft and repentant tone. *"I'm sorry kid, but I need you to come back to work early. Hermes has found new lead and we think this one will finally lead us to the last of Lloyd's co-conspirators."*

"Okay, Hulk," Max agreed without dispute. "Anything you can tell me over the phone?"

"No, the line's not secure. Alpha is on her way to collect you and Flash. She will fill you in on route."

"ETA?"

"She's in a bird about twenty minutes out. Load up."

"Ack. We'll be ready," Max said looking to Flash who knew instantly they were no longer on holiday.

"Thanks kid, I will speak to you when you arrive."

"Understood," Max said putting the phone down on the table and looking at his friends.

"What is it, Max?" Sam asked.

"I'm sorry guys, Flash and I have to go to work," Max said gingerly, looking to Sam.

"That's annoying," Jane said. "We've only been here a day. Can't they get someone else?"

"Sorry Jane, I'll make it up to you, I promise," Flash said placing his hand on the side of her face before turning to Max. "Where are we headed, Max?"

"I'm not sure," Max said. "Kate is on her way, she will be here in twenty minutes."

"Right, well, we better get ready."

"Yeah," Max said as he and Flash stood to get ready. "Sorry, Sam. Sorry, Jane."

Sam followed Max below deck to their room. It was a small white room with maroon curtains and bedding which matched the sails. Max placed his overnight bag on the bed and started loading clothes, toiletries and essentials. He stripped off his boardshorts and underwear and jumped into the little shower in their ensuite. Sam walked over and lent against the door of the bathroom watching him shower.

"Jane's right, why can't someone else do it?" Sam asked angrily. "We only just got here. You haven't had a break in months. They are going to kill you working you like this."

"I'm sorry, Sam," Max said as he washed his hair and bread. "But, it's the job."

"The job. It's always the job. I just wish you didn't have to go."

"I know, Sam," Max said rinsing off the soap. "I wish I didn't either, but hopefully this will be the last time for a while, then I promise we can take some time away without interruption."

"That would be nice. Not just for us, but for you Max. I haven't said anything, but I can see it's getting to you."

"What do you mean?"

"The beard for one. You look like you've let yourself go and I'm worried you might be depressed."

"I just haven't had time to worry about a haircut," Max lied as he continued to shower without looking at Sam.

"I'm just worried about you. Please promise me you will be careful."

Max stood under the water for a moment, thinking about what Sam had said. He opened the door of the shower and waved Sam over.

"I will be careful and I promise I'll get a haircut and trim when I get back," Max said before grabbing Sam and pulling him into the shower. "I'm sorry to put you through all of this, you didn't ask for it."

"I'm sorry I have been putting so much pressure on you. I know what you have been through and I should be more understanding. I just worry about you. Worry you might be slipping away and losing yourself in your work."

Max did not reply, he just held Sam in his arms under the running water. After a few minutes, they got out, dried and got ready, without saying another word. Max dressed into a pair of cream chinos, brown R.M. Williams boots and a navy linen shirt which he rolled up the sleeves on to his elbows. Back in the bathroom, he stole a glance at his reflection in the mirror. Sam and Flash were right, he had let himself go. He took a moment to brush and pull back his hair into a small topknot. He combed his beard and ran some oil through it to soften and control it a bit. *That'll* do, he thought to himself. He walked back into the room and put his glasses on his head, before retrieving his two rings and mobile phone from the charging pad next to their bed. He tossed the changer into his bag and walked over to the cupboard. He entered two four-digit codes into the small safe in the closet and took out his passport, a bundle of Euros, his silenced pistol and his hunting knife, before clicking the safe shut.

Sam had noticed how Max had cleaned up, but did not want to rub it in, so he walked with Max back up onto the deck in silence. Flash and Jane were hugging on the bow. Max noticed the crew had lowered the mast and folded away the sails, opening up the space above the yacht. The same crew member who had brought Max the satellite phone earlier approached.

"Agent Shaw, Hermes has asked me to remain behind with Mr Walker and Mrs Gordon. They will be safe and we'll meet up with you following your mission," the crewmember said with a tone of respect for his superior.

"Thank you," Max said acknowledging his AIS colleague who had been embedded in the crew for this very reason. "I'll let you know how we go and where we can meet up."

"Yes, sir," the undercover agent said as Flash nodded his thanks. "Agent Matthews is about two minutes out."

"Thanks, mate," Max said in a friendly way which treated the crewmember as an equal, not a subordinate, he hated hierarchy.

The couples said their goodbyes as the sound of an approaching helicopter filled the air. The chopper was a dark navy blue with white strips running from the doors to the tail. It moved in above the yacht and its side door slid open before a rope ladder dropped from the side, unfolding down to the deck in front of Max.

"See you soon," Max said kissing Sam.

"Be careful," Sam said with worry in his voice. "Come back in one piece."

Max nodded and squeezed Sam's hand, before turning and following Flash up the ladder to the helicopter. At the top, he threw his bag inside next to Flash's and hauled himself up into the cabin. Flash and Max both took seats in the rear as their colleague Jonnie "Bravo" Bellucci pulled in the ladder. They waved down to Sam and Jane, as their pilot Kate "Alpha" Matthews swung the big chopper around and headed back in the direction from which she had approached.

Chapter Two

Max and Flash put on their headsets as Jonnie climbed over into the cockpit with Kate. The helicopter was a repurposed former army chopper which the AIS had loaned from the MI6. It had a musky smell from years of carrying sweaty troops as well as a copper taste in the air of metal, ammunition, fuel and oil. The seats were a standard hard leather which felt more like plastic and was worn in some places back to the fabric lining and foam inserts. It was decked out with supplies from guns and munitions to medical kits and ration packs.

"Welcome onboard Alpha Fucking Airways boys," Kate said turning back briefly to look at Max and Flash. "I will be your captain for today's short journey across to Rome and Butt-lick Bravo here will be the first officer come flight attendant. If there is anything we can do to make your journey more comfortable feel free to ask him, 'cause I'm fucking busy keeping this old bird in the air."

"Good to see you both," Max said smiling and adjusting his headset's microphone. "It's a pleasure to be onboard, captain. What are today's meal options?"

"We have sweet fuck-all to offer and sadly there'll be no fucking movies either."

"Damn," Flash laughed into the microphone. "Well, why don't you tell us what we are doing here instead?"

"Yeah sorry we had to wreck your trip boys," Kate said genuinely sorry for her friends. "I hope Jane and Sam understand. Hopefully we'll have you back in a day or two. They can go shopping and spend all your money while you're gone."

"Yeah, thanks for that thought," Flash said rolling his eyes. "I'm sure the credit card will be punished for this interruption in our trip."

"Oh, you'll be right, Flash, I'm sure you've got heaps of cash."

"If only."

"Bravo, read them in, will you?" Kate asked laughing at Flash.

"Sure," Jonnie said eagerly. "I've been in Italy for three days following up on a lead we recovered from Lloyd's files. We have verified the contents with the Irishman you picked up in Adelaide. Basically, we traced a payment made to Lloyd from an Italian woman named Gloria Russo. It was well hidden and had been routed through hundreds of banks around the world. Certainly not the work of an amateur. Hermes nearly ripped his hair out in frustration at the blocks the banks kept putting in place, but he got there eventually and traced the money to Russo."

"She's a bad bitch," Kate added.

"How so?" Max asked.

"Once he found her, Hermes started tracking all payments in and out of her account," Jonnie said with wide, excited eyes. "It seems she has been financing a number of pretty awful people around the world, including our former boss, Greg Lloyd. We can't exactly figure out where the money is coming from, but we are thinking she might be raiding it from her workplace. She is the Chief Financial Officer of Valentina Punto di Vendita. It's apparently the largest online women's fashion retailer in the world."

"That's probably where Jane is going shopping with Flash's cash today," Kate laughed.

"Jane loves their stuff," Flash exclaimed, "we can't afford any of it though!"

"Certainly a fair bit of cash flowing through there I imagine," Max said before returning to Russo. "So, we don't know who else she is connected to?"

"No," Jonnie said shaking his head. "But we are certain she is a major player. Hermes has linked payments from her account to several terror-related incidents across the globe. MI6 is very interested in her and the French have more than a couple of questions for her too, which is interesting given her other personal connections.”

“Personal connections?”

“She socialises with everyone from Hollywood stars to Royals to political heavyweights across the globe. She’s a high-profile celebrity in her own right and goes to all the fashion shows. She’s on a magazine cover every few weeks.”

“Okay, well that’s probably why the UK and France are interested, but haven’t moved on her yet. So, what was the payment to Lloyd?”

“We ended up finding more than one payment, it was several, over many years,” Jonnie said. “Totalling somewhere around seven hundred million dollars. He used it to buy shares in NorthStar Defence Industries, which he tried to takeover, and he used the rest to pay his co-conspirators in Australia, most of whom we have arrested or killed in the last few months. AIS agents are taking down the others as we speak.”

“Good, so, how did they meet?” Max asked. “Lloyd was hardly a fashion icon. He spent thirty years in the military and several with AIS, and as far as I know, he never watched a Hollywood movie in his life.”

“We’re not sure yet,” Jonnie said. “Hulk wants us to ask her.”

“We’ll be asking alright, fucking terrorist bitch,” Kate said.

“Seven hundred million dollars is a lot of money, surely someone must have noticed it missing?” Max asked.

“Hermes, thinks a big chunk of it is coming from her company, but he’s going to keep looking for other sources too.”

“Okay, well, he’ll keep us updated I’m sure. So, what’s the plan?”

“We are headed to the Embassy for the brief from Hermes and Hulk, then I’d say we’ll be heading out to find her,” Kate said.

“Ack,” Max said as the helicopter made its way across the Italian skyline towards the capital.

After about twenty minutes, Kate brought the helicopter in slow and landed it on the roof of the Australian Embassy in Rome. The four agents headed downstairs into a secure briefing room. It was a plain room painted off-white with large metal and glass topped cabinets running the length of the longest wall. Televisions, computers and communications gear lined the reinforced and soundproofed walls.

The Ambassador greeted them and said he had set up a videoconference link with the AIS bunker in Sydney. He offered tea and coffee which was placed on the table, before leaving the room, so the agents could make their call.

Jonnie pressed a series of buttons on the keyboard which sat on the large glass conference table. The agents all took up a position around the table in large black leather business chairs. One of the wide-screen televisions at the end of the table came to life. The screen was split in two. On the left side of the screen, Hulk was sitting staring down the lens from his office in the AIS bunker in Sydney. A gruff expression fell on his tanned, rugged and leathery skin, but as usual he was calm in the face of the incredible pressure which came from running the AIS. On the right, Captain Blake "Hermes" Smyth sat in his Navy dress uniform in an oversized leather business class seat onboard one of the AIS Gulfstream jets. He was beyond handsome, especially in his dress uniform. Max and Blake were very close, having first met when Max was in training at the Wool Shed and their friendship had continued to grow over the years, including many missions they had worked together, frequent dinners and drinking sessions, and early working workouts when they were in the same city. He smiled seeing Max in the screen then looked down at his notes. He was Chief of Staff at AIS, effectively making him Hulk's deputy. In the months following Lloyd's death, Blake had taken on most of his duties and was making waves in intelligence and political circles around the world with people impressed at his aptitude and leadership for someone relatively young.

"Good morning everyone," Hulk said looking to each of his agents on the monitor. "Prince, Flash, I'm sorry we had to tear you away from your leave. I know it's well overdue, but there will be time soon enough. For now though, we need to get to work."

"It's fine, Hulk," Flash reassured. "Alpha and Bravo briefed us on the way across. What else do we need to know?"

"I'll let Hermes fill you in, but I've been speaking to my counterpart at MI6 and they are very keen to have a chat with her, very quietly given her relationships with the Royal Family and Britain's elite. They want us to pick her up and they will provide support, but it's our show. Arm's length in case it turns to shit. Hermes?"

"Thanks, Boss," Blake said staring down the lens of his webcam. "MI6 have forwarded through their dossier on Ms Russo. They have credible evidence she financed two attacks in London and one in France. They have had her under surveillance for a couple of days. Looks like she has a group of four or five bodyguards with her around the clock, plus a permanent long-term driver. Her apartment is in downtown Rome and has a lot of security, so they suggest it would be best to grab her in the street. They have offered us access to their surveillance site down the block from her apartment."

"Why would she have all that security?" Max asked. "It's a bit over the top."

"MI6 said the security is a new thing. We're guessing that, if we are right and she is connected to all this, that she's added security after what happened to Lloyd."

"Nothing says innocence like five bodyguards. If MI6 have credible evidence why don't they just pick her up?"

"Because of her connections."

"How fucking ridiculous."

"I agree, kid," Hulk murmured. "Fucking politics. It's worse over there than here at home. Hermes, how far out are you?"

"I'm still several hours away, Hulk," Blake said pressing a couple of buttons on his seat remote. "Eight hours."

"Okay, Prince, Flash, Alpha, Bravo, you guys head to the MI6 surveillance unit and keep watch. If you see a window to take her, do it. Rendezvous with Hermes for an extract to London."

"London?" Max asked.

"Yes, we will work with MI6 to get what we can on Russo and her connections, but I could have had anyone pick her up, it's just convenient given you're nearby. The reason I called you in was because I want your team in London, close to the Prime Minister for CHOGM. I'm thinking about ordering a Section Twenty."

"Of the AIS Act?"

"Yes. Section Twenty gives me the power to take over the Prime Minister and senior ministers' personal security in emergency situations with support from the federal police."

"An emergency situation, you think someone would make a move at the meeting?"

"We don't know how far this terrorist network spreads, but we are also picking up increased chatter about the new terrorism laws the PM has been spearheading and his keynote address at CHOGM. I think I would prefer to have your team in place until we get him back on home soil."

"Okay. Thanks, Hulk. We will pick up Russo and head to London. See you soon, Hermes."

"See you then," Blake said. "Good luck and Godspeed."

"Thanks everyone," Hulk said ending the conference call.

Jonnie typed in a command and the television switched off. Max looked at his crew. Kate was a tall masculine figure about the same height as Max – six feet three inches. She was rough around the edges, but she had a sensitive and caring side under it all, especially when it came to her team, although she would never admit it. She had a short peroxide blonde crewcut with shaved sides and she could match it in one-on-one combat with the best of her male colleagues. In fact, she got her nickname after beating all her male counterparts in weapons, endurance and hand-to-hand combat training to become the "alpha" of the group. Kate was the first woman to successfully join the Australian Special Air Service Regiment. After several years as a non-commissioned officer and many missions under the command of Hulk, and at his urging, Kate worked her way through command studies at the Australian Defence Force Academy and Australian Defence College to become a Lieutenant taking command of her own SAS unit for several years before Hulk recruited her to join the AIS. Kate was part of the team which trained Max, but he soon took on the leadership role within the team and she happily followed.

Jonnie was a new member of the team. He had been with AIS for only a year, after working for the Department of Foreign Affairs and Trade based out of the Embassy in France. The Ambassador noted his performance and intelligence, and recommended him for AIS training. He attended the Wool Shed, like Max had many years before, and excelled in many areas and was fast-tracked for field work on completion of the course. Hulk recently embedded him in Max's team for further field training, but Max was already impressed by his skills, especially behind the wheel and behind a sniper rifle. He was naturally skinny and worked hard to build up muscle mass by eating five times a day with added protein shakes on the side. He was about ten years younger than Max. He was an endurance runner and pretty quick in a sprint too. He had easily beaten Max and Blake on a morning run a few months ago, but neither of them wanted him to know how hard they were pushed to try to keep up. He had short dark hair, olive skin and stood at six feet tall.

"Well, we have our orders," Max said turning to Jonnie. "Jonnie, do you have a vehicle here? Can you get us to the safehouse?"

"Yes, it's downstairs," Jonnie said almost jumping out of his seat in excitement to be part of the team and helping Max.

"Alright, let's move out," Max ordered as his team got to their feet.

Chapter Three

The eleven members sat down around the conference table without speaking. The men and women who had assembled at the large hardwood table sat waiting for their last member to arrive. No one said a word as a young aide moved around the table filling glasses with water for the group. Once the water was filled, the aide moved to the far end of the room and retrieved a small black box. She pressed and held in a button on its side and a small green light illuminated. She sat it in the centre of the conference table and stood back.

"You are free to speak now," she said looking to each of the members. "The box on the table disrupts any listening devices and blocks mobile signals. He will be here shortly. If there is anything you need, please feel free to press the blue button in the control panel on your armrests."

She left the room through the large solid metal sliding door of the conference room and shut it behind her. With the heavy door closed, the room was dimly lit. Most of the light was coming from a large wide-screen television hanging on the wall where the conservative commentator on Sky News was starting his show.

"Good evening and welcome to the Phelps Files," the commentator Kevin Phelps said in his harsh and haughty tone as the banners and music played. *"Tonight, I want to start the program with a discussion on the upcoming Commonwealth Heads of Government Meeting which is being held in London this week. As I am sure my viewers know, this meeting, CHOGM, as they call it, is an assembly of all of the Heads of Government from every nation in the Commonwealth. It is held every two years and the hosting rotates between member states for each meeting. This year, it is London's turn."*

"Much of the city has already been placed into lockdown to prepare for the arrival of the world leaders and I can tell you that I have heard from sources within the Government that say

this will be the most secure event on the face of the earth in the coming days. It is quite fitting that security is so tight, because at this meeting the focus of the Commonwealth leaders will be on security. A broad, wide reaching overhaul of our nations' security laws to protect our citizens for extremism. The same extremism that has given rise to attacks around the world, from here in London to the devastating attacks we saw only months ago in Australia."

"The Australian attacks saw their Parliament targeted and thousands of citizens killed in orchestrated murders in Sydney, Melbourne and the nation's capital, Canberra," Phelps thundered to add drama to his monologue. *"The Australian Prime Minister, Edward Kirby, who witnessed some of his own colleagues' assassinations during that horrific day, as been spearheading ground breaking anti-terror laws for their country and he is due to speak to the conference to try to convince other Commonwealth Leaders to adopt similarly tough national security laws. Now, these laws are not without criticism. The left is up in arms about civil liberties and privacy, and so-called human rights activists are taking to the streets to publicly demand changes to these laws with escalating threats of their own violence."*

"Well, I for one, am outraged by these protestors and the protestors who are already picketing outside the CHOGM conference centre here in London," Phelps raged getting redder and angrier as he went on. *"Terrorism is a reality we face, and we need to have sufficient and ruthlessly effective laws to empower our intelligence, police and defence services to be able to respond, hopefully before an attack even occurs. These protestors and activists will be the first ones to complain when it is their brother or father or partner or mother or aunty who is killed in the next attack. They know nothing, but how to complain, these people. They insight hate and instil fear in the very governments and leaders who are working tirelessly to protect them. They just do not get it. When will they learn? Do they need to see it with their own eyes or lose a family member before they see how close terror is to our doorstep?"*

"I encourage all of my viewers to watch the events of CHOGM, especially Prime Minister Kirby's address, to see what real leadership is and to hear how he plans to help save lives, even the protestors' lives, though it is questionable they deserve such protection," Phelps spat. *"The Commonwealth is an important institution for promoting peace and security throughout the world and the Monarchy has served us well in providing stability and hope for all our citizens. The former Royal Family, may God bless them, moved on following some incidents which were completely taken out of context. But, the humility and grace they showed in vacating the palace shows the power and the strength of the Monarchy and its enduring legacy. His Majesty the King of England, although he is getting on in years, has tirelessly and expertly guided our nations with that same grace and will continue to do so for as long as he rules. And, his adult children and successors, the Prince of Wales and Duchess of Cambridge, continue to uphold his unwavering loyalty to the people and selflessness in service of the Commonwealth. We should all be thankful for the role they play in our society in protecting us from terror and providing for our ongoing prosperity and security."*

A man in his late seventies came through the sliding door and took his seat near the centre of the table as the young aide closed the door behind him.

"We should put him on the payroll," Robert said settling into his seat and nodding towards the television and Phelps who was still in full flight extolling the virtues of patriotism.

People nodded and smiled around the table as Robert muted the television just as Phelps was revving up again.

"Thank you all for coming," Robert said taking a moment to look at each member assembled around his boardroom table. "You know why we are here. Six months ago, Greg "Shadow" Lloyd conducted a number of successful attacks in Australia on behalf of The Sixteen. He carried out his mission and almost succeeded in getting away with it, but unfortunately, he was caught by the Australian Intelligence Service, where he had been the second-in-command for many years after a distinguished career in the military. He was assassinated by Agent Max "Prince" Shaw of the AIS. I am told that Agent Shaw is a particularly ruthless field agent. My contact with MI6 sent me his file and I can tell you he is one of the AIS's best at information extraction by use of torture and psychological techniques. He is an expert with a variety of weapons with his favourites being an MP5 rifle, a silenced pistol and, charmingly, a large carbon-fibre hunting knife which is how he killed Lloyd. Agent Shaw's fiancé, Mr Lachlan Farrell, was murdered by Lloyd in an attempt to break the Agent's spirit and throw him off The Sixteen's trail, but unfortunately, it had the opposite effect. He has spent the years following Mr Farrell's death, hunting down anyone connected to The Sixteen and, MI6 note, he has a brutal and unwavering drive to end terrorism to the point of obsession. In other words, Lloyd fucked up and turned him into our worst nightmare. So far, Agent Shaw and his AIS team, as well as MI6 and the CIA have only been able to arrest or kill low level associates of Lloyd's, however I have been informed that they have made a connection to Gloria Russo in Rome which is why she is not with us today."

There was awkward shuffling around the table.

"Friends," Robert said holding his hands up and gesturing for them to calm down. "Please, do not be alarmed. They are a long way off finding any of us and I am making plans to ensure they never do, but I called you all here today to authorise an accelerated schedule. We need to move on some of our main targets sooner."

"How soon?" one of the women at the table asked bluntly.

"Days, not weeks, Janelle," Robert said holding her gaze.

There was more awkward shuffling.

"The targets have been identified and with your support, today we will move into the home stretch," Robert said encouragingly. "The final stage of the journey we started together many years ago. The road to peace in our time. The path to global stability. A world free from terror. A new world, a better world. Do I have your agreement to proceed?"

One by one the members sitting around the table agreed with Robert's plan.

"Excellent," Robert said smiling at the assembled members. "The plan starts with protecting Gloria. I have sent two teams to head off any advances from AIS or MI6 who have her under surveillance in Rome. They will get her to safety and stop AIS's advance in its tracks. You will know when the first strike has occurred, but in the interim, I encourage each of you to make your preparations. It is time."

"Robert," Janelle said interrupting Robert's flow. "If they get Russo, our plans could be uncovered."

"Our team will be able to get to her in time. I have already got five bodyguards with her and one of our best drivers."

"But, if they are able to get to her, we need to make arrangements."

"What do you suggest?"

"We need to get her manual back."

"This is exactly why the plans in the manual are in code."

"The AIS and MI6 have thousands of codebreakers on their staff," Janelle said looking to each of the members of the boardroom. "It may take them sometime, but they could work it out eventually. We cannot let them know our plans, but more importantly, we cannot afford them linking all this back to us. Our goal is only achieved if the people believe it necessary."

"Of course, you are right," Robert said reassuringly. "For everyone's peace of mind, I will call the team and ensure they get the book back."

"Thank you, Robert. I know we all had the new sections added to our manuals in the last few hours, which no doubt reflect your accelerated schedule, so we cannot afford it falling into AIS or MI6s' hands."

"I agree. I will make the arrangements. The next order of business is electing a new member. Since Lloyd's unfortunate demise, we have been a member down. With the King and Queen absent, and Russo not present, the empty chair left by Lloyd is even more noticeable. The bylaws state seats must be filled within forty weeks. As you know, Shadow's seat is one of the two Pacific seats on the board of The Sixteen. We have three contenders who are next in line for the seat. The portfolios in front of you hold their biographies. The first candidate is Mr Alistair Turner. Alistair has been controlling our financial interest in the Asia-Pacific region for a number of years. His father, Harold, was one of our finest recruiters in the region. He is based in Sydney and works for the Minister for Foreign Affairs in the position of Chief of Staff. He is currently in London with the Minister for the Commonwealth Heads of Government Meeting and has asked for an opportunity to address this room at some point in the coming days."

"I would like to hear from him, if possible," Janelle said to the nods of the other members of the group around the table. "And, the other candidates."

"I will make the arrangements," Robert agreed making a note on his file. "The second candidate is Jillian Ashfield who heads up one of our largest propaganda departments. She is the general manager of Cerberus, a public affairs agency in Auckland, New Zealand."

"And the final candidate?"

"The final candidate is Enoka Ioane from Kiribati, a small nation in the Pacific. He has done some fantastic work rallying the island nations in the Pacific to our cause. He studied in Melbourne and has a PhD in legal systems. His thesis was on the governance and strength of the Commonwealth. He has also recently joined our global propaganda teams traveling the world delivering keynote addresses."

"They are all suitable, when will we be able to meet with them?"

"All within the week."

"I think I speak for everyone when I say we are looking forward to it."

"Thank you, everyone," Robert said standing. "The meeting is adjourned for today, I will be in touch to arrange a time to meet with the candidates. The King will also want to attend the ceremony once we have made our choice, so please stay available throughout the week."

"We will," Janelle said as Robert headed for the door. "Before you go, Robert. Is she ready?"

Robert stopped and stared at the door, while others in the room waited anxiously for his reply.

"She has been preparing her whole life," Robert said letting his frustration give way to reassurance. "Yes, the King is ready."

Chapter Four

Max and his team had gathered their equipment before leaving the Embassy, but stayed dressed in their civilian attire to blend in. Jonnie drove them through the tight streets of Rome until he reached the MI6 surveillance building. Jonnie had pulled his sporty Subaru WRX into the available space under the apartment building and the four agents had made their way upstairs. The surveillance room was a small and cramped lounge room of an old one-bedroom apartment. It was furnished with 1970's decor and fittings, and Max guessed the last time it was painted was forty years ago. Paint was blistering off the wall and water damage was staining the roof. It had a musty-wet smell which was only slightly worse than the smell of the MI6 agents who had been on duty for the twelve hours leading up to their arrival.

Following introductions with the MI6 surveillance team, the AIS agents took turns of observing the Italian woman in the penthouse apartment down the block through a short scope. The MI6 team had video cameras recording her every move. The small room was lined with televisions showing the various camera feeds. Wires and power cords were strung across the suite powering their gear, and mobile phones, tablets and computers were sitting on small portable metal worktables the team had brought in.

Max and his team had been on site for a several hours without anything of note happening. They took the time to check their gear, eat and discuss Russo's movements in the previous days with the MI6 team. She had been backwards and forwards to her place of work, and had been to a fashion launch the previous night, which they guessed was why she was having a relaxing morning at home to recover. They had also set in place a plan to take Russo when she left the apartment.

"Prince," Jonnie called animatedly standing at the scope. "I think you should come look at this."

"What is it?" Max asked as he made his way over to the window.

"It looks like she is getting ready to head out," Jonnie said stepping back. "She's just laid out clothes and headed for the shower, and her bodyguards are checking their gear and milling about."

Max looked through the scope and saw the woman in the shower, then panned it down one level to where the guards were checking their weapons and anxiously shuffling around the kitchen waiting for their protectee.

"I think you're right," Max said stepping back. "Keep watch and let me know when you think they'll be heading out. Flash, Alpha, weapons check, then let's get into position."

"Got it," Flash said standing and holstering his weapons.

"Ack," Kate said turning to Jonnie. "Hey Bravo, don't get a hard-on watching that old woman in the shower. Keep focused."

Jonnie blushed and gave Kate a nervous, but cheeky smile. Max patted him on the back.

"Don't worry about her, you get as hard as you like," Max said smiling at Jonnie who looked away in embarrassment. "But, when they get into the lift, it's game time, you get your arse downstairs to join us. Until then, call the play over the comms units."

"Roger," Jonnie said getting focused again and pressing the small device in his ear. "Comms check, one, two, three."

"Loud and clear, Bravo," Max said pressing his own device. "Alpha, Flash, let's go."

Kate handed Max his silenced pistol and hunting knife, and they gathered their phones and tablets.

"Leave the kid alone, would you?" Max whispered to Kate. "You make him nervous, I think he likes you."

"He could be so lucky," Kate laughed turning and winking at Jonnie who shuffled back to the scope blushing again.

Once Max had holstered his gun and knife under his linen shirt, he led Kate and Flash downstairs. Max checked the street, left and right, then started across the road, weaving in and out of the vespers and other vehicles in the busy little Italian street. There were overflowing cafes and restaurants, and little bakeries lining the road. Tourists and locals alike were busily rushing between venues looking for tables. A small market was set up a few doors down from Russo's building selling street food and souvenirs which was proving to be a popular spot during the lunch break and early afternoon.

"I've got you crossing the street, Prince," Jonnie said over the comms unit.

"Ack. Moving into position," Max acknowledged leading Kate and Flash to a small courtyard near the Italian woman's apartment building.

Kate and Flash sat at a table in the courtyard looking at a map of Rome as if they were lost tourists taking a moment to orientate themselves. Max lent against a nearby fence scrolling through his phone. While it was just for cover, he did notice several missed messages from Sam. He read the first couple. Messages of love and how he was missing him already, how he wished Max had stayed on the yacht. Max hesitated then quickly typed a reply.

Miss you too Sam. Hope you and Jane had a nice day shopping – and I hope you bought yourself something nice! All good here. Talk soon x.

"I've got movement, Prince," Jonnie almost shouted through the comms unit.

"Keep it in your pants, Bravo," Kate joked.

"Enough now, game time," Max said. "Call it, Bravo."

"Two guards are in the lift on their way down. She's just put on a neckless, put her diary in her bag and is heading down towards the kitchen. Three guards standing by the elevator."

"Ack," Max said still pretending to look at his phone. "As soon as she's in the lift, get moving."

"Roger," Jonnie said making sure he had his keys and pistol ready. *"The first two guards are walking out of the lobby, you should have them in three, two, one."*

"Got them. They're making their way to two cars, silver BMWs, must be the drivers."

Flash and Kate casually glanced over and sighted the drivers climbing into their respective BMWs.

"She's at the lift, moving now," Jonnie said before heading for the door.

"Haul arse, kid," Max said as he started casually walking towards the woman's building still glancing down at his phone.

Kate folded up the map and stuffed it into her back pocket, as the two agents stood to follow Max's lead. Max lent against the wall near the lobby entrance doors to Russo's building. The driver in the first vehicle looked over to him, as Max held his phone up to his ear pretending to make a call. The driver watched for a few seconds as Max had a conversation with no one, before turning back to look down the road.

Max watched through the lobby doors as the elevator arrived and Russo and her guards exited the lift. Max walked towards the door and held it open for them, still having a fake conversation on his mobile phone. Once they had walked by, Max put the phone back in his pocket and fell into step behind them. He reached for his pistol as he heard the screech of car tyres rounding the corner. He looked, anticipating Jonnie in his WRX, but instead saw a black four-wheel drive with four guys in full tactical gear and balaclavas standing on the side steps, two either side. For a moment, he stopped in his tracks wondering if MI6 had decided to move in themselves. He had used the same technique many times. The black SUV mounted the kerb between Max, and Flash and Kate. The two men on the far side pointed their rifles at Flash and Kate.

"Get on the ground!" one of the men yelled in broken Italian at Kate and Flash.

Russo was being rushed forward by her security guards. One broke from the group and jumped into the rear vehicle. The other two ushered her quickly into the lead BMW before moving to take their own seats.

"Get on the fucking ground!" the two guards on Max's side of the vehicle yelled in Italian as they stepped off the side rails, their guns trained on Max. Max put his hands up, as did Flash and Kate.

"Bravo, pull back," Max said into his comms unit. "We're burnt. Abort."

"Max, wait," Jonnie said anxiously. *"I'm nearly there."*

"No!" Max said forcefully. "Abort. That's an order."

The first balaclava clad man reached Max and held the barrel of the gun to Max's head. When the second man arrived a few seconds later, he smashed the butt of his gun down hard on the side of Max's head. Max fell down on one knee and clutched the side of his head. The second man who had hit him retrieved Max's gun and his knife from under his polo shirt, then the pair dragged Max to the waiting SUV. The Italian woman's car and the chase car left the scene with Russo smiling broadly through the rear window as it sped off.

Max got just a moment to look through the window of his SUV, as he was pushed in, to see Flash and Kate lying face down on the concrete footpath. His heart raced and he stopped breathing as he watched the two men on the far side run back towards him and the waiting SUV. They climbed aboard and Max kept staring out at his friends waiting, hoping, for them to move. The four-wheel drive sped down the footpath scattering people before it bounced back onto the street. Max turned to see Jonnie arrive in his WRX, fling open the door and run to Kate and Flash. He breathed out in a sigh of relief as the pair got back to their feet to watch as his vehicle made a sharp turn and raced away from them. Max smiled, knowing his friends were safe, before his world went dark as he was hit for the second time with the butt of a gun, knocking him out.

Back in the street, Kate and Flash were on their feet and Jonnie was anxiously encouraging them to get to the car.

"They took Max!" Jonnie shouted running towards his car. "Come on, we have to follow them. We have to rescue him."

"If they see us, they will kill him," Kate said trying to calm Jonnie down. "We need to regroup and come up with a plan."

"Flash, you agree with me, right? We need to go and get him back."

Flash stood staring at the corner the SUV had rounded, willing, hoping, for his best friend to speed back around the corner. He felt sick to the stomach. All he could see was Max's face looking back through the rear window of the four-wheel drive, moments ago.

"Flash?!" Jonnie snapped.

"Kate's right, mate," Flash said sadly turning to Jonnie. "Every inch of my being wants to chase them and get him back, but they will kill him. You need to get us back to the Embassy. We need to talk to Hulk and Hermes. They will know how to find him."

"What? We know where he is! He's in that fucking car!"

"Remember your training, Jonnie," Kate said calmly. "They have at least four guns only inches from our friend. It would take only factions of a second for them to end him. We need to be smart. What would Max want us to do?"

"If it was one of us, he would tear this city apart looking for us."

"And, so will we," Flash said resolutely. "But, more importantly, he would also want us to be safe. He couldn't live with himself if one of us got hurt or killed to save him. He would rather sacrifice himself and so would I. We will get him back Jonnie, he's a tough bastard, but we do it on our terms, not theirs."

"Okay," Jonnie said crankily climbing in the car. "Hurry up then, let's get back to the Embassy."

Jonnie drove fast, punching his car through traffic as he wound his way back to the Embassy. The bollards lowered on sighting his car and he sped through the gates, braking hard by the front door. The three agents ran into the Embassy as the bollards rose back into place and the gates shut. Security let them pass and they ran up the stairs to the conference room.

Blake was sitting in the conference room with the Ambassador discussing the latest intelligence gathered on the Italian woman and her local connections.

"What are you doing back here?" Blake said with a confused expression on his face. "I thought you were going to call in once you had her and meet me at the airport? Where's Max?"

"They took him!" Jonnie said in a nervous half-yell.

"Okay, calm down. Breathe. Who took him?"

"We don't know, Boss," Kate said. "We moved into position to take the woman. Max was behind her and the bodyguards readying to take them down when a black SUV came out of nowhere and jumped the gutter. Four guys, full tact gear, weapons ready leapt from the side of the vehicle and forced us to the ground, and they bundled Max into their car and drove off. The Italian bird got away too."

Blake had spent many years perfecting his stoic look, hiding his true feelings, a trait which had helped him shield his emotions from his enemies; from Senators and Members of the House of Representatives under intense questioning about the operations of AIS; from foreign intelligence sources and diplomats; and even on occasion from his closest friends, including Max, who he had loved since the moment he met him. But now, his emotions were starting to betray him. He rubbed his hand through his hair and looked down at the table trying to compose himself.

"Mister Ambassador," he finally said without looking up. "Please get General Scott on the line."

Chapter Five

Max woke, his head was throbbing and felt dizzy and disorientated. He opened his eyes, but could not see, it took him a moment to realise it was because he had a hood over his head. It felt damp against his face and smelt of putrid musk. Part wet and mouldy, part body odour, and maybe even blood and vomit from previous wearers. He felt nauseous and for a moment thought he may be sick, but he took short, shallow, quick breaths and let the feeling subside.

He ran through his mental checklist, assessing his body from head to toe as he was taught during his training. 'Know your body' they had said. 'Figure out what's broken, figure out what's working and figure out how you might be able to get out of the situation,' he remembered them saying during one the long afternoon lecture sessions at the Wool Shed.

He started at his head. *Throbbing pain, possible cut left side of my head above my ear. Prime for infection in this filthy hood, I need to get rid of it soon,* he thought to himself. *Neck and shoulders okay, arms tied at the wrist to the arms of a chair. It's cold on my forearms. Metal. It's cold down my back, and on my arse and legs. I'm naked on a cold metal chair. Legs tied together at the ankles. No other feelings, everything else seems fine. Only pain is the side of my head,* he thought to himself as he felt a pain in the side of his head.

Max sat on the cold chair thinking back to his training. After accepting Hulk's offer to join AIS, Max had spent months training to become an agent. It was over a decade ago, but he remembered it like it was yesterday. He remembered the countless hours and days of training, including that night where he had been dragged out of his bed and tortured in the nearby shed.

Initially, Max was led to believe it was a disgruntled and homophobic fellow recruit who was torturing him and threatening to kill him, which built his fear. Even after Max had found out it was all part of the training, the instructors put him through various torture techniques from hosing him down with ice-cold water to sight and sound deprivation, and waterboarding. Max was pushed to his limits, then left in the pitch-black shed tied naked to a chair on a freezing winter's night, on the AIS property in a remote location in outback New South Wales.

After hours on shivering in the dark, Blake had entered the shed and spoke to Max. It was part of the training, trying to get Max to break and quit, but he didn't. When Blake saw the resolve and courage in his eyes, he knew Max would not quit. He told Max to 'find a reason to fight, find a purpose, find something to keep you grounded. Why are you doing this? What is your motivation? Find it Max and I won't lie, you will still feel the pain, but it will become more tolerable, more manageable and you will be able to delay any breaking point beyond what is thought to be humanly possible. Good luck.' Blake then reached down and squeezed Max's hand which was cold and turning blue from the freezing night air. He held it for a few seconds, its warmth flowing into Max, before he left Max tied up in the shed.

Max sat in his chair tied up in Rome and wished Blake would come in this time and save him, offer him a way out. It was certainly warmer than that winter's night, but he knew he was surely going to be tortured and he knew, better than most, what that entailed given how many times he had tortured people for information during his career. He knew the psychology of breaking points and he was an expert at finding people's weaknesses and using them against his targets. When he was in training and during the first part of his career, he was sceptical of the use of torture, the barbarism, the pain, the inhumanity of it all, but he learnt in a hurry that it worked.

After Lachlan was murdered by Lloyd, Max redoubled his efforts at work chasing down terrorists and doing whatever it took to get information and use it against his enemies. Anyone who planned to harm innocents, anyone who had harmed innocents, anyone aiding terrorists or rogue States who came to Max's attention suffered his wrath and he fast became AIS's best agent and one of the best spies in the world. All of it to stop others feeling the pain he felt, stop them from experiencing the loss he had felt and stop them from having to live forever without the love of their life by their side. He was still hurting and had spent years using that hurt against his enemies.

At the Wool Shed, Blake had told Max to find his motivation to survive and it was Lachlan. Lachlan got him through that long night. Lachlan was his world, he knew he loved him from the moment they had met. In that moment, he knew Lachlan was the one and that they were going to spend the rest of their lives together. He just did not know that for Lachlan that was only a matter of a few years. He had joined AIS to keep Lachlan, and innocent people like him, safe. He wanted to protect people, especially Lachlan, from pain and from suffering. He wanted to stop terrorists and he wanted to end those who sort only death and destruction. Lachlan was the key to his motivation and his determination. He remembered after Blake visited him in the Wool Shed, on that freezing night, thinking about Lachlan and he remembered feeling warmer. In that moment, he knew he would make it through the torture and through the training.

He heard the door open and a man walked into the room.

"You will tell us who you work for and why you were stalking Ms Russo," the man said in broken Italian. "You will talk or you will suffer."

Max thought back to Blake's advice. 'Find a reason to fight, find a purpose, find something to keep you grounded. Why are you doing this? What is your motivation? Find it Max…'. He thought about Lachlan and how he had failed to keep him safe. He thought about how being an AIS Agent was the reason Lachlan was murdered. *I am the reason Lachlan was murdered,* he thought to himself, not for the first time. He thought about how his drive to keep Lachlan and the world free from harm, had backfired so catastrophically. He remembered how Lachlan had died in his arms and how he ached every day from his loss and how he was not sure if he would ever be able to truly love someone so deeply again. He thought about Sam and how sweet he was and felt tremendous guilt that he could not love Sam as much as Sam loved him.

This is going to hurt, he thought to himself as the man walked over to begin his torture.

Chapter Six

Robert looked down at his phone resting on the conference table. His guests had long since left the boardroom and he was putting his plans into action. One of his agents in Italy had just phoned to say they had picked up Max "Prince" Shaw of the Australian Intelligence Service and he was pleased to hear the news, as well as the advice that Russo had gotten away safely. The plans he put in place were working and he was proud to be getting results. When all The Sixteen's plans were carried out, he would take his place in the leadership of the new world order. A world free of violence and terror. A world he was helping create. He looked at the phone and decided to make the call. After several rings, the woman answered.

"Robert, I trust you are well?" the woman questioned.

"Yes, ma'am," Robert said anxiously.

"What can I do for you?"

"The Sixteen have agreed to our accelerated schedule. I have given the orders and the first strikes will begin soon. We are on the home stretch now, ma'am."

"That is excellent news, Robert. I will not forget the role you have played in all of this, you are doing your country and the world a great service, and you will be responsible for setting the globe on course for peace in our time."

"Thank you, ma'am. You honour me."

"Please keep me informed on your progress."

"Yes, ma'am. I will. I do have something else I need to inform you of though," Robert said nervously.

"Yes?"

"They tracked down Gloria Russo."

"Oh dear, that is not good news. Is she okay?"

"Yes, I intervened in time and she got away, and I have an AIS agent in my possession."

"Good, thank you for stepping in to protect her."

"I know how you feel about her, it is the least I can do. I have just given my team on the ground in Italy the order to torture Agent Shaw to see what AIS and MI6 know, then to kill him and discard the body."

"Excellent. Let's continue to stay ahead of them this time."

"Indeed."

"Thank you, Robert. Keep me updated. If that is all."

"Forgive me, ma'am, there is just one more thing."

"What is it?" she answered getting frustrated.

"I have arranged for the three Pacific candidates to address The Sixteen in the coming days to select Lloyd's replacement. Would you like to attend?"

"I think given the timing I should come along. We will need people we trust following this week's events. I will speak to my assistant to find the gaps in my schedule. It will be difficult given my CHOGM commitments, but I would very much like to attend."

"We will arrange our meetings at your convenience, ma'am."

"Thank you, Robert."

"Yes, ma'am."

The line went dead. Robert felt good, his plans were coming together. The King, a codename bestowed on the head of The Sixteen, said she was pleased with him. He was sorry for the decisions they had to make and the actions they were taking, but he knew what they were doing was right. In the long run, the world would be a better place and he had played a large part in making that a reality. He smiled knowing he was part of the solution to the world's problems and part of its future. He sat the phone down and went back to his files.

Chapter Seven

Jonnie paced back and forth along one of the long walls of the Embassy's conference room, past the photos of the Ambassador, Prime Minister, Foreign Minister and the Monarch. His hands were in his pockets trying to control his nerves and he was frantically chewing gum. He walked staring at the floor until he reached the door then turned and marched back towards the window over and over.

Flash and Kate were sitting at the conference table in silence, collecting their thoughts, recharging and emotionally preparing for whatever was to come next. Flash was contemplating how long he could hold off calling Jane and Sam to tell them about Max. He was filled with anxiety and starting to get impatient. His best friend was missing and in grave harm. He wanted to find him and get him back. He owed Max his life and he was not going to let him down.

Blake was frantically typing on his laptop stopping every few minutes to take phone calls and give orders.

"Oh, for God's sake, Jonnie, will you sit down or stand still, please?" Blake barked letting his normally cool demeanour slide. "You're driving me crazy!"

"Sorry, sir," Jonnie said walking over and leaning on the back of a chair opposite Blake.

"Okay, now the standing still is kind of annoying me," Blake said after a couple of minutes. "Why don't you and Kate go down to the weapons hold and start gearing up? Once we have a location, we will need to move fast."

"Come on hotcakes, let's go," Kate said standing and slapping Jonnie on the arse as she walked past.

Blake and Flash laughed at Kate and Jonnie's reaction as the door closed.

"She's having a lot of fun with him," Flash laughed.

"How's he fitting in with the team?" Blake asked.

"He's young and very eager to please, and he's got a lot of talent, especially with the sniper rifle, but he needs to learn when to just stop and follow orders without the twenty questions."

"I hear he can drive too?"

"Yeah, he can handle a car pretty well, one of the best I've worked with actually. I just wish he'd pick a bigger car, I hate that WRX, its fast but with a few of us in it, it's not really practical."

"Good to know, about the driving I mean, as for the car, well, I don't really care as long as he gets there and back in safety, and can get the job done."

"Well, you can sit in the back on the way to the airport."

"I have a car and driver," Blake said sheepishly.

"Oh, that's right, I forgot. Good to be at the top of the world, cars and chauffers, la-de-da," Flash said jokingly. "How are you finding it, being second in command?"

"Hardly, top of the world. It's weird to get used to, especially the work I have to do with politicians and the media, and I'm still not used to the people employed to do stuff I used to do myself, like driving to and from work. It's weird. Other than that, it's just more work and more pressure, like my social life needed any more excuses to not exist."

"I get that, I'm on holidays remember?"

"True, sorry about that. Anyway, how's Max find him?" Blake said apologetically before changing the subject.

"Jonnie?"

"Yeah."

"Max has been keeping a close eye on him, I think he enjoys the role of mentor and teaching the kid. It's been a good outlet for him during this difficult period."

Blake sat thinking about that comment for a moment.

"And, what about Sam?" Blake asked coyly.

"What about him?" Flash asked.

"Nothing, I shouldn't have brought him up."

"Oh, no it's okay, Blake. Max is still pretty distraught over Lachlan. Understandably. I'm actually not sure he'll ever completely let go. God, if something happened to Jane, I don't think I would. He was making so much progress, but Lloyd really fucked that up. Fucking arsehole, I can't believe he took him back to that warehouse. It is amazing Max got through it at all. Sam was there to help him through it, but I'm not sure it'll go the distance. I don't think Sam can handle the time Max is spending away. I just want him to be happy, he's been through more shit than most people will ever have to endure and the things he has done for the country, fuck, it would break a lesser man."

"Yeah, I want him to be happy too, of course. I just thought it must have been getting pretty serious taking him on an overseas trip?"

"Given how much we've been working lately, I don't think they have spent that much time together. I think Max feels guilty, but I'm not sure what will happen."

"Fair enough, I'm sorry, I shouldn't have asked. I don't mean to pry, I know how close the two of you are."

"It's fine, mate. You two are very close too."

"Yeah," Blake said quietly looking down and starting to type on his computer.

"I'm always here if you need to talk about anything too, Blake," Flash said genuinely.

"I appreciate that, Jacob," Blake said before being interrupted by his ringing phone. "Excuse me please."

He picked up his phone, swiped and answered the call.

"Good, let me put you on speaker," Blake said resting the phone on the table. "You're also on with Flash."

"We've found him," Hulk explained. *"The map should be coming up on the screen in your room."*

"Confirmed, Hulk," Flash said watching the map load on the conference room television. "Did you track his phone?"

"No, it's his AIS access key," Hulk said referring to one of the rings Max wore which acted as a security key for AIS

buildings and vehicles, and it also connected to their mobile devices to securely transport electronic files.

"I didn't know they had trackers in them," Flash said.

"They don't. Blake figured out how to ping the mobile towers in the city looking for the ring's electronic ID."

"Where is he, Hulk?" Blake asked.

"He is still in the city, well sort of. He's actually in Vatican City."

"The Vatican?" Blake asked giving Flash a concerned look.

"Yeah, hang on," Hulk said as he pressed a series of buttons on his computer terminal and a blue dot appeared on the map above the Vatican.

"What building is that?"

"Elemosineria apostolica, the Office of Papal Charities. It's supposedly the Vatican's office for helping the homeless."

"Well, what the hell is he doing there, are you sure the track worked?" Flash asked.

"Yeah, I'm looking at the track now," Blake said spinning his computer around for Flash to see.

"I have no idea what any of that means," Flash said confused looking at the black and white computer code on the screen.

"It means you've got to go get a bit of religion in your life, oh and figure out how to get him back across the border – it being a nation-state after all," Hulk said. *"That ain't going to be easy. I'm sorry I'm not there to help."*

"I will go with them," Blake said determinedly.

"You're not exactly a covert operative these days, Hermes. You're going to be pinged as soon as you cross the border."

"I'm on holidays, back fill the forms on our systems to reflect that, will you?"

"If you get caught, I'm not sure I'm going to be able to help you."

"He's worth the risk."

"Sorry?" Hulk asked as Flash looked over to Blake who had a determination in his eyes.

"The mission is worth the risk, boss."

"Okay, well I'll have the forms processed in case anyone gets into our systems. If you get caught you are on your own."

"I understand. Thanks, Hulk."

"Do you think this is related to the Archbishop?" Flash asked referring to a previous mission Max conducted at the Vatican.

"It is certainly worth considering."

"It's an awfully big coincidence. Max kills the Archbishop of Sydney, a man soon to be made a Cardinal, on the grounds of the Vatican and the first time Max gets near them, he gets captured and ends up there."

"I'll look into it."

"It doesn't matter," Blake stated standing up. "Archbishop Wright was a terrorist piece-of-shit and deserved more than he got. We let him off lightly as far as I'm concerned and I know Max would agree. Hulk, we're going to get Max back and I'll kill everyone who stands in the way, even if they are wearing Catholic robes."

"Let me know when you're moving out."

"Yes, sir," Flash said ending the call and following Blake out of the room.

"Are you sure you want to do this, Blake?" Flash asked. "It's a big risk if we get caught. You and Hulk are the only two visible agents of AIS, the rest of us are anonymous."

"I meant what I said," Blake said without turning back. "He's worth the risk."

Chapter Eight

Max screamed in pain as one of his kidnappers, turned torturers, injected him with a syringe full of a chemical used by some special operations and intel groups around the world to inflict pain. It felt like acid pumping through his veins. He had felt it before, at the Wool Shed, but in a much smaller dose, and he had used it many times on others. Every nerve end burned, his heart was thundering in his chest, and his already throbbing head pounded with the beat of his heart. He was close to blacking out again, but somehow remained conscious.

"Who do you work for?" the man asked calmly, but Max refused to answer breathing deeply trying to recover from the pain he had just experienced.

The torturer left the room to give him time to recover. Max knew too much of the toxin was deadly, so they clearly needed some information from him, otherwise he would be dead already. He could not tell how long it had been since he was taken from the street in Rome, but he figured it must have been at least two hours ago. He imagined Flash, Kate and Jonnie in the Embassy planning a rescue mission. He wondered if they knew where he was. He was completely naked and had no idea where his phone would have ended up. *I'm sure Blake will figure out how to find me,* Max thought to himself. *He always comes through in these circumstances.*

Max was using his hatred for his captors to delay his breaking point. Hate was effective, although not as effective has he had found love to be in the past. He was determined to die rather than give away secrets, but he was not sure how that was going to work out. He knew everyone broke eventually. The best he could hope for, other than rescue, was to hope his captors were poorly trained and went too far and killed him before he gave anything away. The problem was, so far, they seemed like professional interrogators or at least had done it before, which meant they would keep him right at the edge until they got what they came for. Max thought about his next steps. When he felt the breaking point getting closer, he would start feeding them false information to throw them off, giving Blake and the team time to do what they needed to do. The one thing he was certain about was the fact that he was not going to make it easy for his captors and if he was going to die, he was going to piss them off in the process.

The torturer walked back into the room and ripped the hood from Max's head. The large wooden door was swinging back, but Max looked up in time to see a dark shadowy hallway and small anteroom outside the door as his eyes adjusted. He could not be certain, but he thought he was being held downstairs. The air felt damp and mouldy, and a bit cool, but it was a welcomed feeling compared to the disgusting hood he had been wearing. The brickwork looked ancient, the building must have been hundreds of years old. Grout was falling out in several places and some of the bricks had chips out of them. There were some metal chains and loops hanging from the walls, and old wooden crates lined the room. A small lightbulb hung from a rusty old chain above his head.

"So, where were we?" his torturer asked in broken Italian. "That's right, you were about to tell me who you work for and why you were following Ms Russo."

"I'm not telling you shit," Max spat in Italian. "You might as well just kill me."

"You and I both know, everyone eventually talks. Why don't you save yourself some pain?"

"I'm good," Max said sarcastically while trying to mentally prepare himself for the next wave.

Blake's advice from the Wool Shed was playing on repeat in his mind. 'Find a reason to fight, find a purpose, find something to keep you grounded. Why are you doing this? What is your motivation? Find it Max…' His mind calmed as he remembered the warm hand in the freezing cold of the night. The reassurance it had provided and the gorgeous, perfect man and new friend who had been there for him. The calm, warming embrace that had broken the cycle of torture he had endured. While Max spent a majority of his time in and out of work with

Flash, so much of it had been spent with Blake. They had spent countless mornings training together following his time at the Wool Shed, they had worked together on hundreds of missions, and through so many late nights at AIS reading intelligence reports and planning missions. Max remembered every conversation and interaction, every smile and blush, and for the first time he realised Blake's true feelings for him. It had been right in front of him the whole time and he had completely missed it. At first, no doubt, because of his love for Lachlan, but now he felt different. Blake was there that night, after countless injuries and in the days and months following Lachlan's death. Blake had been there for him before, during and after every mission, and Max knew it was because it was his job to be there, but now he realised there was much more to it than just doing his job.

"Well, you are going to suffer until you tell me why you were following Ms Russo," the torturer stated.

"Fuck you," Max said dismissing the torturer. "Do your worst."

The man walked across the room to Max and punched him in the face. Max laughed, a deep guttural laugh, trying to piss off the torturer. It worked. The man punched him again.

"Who's laughing now?" the man asked causing Max to roar with mocking laughter again.

"Oh, so tough," Max said giggling and heckling his torturer. "Any men out there you can send in to punch me properly?"

The man punched him again and this time Max's head fell to his chest.

"Not fucking laughing now you piece of shit!" he yelled.

Max mumbled and coughed.

"What was that?" the man asked moving forward.

Max nodded his head back twice summoning the man closer. The man smiled and lent in to hear his subject's confession. Max threw his head forward with lightning speed and he heard the man's nose break on impact. Warm blood rolled down his forehead as he lent back in his chair and bellowed with laughter again.

"Fuck you, Prince, you broke my nose, you arsehole!" the man screamed in English.

"Well, that's interesting, I knew you weren't Italian because of your shit accent," Max said reverting back to English. "But, I didn't know you were Australian and you called me Prince. It seems you know more than you let on, so why don't you tell me who you work for you traitor?"

There was a metallic thud as a bolt slid back and the big wooden door opened. One of his other captors came into the room.

"Well, that was a pretty big fuck up," the new man said to his friend with the broken nose. "How could you be so stupid to get that close to him?"

"Fuck you," the man spat spluttered "We need to kill him now, he knows where we are from."

"Yeah and who's fault is that?"

"Oh, don't fight over me boys," Max joked. "You'll make me blush."

"We know who you are, Agent Shaw," the new man said. "We will break you eventually, so why don't you tell us what AIS knows and we can put you out of your misery?"

"Misery?" Max laughed. "Watching you two work is a pure joy. I hope it continues for days. I haven't had this much fun for years. I presume you are friends of Shadow's?"

"He was a good friend of mine and a mentor, and you killed him."

"Sure did, I enjoyed it too," Max said sarcastically as the man punched him in the face again. "If he was here now, I'd happily kill him again right in front of you."

"He hated you and now I can see why, you are a smart arse."

"And he, like you, was a traitor and eventually you, like him, will get what's coming to you. So, do your worst to me, I'll die happy knowing my friends will find you. There is nowhere you will be able to hide from them and one day they will send you to meet your mentor in the next life."

"We will get the information we need," he said moving in closer to Max. "And, once we have, your friends will find your dead, naked body washed up on the shoreline."

Max spat blood onto the new man's face and he grabbed Max by the throat as he laughed.

"I am going to enjoy this," the new man said excitedly getting ready to torture Max, before he was distracted by a commotion outside the room.

Four gunshots rang out beyond the door of the holding cell before it exploded inwards. Anticipating what was coming, Max had instinctively closed his eyes and pressed one ear to his shoulder as a flashbang bounced into the room. His unprotected ear was ringing loudly after the explosion and he opened his eyes as the blinding light subsided.

"Don't kill them!" Max yelled as three figures entered the room.

One of the figures broke right, putting a bullet into the leg of the captor with the broken nose. Max knew it was Blake from the way he moved and he watched him as he held the gun level with the captor's head. A second rescuer entered the room, undeniably Flash, Max watched as he broke left charging for the second captor who had fallen to one knee when the door had exploded. Flash pistol whipped him hard in the back of his head and he fell to the floor face first unconscious. Kate was through third, dropping to one knee and scanning the room with her pistol. It is a move the agents had practiced so often and they had executed it flawlessly.

"Clear!" Kate shouted as Jonnie followed them into the room dragging a third captor by the back of the shirt.

"This one is unconscious, but still breathing," Jonnie said was contempt dropping the third guy on his back.

"Good job, kid," Max said making Jonnie smile. "Tie him up and prep these other two arseholes, it's my turn to ask some questions."

"You got it, boss. Glad you're okay," Jonnie said enthusiastically running off to get supplies for Max.

"I'm glad you guys got here when you did," Max said as Flash and Blake walked over to him, and Kate and Jonnie set about tying the men up.

"You look fresh as a daisy, Max," Flash said sarcastically. "Did they even touch you?"

"Very funny, dickhead. I'm fine though, thanks. Why don't you be useful and cut me free?"

"Roger that," Flash said smiling and pulling out his hunting knife to cut the tape. "Glad you're okay, mate."

"I am, thanks to you guys, thank you all," Max said sincerely looking to each member of his team.

"We were always coming to get you, Prince," Blake said tenderly holding Max's hand. "Sorry we took so long. Are you alright, anything broken?"

"I'll be fine, Hermes. The only thing hurting is my pride at being captured in the first place. I want to know who these fuckers are and then I'm going to hunt down every single last one of them and put them in the ground."

"I'll be right by your side."

"Thanks for rescuing me, Blake," Max said squeezing his hand for a second and looking into his eyes.

Flash watched as Blake let go of Max's hand and moved it to the side of Max's face. Max felt overcome by the gesture, one which had gotten him through his torture, and he closed his eyes and softly lent his head into the cup of Blake's palm feeling the warmth pulse through him. It was almost overwhelming.

"Here you go," Flash said handing Blake the knife so he could cut Max free on the opposite side. "I'll go help the others."

"Thanks, Flash," Blake said pulling his hand away, suddenly self-conscious.

Once Max was free, he left the room to clean himself up and get dressed again. He found his clothes and all of his equipment in the room next door. He got dressed then found a small bathroom the washed his face. He wore a couple of battle scars from the beating he had taken, but looked okay considering.

"Where are we?" Max asked Flash as he entered the room holding an icepack on his face. "Still in Rome?"

"Sort of," Flash said. "We're in Vatican City."

"What?"

"We're at the Vatican under some building which is supposed to be a place to help the homeless."

"You're kidding, right?"

"Afraid not."

"What is going on here? Our attempt to capture the Italian woman was blown in a big way, I get kidnapped and brought to the Vatican? Last time I was here, I killed that arsehole Archbishop who released those virus vials at home. Remember him?"

"Yes, well, I remember hearing about it. I was in hospital. Blake and Kate were with you. I guess I've returned the favour today though brother, saving your arse. Does that make us even?"

"Yeah, I'm not sure how much longer they were going to keep me before they killed me, so I guess you're right. Thank you."

"Least I could do and I know you would tear this whole city apart if it was me or any of the team in your position."

"You know I would. Can't be coincidence though, right?"

"Being brought here?"

"Yeah."

"No, I don't think so. Hulk is looking into it for us."

"Good. Can you let him know I was tortured by Australians, maybe that will help narrow the searches?"

"Australians?"

"Yeah, I played possum and headbutted one of those torturing fucks and he reverted back to Australian English instead of his shithouse Italian."

"I think we both need to talk to Hulk, we might have another mole?"

"They aren't AIS, they wouldn't have survived the Wool Shed. Trained for sure, but not well enough. They are definitely Australian though and they are connected to all this somehow. So, why don't we go find out how, then we can give Hulk a call?"

"After you," Flash said opening the door for Max.

The pair made their way back to the interrogation room. Kate and Jonnie had been busy. Each of Max's captors had his hands tied above his head, held in place by a thick rope which was looped around a steel bracket in the roof and pulled tight to a tie off point on the floor. The result was three men tied to the roof with their arms painfully outstretched, balancing on the tips of their toes, trying in vain to take some of the pressure off their shoulders. Blake was pacing down one wall talking on his mobile phone.

"What are the odds of us being discovered in here?" Max asked looking around the room.

"We knocked out three Swiss Guard on the way in, took their weapons, tied them up and stashed them in a small room we found," Flash explained. "They won't be out for too much longer. So, we should act quickly."

"Exit strategy?"

"Hopefully Blake is on the phone working that out now. We're a bit worried they might have made us on entering the city."

"Surveillance?"

"Yeah, Blake is hardly an unknown player anymore. His face would have set off the alerts, especially given the Vatican's private suspicions of AIS involvement in the Archbishop's death. If they flag him, they'll want to ask him some questions."

"Well, let's get to it. Wake them up. One each."

Flash, Kate and Jonnie all snapped ammonia sticks under the nose of their respective prisoners, each woke in a start, shaking their head from the smell. The guy with the broken nose was the last to come to when Kate forced the broken stick up his nose. Max was not sure if it was the ammonia or the pain which woke him, but he did not care. Max tossed his ice pack on the nearby table then turned to face his torturers.

"At least two of you know who I am and I'm sure you know my team," Max said looking around the room to his team, noting the looks on their faces as they recognised every one of his colleagues, including Blake, who they all spent an extra few seconds staring at. "That's right boys, you tortured me and my team busted your arses. Now, it's my turn. If you know me as well as I presume you do, you would have heard how good I am at getting information out of suspects and the pain that I am capable of inflicting to make them talk. So, with that in mind, I have a little rule I'm going to try today which is, the first one to talk doesn't get hurt. So, who wants a leave pass?"

"I do," the guy with the broken nose said. "What do you want to know?"

"I knew it would be you" Max said smiling and walking over to his original torturer. "After what you did to me, I'm not surprised. So, what do I want to know? I want to know which one of your friends here is going to bleed first?"

There was a quick, nervous exchange of looks among the three.

"Times up, who will it be?" Max asked drawing his carbon fibre hunting knife.

"Blaine," the guy said nodding his head to his former comrade on his left who Jonnie had dragged into the room.

"Blaine, hey? Good name. What's your friend, hanging on your right, what's his name?"

"Cameron," he said pointing to the man who had berated him after giving away their nationality.

"And, yours?"

"James."

"Blaine, Cameron and James," Max said pointing to each with his hunting knife as he said their name.

"Cameron," Max said stepping to the side and stopping only inches in front of him. "James is a dick, we both know that, so why don't you and I have a conversation. He just gave up Blaine for torture, at my hands, and you know what these hands have done. Look at Blaine over there shitting himself. James gave him up, so my guess is he's the lowest ranked of your little cabal. So, that means you or James are in charge. James is too stupid, that means you're my guy. I am going to carve the word traitor into your forehead, followed by my initials, unless you tell me what I need to know. Got it?"

"Yes," Cameron said with a defeated look in his eyes.

"Cameron, who do you work for?"

"I work for Air Force Intelligence. Shadow recruited me and I stayed loyal to him and to our cause, even after you murdered him."

"What cause would that be? Money like him?"

"You of all people should know, Prince, there are always more pawns and bigger moves at play. Don't just look at the one move, see the whole board."

"So, you think this is a game?"

"No, but our employers do."

"The Sixteen?"

"Yes."

"What are we doing at the Vatican? Why did you bring me here?"

"After you killed Lloyd, we fled the country, but we have stayed in contact with his superiors. They told us you were in the country and we told the church. The Vatican was understandably interested in asking you some questions about the death of Archbishop Wright and The Sixteen wanted to help them get to you. The church asked us to intervene on their behalf. We were to torture you, then give over all information we received to them, including whether you killed the Archbishop. Then we were ordered to kill you."

"Shut up, Cameron, they will kill us," James nervously blurted out.

"Why don't you shut the fuck up, James, you know what they will do," Cameron said angrily before turning back face Max. "Prince, promise me this, please promise you'll kill me before you leave?"

"Who are you afraid of? We can protect you."

"No, you can't. You have no idea how far their reach extends."

"Why don't you tell me?"

"Our reach is far and our hands never idle. That's what he used to say."

"Shadow?"

"Yes."

"Who was he talking about?"

"Don't, Cam," James said.

"Just a second, Cameron," Max said walking over and punching James as hard as he could right in the face, knocking him out.

James hung limply from the chains, his head hanging down to his chest.

"Sorry, where were we?" Max said walking back over to Cameron.

"Shadow was just a knight and I am just a pawn, but they have their fingers in every pie. They control everything. A global organisation responsible for more death and destruction than you can imagine, but with one goal in mind."

"And what's that?"

"Peace."

"Peace? Through death and destruction?"

"How else are you going to get it? Negotiation, democracy and freedom aren't working. The Sixteen aim to speed up the process and they are going to do so by promoting terrorism, until the people are too scared to function, until they scream for change, until the world as we know it is burned to the ground, so a new world can rise from the ashes."

"And, this group, The Sixteen, they intend to help shape this new world?"

"Yes."

"So, the Italian woman, Ms Russo, is she a pawn or a knight too?"

"More like a rook."

"Moving up in the world."

"How right you are."

"Sorry to interrupt, Prince, have you got a minute?" Blake asked from the doorway.

"Sure, what is it?" Max said following Blake out into the hallway.

"Hulk says our guys are getting questions from official channels about what our team and me in particular are doing in the Vatican."

"That's quick by anyone's timeframes, Blake. They are looking for you."

"That would be my guess."

"One of them said the Vatican wanted information from me. The Sixteen told the Vatican we were in town and these three arseholes intervened on their behalf."

"My plane logs and embassy visit would have been registered pretty quickly by their intel agencies, and I would have set off the facial recognition systems in the square, but it is still too quick. They knew they had you and they are now going to try to stop me from getting you out."

"I agree we need to move. The three in there are Australians. As I said, one is talking, but he's freaking out. He wants to get it all out without pain and then he wants me to kill him. He basically said either way he's dead anyway, so he just wants to go without pain."

"Australians?"

"Yep. One is Air Force Intelligence, haven't gotten to the other two yet. He said Shadow was a minor player. He used a

Chess analogy where he was a pawn and Lloyd was a knight, which is only one step above a pawn."

"So, we are looking for knights, bishops, rooks, queen and king?"

"Yeah, he said Ms Russo is a rook."

"Well, that's jumped a couple of ranks, we are definitely on the right track. How much longer do you need? Those Swiss Guard will wake soon and if they already flagged me, it won't take too long for them to come find us."

"Let's move, we can just take Cameron with us, the other two are worthless."

"Your call Max, you're the mission leader."

"Yeah, but you're the boss."

"I might very well need to keep a low profile after what is coming next, so it's your call Max, it's your operation, you call the shots."

"Okay, he comes with us, the other two stay here. Now, how are we getting out of here?"

"Well, that's the thing, it could get loud, but it should be quick. I just need to make the call when you are ready."

"Make the call, I'll get the others."

Max walked into the interrogation room as Blake made his phone call.

"Cut him down," Max said to Jonnie, pointing at Cameron. "He's with us."

"What about these other two?" Jonnie asked pointing at James and Blaine.

"They stay, but Blaine," Max said turning his full attention on the third man. "If I let you live, what will you tell people when you get out?"

"Nothing, Prince," Blaine nervously cried, viably shaking. "I will just walk away, I'm not even a pawn, I'm a henchman to a pawn, they won't miss me."

"Well, if that's not the case and I find out you told them what happened today, let me make this very clear. There is literally no place on earth you can hide. I will make it my life's mission to find and kill you if you open your mouth, but first I will make you suffer. So, so, so much pain. Am I understood?"

"Yes," Blaine said shaking from fear.

"You'll pass on the message to James when he wakes?"

"Yes."

"Good," Max said walking over to Blaine. "Time for a nap."

Max punched Blaine and knocked him out. He hung loosely from the rope above his head.

"Should we really leave them here?" Flash asked.

"I'd prefer to take them, but we need to move quickly," Max said.

"Fair enough. You know they'll talk right?"

"Yeah, but we can't take them with us and can't kill them, they are tied up. It goes against the rules of engagement."

"You're right, we'll find them again if we need to."

"Okay, Prince," Blake said urgently entering the room. "Time to move."

"Alpha, Bravo, help Cameron. Lead on, Hermes. Let's move."

Blake led the team through a series of small tunnels until he got to a blue indicator flashing on his phone's map. He typed something into his phone and told everyone to stand back. Within a minute, a doorframe sized hole was blasted out of the wall in front of the team. When the dust cleared, Max could see tourists and locals alike running for their lives worried about the source of the explosion. He could hear the screams, then a strong British accent rang out through the opening.

"Hull arse, Hermes," the agent said.

Max and his team rushed through the gap in the Vatican's ring wall into the Roman street and climbed aboard the waiting getaway cars. Hermes, Max and Flash got into the first car with two MI6 agents, while Jonnie and Kate bundled Cameron into the boot, before jumping into the second car with two other agents.

The two cars sped down the small winding cobbled street with sirens wailing and lights flashing, impersonating the Italian police force. Pedestrians fled and the police and military guards on each corner screamed at people in the streets to clear the way for the vehicles to pass, but within several blocks the looks on the uniformed officers' faces changed as they received new commands via their radios. Max and his crew flinched as four Army personnel, two from each of the upcoming corners at the intersection, raised rifles to their shoulders and began firing at the two getaway cars. The MI6 agents did not flinch, the cars were bulletproof and threaded between the Swiss Army guards without as much as a crack in the windscreens. It was noisy though as the bullets impacted the side of the heavy vehicles. Max saw the stunned and angry looks on the faces of the officers as they drove past and he watched as people in the streets ran for their lives from the vehicles and gunfire. They looked like they were in pure terror.

As the two large MI6 cars sped around a corner, three Swiss Guard unmarked cars with lights flashing and sirens blaring raced out of the Vatican gates to give chase and four Italian police cars were rushing down a side road to join the pursuit. The drivers beeped their horns incensed by the pedestrians and vehicles blocking their path.

"So, Hermes, what's the plan?" Max asked.

"We have a package to collect, then we are going to the airport," Blake said calmly checking his phone. "Hopefully by the time we get there, Hulk will have found a way to clear the flights and get us out. Otherwise, well, it's going to get interesting."

"Interesting is not one of my favourite terms to describe a getaway I have to say."

The vehicles wove in and out of traffic, their sirens helping to clear the way, but occasionally a vehicle blocked the street. The drivers, without hesitation, mounted the kerb and barely dodged Romans going about their lives and tourists with cameras and smartphones in hand. Max thought about how hitting one of them would definitely wreck their holiday, then he felt guilty, but not just for that thought, but also for Sam who he had left on a boat sailing with Jane at the start of their first holiday together. He thought about the feelings he had when he was being held by his captors, when he was being tortured. He looked between the seats and saw Blake in the front passenger's seat busy on his phone and shouting orders at people. He was so firm and direct and in control, but Max knew he was caring and compassionate. Before he could finish his thought, his vehicle sideswiped a so-called smart car. Their heavy four-wheel-drive nearly tore the whole side off the little car. It hardly felt like a bump, but Max was sure the other car's occupants knew they had been hit. The MI6 driver just kept going and Jonnie and Kates' car followed only a few feet from their tailgate.

"Hermes," the driver said pointing to his satellite navigation system in the dashboard. "We're closing in, get your team ready, my boys in the other car will update your other two members on the plan."

"Okay, thanks Turk," Blake said turning back to face Max and Flash. "Prince, Flash, we are coming up on two silver BMWs that should seem very familiar to you. We are going to pull up beside them and get them to stop, then we are going to get the package."

"Russo?" Max asked smiling as he remembered her driving off earlier in the day.

"You got it."

"I have a visual," Turk the driver said. "Three blocks ahead. Guns up."

The cars pulled in beside Russo's little convoy. Max and Kate in their respective vehicles stood and took aim at the target vehicles through the sunroofs. The noise of their sirens and those of the chasing Swiss Guard and Italian police cars was almost deafening. Max saw Russo in the backseat of the first car. She looked panicked and started to scream at her driver. He clearly had slammed his foot down because the BMW accelerated forward. Max took aim at the driver and fired a single shot. It struck the driver in the throat and the car immediately began to slow as he braked and gripped his bleeding neck. Russo was screaming before being thrown back in her seat as the second car rammed into hers from behind. The second vehicle pushed Russo's car into a parked car and they both stopped dead in their tracks. Turk and his chase car slammed on their brakes and hammered their cars into reverse. Max and Kate both lined up high and wide shots at the incoming police and Swiss Guard vehicles to slow them down. They all stopped around a hundred metres down the road from the accident, not wanting to get any closer to Max and Kate's bullets. Flash and Jonnie were already moving, and within seconds they had a bloodied and unconscious Russo in their arms dragging her towards the boot of Turk's car. Once she was in, the two agents climbed back in their respective cars as Max and Kate provided very loose cover fire, not wanting to actually hit the chasing officers.

"Go!" Max yelled lowering himself back into the car as the doors closed. "Get us out of here!"

"The engines have already started on the jets," Blake said relaying information from the pilots. "My AIS one is waiting to get us airborne and the MI6 one is waiting for our friends here."

"And, Russo and Cameron?"

"They are coming with us, but it doesn't matter, we are all going to the same place."

"Where?"

"London."

"Okay then," Max said as their cars wound through traffic until they approached the Leonardo da Vinci airport and Max pointed through the windscreen. "That doesn't look good."

Up ahead police and army vehicles were already blocking the entrance to the airport. Their lights flashing and sirens blaring, and a line of well-armed officers standing behind the cars aiming in their direction.

"Hold on," Turk said as he drove the car off the roadway onto the grass and smashed through a small sculpture before sliding back onto the road just past the blocking vehicles, as bullet bounced off the car harmlessly.

"God, I hope that wasn't some priceless ancient artefact," Max grimaced.

"They've got hundreds," Turk said cynically.

Max frowned at the thought before noticing more vehicles blocking the VIP entrance to the airport.

"Hold on again," Turk said and with that he turned hard smashing through the security fence near the entrance.

A mess of wire and steel poles tangled and surrounded their car, and was dragged along behind them as they sped down the taxiway to the waiting planes. Max could hear sirens approaching from every direction as they all got out and made for their respective planes. Max and Flash grabbed Russo, while Jonnie and Kate recovered Cameron who looked green from the car ride. Blake spoke briefly to Turk, before leading the AIS team onto the waiting Gulfstream 650ER. As soon as Jonnie boarded, carrying Cameron over his shoulder, Blake hit the close button and shouted an order to the pilots. The engines revved hard as the door raised itself and locked in place.

The two jets followed each other down the taxiway towards the runway as security vehicles began to give chase. Russo and Cameron were handcuffed to their seats for take-off. As Max was taking his seat, the pilots ordered everyone to be seated for an emergency take-off. Max had only ever experienced a proper emergency take-off leaving Baghdad after a mission, but that was in a Globemaster, not a Gulfstream, so he was not sure what to expect. With that, the engines accelerated and the plane began racing to take-off speed, on the taxiway. No sooner had it reached the right speed than it lifted from the ground and raced into the sky at what felt like a ninety-degree incline, straight up, hard and fast. They were at cruising altitude in seconds and banked hard for London as they levelled out. Cameron already motion sick from the journey to the airport, had thrown up all over himself.

Chapter Nine

Max and Jonnie had dragged Cameron to the bathroom at the rear of the plane and threw him fully clothed into the tiny shower cubicle. They let the freezing cold water clean him up, then left him tied up in the shower soaking wet. The bathroom was small, but well appointed. It was clean and gleamy white, with all the toiletries needed for AIS agents on the move. There was even a storage area which held spare clothes for the agents in various style and sizes, plus tactical gear and weapons.

In the main cabin, Russo was coming to, disorientated and slurring her words. She was still handcuffed to the big leather business chair.

"Tie her up in the luggage hold," Max ordered.

"You got it, boss," Kate said getting to her feet. "Want me to make a start?"

"Yes, you know what to do. We need to know how she fits into all this and we need to know what their end game is and how it is going to unfold. Our friend in the bathroom, Cameron, says she's a rook, so she's obviously more important than she will let on, but let's not tell her know we have Cameron just yet."

"A rook?"

"Yes, like in chess."

"I don't play fucking chess."

"Pawn, knight, bishop, rook, queen, king."

"Got it," Kate said dragging Russo up out of the chair and towards the rear of the plane. "Told you she was a bad bitch."

"I'll be in soon."

"Max," Blake said motioning for Max to join him, "come sit down."

"What's up?"

"I just wanted to see if you were okay. Did you want to talk about what happened?"

"I'm fine, Blake, thanks. I got a bit beat up and had some nasty shit coursing through my veins for a few minutes, but I'm okay. You got me through it actually."

"I did?"

"Yes. I remembered your advice from the Wool Shed, that night you came in during my training and told me how to delay the breaking point."

"I remember it," Blake said sheepishly remembering Max tied naked in the Wool Shed.

"Well, it helped, so thank you."

"Glad it worked and I'm glad you are okay."

"You're a great friend, Blake, thank you for always being there for me."

"Of course, Max. I'll always be here for you."

"I hope you know I'm always here for you too."

"Thanks, Max. Yes, I know and it means a lot."

"So, where are we up to?" Max said changing the topic.

"Let's get Hulk on the telecon," Blake said turning to look over his shoulder. "Jonnie, can you please call Hulk?"

"Yes, boss," Jonnie said pressing a series of buttons on his tablet computer.

A repeating ring of circles lit up and faded as the television on the wall waited to connect to the AIS bunker. A message in white text displayed on the black screen which simply said *Rerouting.*

"Hello?" Hulk said over the television's tiny speakers before an image of him flickered then materialised on the screen.

"Hulk, it's Hermes," Blake said checking out the background behind Hulk. "We have Prince and we are on route."

"Good work, Hermes. Prince, how you doing, kid?" Hulk asked from his seat on another AIS jet.

"I'm doing just fine, Hulk, thanks to these guys. Ready and raring to go get these fuckers and put them to an end."

"Good to hear it, so where are we up to?"

"I think we should do a bit of a summary," Blake explained. "Prince killed, Shadow, a traitor at the highest ranks of our intelligence community only a few months ago. At the time, we suspected him to be the leader of an Australian-based terrorist organisation. In the months following, we have set about pulling down what was left of his network arresting or killing people as the situation dictated. The last Australian-based takedown we had was the Irishman in Adelaide. His evidence led us to Italy and Ms Russo who is currently tied up in the back of this plane being interrogated by Alpha. During the first extraction attempt, Prince was captured and tortured, but it would seem he got more out of them then they got from him. Prince?"

"As he was parading around in front of me, I noticed his broken Italian accent," Max quickly summarised. "I knew he was not Italian. So, when I had the chance, I tormented him and ridiculed him, until he was stupid enough to come close to me. I headbutted him and broke his nose, at which point he started cursing in Australian English."

"He's an Australian?"

"Yes. When these guys busted in, we took three captives, including my torturer. To cut to the chase, one very talkative combatant is in our possession, tied up in the back of the plane. His name is Cameron, more details to come, he has confirmed he worked for Shadow in Air Force Intelligence before joining him in his crusade. Cameron said he believed in their cause, which I now do not believe is money. I think it is something much bigger. Most alarming though, Hulk, he claimed he was only a pawn and, Shadow, only a knight."

"Chess?" Hulk questioned with an inquisitive look.

"Yes and he says Ms Russo is a rook."

"It's been a while, tell me, there's still a queen and king, and bishops left in the hierarchy?"

"Yes, but the rook is ranked third most important," Blake added. "Pawn, Knight, Bishop, Rook, Queen, King."

"Well, it would seem Ms Russo is more important than we thought and this organisation it would seem is a lot bigger. If Shadow was able to unleash what he did on our country from such a relatively low-level position, what are the rest of them capable of doing?"

"My thoughts exactly," Max agreed. "I think we are going to need to loop in some friends to help out."

"Hermes already has, MI6 is assisting, but I'm on my way to formally make this a joint operation."

"You're on route to London too?"

"Yes, Hermes and I had planned to take over the mission hunting down The Sixteen, and let you and Flash head back to Italy for your break after CHOGM."

"Due respect, boss," Flash interrupted. "But, no way, we're with you 'til this is done."

"You didn't let me finish. I was going to say that, but things have changed. We will still be running things from on the ground in London, but we'll need you two, plus Alpha and Bravo in the field with the Prime Minister at CHOGM and chasing down any leads we find."

"Ack, sorry. We're in," Flash said.

"I knew you would be. Let me know how you get on with your two guests."

"Will do."

"See you in London soon."

"Thanks, boss," Blake said nodding to Jonnie who cut the connection and the screen went black.

"I'm going to go check on Kate," Max said standing and walking towards the rear of the plane.

Inside the luggage hold he found Kate and Russo, who was tied up with her arms outstretched above her head, balancing on her tip toes. She was a beautiful woman in her late fifties with short snow-white hair and she was wearing a white dress and red high-heals, and a collection of white-gold jewellery covered in diamonds adorned her wrists, fingers and neck. Her makeup was running from a combination of sweat and tears, contrasting hard with her glamourous outfit.

"How are you going in here?" Max asked not taking his eyes off Russo.

"She's not talking yet," Kate said starring at Russo with a look of disgust.

"Hello, Ms Russo. Do you know who I am?"

"No," Russo said with a look approaching fear in her eyes.

"Your eyes tell a different story, Gloria. Want to try again? Do you know who I am?"

"Yes," she said softly looking down at the floor.

"Good. So, you will also know how I operate, how I extract information from people and how good I am at it?"

Russo nodded and stifled a sob.

"I didn't quite hear that."

"Yes, I know," Russo whispered through her tears.

"Excellent. Now tell me, in your organisation's file on me, did it mention this," Max asked withdrawing his knife from under his shirt.

Russo nodded.

"I'm not going to tell you again!" Max yelled throwing his knife and pinning into the wall next to her face with its blade edge facing Russo, "use your words!"

"Yes, it mentioned your knife, Agent Shaw."

"So, why don't you save yourself some time and a lot of pain, by telling us what we need to know?"

"Because Agent Shaw, this is bigger than you and me, and I know that very soon I will be out of here and you will find yourself in more trouble than you have ever experienced."

"Oh and how do you image that is going to happen?"

"Our reach is far and our hands never idle."

"I'm sick of playing games with you people," Max said angrily walking over and grabbing Russo by the neck. "Tell me what I need to know!"

Max grabbed Russo by the hair and slowly used both his hands to push her face towards his hunting knife which was still lodged firmly in the wall. She was fighting back with as much force as she could, but Max was easily too strong and she was on her tip toes which meant she could not get traction. Max stopped as the blade rested against her forehead.

"Why are you funding terrorists?" Max demanded. "What is your goal?"

"We are not terrorists!" Russo yelled.

"Could have fooled me. So, what are you then?"

"Visionaries. Leaders. Patriots."

"Oh please, you think the death of innocent civilians makes you a patriot? You think killing the defenceless is leadership? How visionary do you think it was to kill my fiancé?"

"That was a mistake."

"A mistake?"

"Your old boss, Greg "Shadow" Lloyd hated your insubordination, hated your devotion to General Scott and the AIS, and he thought you were getting too close to his plans. When you took one of his pawns into custody and killed several others, he tried to slow AIS's progress by hurting you, the lead agent on the case. I tried to talk him out of it."

"You failed and the man I loved died in my arms," Max choked out pressing Russo's head against the blade, slicing a thin line above her eye and drawing blood which ran down her forehead, across her eyebrow and down her cheek.

"Prince," Kate said softly, gently touching him on the shoulder. "Why don't you leave her with me for a while?"

After several long moments, Max punched the wall beside Russo's head cracking the plastic and causing Russo to flinch and close her eyes. Tears rolled down her cheeks.

"Tell Agent Matthews here everything she wants to know or I will be back in here and she won't stop me again."

Max left the room with Russo trembling in tears. He could feel the hurt and pain coursing through his whole body. He was angry. He wanted her to suffer.

"How'd it go?" Flash asked pointing at the luggage hold.

"She'll talk eventually," Max snapped.

"Are you okay? You look shaken up."

"Yeah, I got a bit carried away. Kate stepped in and took over."

"What happened?"

"She said they were patriots, leaders and visionaries. I asked how it was visionary to murder Lachlan and sliced her forehead with my knife."

"Jesus, Max."

"It was just a nick, nothing major."

"Are you sure, Max? You've been through a lot today."

"You all just need to settle and calm down, I'm fine! She just pissed me off!" Max barked.

"Alright, mate, but just so you know, we're here for you, I'm here for you."

"I know, Jacob," Max said calming down. "Thanks. Honestly, I'm fine."

"You don't seem fine."

"Oh, for fuck's sake, Flash!" Max shouted turning his back on his friend to look out the window.

Flash just sat in silence looking at his best friend, more in worry than anything else. In all the years they had known each other, they had never had one argument or fight. Flash had never seen Max lose his cool. He had seen him angry at targets and passionate about his work, and he had seen the highs and lows of Max's love and loss with Lachlan. But this was new, something was not right. His friend was breaking.

"Sorry, I'm sorry, Flash," Max said after a few moments and turning back to face his friend. "It's just."

"I get it, mate," Flash reassured. "It's okay, you need to get some rest."

"Yeah, you might be right," Max said taking a seat and resting his head in his hands.

"I'll leave you alone and let you relax. I'll go check in with Blake."

"Thanks," Max nodded without looking up.

Flash headed for the front of the plane. There was a small office with a door to the cockpit on the far side and a door to the main cabin on the other. Blake was in the office sitting in a high-back leather business class seat at a foldout table which was covered in paperwork and ICT equipment.

"Hey, Flash," Blake said looking up briefly. "How's it going? Any movement with Russo?"

"We may have a small problem," Flash said hesitantly taking a seat opposite Blake.

"What is it?"

"It's Max. He's more shaken up than he's letting on."

"After what they did to him, I'm not surprised, Jacob."

"He sliced Russo's head with his knife after she mentioned Lachlan and he snapped at me for asking questions. I have known him for as long as you have, have you ever seen him snap like that?"

"No, I haven't."

"But?"

"But, I think we should just give him some time. He will come good. He always does. He's been through a lot, just today, let alone the past few months and well, years."

"Yeah, I guess you're right, but I just wanted you to know."

"Thanks, mate. I'm sure he will be okay, he just needs some time."

"Time we don't really have."

"We have time now. Hopefully he can get some rest before we get to London."

"He's resting now," Flash said nodding his head back towards the cabin. "Anyway, where are we?"

"We are somewhere approaching Venice."

"I meant with Russo and the case."

"Oh, of course, well MI6 is working up their evidence and are trawling through her connections with the AIS team we have on the ground," Blake said shuffling through some paperwork when out of nowhere the plane lurched to the side violently.

Flash fell sideways into the cabin wall, hitting his head. Blake clung to his seat, as his paperwork and computer flew off the desk and hit the opposite wall. The plane levelled and for a moment there was calm. The agents sat silently, holding their breaths, then suddenly the plane dropped several feet and banked hard to the other side. Again, Flash who had not fastened his seatbelt tumbled, this time right out of his seat, across the small cabin with all of Blake's paperwork. Blake's laptop screen shattered as it hit the wall and Blake watched helplessly as he clung to his seat. Flash scrambled to his seat and fastened his seatbelt as the plane levelled. Max had been resting towards the rear of the plane, when the first lurch threw him onto the floor. As Flash clipped his seatbelt in, Max appeared at the door of the office.

"What the fuck is going on?" Max asked opening the door. "Are you two okay?"

"Fine, Max," Blake shouted, "you need to strap in!"

"Yeah," Max said ignoring the direction and walking unsteadily to the cockpit door as the plane moved from side-to-side.

He opened the cockpit door and heard the two pilots shouting into their headsets.

"Sir, you need to take a seat!" one of the pilots ordered. "We are going to be in for a rough ride."

"What the fuck is going on?" Max demanded.

"We have two fighter jets on our tail, they have missile lock. We can't shake them. They are asking us to land in Venice or we will be shot down."

"Russo."

"What?"

"Nothing. Hold them off as long as you can, but land if you need to. I don't think they will shoot us with her on board, but we can't take the chance."

"Yes, sir."

"Did you hear all that?" Max asked as he walked back into the office, holding onto nearby chairs as he walked.

"Yes," Flash said pointing to Blake. "Blake's calling Hulk now. What should we do?"

"Talk to Hulk, relay what's happening, then stay strapped in, it could get bumpy."

"What are you going to do?"

"I'm going to talk to Russo. She indicated before that she wouldn't be with us for long and that we would be in trouble when she got away from us."

"Jesus, who are these people? Do you need a hand with her?"

"No, stay here," Max directed as he walked into the main cabin.

"You okay, kid?" Max asked Jonnie as he walked past.

"Yeah, boss," Jonnie said. "What's going on?"

"Seems the Italians don't want us to leave."

"Jets?"

"Yep."

"Oh, fuck," Jonnie said nervously. "I hate planes at the best of times."

"It'll be fine, mate. Whoever ordered them up here, wants her back. They won't shoot, they want us to land."

"You sure about that?"

"I'm going to find out. Stay strapped in."

"Okay, sing out if you need anything."

"You got it."

Max fought his way to the rear door leading to the cargo hold, hanging onto the wall and chairs as he went. The plane rolled to the side, Max fell against the wall, but stayed on his feet.

"Are you okay?" Max asked as he opened the door and looked around for Kate.

"Yeah, I'm fine," Kate said getting to her feet. "What the fuck is going on?"

"Fighter jets. They are trying to force us down."

"To get this stupid bitch back?"

"I would guess so," Max said finally looking at Russo who had blood running from her forehead.

"She hit her head on your knife with the first bump, probably lucky it didn't cut something important, other than her stupid face."

"What'd you get from her?"

"Not much, the organisation is called The Sixteen. They use chess ranks to help structure the organisation and give people some idea of which arsehole is in charge."

"Bureaucracy works, even for the bad guys," Max said walking over and lifting Russo's head.

"I told you my friends would come for me, you better land the plane," Russo smiled. "But, when you do, you should run. Run as fast and as far as you can, and maybe, just maybe, you will live another day or two until we find you and kill you all."

"It is you and your friends who should run. I am going to make it my life's mission to find every last one of you and put you in the ground."

"I believe you think you can, Agent Shaw, but you will not succeed. We are everywhere. Our reach is far and our hands never idle."

"How far?"

"Global."

"And, what exactly is it your hands are doing?"

"We shape global events from the rise and fall of governments to terrorist attacks and business successes and failures."

"You're the puppet masters?"

"That is one way of putting it. We would rather consider ourselves a network of likeminded individuals searching for peace."

"Peace through death and chaos is hypocritical surely?"

"You cannot make an omelette without breaking some eggs."

"These are people's lives you happily trade for your own success and goals. What about them, do you ever think about them and lives you are throwing away?"

"You will never understand. The people are sheep, they need shepherding. If a few need to die for the many, then so be it."

"You are wrong, people have freewill and they will see through your actions. They will see you as the terrorists you are."

"They have not yet," Russo said smugly.

Abruptly the plane dropped several metres without warning. Max and Kate were lifted off the ground, before they were both slammed into the floor as it levelled out. Russo had been lifted off her tiptoes into the air as well, but as she fell and slammed into the wall, she sliced her arm on Max's knife which was still pinned to the wall. She screamed and Max looked up to see blood gushing out of the wound, it must have hit an artery. Max leapt to his feet and put pressure on the cut as Kate retrieved the first-aid kit.

"Jesus!" Kate said grimacing when she got back on the sight of all the blood. "This bitch can bleed."

"Wrap it tight," Max ordered. "We have to land. She will bleed out if we don't get her to a hospital."

"I've got this, make the plans, boss."

"Got it," Max said running out of the room, blood dripping from his hands onto the Gulfstream's carpet.

He stormed through the plane and noticed all the computers and paperwork scattered about the cabin. Russo's bag and belongings were laying on the floor beside Jonnie who was clinging onto his chair for dear life. Max headed past him towards the cockpit leaving bloody handprints on the chairs and walls.

"Christ, Max!" Flash exclaimed. "What happened?"

"She cut an artery on my knife," Max said.

"Fuck, Max. That might have been taking it too far."

"I didn't do it," Max riled, "the knife was stuck in the wall, she fell into it when the plane dropped."

"Oh, sorry mate, I thought."

"I know what you thought, it doesn't matter! We need to land, she won't make it to London."

"Nor will we with these arseholes on our tail."

"Land the plane," Max ordered flinging open the cockpit door.

"Yes, sir," the pilot agreed. "We are looking for a suitable spot. An alternate to where they want us to go. We don't know what will be waiting for us."

"Good thinking. How about we fox them? Make them think we are complying, then at the last-minute abort for a nearby location, one they haven't secured."

"My thoughts too, sir. They will have the runway and airport locked down. They want us to land at Lido, how about we just head for the main airport, Marco Polo, across the bay?"

"Do it. It might give us a chance to disappear in the crowd. Make the approach to Lido, let the jets go by, then head for Polo, when they clear the area. Tell them we will comply over the radio, buy us as much time as possible."

"Yes, sir," the pilot said as Max left the cockpit.

"Hear all that?" Max asked.

"Yes, it's not going to be enough time to get cars in place," Blake said looking up from his phone to Max.

"We will have to figure it out on the run. Flash stay with Blake, whatever it takes, don't let him get captured. Both of you gear up."

"You got it," Flash said looking to Blake. "I'll get him out."

"What are you going to do?" Blake asked.

"I'm getting Russo to the hospital."

"That's suicide, Max. You'll never get her there by yourself, let alone getting away again."

"That's why it's only me going," Max dismissed as he pointed to a map on the table. "I will take her to the main hospital. I'm going to bug her. Get AIS to monitor the chip and we will pick her up when we get the chance. Jonnie and Kate will take Cameron and they can meet you both at the safehouse."

"You'll meet us there too?" Flash asked worried about his friend.

"Yeah, I will make my way there when I'm sure I'm away free."

"As soon as the plane taxis, get ready to move."

"Got it, mate."

Max found Jonnie in the doorway to the plane's bathroom. Cameron was lying in a pool of his own blood. He had fallen through the glass shower screen, a long shard had punctured his throat.

"Guess he won't be coming with us," Max said matter-of-factly. "You alright, kid?"

"Yeah, it's just a lot of blood," Jonnie squirmed. "I got a bit woozy."

"You've killed ten people by my count since you joined my team. A bit of blood is making you woozy?"

"Yeah, normally through a sniper rifle, I don't get this close for a reason."

"Well, don't fucking collapse or anything, you need to get ready to move. As soon as we land, you and Kate need to make a run for it. Blake and Flash will go a separate way, and I'm taking Russo to the hospital. We will all rendezvous at the safehouse."

"I can help you get her to the hospital," Jonnie said again eager to help Max anyway he can.

"No, mate. It might be a one-way trip. I need you to help the others. Get them out, protect them, then track her down again later and finish the job. There are a lot of people counting on you to succeed. Got it?"

"Yes, Prince. If you say so."

"Thanks, Jonnie. For what it is worth, kid, you are doing a great job. You are a vital member of my team and I'm glad I got a chance to work alongside you. You're already a great agent. Keep it up."

"We will finish this together, you'll meet us at the safehouse, I know it."

"I hope so, kid. You look after the others for me when you get there, won't you?"

"You bet, I will!"

"Good. Now gear up."

"Yes, sir."

Max went next door and had a similar conversation with Kate, only she swore a lot more. The general point was the same as the rest of his team, but she told him he was a 'fucking idiot' at least twice for going alone. He pulled rank as team leader and she begrudgingly accepted the order with a few more expletives under the breath.

The pilots told everyone to get ready over the plane's little speakers, so Max and his team took their seats and strapped in. The plane slowly dropped altitude preparing to land at Lido airport. The landing gear was lowered and they made their approach. Only metres from the ground the escort jets banked hard and headed for their home base. On cue, the AIS pilots, both former Air Force pilots, wound the engines back up to full speed and took off into the air again. Max saw the waiting police cars surrounding the runway, he hoped the scene was not repeated at the Marco Polo airport. The AIS jet flew low over Venice, no doubt frightening people in the streets. The pilots were aiming for a smaller side runway which they hoped was not in heavy use today.

The pilots watched the radar and listened as air traffic control cleared planes from the landing and take-off patterns they had been in, clearing a path. The Gulfstream made its second approach, but this time it touched down as normal, well almost as normal. As soon as the pilots had it at a manageable ground speed, they taxied for the nearest fence. The nose of the small jet punched through the fence and the pilots shutdown the engines.

Max threw the unconscious, but alive, Russo over his left shoulder and held his pistol in his right hand. Blake and Flash had opened the door during the taxi, and were on the bottom steps when the plane crashed through the fence. They both took off to the left towards a row of cars as the plane came to a halt. Jonnie and Kate ran right after making sure Max got Russo down the stairs. The pilots followed Blake and Flash.

Blake and Flash hijacked a cab with the pilots climbing into the backseat, while Max saw Jonnie and Kate running towards the long-term carpark. Max ran with Russo bouncing on his shoulder for the terminal as police cars started to approach. He took off over the greying tiles of the terminal for the rear exit. It was a small airport and the rear exit, opened up onto a marina on the Grand Canal. Max found a speed boat and tossed Russo in the rear, then took aim at the driver with his pistol. He ordered the driver to take them to the hospital. The boat driver did as commanded, dropping the ropes into the canal and winding up the boat to full speed within seconds. As the boat pulled out into the canal, a swarm of uniformed police officers flooded out onto the marina's dock and began firing at Max. Bullets ripped into the wood lined vessel, Max threw himself over Russo as the windscreen shattered sending glass flying over the three occupants.

Three police boats sped out onto the canal behind Max and the bullets continued to smash into the boat. The driver dived down a small set of stairs to shelter in the cabin, so Max jumped up to grab the wheel. He turned sharply, racing the boat down a narrow channel off the Grand Canal. He rushed past windows of homes lining the street and under overpasses and footbridges causing nearby tourists and locals alike to scream abuse at him, telling him to slow down. The wake from the powerful outboard motor sent water gushing over the lower walkways, while Max ducked under several stringlines holding locals' washing.

One of the chase boats had successfully made the turn and was gaining on him. The other two were following, but much further behind having missed the turn. Max accelerated hard and swerved to the left narrowly missing a condoler, the wake of his powerful boat rocking and overturning it, tipping its occupants into the water. The police boat smashed through the overturned condoler breaking it in half. Max was relieved to see the two rear police boats stop to help its occupants out of the water. Max steered the boat back out onto the Grand Canal and wove between the water taxis, leisure craft, condolers and ferries to stop the police from firing. He watched the channels and streets whip passed as water sprayed up with each bounce of the boat on the waves, until he finally found the street he was looking for and yanked hard on the wheel. He speared his boat between two passenger ferries, cutting away from the police boat. He entered the channel and brought the boat to a stop next to the hospital entrance. He grabbed the unconscious Russo and fireman carried her into the hospital.

"I need a doctor!" Max yelled in Italian to a nearby nurse. "She's lost a lot of blood."

Several nurses and a doctor appeared, and Max placed Russo down on a trolley. They disappeared, wheeling Russo into surgery. Max stole a look behind him to see the police boat arriving and three officers climbing out, headed for the hospital. He run towards the back of the hospital, weaving through the sterile corridors. As he arrived at the rear doors, three more police were entering led by a man in a dark suit who raised his hands in calming motion on sighting Max.

"Agent Shaw," the man in the suit said. "My name is Agent John Bradley of MI6. Where is Ms Russo?"

"Why is MI6 chasing me?" Max questioned. "Why did you force us out of the sky?"

"We did not have anything to do with that. You pissed off a lot of people in Rome, they were the ones who ordered your plane to land. I'm here to help you. Where is Russo? Is she alive?"

"Why do you want her?"

"We have a mission to complete, to get her back to London. So, where is she?"

"Something doesn't make sense here. We were going to be shot down, then the police just tried to kill me on the way here. Now, you say it's okay and we have a mission to finish."

"We do. I have spoken to the police. They understand the situation. Now, if you could show me to Ms Russo."

It's too quick, Max thought to himself.

"What's the plan?" Max asked Bradley.

"We will collect Ms Russo and head for London."

"And, my team and the AIS jet?"

"We will get a message to them at the safehouse, I presume that's where they were going, you will just need to let me know where it is. You and I can take my plane."

"She's down there," Max said pointing over his shoulder and stepping to the side. "After you."

"Great, let's go," Bradley ordered walking past Max, followed by two of the officers.

The third officer stopped to let Max walk in the middle of the group. *I can't let them flank me*, Max thought to himself. He leapt forward and punched one of the officers in the back of the head, knocking him out. As he fell, Max spun, jumped off his left foot and drew back his right fist, then slammed it into the trailing officer's face. As Max landed, he drove his left fist through the air uppercutting the trailing officer and knocking him out. Not waiting for the others to react, he spun on his heals and fled left down a white tiled corridor.

"Fuck," Bradley yelled to his remaining officer. "He's onto us, take the stairs at the end."

"Yes, boss," the officer said in English before running the length of the corridor to the stairs.

Max had taken the first set of stairs, he took them three at a time, until he reached the third floor and ran down the corridor looking for somewhere to hide. He ducked into a patient's room, there was one old man asleep but the other three beds were empty. He quickly wrote a false name on the white board above one of the spare beds and put a red line through it, then he climbed under the sheets, dragging the top sheet over his head. The soft white cloth fell over his face and he laid perfectly still, slowing his breathing, like he had learnt during sniper training. He heard footsteps at the door.

"Did you see him?" Bradley asked out of breath from the run up the stairs.

"No, boss," the officer said equally exasperated. "He must have found a way out. The Bishop will not be pleased if we let him get away."

"Well, let's not worry about that right now, Shaw's not gone yet. We need to search every room. Have they secured the Rook?"

"Yes, she is in surgery, but he got her here in time. She will make it."

"Well, that is good news at least. You check this level for the little Prince, I'll head to level two."

"Yes, boss."

Bradley left and Max could hear his footsteps trailing off into the distance. The officer walked into the room and looked around, he checked the old man then wandered over to Max's bed. He saw the whiteboard above and read the name aloud. Max sat up and lurched forward towards the sound of the officer's voice, grabbing him by his borrowed Italian police officer uniform. He was stumbling back in shock and Max took the opportunity to stick his silenced pistol in his open mouth.

"Do you work for MI6?" Max asked and the officer nodded in terror.

"Is John Bradley his real name?" Max asked and the officer nodded again.

"Are you both part of The Sixteen?" Max asked and the office nodded, and Max pulled out the pistol. "How far does this thing really go?"

"Right to the top."

"The top of what?"

"The world. We are everywhere. Our reach is far and our hands never idle."

"So I keep hearing, but there has to be someone in charge. Who is it?"

"They will kill me."

"What do you think I will do to you?"

The officer slapped Max's hand away, knocking the gun to the floor and the pair wrestled after it on the tiles. The officer got there first, but Max jumped on top of him, grabbing his wrists and slamming his hands down onto the floor forcing him to drop the gun. It scattered across the tiles, as Max unleashed a flurry of punches to the officer's stomach and chest. He brought his arms up to protect his face, but Max saw an opening and threw his head forwarded violently headbutting the officer, busting his nose. Max rolled off and got to his feet, looking for his gun. He walked over, but as he bent over to pick it up the officer crash tackled him through the locked bifold glass doors out onto the balcony. The glass shattered, raining down on the balcony and over the edge to the footpath below, as Max and the officer crashed into the small rusty iron railing on the tiny balcony. The balcony creaked as they bounced left and right throwing punches at one another, then it tilted slightly, Max felt it move under his feet. He jumped left and kicked the officer square in the chest. The officer tumbled backwards over the railing as the balcony gave way and fell from the building. Max used the kick for momentum to jump back into the room. He watched as the officer fell, three storeys to the concrete pathway below, only narrowly missing the canal. The balcony hit the concrete and shattered next to the officer's lifeless body, the rusty iron clattering across the pathway and into the water as it broke free.

"Freeze, Prince!" Bradley shouted from behind him. "You have delayed their plans too many times and I am sorry to say that it is time for you to die."

"I'm going to find each of those involved," Max said coldly keeping his back to Bradley. "And, I'm going to kill them."

"No, Mr Shaw, you are going to die."

"No, Mr Bradley, I'm not," Max said diving from the third storey window into the canal's murky water as bullets flew through the air then into the water next to him.

Chapter Ten

"It's the Bishop," Robert said into his phone.

"Yes, sir," Bradley answered.

"I received your message. Are you telling me Prince evaded you?"

"Yes, sir. He dived out the fucking third storey window into the canal after killing one of my men."

"I am starting to lose my patience with the Prince. I am starting to understand why Shadow had so much trouble controlling him."

"Yes, sir, but I will find him."

"When you do, you need to kill him. He has been a reoccurring pain for The Sixteen and we have let him disrupt our plans too many times. Kill him and his team, then move to location two."

"Will do."

"What do you need to make that happen?"

"If I find his team, he will come for them."

"Our friends from the Vatican have lent on the local police. It seems they were very unhappy to hear of AIS's involvement in the death of one of their Archbishops a few years ago. So, the locals will help find the agents. You just need to be ready to sweep in and do what's necessary. Your badge should open the doors for you."

"Amazing how that evidence surfaced after all these years and fell into the church's hands."

"Our reach is far and our hands never idle."

"So it is. Are they helping The Sixteen willingly, the church?"

"Not exactly. We have a couple of connections, but they are mostly seeking AIS agents to question and arrest them over the Archbishop's death, not to further our cause. It just so happens that our needs align. So, the local police should give you whatever you need to make the arrests."

"Understood. I will do what needs to be done."

"Good. I need you to do something else."

"Yes, sir?"

"I need you to find Russo's manual."

"Her what?"

"Her manual. It is a small brown leather book, looks like a diary. It has The Sixteen's seal pressed into the leather strap."

"I don't know what the seal looks like."

"It is a diamond with the head of a roaring lion inside it."

"Understood, I will find it. Priority?"

"It is a very high priority. The contents are vital to our operations."

"Okay, I will track it down."

"Thank you, I look forward to hearing of your success and to seeing you when you arrive."

"Thank you, sir."

Robert cut the call and dialled a second number.

"It's the Bishop," Robert said into the phone for the second time.

"Yes, sir," Wes Harris said.

"Is the device in place?"

"We are on route right now, we should be onsite in a few minutes. We will proceed as planned to the construction site and place the device in one of the pillars."

"Any difficulties getting the access passes?"

"No, we stole one of the contractor's trucks. It had a pass in the window."

"Excellent, good job."

"Thank you, sir."

"What about the other two devices?"

"They are on route as planned. Within the next few hour, the first will arrive in America and our team will move it into

*position. The other will take a few more hours, but our team is
ready to move as planned."*

"And the timers?"

"They will be set when they are placed in their positions."

"What is the radius?"

*"Somewhere around three miles immediately levelled, four
more miles damaged and contaminated. Fallout will follow the
cloud."*

"Which direction is it likely to flow?"

"Away from the principal."

"Good, let me know when it is done."

"Yes, sir," the man said as Robert ended the call.

Chapter Eleven

Flash drove their stolen car through the narrow streets leading away from the airport, while Blake called Hulk and explained what had happened. Hulk was understandably pissed off and he felt helpless trapped on his little plane miles away from his team. Blake knew Hulk was upset, partly because he blamed himself for this mess. Shadow had been one of Hulk's oldest friends and longest serving colleagues, and he had betrayed everyone and committed treason right under Hulk's nose. He blamed himself for missing it and for trusting him, he felt somehow responsible for the deaths of thousands of Australians and he felt like he had let his country down. He also felt tremendous guilt for the pain his team had suffered, especially Max who lost his fiancé at Shadow's hands. He had made it his personal mission to root out every last one of those involved with Shadow and to bring them to justice either before the courts or before the end of a gun. Every time he thought they were getting closer to the end, more and more people were uncovered, and now he was faced with news his team's jet had been forced from the sky and he had agents scattered across Venice, surrounded by hostiles. It just keeps getting bigger and more out of control. He wanted to find these people and stop them once and for all.

"Where are you now?" Hulk asked.

"We are headed for the safehouse," Blake said as Flash flung the car left to dodge a slow-moving bike. "I've got Flash and the two pilots."

"Where is Prince?"

"He took Russo to the hospital. He figures she is too important to die, at least for now. He planted a tracker on her, so we can pick her up later."

"And, did he have a plan to get out after dropping her off?"

"He ordered us to split up, he took her alone, just in case he couldn't get away."

"Well, if anyone can, he can. What about Bravo and Alpha?"

"They are making their way to the safehouse too, I'm unsure of their current location."

"This is a great deal bigger than we thought, to have fighter jets track and force the agency jet down, they are more connected than we could have imagined."

"I've been thinking about it, it doesn't necessarily mean they have infiltrated each of these organisations, it could just mean they know people who can pull the strings."

"You might be right, but they are some big strings they are pulling."

"Agree."

"I'm maintaining my route to London, the Prime Minister is already in town for the Commonwealth Heads of Government Meeting. I want to brief him in person and increase his security, I am ordering an AIS takeover of his detail until we can be sure of what is happening."

"I agree, we need to re-evaluate and until we can get a handle on this, we don't know who to trust."

"Get your team to the safehouse and lay low for a couple of hours, I'll follow up with some of my contacts in the European Intelligence community to find out who ordered the plane down, then hopefully get it cleared again for take-off. I want you all here, by tomorrow morning."

"Yes, sir. What about Prince?"

"He knows how to look after himself, he will make it to the safehouse. Leave him to it."

"And, if he doesn't?"

"If he doesn't get back to the safehouse, you will need to just get to London without him."

"Yes, sir," Blake agreed staring out the window as if willing Max to find them.

Out of nowhere, a car pulled out in front of them and Flash hit the brakes. The occupants of the other car raised their weapons and started firing at Blake and Flash. Flash threw the car into reverse and hit the accelerator.

"What's going on?" Hulk asked.

"We've got company, they are firing on us. I will call you when we reach the safehouse."

"Good luck and Godspeed."

"And, to you," Blake shouted as he wound down his window. "I don't know about you, but I'm sick of these pricks!"

"Do it," Flash said as Blake picked up his MP5.

Blake undid his seatbelt and kneeled on his seat facing backwards. He stuck his arm out the window and started returning fire at their pursuers. The chase cars swerved left and right trying to avoid the onslaught, but Blake was patient and only fired when he had a clear shot at the cars. Bullets pinged off the bonnets and slammed into the windshields, but they were unrelenting and kept pace. Unexpectedly a four-wheel drive came rushing at the side of their car, forcing Flash to take a hard turn onto the motorway leading to the city. Blake fired at the new car as its passenger drew similar weapons to his and opened fire.

Flash wove the car through traffic causing some vehicles to brake hard, creating obstacles for the chase cars. The third chase car in the line was not able to avoid a small truck which had braked when Flash cut in front of it. It smashed into the truck's tray with violent force, the bonnet crumpled and the car lifted off the ground and bounced backwards, while the truck ran into the guardrail. The passenger who had been shooting at Flash and Blake was thrown through the windscreen and his body flailed around on the bitumen like a ragdoll, then laid perfectly still face down on the hot road surface.

Flash kept pushing the small engine to its limits as the two remaining cars stayed on his tail. Blake saw an opening, lined up his shot and squeezed the trigger. The bullet spat from the MP5, splintered the windscreen and hit the driver of the four-wheel drive in the face. The result was instantaneous. The big powerful engine roared as the dead weight of the driver's foot pressed down on the accelerator it came up level with their car and they watched as the passenger was trying to wrestle control of the vehicle, but it was hopeless, it careered through the guardrail over a small rocky reinforcing wall and ploughed into the ocean. It came to a sudden, aggressive stop and started to sink, while its engine continued to red line, spluttering water from the exhaust. As they continued along the motorway, Blake's phone rang.

"Hermes," Blake yelled into the phone while still firing at the remaining chase car.

"Agent Smyth," the British accented man said on the other end of the phone. *"This is Agent John Bradley of MI6. I am in Venice and have been asked to provide your team with assistance. Where are you now?"*

"On the motorway, leading to the city."

"Good, can I hear gunfire?"

"Yes, two chase cars down, one to go."

"Take the second exit at the end of the motorway, just after you cross the water, my team will spring the trap for the chase car four blocks down. Understood?"

"Roger that, see you in a few minutes."

"Acknowledged."

"Who was that?" Flash asked.

"MI6, take the second exit when we crossed the water, they will help us with vehicle number three."

"You got it. About time we had some good luck."

Flash hit the off ramp at the second exit and followed the road for several blocks with the chase car half a block behind. At the fourth intersection, Flash jumped the car over a few bumps, but saw a large white object hurtling down the street at tremendous speed. It was too late. As their car shot into the intersection a cement truck flew into the intersection and smashed into the back of the cab. It ripped the boot clean off the car and they spun wildly, somehow staying on their wheels.

"Hermes, Fla..." Max said breaking up over the comms unit as the car came to a stop. *"Can...hear me?"*

"Yes, Prince," Blake answered groggily. "But the line isn't good. Are you okay?"

"MI6...Bradley..."

"Repeat, Prince, I didn't copy."

"Don't trust...Bradley."

"Agent John Bradley from MI6?"

"He's...Sixteen...out now."

A swarm of badged and unmarked police cars surrounded their car, and men and women sprung out drawing their weapons and taking aim at the AIS agents and pilots. Blake looked around at his team. They were shook up, but not hurt following the crash.

"We are burnt, Max," Blake said. "They've got us."

There was a crackling sound on the other end of the line, then it went quiet.

"Throw your weapons out, get out of the car slowly and kneel on the ground with your hands above your head," Bradley demanded over a megaphone.

The two agents and the AIS pilots complied. They drew out their guns and climbed out of the vehicle. They all knelt and raised their hands, as officers circled and placed them in handcuffs.

"It is a pleasure to meet you, Captain Smyth," Bradley said to Blake. "Chief of Staff and Deputy Head of Operations for the Australian Intelligence Service it is an honour, sir."

"Why are we in these handcuffs?" Blake asked.

"You invaded Vatican City, murdered and tortured people on foreign soil, in the process committing several acts of war and other crimes, including ignoring orders from air traffic control and the air force. Did you really think they would just let you get away?"

"You and I both know what was happening there," Blake said switching to Italian. "Why don't you tell all of these officers about The Sixteen, about how you and your friends have murdered and bribed and forced your will on the people, for money and power? Why don't you tell them senior priests and cardinals were involved in assassination and mass murder? Why don't you tell them that they captured and tortured an Australian intelligence agent in Vatican City?"

"I do not speak Italian, Agent Smyth," Bradley said bemused as several of the officers exchanged worried looks. "I am sure that was passionate and moving, but these guys work for me. Take them away."

Blake, Flash and the two pilots were dragged up to their feet and marched over to a waiting police wagon where they were instructed to get in the back. They climbed in and sat on the long benches and Blake stared at Bradley.

"He will come for you," Blake said smiling. "And he will kill you for this."

"If Agent Shaw survived the dive and swim through the canal, and missed taking a bullet, I would be surprised, but if he does come, I will be ready."

"No, Bradley, you will be sorry!" Blake yelled as the doors slammed shut.

Chapter Twelve

Jonnie parked their stolen Opel sedan in a public parking lot. He and Kate had spent over an hour looping back and forth through a mix of narrow streets and large motorways from Marghera to Treviso, doubling back occasionally to ensure they were not followed. Once the were satisfied, they took a winding loop back through the countryside until they found the Liberty Bridge which they took across to Venice. They wound their way through the tiny streets of Venice and over the narrow bridges until they the parking lot and decided to dump the car and walk the rest of the way.

Jonnie had found an empty parking space on the second floor of the lot in the back corner. It was shadowy and dark giving them some privacy to check their surroundings and make sure there was no one following them. They wiped the steering wheel and down handles to remove their prints, then checked outside again. The level was clear, so they concealed their weapons and jumped out of the car. Jonnie went to the rear of the car and drew his pocketknife and began undoing the screws holding the number plate. Kate did the same at the front of the car.

When they had the number plates in hand, they folded them both in half and Jonnie carried them as they walked out of the parking garage. They strolled hand in hand like a married couple, even though their size and age differences made them an interesting couple. When they got close to the canal, Jonnie lent down pretending to tie his laces and when he was sure no one was watching he slid the number plates into the water.

They took their time walking through the streets as if they were tourists, stopping occasionally with a crowd to see a local sight. Jonnie took out his phone and took photos to reinforce the tourist stereotype. They spent some time doubling back on their course and taking wide loops around the safehouse to check for people following them. A few blocks from the safehouse, they stopped at a café and bought coffee. They watched for people who might be surveilling them while they waited for their coffee. While one or two people glanced in their direction, neither agent could spot anyone tailing them. They gathered their coffees and strolled towards the safehouse, taking the opportunity to buy some takeaway sandwiches on route.

Eventually they made their way into the AIS safehouse, which was a rundown old apartment on the third floor of a small apartment block. When they got to the door, they checked the hallway before Kate removed the doorhandle exposing a hidden keypad. She waved her ring in front of the sensor then typed in her access code. There was a soft beep and click as the door unlocked. She replaced the front panel of the door handle again hiding the hi-tech lock and the two agents walked inside.

They were the first to arrive. They tried to radio Max, but could not reach him, so they tried Blake. Blake did not answer either, so they messaged Hulk to tell him they were secure in the safehouse awaiting the team's arrival. Then they waited.

The two agents ate their sandwiches and drank their coffees. They passed the time checking the safehouse's security and equipment, and they charged their comms gear and mobiles. Jonnie paced back and forth along the hallway letting out his nerves and frustrations.

"You should take the time to get some rest," Kate said walking to the end of the hallway. "Pacing like a lunatic isn't going to help you pass the time."

"How do you remain so calm?" Jonnie asked. "Where are the others? Why aren't they on comm? Why aren't they here yet? What do we do if they don't turn up? How long do we give them before we make a new plan?"

"Wow, okay. I told you the fucking pacing isn't helping. Our boys have the best training in the world. They are probably doubling back and checking for surveillance officers like we did. They will probably walk in any minute."

"There is a lot of hope in your voice, Kate."

"It's not hope, it's belief. I believe in my boys. They will get the job done."

"And, if they don't?"

"We have texted Hulk. He will contact us and give us our orders."

"What do you think he will say?"

"Either way, I would say we will be trying to find a way to get to London to meet him within hours."

"With or without Max and the others?"

"Yes," Kate admitted. "But, it won't come to that."

"I hope you're right," Jonnie said deflated.

"Come on, let's have a cup of tea?" Kate said putting her arm around Jonnie and walking him back to the lounge room.

Jonnie pulled the dusty sheet off the lounge and tossed in on the floor. Normally, the safehouse would be cleaned and stocked ready for agents if AIS knew they would be operating in the area. The Embassy would usually send one of the intel team out to get it ready, but given their unscheduled visit the apartment was a bit unkept. All the furniture had been covered in sheets which were covered in dust. He walked over and pulled the cover off the television and coughed from the dust as he tossed it on the floor. He clicked the remote and the television came to life.

"Welcome to the Phelps Files," Phelps said from his studio in London. *"We start today's show with breaking news from Italy where a plane was forced to land by the Italian air force. There is still no official word as yet from the Italian authorities on exactly what has happened and who as on board the plane. My producers have spent some time, prior to coming on air, trying to get a comment, but we have so far been unsuccessful. I will bring it to you as soon as we have it."*

"But, the question we most want answered is this, have the police arrested these people? What will be the price of this breach in not only Italian security, but the security of the entire European continent. We all know the dangers of letting madman take control of aircraft. The police must act to bring

*these people to justice. The police and our intelligence
agencies need the power to be able to stop incidents like this
before they even get off the ground, excusing the pun. We have
eyewitness statements that the jet flew low enough to shake
buildings in Venice, terrifying locals and tourists. Imagine the
damage it could have done. Other witnesses claim to have seen
the plane under escort from air force jets moments before it
skirted the skyline of Venice. It is simply not good enough for
the authorities in Italy to not be providing comment hours after
this incident. I am told the aircraft has done damage to the
Macro Polo airport which is just outside the city of Venice. We
would bring you pictures, but media has not yet been allowed
near the site."*

*"Incidents like this are a reminder of the need for the new
security laws being proposed by the Australian Government
and the need for them across the Commonwealth, and the
world. Viewers will remember I spoke during my last show
about these laws and the strength of the Australian Prime
Minister, Edward Kirby, for enacting these laws and for
sharing them with other Commonwealth leaders here in
London this week at the Commonwealth Heads of Government
Meeting. I again encourage my viewers to tune into the events
of CHOGM in the coming days as our leaders consider these
laws and Commonwealth security. Sadly, Venice looks to be
yet another example of why this legislation is needed to stamp
out terrorism, no doubt perpetrated by radical Islamic
terrorists. I encourage my viewers and anyone who believes in
strong borders and national security to contact their local
members of parliament and demand they endorse the Prime
Minister's message and adopt these laws as a matter of
urgency."*

"God, turn that shit off, will you?" Kate said walking back
into the room holding two cups of steaming hot tea. "He's such
a fuckwit."

"He thinks our jet was being controlled by Islamic
fundamentalists," Jonnie laughed. "Can he just make stuff up
like that?"

"I don't think he really cares about the real truth, just his own truth, constructed in that pea sized brain of his."

Jonnie clicked the remote and changed the channel.

Chapter Thirteen

It had been several hours since the hospital. Max had swum underwater for as long as he could hold his breath, before surfacing and making his way towards the safehouse. He stole a shirt from a rack outside a small men's fashion boutique to cover his gear and ducked into a public bathroom to dry his clothes as best as he could under the hand dryer. He took a circuitous route to the other side of the town, stopping for coffee and something to eat so he could see if anyone was watching him. He doubled back on his route several times to ensure he was not being followed. When he was sure he was away clear, he made his way to the safehouse.

Max flung open the door to the safehouse to find Kate and Jonnie inside laying out equipment on the dining room table. He told the pair about his fight at the hospital and Bradley, then about the conversation with Blake.

"My comms gear is down," Max said throwing the unit on the table. "And I need one of you to have a look at something for me."

"Bravo, go get onto AIS see if they can covertly figure out where MI6 and the Italians might have taken Flash and Blake," Kate ordered. "Then finish getting the gear ready, we will move out as soon as we have a location."

"You got it," Jonnie said heading for the communications room at the back of the small apartment which overlooked a narrow canal in downtown Venice.

"You alright, Prince?"

"No, I've been hit," Max said warily removing his stolen shirt, tactical vest and black t-shirt which he had changed into on the plane.

Kate saw the scars on Max's chiselled torso from knife and bullet wounds, long since healed, but then saw the fresh wound on his lower left side, beside his abs. Dirty water and blood dripped out of the wound and down to his waist, now his vest was not putting pressure on it, and Kate removed the piece of cloth he had shoved in there.

"Fucking hell, Max," Kate exclaimed. "How often do you go to the gym?"

"Every day, why?" Max asked.

"That's one hell of a body you got. Sam's a lucky boy. Pity about all the holes you keep putting in it though."

"It's certainly not by choice," Max laughed then grimaced.

"That hurt?" Kate said opening the first aid kit and pouring an alcohol-based cleaning fluid in the wound.

"I've felt move pleasant things that's for sure," Max said through gritted teeth.

"And worse ones too, you big soft cock, you'll be right. Hold still."

"So, how did you get here?" Max asked taking a seat as Kate retrieved some forceps to remove the bullet.

"We headed out of town and hid out for a bit, then we drove over here and dumped the car and plates. Once that was dealt with we took a leisurely stroll through this weird-arse city, got coffee and food, and came here without so much as a sideways glance."

"That easy?" Max said through clenching his jaw as Kate pressed around inside the wound with the forceps looking for the bullet.

"Yep, don't know what it is with you fucking boys, always getting yourselves in the shit," she said pulling the forceps and bullet out. "Got it! Trouble just follows you lot."

"Fuck," Max groaned as Kate waved the bullet pinched in the forceps in front of his face. "Guess, I'm just lucky."

"That's one fucking way of looking at it, not my fucking way, though," Kate said tossing the forceps onto the dining room table and reaching for the kit. "I wish you would be more like me."

"You're not trouble?"

"Not when it comes to work," Kate winked.

She poured sanitising alcohol into the wound and Max gritted his teeth again from the burn, then she gave him an antiseptic injection right into the bullet hole, followed by some pain relief.

"Next time," Max said with a pained looked on his face. "Can we do painkillers first?"

"I wanted to see how tough you were," Kate said snitching the wound.

"I found them," Jonnie called coming back into the room. "Oh fuck, Max are you alright?"

"Yeah, kid," Max said trying to put on a brave face as Kate continued to stitch the hole closed. "Good as new now Kate's fixed me up. Where are they?"

"Not far from here," Jonnie said passing Max a tablet computer. "We are the blue dot, they are the red one, only a few blocks."

"What's the building?"

"Well, that's the issue. It's Venice's gaol house."

"They took them to the gaol?"

"Looks like it."

"We're going to need the schematics as soon as practically possible, Bravo."

"AIS are on it. I also told them about the MI6 agent. Hulk wants to talk to you."

"Where's the sat phone?"

"Here, I will put you through," Jonnie said speaking to an aide before handing Max the phone.

"Prince," Max stated.

"It's Hulk, how you doing, kid?" Hulk asked.

"I'll be better when I put a few more of these arseholes in the ground. What have you found out?"

"There are some very powerful people involved in The Sixteen and they clearly don't give a fuck about bending or breaking the rules to get their way. I have spoken to my counterpart at MI6 who has increased security around the

Heads of Government meeting and we are working up as many connections to Russo and Shadow as we can find. Russo's accounts have led us to a couple of interesting parties, but it is still in the infancy stages at the moment."

"What about the plane?"

"The order came from the Vatican via Interpol and onto the military. It looks like there are people working within these organisations answering to The Sixteen, now whether the organisations know that or not remains to be seen. Like we were in the dark with Lloyd, they probably are too. But the problem is, they can still give orders."

"Bradley is MI6, he's with The Sixteen for sure, but he is using his MI6 credentials to pull strings with the local cops."

"I've got our guys pulling his file and mission reports apart as we speak, we are trying to find the connection."

"He's got the local authorities jumping to his commands here, can we get MI6 to revoke his authority?"

"Yes, MI6 is about to rip the mat out from under his feet, which should take him out of play, but it won't be enough for the Italians to just let Blake and Flash go. The Vatican is really pissed off and they have lent hard on the local guys. At this stage, we believe it is solely due to the Archbishop's death and nothing to do with The Sixteen, but we are still looking."

"I'm not leaving them in the gaol a minute longer than I have to, you will just need to smooth it over later. Those arseholes tortured me in the basement of a building in Vatican City and one of their people was involved in attacks on our country. Their hands are dripping with blood and bullshit. Fuck them."

"I know, Prince. I'm meeting with the Prime Minister shortly and I will be asking him to make the call."

"Thanks, Hulk. Do you think the jet will be cleared for take-off again anytime soon?"

"I'm working on that too, leave it with me."

"You know what I'm about to do?"

"Yes, I'd do the same if it was my team."

"I know you would."

"See you soon," Hulk said ending the call.

"You sure you can do this, Max?" Kate questioned. "It's a fucking gaol."

"We can do it. Are you in?"

"Fucking oath, I am."

"What about you, kid?"

"Say the word, boss," Jonnie said grabbing his pistol. "Let's go."

"Gear up," Max said heading for the bedroom to get changed.

Chapter Fourteen

Blake had spent his time in confinement thinking through some questions and some counter-intelligence statements he would make to throw Bradley off his game. The room was cold and damp, and layers of paint were peeling off revealing the various shades it had been in the past.

Blake sat handcuffed to a steel table in the interrogation room his face emotionless and still as he watched Bradley and a young Italian agent, who had introduced himself as Antonio Ricci, enter the room. Bradley took a seat opposite Blake, as Ricci stood near the back of the room. Bradley was wearing an ill-fitting suit with a blue business shirt, no tie. He looked a bit dishevelled and untidy like he had run a marathon in his suit. Ricci on the other hand wore a nice Italian suit, not expensive, but clean, ironed and well-fitting.

"Where is my team?" Blake asked staring Bradley in the eyes with laser-like focus.

"They are fine," Bradley dismissed. "Agent Gordon is next door, I will be interviewing him momentarily and the two pilots are in a holding cell down the hallway. So, why don't you tell me what you were doing at the Vatican?"

"You know what we were doing?"

"Why don't you tell me anyway?"

"What is this? MI6 interviewing me about an operation they were involved in. Are you trying to distance yourselves from the operation or is it just you in here, working for The Sixteen to try to get information from me?"

"You sound quite mad, Captain Smyth, considering your rank and title, I am worried about you. Grand conspiracy theories and accusations. Your team invaded foreign soil and undertook a covert intelligence operation. That is an act of war."

"Let's just say for a minute that was true. What would you call the capture and torture of one of our intelligence agents, by the very people who only a few years ago were responsible for a series of terrorist attacks on our country which killed thousands? The same people connected to the brutal murder of the same agent's fiancé trying to get him to stop his investigations into their activities."

"There you go, again. Blaming the Catholic Church and this imaginary group you call The Sixteen for some crimes which have never been reported."

"Their involvement was never reported, but that doesn't mean it didn't happen. Every day we are finding your hidden colleagues and plucking them out of society. Soon enough we will find all of you and bring you to justice one way or another."

"Did you just threaten me?"

"Are you part of The Sixteen?" Blake asked in a mocking tone leaning forward. "If so, then yes, I sure did and I promise it will be justice like you have never felt when we get our hands on you and your friends for what you have done."

"Why don't you tell me exactly how far you have gotten with your investigations?"

"Why don't you call MI6 and ask them?" Blake said looking to Ricci then back to Bradley. "We both know why. You are a rogue agent and the net is tightening around you. Tell me Agent Ricci, how long have you worked with this man?"

"I have worked for MI6 for six years and Agent Bradley for the last two months," Ricci said with a thick Italian accent.

"Are you in on this too, part of The Sixteen?"

"I can honestly say, sir, I have no idea what you are talking about," Ricci said and Blake believed him.

"That's enough, Ricci," Bradley dismissed with a wave of his hand. "Why don't you go get us a coffee?"

"No, sir. I think I will stay," Ricci said defiantly.

Blake nodded to Ricci as a gesture of thanks. He wasn't sure how much of the story he was believing, but it was obvious Ricci was starting to ask some questions. There was a knock on the door and a uniformed prison guard walked in with a note for Bradley.

"I will be back in a moment," Bradley said getting up and walking from the room. "Not a word, while I am gone."

"Agent Ricci," Blake said looking to the younger Italian as soon as the door closed. "Does any of this make sense to you?"

"No," Ricci said shaking his head. "The Sixteen, Catholics and torture, it all sounds ludicrous. Almost medieval. What the hell is going on?"

"Please listen to me, my colleague, we call him Prince, was captured by a group called The Sixteen. They took him to the Vatican and tortured him for information about AIS operations to try to apprehend a woman named Gloria Russo who is the financier for The Sixteen. My team and I rescued Prince and took Russo into custody. She was on our plane and we were heading to London, when we were forced to land. Prince trying to get her to the hospital, after she was injured, and we fled not knowing who was after us. You have to know that these people are responsible for thousands of terror-related deaths across the globe, including the attacks on our Parliament only a few months ago."

"I remember seeing the footage," Ricci said walking in closer to Blake. "This group did that, I thought it was an Islamic fundamentalist?"

"The Sixteen, they used the Islamic group. They funded their operations and helped choose the targets. They were the ones pulling the strings."

"So, where is this Russo now?"

"I'm not sure. Prince was trying to get her to the hospital. She was hurt when the plane was forced down."

"And, Prince, where is he?"

"I don't know that either. Before you picked us up, Prince got a message to me, telling me Agent Bradley was involved with The Sixteen. They must have had a run in at the hospital or on route to the hospital. Any of this sound familiar?"

"He was at the hospital, I picked him up out the front of the hospital to come looking for you."

"Did he tell you why we were here?"

"No. Only that you had breached Vatican security and we needed to take you in for questioning."

"Why wouldn't the Swiss Guard or Italian intelligence be interviewing us if that was the case?" Blake asked leaning forward on the table.

"I do not know."

"Someone up the chain has allowed him in here to question me, maybe they respect his credentials. MI6 pulls a lot of weight and they would be inclined to help. At some point though, he is going to find an excuse to get us out of here, maybe he'll do a deal to hand over information he gets from us to the Italians so he can get us away from here. There are too many people watching us. When he gets us out, he will take my team out. The Sixteen want us off the trail and there is no better way than killing several lead agents. You can't let that happen."

"I am sure that is not going to be possible."

"Please, just hear me out. If I am right, there is a global organisation working against our governments and enforcing their will on the people we are sworn to protect. They are behind the attacks on our cities and for overthrowing governments and democracies around the world at will. My job is to stop them and it is your duty to as well."

"I just, I do not know what to think of all of this, I mean a world-wide conspiracy?"

"Yes, a number of incidents in the last few years can be traced in some way back to these people, the bombings in Melbourne, the attack on our national Parliament, even the virus releases over a decade ago, we know they were involved. We have been working with MI6 too. Call and ask. Your own organisation wanted to question Russo for financing attacks in the UK and France. An MI6 team helped us carry out the Russo capture missions. Please, I know how it sounds, but I need your help. Our countries need your help."

"Even if I did believe you, what would you have me do? We are in the middle of a prison."

"I need you to uncuff me and help me get out."

"That's a big risk I would be taking."

"I know and it would be dangerous too, but Bradley can't be trusted and I need your help to stop him."

Ricci looked Blake in the eyes and thought about the story he had just heard. He did not like Bradley, although to call him a terrorist was extreme, to say the least. But, there was something about Blake, he was believable. Ricci's thoughts were interrupted. The alarms across the prison sounded and red lights flashed throughout the facility. An automated voiceover told everyone the gaol was in lockdown, people needed to find a secure room and prisoners in open spaces needed to lay on the floor and await further instructions.

"My team is here," Blake said calmly to Ricci. "I need you to uncuff me and take me to Flash and the pilots. We can't afford to get backed into a corner with Bradley and anyone else he has on the payroll. Please."

"Let me see what is happening," Ricci said heading for the door.

"No, wait. Please unlock me and let me out of here, I promise I will show you all the evidence we have to date. It's for your own safety as well as my teams."

"I will be back in a moment," Ricci said opening the door, startled by the imposing figure of Bradley standing on the opposite side.

"Where are you going?" Bradley said as the door swung open.

"I came to see what was going on."

"We have a small team trying to make entry into the prison. I am going to take Agent Smyth and Agent Gordon with me, and relocate to another facility to continue their interrogations. We can't let them go. They have questions to answer."

"Where are we going?"

"We are not going anywhere. I need you to stay here with the pilots."

"I think I should come with you. You can't handle two trained agents on your own and you need a witness to corroborate any statements they provide."

"No, that is not necessary. You can stay here."

"Sir, I am sorry, but that does not make any sense."

"That is how it is and it is an order," Bradley said walking in and fumbling with his keys to unlock Blake.

"I think I would rather stay here," Blake said sitting back in his chair. "At least for the next few minutes until my team arrives. You have no reason to take us and no reason to question us. Let me go and you will have a few minutes to get away before my team find you."

"Just shut the fuck up," Bradley said backhanding Blake. "You have gotten in the way too many times."

"You can stop this Antonio," Blake said turning to Ricci. "Think about it. He isn't taking us to be interrogated, he is going to kill us. Isn't that right, Bradley?"

"In the way of what?" Ricci questioned.

"What?" Bradley snapped.

"You said he had gotten in the way too many times. What did he get in the way of?"

"The Sixteen," Bradley huffed as he turned, drew his pistol and fired at his partner.

The bullet slammed into the young officer's chest. He stood for moment clutching his hands over the wound, a look of pure horror on his face which turned to sadness and a tear fell down his cheek in realisation. He dropped to his knees, as Blake looked on helplessly, then he fell backwards through the door into the hallway still clutching his chest.

"You didn't have to do that!" Blake yelled yanking on his handcuffs as he got to his feet and knocked over his chair with a thud. "He didn't need to die!"

"They are onto me anyway," Bradley said coldly, smugly shrugging his shoulders. "I just got a call from my superiors at MI6 ordering me back to London, so I guess someone from your team got a message through. But, it doesn't matter, The Sixteen has other plans for me which include killing your whole team."

"If those alarms are what or, more importantly, who I think they are, you will never succeed. He is coming for you."

"I am counting on it," Bradley said throwing Blake a key, while aiming the gun at his face. "Unlock yourself from the table then re-cuff yourself, arms behind your back. We are leaving."

Blake did as instructed, he uncuffed one hand, pulled the cuffs out from under the metal bar which was fastened to the table and put his hands behind his back.

"Good try, Agent Smyth," Bradley said smiling. "Turn around and show me the cuffs locked in place."

"It was worth a try," Blake sighed clicking the cuffs around his wrists.

Bradley checked the cuffs then pushed Blake through the door. As he walked out into the hallway, he paused for a moment next to Ricci, whose shocked, sorrowful and lifeless face stared back up at him.

"I'm sorry, Antonio," Blake lamented as Bradley pressed his pistol in his back.

"Move," Bradley ordered leading the pair down a dark concrete hallway.

Chapter Fifteen

Max shot out the two cameras hanging on the guard tower, which was positioned as part of the prison's exterior walls, then placed a small piece of explosive cord on the big old heavy wooden door and waited patiently for the signal. He could not risk letting Bradley or anyone connected to The Sixteen to keep Blake and Flash in custody. Their lives were at a risk. He also did not want The Vatican or the court system to subject them to questioning about the Archbishop. He knew they could never draw an actionable line to either man, but the trial would damage the AIS's reputation and Blake's. He was not going to let that happen. He could not allow the terrorists to use their own systems against them. He checked his watch and wondered what the hold up was.

On the opposite side of the prison, Kate drove the stolen truck fast through the street leading up to the prison's loading dock. Once she had it lined up with her target, she braced the steering wheel with a metal lock, extending it through the wheel and gave it a sharp turn to lock it in place. She grabbed a short length of poly-pipe and jammed it down onto the accelerator wedging the opposite end against the driver's seat. The clunky old diesel engine revved and started gathering speed, as Kate used duct-tape to tape down the horn which blasted alerting everyone nearby to get out of the way. A block away from the prison, Kate climbed out onto the sidestep of the truck. It sped over a small bridge. At the midpoint, Kate launched herself from the side of the truck over the little rusty railing and into the canal. The truck continued on, horn blaring, scattering people in the street, then it slammed with ferocious force into the prison loading dock doors. The doors burst open as the truck hit and immediately slowed, its engine suffering catastrophic damage. Kate resurfaced to watch the oil, coolant and diesel begin spilling into the loading dock entrance before igniting sending a pillar of putrid black smoke billowing into the air with stark orange flames. She smiled listening as the horn was still blaring, before the petrol tank exploded, sending a massive mushroom of black smoke up into the air. The horn stopped, but it was quickly followed by the sound of the prison's alarm bells ringing.

"Alpha has hit the gates," Jonnie informed Max through his comms unit. *"She's clear. Prince you can proceed."*

"Ack, Bravo," Max acknowledged firing a round into the explosive cord on the tower door smashing it's lock to pieces. "I'm going in."

"Roger that. Alpha, move to extraction point."

"Ack," Kate said climbing up the bank of the canal.

Max pushed open the tower door and began running up the stairs three at a time. At the top, he snuck a quick look through a porthole sized window in the door. The guard was listening to his radio and watching the smoke billow up from the far side of the prison. Max quietly opened the door and crept into the room silently, then put the guard into a sleeper hold. Less than a minute later he was unconscious and laying on the floor. Max took the guard's radio, access card and a bunch of keys, then undressed him taking his uniform and tied him up. Max got into the guard's uniform, including his baseball cap and glasses, then headed for the door leading out onto the gangway between the towers. He walked briskly, but did not run, not wanting to alert other guards.

"What is going on over there?" the guard in the second tower asked Max in Italian as he walked in, pointing to the billowing smoke.

"I am going to find out," Max said in Italian. "The commander said you should stay put."

"Just a minute," the guard said as Max reached for the door handle. "Who is looking after your tower, while you are not there?"

"Command is sending someone over," Max said not turning around.

"Do you want me to do some laps across the gangway, while we wait for them to arrive?"

"No, that will not be necessary, but thank you for being conscientious. I will make sure the bosses know you offered to go above and beyond."

"Yes, sir. Thank you, sir."

"I better get going," Max said pushing the door opening and walking through.

"Of course, good luck, sir."

Max walked down a large set of concrete stairs which led down into the prison yard. They were centuries old and worn smooth in places. The centre of each step was rounded, shortening the length of each step. Max headed across the prison yard, noting some prisoners were laying prone behind wire fences in the exercise areas. He swiped the guard's access card on the administrative building's door and a short electronic buzz and click sounded as the door opened an inch. He pushed it open and closed it behind him, then walked patiently down the corridor to the security room. Guards were running left and right, and yelling commands. Max slipped into the room behind a row of guards at a panel of security monitors. Several of the screens were showing the truck Kate had crashed into the gates. Flames were taking hold and burning what was left of the truck and the doors, and black smoke was billowing into the air. Max scanned the monitors looking for his team, then he saw a young man in a suit fall clutching his chest on one of the little screens, before Blake was led out of the interrogation room by Bradley. Blake stopped to look down at the young agent before Bradley pushed him towards the next holding cell. At the interrogation room next door, Blake and Bradley got into an argument and Max laughed as Blake headbutted Bradley. There was a short exchange then they continued down the hallway. Max turned and left the room, but this time he ran, dodging guards and administrative officers as he did, unnoticed in the confusion. At the interrogation room, he knelt down and checked for Ricci's pulse, but it was too late. A ran to the neighbouring cell and used the big bundle of keys until he found the right one and unlocked the door.

"Are there always alarms when you go places?" Flash asked sitting handcuffed to the table like Blake had been previously.

"It's fairer for my opponents that way, a bit of warning," Max laughed. "Great leveller. Ready to go? Bradley's got Hermes."

"Yeah, unlock me," Flash said as Max threw him the bunch of keys.

"He stopped Bradley from coming in here, Hermes."

"What?"

"Bradley stopped by the door and looked like he was coming in here, then Hermes headbutted him and they marched off down the hallway."

"He's always got our backs, doesn't he?" Flash asked, realising Blake had likely saved his life.

"Yeah and we are going to get his," Max said checking the hallway. "Where are the pilots?"

"They were taking them to one of the cells down the hall."

"Good, let's go get them too," Max said handing Flash his spare pistol. "Then let's get out of this fucking country."

"Right behind you," Flash said chambering a round in his pistol.

Max and Flash headed out and down the hallway. A few guards gave them a look, but Max waved them off. In the second corridor, they found the pilots in their cell. The first pilot was slumped on the floor face down, blood was gushing from wounds in his head and chest. The second pilot had similar wounds, but he was leaning back against the wall, blood was running from the bullet hole in his forehead and from his mouth.

"We have to go, Prince," Flash pleaded placing his hand on Max's shoulder. "I'm sorry about our guys, they were good men. But, we need to get Hermes back."

"I'm going to kill him," Max stated coldly, his anger hanging in the air, before he marched off with purpose down the hallway.

"I know," Flash said pausing for a moment to look at his fallen colleagues before following Max.

Max followed the stale old concrete walls and walkways with Flash close behind, until they reached a door leading out onto the prison grounds.

"The distraction I used to get in here is now his distraction to get out," Max grumbled. "Fucking arsehole."

"Okay, well at least we know which way he is going," Flash added trying to sound positive.

"Yeah, let's get through the door and across the yard, the far-right corner tower is our exit point," Max said pointing through the glass window to the tower he had come through earlier.

"Ack. On your lead."

"Stop," a guard yelled from behind in Italian. "Please stay where you are."

"Get the door, Flash," Max said turning to face the guard and changing to Italian. "I am taking this prisoner to a secure room, given the attempted entry on the front gate."

"We are holding everyone in place for now."

"I have my orders, we are leaving," Max said giving the guard a moment to pause.

In those brief seconds while the guard was considering what he had heard, Flash opened the door and ducked into the yard. Max quickly turned on his heals and ran through the door as the guard drew his pistol and opened fire sending bullets into the door frame. Max kicked the door closed then pressed a small play-doe like substance to the door handle, then he ran after Flash across the yard. Within seconds, the doorhandle melted as the explosive Max had placed fused the lock shut. Halfway across the yard, bullets started flying at Max and Flash kicking up dirt and grass at their feet. The pair started running in zig-zagging patterns to try to avoid the incoming fire. Max looked up at the guard tower to see Bradley firing with Blake pressed against the railing in front of him for cover.

"Shoot him, Prince!" Blake yelled.

Max drew his pistol but could not get a clear line of sight on Bradley, he was not willing to risk hitting Blake. Flash had made it to the neighbouring tower door and held it open for Max. The pair ran inside and started up the stairs. The guard who had spoken to the Max earlier was dead on the floor of the guard tower with blood already pooling around his head. Flash holstered his pistol, picked up the guard's rifle, checked the magazine and chambered a round. They ran across the gangway to the now empty corner tower and headed down the stairs for the exit. Bullets smashed into the door, as Max kicked it open. He pulled Flash back in behind the concrete walls for cover, just in time.

"Bravo, are you in position?" Max asked into his comms unit.

"Roger, Prince," Jonnie said focusing his sniper rifle scope. *"I have sighted an agent of some sort with Hermes leaving the tower."*

"The agent is the target, Hermes is his hostage."

"Confirmed, Prince. Am I authorised to engage?"

"Yes, but do not, I repeat do not, risk Hermes."

"Acknowledged, Prince. Looking for a shot. Target is on the move towards the canal. Your door is clear."

"Keep on him!" Max ordered running through the door towards the water with Flash in tow.

"Target has acquired a speed boat and is climbing on board with Hermes. I have a shot at the engine. Taking the shot."

Three bullets in rapid succession spat from Jonnie's sniper rifle on a nearby roof and seconds later all three drove deep into the outboard engine of Bradley's boat. Bradley and Blake dived behind the boats hull for cover as smoke, steam and fire erupted from the engine. Bradley grabbed Blake by the neck and stood him in front for cover as he tried to locate the source of the incoming fire, then Jonnie watched as he started screaming into his phone.

"Boat disabled," Jonnie said trying to line up Bradley's head with the red dot in his scope. *"Target was yelling into a*

phone. Now, he is moving to another boat. Hermes is in the way, I do not have a clean shot."

"Ack. Do you see a third boat in case we need to give chase?"

"Yes, there are three more speed boats docked nearby, the red striped one on your right has a man on board, probably the owner and therefore most likely to have keys."

"Roger that, mate. Thank you."

"Can you hear that?" Jonnie asked looking around the skyline. *"Shit. Prince, we have two attack helicopters coming in quick from the north."*

"Get out of there, Bravo!" Max yelled. "Move now, kid!"

"Moving now," Jonnie said rolling to his feet.

He shouldered his sniper rifle and sighted the helicopters. Max and Flash could see Jonnie, but needed to keep moving to secure a boat to chase Bradley. There was nothing they could do from this distance anyway. Max was focused on Jonnie, until Flash crash tackled Max to the ground.

"What the fuck?" Max asked but did not need an answer.

Two smoke trails shot out from the helicopters and streaked across the sky. The first missile hit the boat Max and Flash were running for destroying it in a ball of fire. Splinters of wood and fibreglass, and flames shot out in all directions. Max scrambled across the grass and threw himself over Flash as chunks of the burning boat started raining down on them. The second missile hit the rooftop where Jonnie had been standing. Glass shattered in the windows of both that building and the surrounding buildings, and ancient bricks and metal rained down into the street and canal. Max and Flash rolled the debris off, and laid on the grass surrounded by flaming plastic and wood in complete shock as they watched Jonnie's building burst into flames and start crumbling into the canal.

"Bravo!" Max yelled into his comms unit, the panic clear in his voice. "Bravo, come in kid. Did you make it off the rooftop?"

Silence.

"Bravo?" Max asked impatiently and nervously getting to his feet, still staring at the burning and crumbling building. "Alpha, come in."

"I saw the missile hit, Prince," Kate's sad tone said over the comms unit. *"No way he could have gotten out. He's gone, boss. I'm sorry."*

"Clear the building when you can, see if you can find him, then get to the plane. We're going to get Hermes back."

"You got it, boss. Go get that arsehole and get Hermes back."

"I plan to," Max said resolutely running towards the dock.

Max and Flash checked a few of the boats to find one they could use.

"Over here, Max," Flash said climbing into an old boat. "Keys are in the ignition."

"Hit it," Max ordered climbing aboard as Flash threw the throttle forward.

The old wooden boat lurched forward as the props spluttered to life. Fortunately, one of the helicopters had been following the boat, so Flash sped through the canals chasing Bradley, using the helicopter as a navigation guide. The second had hovered over the crumbling building Jonnie had been in before returning for base. Flash drove the boat through the winding canals, under the concrete footbridges and roadways, and out into the open waters. He dodged ferries and jet skis, as the pair watched the helicopter fly off at pace.

"We've got Bradley and Hermes, straight ahead," Flash said.

"Get as close as you can," Max said drawing his pistol.

Max watched the helicopter for a few moments, then it hit him.

"It's at the hospital," Max said turning to Flash. "They are going for Russo."

Flash accelerated, bring their boat in near Bradley's. Max and Bradley began trading shots, the bullets ripping into the boats and water. Max was being extra careful with his shots to avoid hitting Blake. Flash moved the boat in close and Max climbed through the hatch leading to the bow. As soon as he was through, he sprinted forward and jumped, just as Flash hit the throttle and drove his boat right into the back of Bradley's. As Max landed on the deck, Bradley who had been near the stern of the boat turned to point his pistol at Blake. Blake had been driving the boat, but fell to the ground as Flash rammed him and rolled in behind the passenger seat.

When he could not see Blake, Bradley spun back around just as Max stepped in behind him. Bradley fired a shot at Max, which sailed past him and hit the side of the boat. Max dived clear and rolled to the side, then lined up for a shot, but Bradley was already moving, he kicked the pistol from Max's hand and aimed his own at Max's face. As he tightened his finger on the trigger, Blake reached up and swung the boat wildly to the left causing Bradley to fall, giving Max the window he needed. He sprung forward from his left foot into the air, drew back his right fist and brought it down hard on Bradley's face, hearing a sickening crack. As he landed, he threw a short hard hook into Bradley's jaw and Max instantly felt it break. Bradley stared for a moment, groggily, and moved a hand up to hold his jaw, but before it got there he passed out.

"Pull up at the hospital," Max yelled to Blake who was now back at the wheel.

"Got it," Blake said steering the boat into the dock beside the hospital's emergency entrance at speed, sending the wake of water up over the concrete pathways as he stopped.

"Flash, get to Alpha and then head to the airport. If we aren't there in thirty minutes, take off."

"Yes, mate," Flash said over the comms unit before turning his big old boat around and speeding off back to get Kate.

Max took Bradley's phone then he and Blake ran into the hospital and headed for the operating room where Russo had been earlier. There was a slightly elevated atmosphere in the ward.

"Where is she?" Max asked a nearby nurse who looked shocked.

"They took her," he said pointing towards the elevator.

Max and Blake headed for the stairs and spirted up as fast as their legs would carry them. At the exit to the roof, Max kicked the door open and the two agents headed for the helicopter. Two men were loading Russo on her bed into the chopper, while a third kept the engines running. Without warning Max shot the pilot through the side window showering him with glass, as his blood and brains sprayed the far side of the cockpit. The other two men heard the sound of the shot over the rotor wash, but it was too late, they turned and were both immediately hit in the head and chest by a pair of bullets from Max and Blake.

"I hope you remember how to fly that," Max said as the pair walked for the chopper.

"This is easy compared to what you are going to have to do in a minute," Blake said holstering his pistol.

"We will cross that bridge when we get there. Let's get her in the chopper."

"You got it," Blake said as they pushed Russo into the chopper, locked the bed in place and shut the door.

Max climbed into the passenger seat, as Blake opened his door. Max kicked the pilot's body out and it dropped at Blake's feet.

"Thanks," Blake said raising an eyebrow. "Can you clean the brains up now too?"

"I'm sure you've sat in worse. Hope that office job isn't making you soft."

"Let's just go, hey?" Blake said smiling until he was interrupted by gun fire and bullets pinging off the side of the helicopter.

Three men ran out onto the roof and opened fired at the helicopter, as Blake hauled himself into the pilot's seat. Max returned fire as Blake accelerated to get the big chopper to lift off. Max's gun ran dry, so he climbed over next to Russo, opened the door and swung the big mounted machine gun around to the doorway on the roof. A line of bullets sprayed from the gun, tracing a line in the concrete towards the three men, the first guy was cut down violently as his two comrades jumped for safety. The chopper lifted off and Max got a line of sight on the second guy whose head exploded as a round from Max's gun hit its mark. The third guy had a similar experience only seconds later. His lifeless body fell to the roof of the hospital as Blake pulled the helicopter around towards the airport.

"Umm, Max," Blake hesitated as he stared out the windshield. "We've got a bigger problem."

"What is it?" Max asked as he climbed back over to take his seat. "Oh, fuck."

The second attack helicopter was coming in fast.

"Get us over a non-populated area," Max said pointing to the canal and the opening onto the sea.

Blake banked the chopper hard and accelerated towards the open water with the second chopper giving chase. When they were over the water, Blake slowed the big bird into a hover and quickly swung it around one-hundred and eighty degrees. Max sighted the second helicopter, squeezed the trigger and fired two missiles. The smoke trails streaked across the sky before both missiles hit the chopper. It exploded in a huge fireball and dropped straight down into the water as a black smoke plume mushroomed into the sky traced with lines of whipping flames. Blake banked the chopper around and headed for the airport.

"Flash, do you copy?" Max asked into the comms unit.

"Roger, Prince," Flash yelled over the sound of his boat's whining engine. *"I've got Alpha, we're pulling up to the airport. Hulk got the jet cleared for take-off."*

"We're in a chopper coming in hot. We have Russo. Go to the cockpit and start the engines."

"You've got it, mate."

A few minutes later, Blake landed the helicopter near the AIS jet on the tarmac at Marco Polo airport across the bay from Venice city. The two agents pulled Russo from the bed and carried her up into the jet. Blake and Kate secured her in her seat and hooked up to a drip. Max hit the close button on the door and the steps folded in as he headed into the cockpit. Flash was sitting in the co-pilot's seat.

"You ready for this?" Flash asked as he adjusted his headset.

"This is what we train for, right?" Max said climbing over into the pilot's seat. "Should be fine."

"Fine or fun?"

"Maybe both, but either way it will be interesting," Max said clicking buttons and flicking levers, before accelerating the jet to taxi for the runway. "Tower this is AIS four, six, two, zero seeking immediate clearance for take-off."

"Roger, AIS four, six, two, zero, you are cleared for take-off, please proceed to runway one. Skies are clear, have a safe flight and thank you for visiting."

"Thank you for your hospitality, Venice Tower," Max smiled throttling forward before switching to the intercom. "Every take your seats and strap in, it's been a while, but I for one don't want to stay in this fucking city any longer."

Max pushed the plane up to full speed and the jet shot down the runaway fast, he pulled back on the controls and it took off into the blue sky, and banked for England climbing hard to their cruising altitude.

Chapter Sixteen

"That wasn't so bad was it?" Max asked as he put the plane onto autopilot and turned to Flash. "You look a bit green."

"I'll be okay in a minute," Flash said trying to steady himself by holding the seat. "Good job."

"Jonnie?" Max asked after a few minutes of silence staring out the window.

"I'm sorry, Max," Flash lamented, shaking his head.

"Where is he?"

"We couldn't find him. I had to get Kate out of there."

"Okay," Max said getting up from the controls and heading for the back of the plane.

Max walked past the unconscious Russo. Her colour had returned and she was breathing steadily. After what happened to Jonnie, Max was regretting not letting her die. He knocked on the door and opened it to find Kate pacing back and forth. In the years the pair had worked together she had proven time and time again how tough she was. She was one of the strongest people, both mentally and physically, that he knew. But, as he watched her pace, he saw a sadness he had never seen.

"Hey, boss," Kate said wiping her eyes and trying to sound fine. "I'm sorry we couldn't find him. I feel nothing but pure guilt."

"It's not your fault, Kate," Max said placing his hand on her back. "This is Bradley and Russo, and The Sixteen."

"I'm going to hunt down every single one of them and fucking end them. He didn't deserve to die like that. Fucking cowards. Couldn't even face him man to man. Had to blow him out of the sky from afar."

"You know I'll be right by your side. He was a good kid."

"He was a fucking great kid. This is the first time I have ever left a man in the field. I feel sick to the stomach. I shouldn't be on here. I should be back there looking for him."

"I needed you here. It was my call."

"I know, boss. I'm not blaming you. I just feel like I fucking let him down and let you down."

"You could never let me down, Kate. You are an extraordinary agent, a great person and an incredible friend. And, so was Jonnie."

"Fucking aye. Are you okay?"

"No, Kate. You're right, he was a great kid and he was on my team. I asked him to be there, in that position."

"As you said, this isn't your fault either, Max."

"I know, but it's my team, my command. I am responsible for everyone on it and I failed."

"He idolised you, you know? He was so thrilled when you accepted him on the team. All he wanted was to impress you."

"He did. Constantly. That's why he's on the team."

"He knew that and he was so proud serving with you. He was always talking about you and seeking feedback on his performance. He wanted to impress you, so badly. Always so eager to please."

"He got me out of a couple of very serious situations with that rifle and boy could he drive."

"Yeah, he could," Kate said wiping away more tears.

"Are you sure about what you saw?"

"On the roof?"

"Yes, the missile hit the centre of the roof. There is no way he could have escaped. Just no way. I'm going to take The Sixteen apart one-by-one until they are all simply dead."

"God help the people responsible for this, they don't know what they have unleashed."

"I've asked the embassy to find his body and prepare for the return to Australia."

"Thank you."

"Least I could do," Kate said looking up at the roof as if trying to force the tears back into her eyes.

"Get your thoughts under control and then come join us in the boardroom," Max said hugging Kate. "Take your time."

"You got it, Max," Kate nodded as Max left the little room.

Max dodged the debris on the floor of the plane to join Flash and Blake in the office upfront. Hulk was on the teleconference screen on the side wall.

"Hey, boss," Max said taking his seat. "I'm sorry about Bravo."

"Me too, kid," Hulk said sorrowfully. *"He was one of the best rookies I've seen go through the Wool Shed, but there will be time later for us to mourn."*

"Alpha said she's made arrangements with the embassy to find his body and get him home."

"Yes, the ambassador is making the arrangements."

"What the fuck happened, Hulk? How is it possible they had jets and attack helicopters? Is their reach really that big?"

"The jet order came from senior people with the power to make those calls and the air force were just following orders as far as we can tell. As for the attack helicopters, we aren't sure who was flying them yet, but they match two stolen from the manufacturer last year."

"How the fuck do you steal a helicopter?"

"My bigger problem isn't that it was stolen, although that is of course a concern. My problem is that the manufacturer didn't report it stolen."

"Anyone looking into the company?"

"Yes, MI6 and Interpol."

"I want a fucking name as soon as possible."

"You'll have it as soon as I do."

"Thanks. What's the plan?"

"I have arranged office space in the High Commission and with MI6 for our team. Hermes and I will be reviewing Russo's connections in detail with MI6 and we will be helping Interpol weed out the arseholes who tried to take you out in Italy."

"Ack. What about Kate, Flash and I?"

"I decided to enact Section Twenty. As soon as you arrive, I need you to get to the Hyatt. You will be providing close personal protection to the Prime Minister, supported by the feds. Prince, you've got the lead."

"How were the feds?"

"They will be fine."

"And the PM?"

"Too occupied with his speech to care about his security at the moment."

"I've got their plans and protocols," Blake noted bringing up the files on the second screen. "Here is how they plan to secure the PM during the conference."

"We need to start again," Max directed. "Let's go back to basics, rearrange the entrance and exit protocols, and the agent positioning. We can't be too sure who may already have these original plans, so let's mix them up."

"You got it, Flash and I will work on it."

"Hermes," Hulk interjected from the television on the wall. *"Give Prince the profiles and intel files on the chatter we have collected so far regarding the summit. Prince, work with Alpha to sift through the profiles and figure out potential targets and potential perpetrators, also see if there is anything in the briefs provided by our analysts on times and dates."*

"Got it," Max agreed as Kate walked into the room.

"Sorry," Kate said, her eyes red from crying. "Where do you want me?"

"You're with Prince," Hulk said before pausing when he registered the distress on his long-term colleague's face. *"We will get him back to Australia, Kate. You didn't fail anyone."*

"Yes, sir. Thank you for saying that, sir. I just feel guilty."

"We all do," Hulk said acknowledging the trauma his team had been through and feeling it too. *"But Prince made the right call."*

"I know, boss."

"Use it to get these arseholes."

"You fucking know I will."

"Good. How is the Italian bird?"

"That bitch is still breathing sadly, but I'm happy to turf her out the door," Kate said angrily looking back towards the main cabin. "Just give me the word."

"Well, let's hold off on that for now. Get whatever you can out of her and we will hold her at MI6 until we can figure it all out."

"Got it."

"Alright, see you all when you get here," Hulk said ending the call.

"We've all got our assignments, let's get to it," Max ordered heading back into the main cabin.

Max walked over to a small cupboard and removed a red satchel with a large cross on it. He took some time to redress his wound with clean bandages, before withdrawing a small needle. He drew in a small dose of a clear watery product into the needle then sat the needle on the bench and replaced the small bag in the cupboard, clicking the door shut. He collected the needle, walked over to Russo and injected the contents into her drip before taking a seat opposite her.

He sat in the cabin and noticed his bloody handprints on the wall from earlier. He briefly looked at Russo who was starting to wake from the needle he had given her, then he continued looking around the cabin. It looked like an office warzone. His laptop was resting against the seat across the aisle. He got up and walked over to it. Glass from the shattered screen fell onto the carpet when he picked it up. Without bothering to open it, he tossed it onto the floor which is when he saw Russo's bag and belongings. Max sifted through her bag, lipstick, pens and various items fell out. Nothing of interest so he tossed it on the ground next to the laptop.

As he was starting back for his seat, he saw a mobile phone and a small brown diary under a nearby seat. The mobile was locked so he put it in his pocket. He picked up the diary and studied its logo, a roaring lion with its teeth bared, it looked angry. There was a thick diamond carved out around it and it was covered in flowers and thorns. Sixteen of each. He undid the small buckle and leafed through the pages.

It was divided into sections. Those at the front were well worn and ratty, while the ones at the rear were near new. Colour dividers separated each section and they were adorned with excessive and dramatic calligraphic text and symbols. Each one had a similar diamond to that on the front, covered in flowers and thorns, and counting up in phases – phase one, phase two, phase three. The last was phase twenty-four. Beyond each divider there were pages and pages of letters and numbers. Some individual symbols were circled in red, others had blue squares around them. Two on each page were marked with a yellow diamond and there was a green cross through others. Russo coughed and started to open her eyes, she was groggy from the anaesthetic and slowly blinking trying to take in her surroundings, until she saw Max and her eyes widened in horror.

"A friend of mine was killed an hour ago as a rogue operative from MI6 tried to escape after killing two officers who worked for me," Max stated in a stony calm voice still looking at the diary. "We have had fighter jets and attack helicopters after us, and to say I'm upset would be an understatement. My colleague, who you were talking to earlier, wants to throw you out the door of this plane and I am strongly considering letting her."

"You need me," Russo said weakly, clearly frightened by Max.

"Maybe, but we'll figure it out eventually and you will be dead, so that will give me some closure for the friends I have lost today."

"And, what about Lachlan?"

"I told you earlier you don't get to say his name," Max said his voice tightening before he stood and walked through the office into the cockpit.

He took his seat and sat staring out the window for a moment thinking about what to do next. He needed information and he needed to stop these people whatever the cost.

"Everybody hold on," Max yelled behind him through the cockpit door before taking the plane off autopilot, dropping altitude and lowering the speed.

"What's going on, Max?" Flash asked climbing into the co-pilot's seat.

"I thought Kate made some good points," Max said hitting the autopilot button and climbing back out of his seat. "Stay here and let me know if there are any issues."

"What?" Flash asked confused. "Wait."

Max did not stop, he walked back into the main cabin to see Russo sitting smugly staring at him. He marched over, grabbed her by the shirt and dragged her out of her seat. He pushed her towards the door, trailing her drip behind, and pulled down on the lever, the seals of the door hissed and wind started gushing in around it.

"You wouldn't dare," Russo yelled over the sudden decibel increase.

"I told you, you don't get to say his name," Max said kicking open the door.

The wind rushed in and out of the door, swirling in the cabin. The plane was flying low over the ocean and Max watched as the waves beneath were crashing with whitecaps in the high swell. He dragged her into the doorway and she clawed at his arms and chest trying to fight him. Paper whipped round the cabin, as she tried to fight him off. Even in her weakened state she was fighting hard, but he was just too strong. He held her by the door.

"Your feelings betray you, Agent Shaw," Russo yelled over the roar of the engines. "You will never find his killer without me."

"Shadow killed Lachlan," Max shouted. "And, I already killed him."

"Shadow was just a player in the game, don't you want to find out who was pulling his strings?"

"Tell me."

"Pull me back in."

"Not until you tell me how this all works. Who is in charge?"

"I won't say a word until I am guaranteed immunity and we are safely on the ground, that's the deal."

"The deal is you give me some names or you will be on the ground before we are," Max said increasing the force of his push.

Russo's back was assaulted by the wind racing past the door and she grabbed the doorframe desperately trying to cling to the safety of the plane.

"Alright!" Russo yelled. "Alright, I'll give you details and some of the names of our members."

"I want them all," Max snarled.

"I do not know them all, but I will give you the ones I have. Please just bring me back in the plane."

Max pulled her back through the door and shoved her towards the seating area. He pulled the big lever and the door automatically folded back in and clicked shut.

"You're a fucking maniac, Prince," Kate laughed walking into the main cabin. "I love it. I've got fucking paperwork blown all to fuck in there though, you better help me put it all back together."

"After Ms Russo and I have a chat about her friends in The Sixteen, I will be there to give you a hand," Max said dodging the mess and heading for the cockpit.

After he got the plane back to its normal cruising altitude, Max resumed his seat across from Russo.

"You have had some time to think," Max said crossing his legs. "I want names – who is in The Sixteen and how do I find them?"

"I only know a couple of names."

"Well get on with it."

"You have to understand The Sixteen is bigger than any one person. It exists to serve one purpose."

"Which is?"

"Global order."

"And how does it do that?"

"By creating chaos and terror when necessary to eliminate our opponents and to remind the people that they are sheep and like any good flock they need a good shepherd."

"So, who is the shepherd?"

"The Sixteen is the shepherd."

"Okay, so back to my original question, who are the members of The Sixteen?"

"There are sixteen members of our organisation at any one time throughout history."

"Throughout history?"

"Our organisation has existed for generations, Agent Shaw, and when one of our members dies or becomes unavailable, for whatever reason, we find someone to replace them, always keeping the number at sixteen."

"And, Shadow was one of the sixteen members?"

"Yes."

"Has he been replaced?"

"Not yet."

"When?"

"I imagine it will happen within days. The rules are clear. There are strict timelines. He will need to be replaced very soon."

"Do you know who will replace him?"

"No."

"Why not?"

"I run a major international company, I don't always have time for trivial details."

"Trivial? This man or woman will be added as a member of your so-called global order, to bring chaos and terror to the world, and you don't know who they are – just how out of touch with reality are you?"

Russo said nothing.

"So, I presume he or she will be a pawn or do they get to be a knight immediately?" Max asked.

"The elected members of The Sixteen all start as knights," Russo said giving him an inquisitive look. "But, there are many, many pawns."

"I've met some of the pawns."

"They are not members of The Sixteen per se. They are just tools of The Sixteen."

"John Bradley?"

"I do not know him. Each of the knights has their own pawns to command and their own territories to control. He could belong to someone else in the organisation. I do not know."

"And you are a rook, I'm told."

"Seems you know more than you originally let on."

"You handle the finances?"

"Something like that."

"So, how many of your group would be considered knights?"

"There are twelve knights."

"And the other four?"

"A bishop, a rook, a queen and a king."

"It's a hierarchy? Command and control?"

"Yes, although we all have our roles to play and a significant amount of power, even as a knight you can be responsible for some notable actions and wield significant resources. As I said, they each have a territory to control."

"What are the territories?"

"There are two knights from every continent or region on the planet, except Antarctica."

"So, why don't we just cut to the chase, who are the king and queen?"

"I do not know."

"They give the orders and sit at the top of the structure and you don't know who they are?"

"They are protected by the bishop. Their orders are given via the bishop and we all report back through the bishop. They are nominated and elected by the members of The Sixteen, but only members present during the election know who they are and those details are then protected. I was not a member of The Sixteen during the last election of the king and queen positions, thus I do not know who they are."

"So, you blindly serve a faceless master?"

"No, I serve a cause, one that has outlasted any agent or government seeking to bring us undone and one which has adapted as necessary to survive for the good of all people."

"Adapted?"

"We were not always known as The Sixteen. We have held many names that have been lost to the ages, but it is not important, what is important is the role we play in society. We shape it with a goal of creating a world which thrives and survives, rather than the one we have now built on competing interests and struggle."

"This sounds like some new-world order conspiracy theory bullshit."

"No world leaders can act in the best interests of the people all the time, especially when they are so easily replaced. We are there to provide advice, provide balance and provide knowledge to control them. We exist outside governments to keep them in check and to ensure global order."

"How?"

"You name it. Assassinations, political appointments and donations, funding terrorist attacks and business takeovers. Whatever it takes."

"This is ridiculous."

"No, Max, it is how the world really works."

"What about the book?" Max asked showing Russo the diary he found with the lion on the cover. "What are the codes?"

"It's a find a word puzzle book."

"Do you think I am stupid? How do I decode it?"

"You don't."

"We will in time, with or without your help," Max said tossing the book onto a nearby seat and pacing before Russo. "Let's say I believe your ludicrous story, tell me who the bishop is and where to find him."

"His name is Robert and he lives in London."

Chapter Seventeen

The Sixteen sat at the boardroom table in London. The aide had arranged water and coffee and tea, and had sat the little box on the table again for privacy. The members all sat starring at the television while they waited for Robert to arrive.

Kevin Phelps had been labouring on and on about the threat of Islamic terrorism and outlining the proceedings of the Commonwealth Heads of Government Meeting. He had spoken to experts in the fields of government relations, international relations, terrorism and intelligence. He would occasionally break his long preaching monologues for the news headlines. The potential terror situation unfolding in Italy continued to run as the lead story, but details were still unclear. Eyewitnesses were reporting boat and helicopter chases and explosions.

Robert walked into the boardroom.

"Thank you all for coming back so soon," he said taking his seat at centre of the table. "I spoke to the King, she is happy with our progress. Unfortunately, since we spoke, an issue has occurred. Russo was injured and taken to a hospital in Venice."

"Is she okay?" Janelle asked pointing to the television. "Is she in the middle of all that?"

"Yes, I am afraid she is."

"But she is okay?"

"She had a cut on her neck and she lost a lot of blood, however the doctors tended to her injuries and she was given blood. She was on a drip and recovering well."

"Was?"

"I ordered her be moved to a secure facility, however the Australian Intelligence Service agents again intervened and took her into custody."

"I thought you ordered them to be killed."

"We forced them out of the sky. I lent on some mutual friends in Rome, who lent on the government, military and local police. They set up a net across Venice, however they managed to evade our teams."

"Robert, I was told half of the AIS team was being held in the Venice prison. How did the remaining half of the team manage to get Russo and get out of the city undetected?"

"Prince," Robert said in frustration.

"He is becoming just as big a problem for you as he was for Shadow."

"He is a problem, however I am making arrangements for him to be taken care of."

"Taking out half his team should slow him down. Have you killed them yet?"

"Actually, he broke into the prison and freed them."

"What?"

"We do not have any of the agents in custody. They escaped."

"That is disappointing. Where are they now?"

"They are on route to London and are being escorted by two Royal Australian Air Force Super Hornets."

"They are coming here?"

"Yes."

"Do we know why?"

"General Patrick "Hulk" Scott the Head of the AIS has used his emergency powers to take over the protective detail of their Prime Minister while he is out of Australia. He has ordered his agents, Prince, Alpha and Flash, to protect the Prime Minister at all times until he returns to Australian soil after the Commonwealth Heads of Government Meeting."

"And, their investigation?"

"Hulk and his deputy, Captain Blake "Hermes" Smyth, are setting up operations in London with MI6."

"Do we have people at MI6 we can use?"

"Unfortunately."

"You have been using that word a great deal today."

"Unfortunately, my main point of contact and inside man, Agent Bradley, was just found unconscious with a broken jaw and fractured eye socket, on the deck of a boat floating outside the Venice hospital."

"So, his role has been uncovered?"

"Yes, but I have made arrangements for him to avoid custody."

"You should put a bullet in his head and move on. Does he know who you are?"

"Unfort…" Robert interrupted himself. "Yes, he does."

"I am very uncomfortable. They are getting closer to us, literally, by the minute."

"Once the suitcases are in place and the attacks begin, they will be too distracted to look for us, then it will be too late."

"There is a great deal of hope in that statement."

"That is why we are here is it not? Hope."

"Hope is a foundation of The Sixteen and its predecessor organisations, and as members of this group we need to pull together in service to our king and our cause. Please do not misinterpret my questions as any sort of misbelief or disloyalty to our cause, Robert."

"I am pleased to hear that, because faith is another pillar of our organisation and I am asking you to have faith that our plans will come together."

"Then faith you shall have, Robert. We are in this with you and the king all the way."

"Our reach is far and our hands never idle."

"Our reach is far and our hands never idle," the collective members of The Sixteen said in their London boardroom.

"Now, as promised, I told you one of our candidates for the vacant seat was in town and he has ducked out of the Heads of Government meeting to be here to address us," Robert said pressing a small button on the table in front of him. "Please welcome, Alistair Turner."

The big metal door slid to the side and a tall attractive young man in his mid-thirties walked into the room. He was wearing an expensive navy suit, white shirt and blue and red tie.

"Good morning," Alistair said as the door rolled shut behind him. "I am honoured to be here. Long live the real king."

"Long live the real king," the room echoed collectively.

Chapter Eighteen

Max sat in the back seat of the bulletproof four-wheel drive as it rolled through the security checkpoint outside the conference centre. He was purposefully staring at a page in Russo's brown leather diary trying to work out the codes. On the flight, she had provided him with details on the man named Robert, but she refused to talk about the diary and the codes within. Max had considered using more invasive torture, but for some reason he knew it would not help, she was not going to tell him how to break the code. There was a resolve and a strength in her, he had not seen earlier, when the book was mentioned. She was currently on route to the Australian Embassy with Blake where she would be detained and questioned further on her role and The Sixteen. Max had snapped hundreds of pictures of the codebook and sent them to a team of analysts at AIS in Canberra, he knew they would eventually figure it out, but he could not shake the feeling that it was important, so he kept at it.

The car pulled into an available spot outside the conference centre. Max, Flash and Kate climbed out and walked up the concrete steps. Max could hear the protesters being held back by police only a block away. They had driven through the crowd with police holding the protestors back with steel barricades and plastic riot shields. They waved banners and homemade signs. On one side of the road there were people protesting for civil liberties and freedoms, while on the other people were protesting against terror and for increases in national security. It was a melting pot readying at any minute to boil over as the reviling sides got angrier and more passionate.

The Commonwealth Heads of Government Meeting banners flicked back and forth in the breeze as Max stepped out of the car. Security guards at the entrance checked their credentials before Max and his team were allowed into the centre. They had changed into black suits on the plane and their pistols and knives were discreetly hidden out of sight. The metal detectors sounded as they walked through, but the security agents waved them through, given their protective role and clearance levels. Outside the Prime Minister's temporary office, they found the Australian Federal Police standing guard all wearing dark suits and reflective glasses like Max and his team.

"Agent Shaw," one of the officers said walking over to shake Max's hand. "Welcome to London. The Commander is inside with the Prime Minister, please go on through. They are expecting you."

"Thank you," Max said as he and his team knocked then entered the Prime Minister's suite.

"Max!" the Prime Minister Edward Kirby said standing and walking over to greet Max.

"Prime Minister," Max said respectfully shaking the Prime Minister's hand. "It is a pleasure to see you again. Please let me introduce Agent Kate Matthews or Alpha as she is better known in our circles."

"Pleasure, Agent Matthews," Kirby said holding out his hand.

"Sir," Kate said shaking his hand.

"And, you may remember Agent Jacob Gordon, from the incident at Parliament House several months ago."

"Yes, of course, Flash Gordon, how could I forget," Kirby said shaking Flash's hand. "I'm very glad you are all here. And, I am sure you remember Special Agents Tim Carrol and Jill Stevenson of the federal police."

"We do," Max said shaking the agents' hands. "Tim, Jill, nice to see you again."

"Glad to be working with you again, Max," Carrol said. "Maybe we should let you get back to your speech Prime Minister and we will head out to ensure everything is ready."

"Ah, yes, thank you all," Kirby said walking with a cane back to his desk.

Max and his team followed the police agents to an adjacent room where they all took a seat around a large conference table.

"He's still got the cane," Kate said smiling and elbowing Max. "Still can't believe you shot the fucking Prime Minister. How many people get to say that?"

"He seems to have forgiven me anyway," Max said smiling. "Let's just hope I'm the last person to do it."

"Fucking oath, boss."

"We received your updated configuration for our troops and we have redeployed as requested," Carrol stated.

"Thanks, Tim, appreciate your understanding," Max said acknowledging the slight the police may have felt having their plans and teams taken over. "Flash worked them up on the plane. We will be continuously changing and altering plans as we progress."

"Don't want to set and forget?"

"No."

"Worried about a leak?"

"Yes."

"Roger that, we will adapt as necessary."

"Thanks, Tim. I'm sure this was unnecessary and frustrating for you, having AIS take over."

"Higher powers made the call, I will do what is asked mate. You've got our full cooperation."

"Thank you, I appreciate that."

"Alright, here are your comms units," Carrol said handing over three devices. "We are on channel twelve today."

"Thanks," Max said placing the unit in his ear. "Test one, two, three."

"Got you."

"How long have we got until the speech?"

"Thirty minutes."

"Flash, Alpha, head down to the conference hall and take a look, will you?"

"Jill, take them down and introduce them to the team."

"Yes, boss," Stevenson said escorting Flash and Kate out of the room.

"What's the latest chatter?" Max asked turning back to Carrol as his team left the room.

"Given the size of the event, social and traditional media around the globe are drowning in news and comments. It is creating a lot of content to sift through. Our darknet teams are also seeing a lot of increased activity, but nothing specific as yet. Anything on your end? Want to tell me why you are here?"

"Nothing specific. We are following a number of leads all still related to the incidents a few months ago, at home, which you helped us out with. It is a weirder world now, that's for sure."

"Hence the PM's address."

"Yeah, I guess."

"You don't sound convinced about the speech."

"It's not the speech, it's the content. Mass surveillance, hostile border protection, open discrimination and profiling. It all sounds like we could be going a bit far."

"A bit far? Your agency is leading the charge."

"I know and it will help us do our job, but what do we sacrifice along the way to get it done?"

"I wouldn't bring that up with the PM."

"Agreed," Max said smiling. "I do wonder though if their exposure to all this, you know, in the Parliament attack, I wonder if it may have caused them to overreact. It would be a perfectly natural human reaction, friends were killed and you reacted. In this case, the only way they knew how, by altering the laws."

"You might be right, but it's not our place to say."

"That's true, but we need to see it from other viewpoints, like those protesting down the block. How passionate are they? What will they do to stop him? Let alone what people who actually have something to hide might want to do to stop these laws."

"You think an attack would stop the laws going through?"

"No. Having worked there for several years, I know politicians, they would double down and say this is exactly why we need these laws."

"I think you're right," Carrol said standing. "Let's just make sure he gets home safely, shall we?"

"You got it," Max agreed following Carrol back to the Prime Minister's suite.

"Ready, gents?" Kirby asked walking out into the hallway.

"Yes, sir," Max and Carrol said together leading the Prime Minister down the hallway.

"Slow down a bit, will you please?" Kirby said limping a few metres behind the two agents. "Max, I'm not as fast on my feet as I used to be. Thanks to you. So the least you can do is slow down to a respectable speed."

"Yes, sir. Sorry about that, sir."

"You saved my life, Max. No need to be sorry, although I should give you a belting with this cane while I've got you close."

"Yes, sir."

"Not scared of an old man whooping your arse?"

"I'm sure you would give it a red-hot go, sir," Max said looking back and smiling at the Prime Minister.

"You could pretend to be a little worried," Kirby laughed. "I used to be a boxer."

"I'm sure you would get one or two in," Max said as he held the elevator door open.

"You hear that Agent Carrol?" Kirby said entering the lift. "He's not a very good liar. Not intimidated at all, is he?"

"It doesn't seem fair like a fair fight, PM," Carrol smiled. "Maybe that's why he shot you in the leg, to slow you down."

"Case solved!" Kirby bellowed throwing his head back in laughter. "That's got to be it."

"I would have you down on the mat in fractions of a second, with two good legs, sir," Max said smiling and pressing the button for the conference floor. "But, that is what you pay me for."

"Indeed, it is, Max," Kirby said laughing. "Indeed, it is."

The doors to the elevator opened and Max and Carrol led the Prime Minister out into the entrance hall to the auditorium. Kirby stopped to shake hands with a few people, including a short woman in a green pants suit. Max recognised her as the new foreign affairs minister. As she spoke to Kirby, Max noticed her sneezing and coughing. Kirby wore a concerned, friendly look on his face as he patted her on the arm and told her to get some rest after the speech. She was only new in the job, following a reshuffle of the government front bench and Max could not help but wonder if the job was knocking her around a bit, hence the flu.

A tall handsome man, about Max's age entered the hall and stood beside the foreign affairs minister. He looked Max up and down a few times, but looked away when they locked eyes, then he shook hands with Kirby. He spoke briefly to Kirby, then headed into the auditorium to take his seat. The lights flashed and an announcement told those gathered outside to enter and find their seats for the keynote address. The crowd gradually filed into the auditorium then the announcer introduced the Prime Minister. Kirby walked into the room and took the stage to a standing ovation and stirring round of applause. Max took up position on the side of the stage, out of sight in the shadows, where he could watch the crowd, while staying close to Kirby. The auditorium was massive. It had chairs for around five thousand people. It had been recently restored and renovated for the conference, and it smelt like fresh paint and new carpet. It had a gentle sloping circular seating area which looked like ripples leading to the rear of the hall. A large open space ran from the front row up to the elevated stage where Kirby was walking to the lectern.

"Thank you," Kirby said adjusting the lectern's microphones and gesturing for the crowd to be seated. "Thank you all very much. These are confronting times. My country, like many others around the world, has been subject to a series of terrorist events, including the terrible attacks which took place only months ago in our Parliament, on our streets and in some of our iconic buildings and largest cities. It is no secret that some of the people involved had worked their way into positions within government and senior roles in the private sector with a view to undermining our national security. I am sorry to report that terrorism as we knew it no longer exists. Instead, in its place stands a darker and much more sinister force. These people hide in plain sight. Their motives vary from religious zealotry to financial gain, and some, I hate to say, are passionately motivated to overthrow and destroy the very foundations of our democracies. They stand ready to crush the liberties and freedoms we take for granted. They seek nothing but their own will imposed on us all and nothing will deter them from their goals. They would see this very organisation, the Commonwealth, a symbol of democracy and freedom throughout the world, shattered and disbanded. But, I ask you this, should we let them? Should we let these people takeaway everything our nations have worked to achieve for our people? Should we let these people overthrow democracy and destroy our way of life? Should we fall to our knees and give in to their demands?"

Kirby paused briefly as the crowd started responding with chants and calls in reply to his questions. The crowd were clearly onboard with the Prime Minister's address. Shouts of 'no way' and 'who do they think they are?', among other more inflammatory remarks, were being yelled back at Kirby, until he held up his hands and quietened the crowd.

"And the answer, in case any of them are watching is of course, no!" Kirby thundered to rapturous applause. "No, we will not sit by let you trample on our dreams and on our history. No, we will not allow you to force your will on us. No, we will not permit you to hurt or kill our people, or your people for that matter, simply to boost your bank account, in your quest for power or in the name of your God! And, if you choose to fight us, we will rain down our vengeance with everything we have in our arsenal. There is no boardroom, nor cave, you can hide in. No desert, nor city, in which we cannot or will not find you. If you come for us, know this, we will come for you and we will end you!"

The Prime Minister was interrupted by a hearty round of applause.

"I urge the members of this great organisation, the Heads of the Commonwealth Nations, to urgently support new legislation in your parliaments mirroring Australia's new *Secure Nation* laws. I urge you to support our motion at the United Nations in the coming months to increase the world body's escalated response ability to help stamp out terrorism. And, this week at the Commonwealth Heads of Government Meeting, I am asking on behalf of the thousands of people who died in Australia this year at the hands of terrorists and for the survivors, please support my motion to increase our intelligence sharing and surveillance powers across the Commonwealth, so together we can eliminate terror in our nations. And, I urge the people of Australia, including my political opponents, to abandon their plans for a republic. Australia is strong and the Commonwealth is strong, thanks to our shared values and history. Only together can we succeed."

Max watched as parts of the crowd rose to their feet to applaud the Prime Minister. Kirby took a moment to gather his thoughts and have a sip of water as the applause rolled on. Then Max noticed a man in the front row. He was not clapping, he was staring intently, almost angrily, at Kirby.

"Eyes up," Max said into his comms unit. "Front row, ten seats from the left wall."

"Got him, Prince," Flash replied. *"Unhappy customer, want me to get him out of the room."*

"Just watch him for now."

"Ack."

Max continued to watch the man in the front row, when suddenly he and four others from the front row stood and ran for the stage.

"Take him down, Flash!" Max yelled. "Get the PM, Carrol!"

Carrol was already moving, he grabbed Kirby and quickly moved him towards the back of the stage as two other officers shielded him from whatever might be coming. Flash tackled the man from the front row as two of the others made it to the stage. Max was running at full pace across the stage and leapt up off his left foot and slammed his right hand down hard on the side of one of the men's faces, knocking him out instantly, and sending him flying back off the stage. The second man froze instantly and held his hands up just as Max dived and tackled him. The force of the tackle sent the pair flying off the stage into the wing as the crowd from the auditorium fled in fear. Max could hear their screams and shouts as they jostled for the doors. Max drew back his hand and prepared to punch the man he had tackled, but stopped. He was just a teenager, barely out of school and the look of fear on his face said it all. He was not a terrorist, he was a protestor. How he had gotten inside was going to be a topic of discussion in the very near future, but for now, Max flexi-cuffed him and let two police officers escort him away. The man he punched was still unconscious on the floor, a police officer was leaning over him calling for a medic. Flash had tackled the original suspect and the last guy was held at gun point on the far side of the stage, both were being cuffed and dragged away.

Max jogged out of the room and up the stairs. He caught up to Carrol who was escorting Kirby back to his suite a few doors down from the room.

"Jesus Christ!" Kirby shouted waving his walking stick at Max. "Who were they, Max? How the fuck did they get in here? The security is tighter than a fish's arsehole! It should be impossible to get in without the right credentials."

"Unclear, at this stage, sir," Max said calmly. "I think they may have been protestors."

"Fucking protestors. You should have punched the other one too, while you had him close. Don't they know we are doing this for their safety?"

"It's not my place, sir."

"It used to be, remember when you worked as an adviser to the government? You must have a view."

"It is not my role anymore, sir, and I would not presume to know. I have spent too much time out of the game."

"Well, that is bullshit, Max," Kirby stopped at the door of his suite. "What do you really think? I want to know. I am ordering you to tell me."

"These new laws will help me do my job, sir," Max said looking to Carrol, "and will help Agent Carrol and his teams too."

"But?"

"But, they may also take away some of the very liberties we are trying to protect."

"Not turning into a bloody lefty are you, Max?"

"I am sure you will do what is right Prime Minister," Max said ignoring the comment.

"Thanks, Max. Please let me know when I can finish my address. This is bullshit, it was my moment."

"Yes, sir," Max said allowing the Prime Minister to enter his office, then pulling the door closed behind Kirby to remain in the hallway to speak to his team. "I want a full security sweep of this building. Every person's credentials checked. Anyone without valid passes or without a valid reason to be here needs to be removed now."

"I will contact the security teams and make it happen," Flash said over the comms unit.

Chapter Nineteen

"I'm a block away," Robert said into his mobile from the luxury cream leather backseat of his BMW. *"Do you have my credentials?"*

"Yes, I do," Alistair whispered as he walked out of the Foreign Minister's temporary office in the convention centre. "But it was not easy. AIS has used their conference security status to clear the building. Everyone is going back through the security checkpoints and their credentials are being scrutinised. They literally emptied the whole building to recheck everyone."

"Excellent, that gives us a window to get into position."

"Us?"

"Yes, we're pulling up now."

"We?" Alistair probed walking out the rear VIP door to the conference centre.

The VIP entrance had lower security checks given it was for Heads of Government and staff, but there was still a checkpoint and scanners. Robert and Bradley climbed out of the luxury BMW and walked over to Alistair.

"There are two of you?" Alistair said nervously as he tried to look unsuspicious to the nearby security guards. "I didn't get two passes."

"Relax, he has his own pass," Robert dismissed pointing to Bradley's access pass. "Alistair, this is Agent John Bradley MI6."

"Nice to meet you," Alistair said shaking Bradley's hand.

"He cannot speak. His mouth is wired shut. Your friend, Agent Shaw, broke his jaw a few hours ago."

"Jesus, Robert. Why is he here? Agent Shaw is in the building. He is the one who ordered the security sweep. If he knows this man, he will remember him and he will start asking question, like how the fuck did he get in?"

"You need to calm down."

"You're joking, right? You've read what that psychopath does for a living, haven't you? I don't want to get anywhere near him. I saw him earlier and my blood ran cold."

"You sound like you are losing your nerve. Not a good start for someone who wants Shadow's seat at the table."

"I believe in what we are doing, of course I do, but I don't want to be on the other end of Agent Shaw's knife or being tortured by him for information. He's fucking ruthless!"

"So are we," Robert said calmly and coldly. "It is the mission we signed up to and the only way we can achieve our goals."

"You are right, of course, you are right, Robert. But, if this man has been anywhere near Agent Shaw, he will recognise him. So, why is he here?"

"To do what you and I cannot do."

"And what is that exactly?"

"Do you really want to know?"

"If I am going to be involved in all this, yes, I would like to know."

"He's going to assassinate the Australian Prime Minister when he retakes the stage."

"Jesus Christ, Robert."

"Do you want your seat at the table to become The Sixteen's knight in Australian?"

"Yes," Alistair declared more determinedly.

"Do this and I will make it a reality."

"Okay, Robert," Alistair agreed, encouraged by Robert's promise and pointing at Bradley's bag. "Is it in there?"

Bradley nodded.

"Can a metal detector pick it up?"

Bradley shook his head.

"It's ceramic," Robert added.

"What about x-ray?" Alistair asked.

"It is in multiple pieces which look like pens and stationery."

"Okay, well just as a precaution I brought this down too," Alistair said retrieving a diplomatic sticker from his pocket, peeling off the label and sticking it to Bradley's bag. "Now, they can't open it even if they wanted to."

"Good thinking," Robert said impressed.

"Okay, come with me," Alistair said escorting them towards the security checkpoint.

"Good afternoon, gentlemen," the security guard said waving his hand towards the scanners and x-ray equipment. "Please place all bags and items from your pockets into the trays for scanning, then proceed through the metal detectors."

"Thank you," Alistair said dropping his mobile and belt into the tray before walking through.

"Credentials?" the guard on the opposite side said.

"Oh, yes, here they are," Alistair said fumbling the passes before handing them over for inspection. "These men are here to meet with the Australian Foreign Minister."

"Yes, sir, but we need to check everyone after the incident earlier."

"Understood," Alistair said putting his belt back on and retrieving his mobile from the scanner.

Alistair watched nervously as Robert made his way through, followed by Bradley. As the pair were gathering their belongings from their plastic trays, the bag went through the x-ray scanner. The guard stopped the conveyer and studied the image on his little screen. He called over one of the other guards and started pointing at a few items in the bag. Alistair felt his chest tighten and he stopped breathing.

"Whose bag is this?" the guard asked turning to face the three men.

Bradley raised his hand.

"We need to have a look at one of the items," the guard said pulling the bag up onto a nearby desk.

"He's got a broken jaw," Alistair said walking over to the desk. "He can't speak. Rugby accident on the weekend. That bag has a diplomatic seal on it, I'm afraid you cannot open it."

Bradley grunted and waved his hand, gesturing to the guards that it was okay to open the bag and dismissing Alistair. He walked over and opened the bag. Alistair just starred, half in shock. The guard reached in and retrieved a small white cylindrical item. He pulled it into two pieces revealing it to be a pen. Alistair wondered if it was in fact a pen. The guard scribbled on some paper with it and wrote his name. Satisfied, he replaced the lid and handed it to Bradley.

"Nice pen," the guard said looking from the pen to Bradley. "Strange design, but it is okay, you are free to enter. Thank you for your understanding. I hope that jaw heals soon."

"Anytime, gentleman," Alistair said anxiously corralling his two guest and pushing them for the entrance. "Cannot be too sure these days."

"Agree, thank you, gentlemen. Have a good day."

"And you too," Alistair said walking his new guests into the conference centre and down the hallway into the auditorium which was starting to refill after the earlier incident. "You could have told me you could just open the bag."

"After your protest, when Bradley agreed, it immediately disarmed them," Robert said looking around the big hall. "It worked well, they did not do a thorough search, thankfully."

"Yes, thankfully. Anyway, I am going to have to leave you here for now. I am late for a meeting and the Minister is expecting me. Given she is unwell, I will be caught up in meetings sitting in for her all day."

"Thank you, Alistair," Robert said shaking his hand. "I will be in touch."

"Good luck," Alistair said turning and leaving the room.

"We should separate," Robert said to Bradley who just nodded. "Do you have everything you need?"

Bradley nodded again and took the pen and other items from the bag getting ready to assemble his ceramic pistol.

"Good luck my friend," Robert said shaking Bradley's hand. "Thank you for everything. If you are captured after, I will do everything in my power to get you back out. You will just need to hold your nerve and trust me. I will not let you down, especially after all you have done for us."

Bradley nodded and placed the pistol components in his pocket, before finding a seat near the front of the room. Robert walked towards the middle of the room and took a free seat and waited patiently to watch the death of a world leader.

Chapter Twenty

Max sat at the conference table in the room next to the Prime Minister's suite. The conference facility was beginning to refill after he ordered a full security sweep. The Prime Minister was not happy with him and had let him know as much. This was supposed to be his moment and now protestors had managed to interrupt him. Thanks to Max and his team, protestors against the Prime Minister's new laws were calling the arrests of their comrades heavy-handed and over the top. Kirby had just moments ago berated Max letting his stress and anxiety out. Max was the easy target, given he ordered the security sweep and he had been part of the arrests. Kirby did not really care what the protestors were saying, he knew they were just overegging it like always to try to steal the spotlight. No, he was annoyed because Max had delayed his return to the stage for a few pimply kids. There was no real security risk, the place was like Fort Knox. Max just took the verbal lashing then explained to Kirby that if protestors could get through, anyone could. He did not want to take that risk. Max could tell Kirby understood, but it did not stop him stomping out of the conference room and slamming the door.

Max and Flash had sat in relative silence with Carrol and Stevenson ever since. Max and Flash took the chance to recharge a bit, given the ordeals they had been through. Flash had suggested Max should try to take a nap, but he could not sleep, even if he wanted to, he couldn't get his mind to settle. He thought about being tortured, about the hunt for the people behind the attacks, about Sam and Lachlan, but mostly his mind was stuck on repeat watching the rooftop explode killing Jonnie. He was not sure he would ever forgive himself for getting the young member of his team killed. Jonnie had been on the roof, under Max's command. The guilt was crushing, but it was nothing compared to the shame he felt in leaving the young agent's body behind. His mind was on fire and he felt like he was torturing himself with his thoughts. But, he guessed it was the least he deserved.

"Ladies and gentlemen," the announcer said over the conference centre speakers. *"Thank you for your understanding. We are now ready to proceed with the conference. Can you please move into the auditorium for the remainder of the Australian Prime Minister's keynote address. The Prime Minister is due to retake the stage in ten minutes."*

"Alright," Max said getting to his feet and stretching his back, glad to be able to focus on something else. "Let's get this show on the road."

"I will get the PM," Carrol said walking from the room and leaving the door open for the others.

Max and the team surrounded the Prime Minister for his walk to the auditorium. They walked at a relatively slow pace, so Kirby felt comfortable with his cane. On the walk, Max's phone rang.

"Prince, it's Hermes," Blake said breathlessly.

"Go ahead, Hermes," Max answered, "what is it?"

"We have been trying to track down Robert Hardy from the evidence provided by Russo on the plane."

"Tell me you've found him," Max said impatiently.

"Yes."

"Great, I will send Alpha and a team to pick him up."

"No need. We tracked his mobile phone. He is in the conference centre."

"What? He's here?" Max said abruptly stopping the group in its tracks with a closed fist.

"We think so."

"Think or know?"

"I would not be calling if I wasn't fairly sure."

"Understood, got a picture of him?"

"Sending to your phones now," Blake stated as Max's phone buzzed.

"Got it, thank you," Max said ending the call and turning to face Kirby.

"What is it, Max?" Kirby asked. "Why are we stopped in the middle of a hallway? I need to get to the stage."

"Sorry Prime Minister, but I need you to return to your suite. We have another security breach."

"You have got to be kidding me!" Kirby boomed. "This is unacceptable!"

"Yes, sir, I understand your frustrations, but it is my job to keep you safe and I will not put you at risk. Carrol, Stevenson, get him back to the suite. Guard the door. No one in or out."

"Max, wait," Kirby protested as Carrol and Stevenson took an arm each and essentially carried him at pace back to his suite.

"Robert is here," Max said to Flash as the pair headed for the lift.

"Well, that's stupid of him," Flash guffawed in disbelief.

"He obviously doesn't think Russo would give him up."

"Yeah, pretty arrogant. So, where is he?"

"I can only assume he is in the auditorium. Blake sent through a picture."

Both agents studied the photo before heading to the door of the auditorium.

"Prince, I got the photo from Hermes," Kate noted over the comms unit. *"I'm in the auditorium, I've got him. He is sitting almost exactly in the centre of the room. Middle of the row, fourteen rows back. How do you want us to proceed?"*

"Great, Alpha," Max responded. "Hold position and keep watch. Flash and I will circle in from behind."

"Ack."

Max and Flash took the stairs outside up to the second floor, entered the auditorium from the rear and started down the stairs on opposite sides of the room.

"Alpha, come up to the centre of row twelve right in front of him and move towards that free seat," Max ordered.

"Got it. I see it. Moving now."

Max and Flash slowly walked down the steps, as Kate climbed the stairs towards row twelve. Max watched as she shuffled past a group of already seated officials. They looked annoyed, but moved uncomfortably to let her pass. She was in position two rows in front of Robert and only one or two seats to his right. She just stood looking around the room, as if stretching her legs before the show started. Flash moved along row fifteen to get closer to him, while Max stood at the end of Robert's row and waited. When Flash was in position, Max made his move drawing his pistol and aiming it in Robert's direction.

"Robert Hardy!" Max yelled down the row, scaring people all around him. "You are under arrest, please stand and make your way towards me with your hands in the air."

Robert stood up, shocked at the booming voice. As he turned away from Max to look for a way out, Kate spun and pointed her pistol at his face.

"Don't you fucking move," Kate commanded making sure he noticed her sliding her finger onto the trigger.

Robert turned and looked over his shoulder to find himself looking down the barrel of Flash's pistol. It was pinned down with nowhere to go.

"Like she said, don't you move," Flash said locking eyes with Robert.

Surrounded, Robert threw his hands into the air and started to awkwardly shuffle towards Max, as the people all around them sat perfectly still in nervous silence. A shot rang out and Max watched as Kate fell forward onto the chair.

"Fucking, motherfucker!" Kate screamed to Max's relief; she had been shot in the bulletproof vest which was under her jacket. "Son of a bitch shot me in the back, fuck that hurts!"

Max spun and looked down the auditorium and saw Bradley aiming a white pistol in his direction. Max dived behind a chair as the bullet smashed into the steps where he had been standing.

"Go, Max!" Flash yelled over the screams that filled the auditorium. "He's moving for the exit. We've got Hardy."

Max leapt up from behind the chair and sprinted down the stairs pushing through the crowd who were all running up the stairs away from Bradley.

"Move aside! Federal Agent!" Max roared firing his gun into the air causing people to scream and clear the aisle.

Max got to the door and ducked his head around. There was a body lying in the hallway. Max raised his pistol and started down the long walkway outside the auditorium.

"I have a victim, hallway two," Max said into his comms unit. "We need an ambulance ASAP."

He did not stop at the body, help was coming, he had to keep moving. He rounded a corner and found a second victim, this time a security guard. The guard had a pen sticking out of his neck and was bleeding out. He called it in and told the guard to keep pressure on the wound, but he kept moving. The guard pleaded for help, but Max could not let Bradley get away. As he moved past the dying guard, Max noticed his gun was missing. Bradley must have taken it. Max moved quickly down the corridor leading to the rear of the facility. He could still hear screams and people running throughout the centre, then he heard four shots up ahead. Max ran towards the sound.

Just outside the rear door, Max found four security guards slumped over. Three of them were still seated, shot in the back of their heads. The other guard had been shot in the chest and she was struggling to breathe. She coughed and blood splattered her face, as she began to cry in pain and fear. She looked at Max and he could see her willing him on, as if begging him to go get the man who had done this to her. She pointed her blood hand in the direction Bradley had fled. Max nodded his thanks and sympathy as the woman's head fell to the ground.

Max sprinted through the carpark, searching between cars and under others trying to find Bradley. As he ducked to look under a row, a windscreen shattered beside him, showering him with glass. Max hid behind the car tyre trying to determine where the shot had come from. He snuck a look over the bonnet as two bullets hit the metal in front of his face forcing him back into cover. Max inched forward to glance around the front bumper of the car when he heard screeching tires on the concrete. He looked over the bonnet to see Bradley behind the wheel of a police car, accelerating hard it hard in reverse in his direction. Max jumped clear, up onto a nearby car, as the police vehicle's boot smashed into the car he had just been using for cover.

Max rolled off the bonnet and got to his feet as Bradley stopped the car and threw it into drive. Max started firing shots into the windscreen, but it did not crack, it was a VIP escort vehicle with bulletproof glass. Bradley smiled as Max fired a shot into the side window of the stolen car as he drove past. Within seconds Bradley flew out of the carpark and out towards the perimeter barricades.

"This is Agent Shaw, AIS!" Max thundered into his comms unit. "Stolen police vehicle approaching vehicle checkpoint delta. Stop it with extreme prejudice."

Max waited for a response.

"Delta, do you copy?" Max asked but again there was no reply. "Delta, what is your status?"

"Agent Shaw, this is delta one," the guard said almost a full minute later. *"We were unable to stop the vehicle, it smashed through the barricade, two of my men were run down."*

"Roger, Delta. This is Agent Shaw. I want an immediate search started for that vehicle and its occupant. Male, mid-fifties, dark suit, white shirt, armed and dangerous, carrying UK government security identification, MI6 Agent John Bradley."

Chapter Twenty-One

Max and his team, along with Carrol and Stevenson, had moved the Prime Minister and a number of government officials back to the Australian Embassy for security reasons. They put the building into lockdown as soon as they had arrived and armed federal agents were on every door. The conference centre security was being upgraded with more barricades and checkpoints, as well as additional screening and officers on site. The Heads of Government had all agreed to continue the meeting once the additional security measures were in place. It was already an embarrassing incident on the world-stage, but to cancel would prove they could not handle things, so they were determined to push on. At least to save face and ensure the world knew they would not succumb to terror.

As for Robert, he was being held in an interrogation cell under the Embassy next door to Russo. Max had spent some time interrogating him, but was not getting far and he was starting to lose his patience. He stepped out of the room to get some air. Across the corridor he found a small kitchenette and made himself a cup of tea. He absently watched the small television while the water was boiling.

"That footage was taken several hours ago now," Kevin Phelps said as the screen changed to show him sitting at the studio desk. *"We have reporters on the ground who are telling me that the police and riot squads have moved in to move the protestors back and away from the conference centre. At this stage, CHOGM security has not released the name of the man they have in custody, but they have only moments ago provided us with a name and photo of the man they are wanting to speak to after the attack."*

"His name is John Bradley," Phelps said as a photo of Bradley popped up on the screen. *"He is said to be armed and dangerous. Anyone who sees this man is to not approach him,*

but instead contact your local police. I repeat, do not approach this man, report him."

"I want to let my viewers know that sadly a number of people were killed, including several security guards. Our thoughts and prayer go out to the families of these victims. Now, as I was saying earlier, these events only serve to highlight the growing need for stronger anti-terrorism laws. The Australian Prime Minister, Edward Kirby, was in the middle of his keynote address when he was rudely interrupted by protesters. The left is calling for the police to be arrested after what they call heavy-handed arrests of these protesters. Can you believe that? Our police officers threw themselves into danger, not knowing these people were protesters. These lunatics were running at the stage and the agents stepped in to protect the Prime Minister. Fast forward a couple of hours and boy, don't they have egg on their faces now. Kirby was only moments away from taking to the stage and someone in the crowd has opened fire, killing a number of security guards."

"It is a tragic and senseless crime, but it only goes to show you the hypocrisy and insanity of anyone who would protest the need for strong laws and law enforcement. We will wait to see who is behind these attacks and we will bring you any new information when it comes to hand. I have been told CHOGM will go ahead once the security arrangements are reviewed and I promise to stay with you, until this crisis is behind us and to provide rolling coverage once CHOGM resumes."

Max shook his head at the screen as the kettle came to a boil. He poured himself a black tea, then headed back to Robert's holding cell. He took a seat opposite Robert and sat in silence for a moment, blowing on his tea.

"Why would a man with so much wealth and so much success get tied up with all this?" Max asked as he his tea on the table in front of Robert. "Your business empire stretches throughout the world, it can't be for money. What is it, power? You want to run the world without the unnecessary burden of democracy?"

Robert scoffed. It was the first thing he had said or done, other than when he asked for a lawyer, since they arrived.

"Do you think you are smarter than the people?" Max asked slapping the table. "Seriously! Do you think you have some right to control them and force them to your will? I want to know. Why do you think you know better? Why is it Robert Hardy wants to impose his world views on innocent people?"

"The people are stupid," Robert said with his words dripping with distain. "They do not know what they want and they do not know what is best for them."

"And you do?"

"Yes."

"And what's that?"

"They seek to live their quiet, little, pathetic lives in their modest houses, simply getting on with their lives. They want to just be, never more, never less, completely devoid of grand ambition. But they elect other stupid people to run their governments and the results I am afraid are not good. Ignorant people, elect ignorant peers and they make ignorant decisions which lead us to economic hardship and eventually to war. The revolving door of idiots at Number Ten and in Canberra are just some examples of the calibre we have come to accept. There is no stability, no security and without these key pillars, our nations are driving closer and closer to war. The people do not want war, but sadly the people they put in to represent them are not doing their jobs and if action is not taken, war is inevitable."

"You think very little of the people and democracy."

"Oh, you miss understand, Agent Shaw. Just because I think they are stupid and can be controlled does not mean I do not care for them. I do not want to destroy them, I want to save them, from themselves."

"How?"

"They elect incompetent governments and chose systems which promote freedom and liberty, but deliver neither. They sit by and allow so called equality and diversity to spread, without realising their true potential for harm.”

“So, to stop this harm, you inflict war and terror on the people you claim to care about?”

“Global change does not happen overnight and it is far from bloodless.”

“So, sacrifice is okay, as long as it serves your purpose.”

“It is for the greater good.”

“Shadow spoke like that too, right up until the moment I killed him.”

“Do you think you can intimidate me? I know all about you, Agent Shaw, and your methods.”

Max lifted his cup to his lips to sip his tea as Robert starred defiantly. Max blew the steam from his tea, enough clear his line of sight to Robert, then he abruptly flicked his wrist and threw the scolding tea into Robert’s face. Robert instantly when red and screamed, as he wiped his eyes.

“What you have heard or read is nothing like experiencing the real thing,” Max said getting to his feet. “Why don’t you think about that for a while? Think about my file. Think about the people I have tortured and killed. Think about how I did it. And, think about how much it is going to hurt.”

Max walked out of the room, clicked the door shut and walked into the observation room next door.

“He is pretty strong willed,” Blake said kicking a chair out for Max.

“Tell me about it,” Max said taking a bottle of water from the table nearby before sitting next to Blake.

“Are you going to ramp it up?”

“Yeah, he’s a seventy-year-old man though. I was hoping I wouldn’t have to. He might not be able to handle it. Let’s just leave him to sweat for a bit longer first.”

“I’m sure he’s warmed up now, thanks to the tea,” Blake laughed. “Maybe that will encourage the sweating.”

"It was an impulse, I couldn't help myself. I'll leave him to think about it for a bit."

"Your call, Max."

Max and Blake spoke briefly and checked on the progress at the CHOGM site. About an hours later, he walked back into the interrogation room. Robert was sweating heavily and looked worse for wear. His shirt was soaked through from sweat and stained from the tea, and his pants were clinging to his legs. He had not had water for hours and the heating was turned up on high in the room.

"I need my medication," Robert coughed with a look of desperation on his face. "It's my lungs."

"Hermes, get the embassy doctor to come down, will you?" Max said to the mirrored wall between the cell and the observation room.

"Did you say embassy?" Robert wheezed.

"Yes," Max said turning back to face him. "Why?"

"The Australian Embassy?"

"Yes, why?" Max asked as the door to the cell opened and the doctor walked in, but Max stopped him from seeing to Robert. "Hold on, doctor. Why do you care where you are?"

"Please, I need the reliver," Robert begged motioning for the doctor to give him the puffer.

"Wait, doctor," Max said putting his hand on the doctor's chest and stopping him from getting any closer. "Why do you care about the embassy?"

"The attack," Robert said between short breaths and straining to fill his lungs without coughing. "We will be killed."

"I need to give him the reliever," the doctor said trying to push past Max, but Max held him back. "A man his age could go into cardiac arrest if his lungs are failing."

"Did you hear that, Robert?" Max asked getting his face down lower near Robert's. "Want to die here today?"

"No, I do not," Robert said clutching his chest dramatically and wheezing.

"Tell me about the attack."

"It's a bomb, not far from here. It will level this building and everything around it."

"Why are you telling me this? Your cause not good enough for you to die for? Only send your pawns and your innocent victims to their deaths, but won't take one for the team yourself?"

"Please, I do not want to die. I will tell you where the weapon is."

"And you will tell me about The Sixteen?"

Robert looked up and locked eyes with Max.

"Yes," Robert said defeated and in pain.

Max let go of the doctor who gave Robert the reliefer then put him onto an oxygen supply. He checked his heart and gave him some medication to bring the heartrate down from its dangerous level.

"It will take a few minutes to work," the doctor said as Robert sucked oxygen in through the cover on his nose and mouth. "Call me if you need anything further."

"Thanks, Doc," Max said as the doctor left the room and he turned back to face Robert. "Tell me what I need to know."

"The first thing you need to do is stop the bomb," Robert said in a panic. "When you have done that, then I will speak to you."

Chapter Twenty-Two

Max and Flash raced through the traffic in a V8 Chevy, Max's vehicle of choice. It had been fitted with blue and yellow flashing lights and a siren which they were making use of to try to clear some of the London traffic. Robert had told Max that a Russian-style nuclear briefcase bomb had been planted at a construction site near Trafalgar Square. The blast radius was several miles, enough to level everything, including the Australian Embassy. Several miles surrounding the blast zone would suffer tremendous damage and would be contaminated for thousands of years, and the fallout cloud would contaminate everything in its path. Robert had originally planned to be far away from the site when the weapon detonated, but now he was locked up inside the blast zone he had a change of heart and did not want the bomb to go off. He had explained to Max that the device was to be buried in a small concrete slab towards the back of the site.

"Do you have the site foreman?" Max yelled into his mobile phone over the sound of the sirens.

"Yes, John Statton is the foreman. He knows you are on the way and will have blueprints ready," Blake replied.

"And, the device, any luck on a schematic?"

"We have a couple of design plans ready for when you locate it. We will pick the right one when you give us the description."

"Got it. We're going onto comm now," Max said entering the call and placing the comms unit in his ear. "Test one, two."

"Acknowledged," Blake said. *"We've got a clear signal."*

"Did Robert give you any other details of the device? Size, casing, triggers?"

"No, he didn't know."

"It goes without saying, if this thing goes off, they will have successfully changed the world. The world as we know it will never be the same. The damage to global financial markets and the world economy. A nuclear device in London. Jesus, it's unthinkable."

"We have time, Prince. We will get through this."

"We will be dead, if we don't get there in time, so I guess it won't affect us too much."

"Let's not let that happen hey?"

"Agreed. We are pulling up to the site now."

Max turned onto the construction site and a small boom gate opened, as Flash killed the siren. The agents climbed out and greeted the foreman.

"Mr Statton?" Max asked shaking the older man's rough hands.

"Yes, Agent Shaw?" Statton asked.

"Yes and this is Agent Gordon," Max said as Flash shook hands with Statton.

"What is going on here?"

"We believe a suspected terrorist has gained access to your site in the last few hours and that they may have planted a weapon of some sort."

"Shit, are my guys in harm's way? I better evacuate the site."

"No, please. We cannot have panic. We just need to get in and find the device, then we will be out of here."

"Are you sure my team is safe?"

"They will be fine, Mr Statton. I appreciate that you care for your workers, it is very noble, but we should be in and out soon, and as I said, I can't risk confusion or interruption to our search. A couple of hundred workers walking off site would not be very helpful as we were looking around."

"I understand."

"Thank you, sir."

"Your colleague said you needed to see blueprints," Statton said placing the blue paper rolls on the bonnet of Max's car and rolling them out. "Here we are. We are standing here at Gate One."

"How big is the site?"

"It runs from the A4 under the square to the A400 west to east, and from basically the steps of the National Gallery to the Statue of Charles I on the horse," Statton said running his finger over the blueprints on Trafalgar Square.

"What's the project?" Flash asked.

"We are shoring up the foundations of the monuments and replacing some of the services which run under the square."

"Services?"

"Water and sewer systems mostly, but also a few telecommunications lines," Statton said tracing lines across the blueprints. "We had a couple of burst mains which flooded the square and damaged the area. We are replacing most of the pavers too and some of the tiles on the statues and the obelisk."

"Has there been any concreting down there today?"

"Yes, we have poured a few pillars underground and some surface level work."

"The pillars, can you take us there?"

"Yes, of course, please follow me," Statton said rolling up the plans and leading Max and Flash towards a stairwell which had been cut out of the old forecourt and led under the square. "I find it hard to believe anyone was able to get on site. We have very strict procedures in place."

"The people we are looking for are very well connected and sadly they have gotten past some sophisticated systems in recent days."

"That is frightening."

"Yeah, sorry, but don't worry, we will find them."

"I am sure you will," Statton said passing Max and Flash hardhats equipped with lights which they turned on. "The pillars are down this way."

Statton led Max and Flash through a series of tight underground tunnels held up by metal scaffolding. Workers were all busy drilling and shovelling, and moving out wheelbarrows full of old bricks and mud, and rusty piping.

"You see the state of these old pipes," Statton noted pointing to a nearby worker who was wheeling out a barrow full of rusty old metal and terracotta pipes. "It is a wonder they lasted this long."

"Tell us about the pillars you were pouring today," Flash said.

"They are rebar and concrete, replacing these old red brick supports," Statton said tapping on an old support as they passed. "We are placing a couple either side of these existing ones for additional support and in some places, we are replacing supports which crumbled during the water main burst. They were obviously the priority."

"How many have you poured today?" Max asked dodging some loose bricks on the path.

"Three. They are just around the bend up here."

Max could hear a jackhammer working away around the corner. It stopped as they got to the bend and he heard a loud bang as the jackhammer hit the scaffolding, like it was dropped from a height.

"Jesus, these blokes will be the death of me," Statton huffed marching around the corner. "Dropping and breaking this shit, it is expensive to replace, some of them just do not give a fuck."

As Statton turned the corner and tripped. He fell to his hands and knees.

"What the fuck is this laying in the walkway?" Statton grumbled moving his headlamp to see what he had tripped on. "Fuck me."

Max and Flash were just behind him and saw the body of one of the construction site workers lying dead at their feet. Statton felt the body anxiously and fast, trying to feel for injuries and signs of life. Flash lent down and felt for a pulse, the guy was gone. He put a hand on Statton's back.

"Flash, contact front!" Max yelled raising his pistol and jumping over Statton.

Flash pulled his pistol and scanned ahead looking for whatever Max had seen. In the distance he could see the outline a man running away from them with a briefcase in hand.

"Get back up to the square," Flash said to Statton before following Max who was already at a full sprint down the dark corridor.

Max had seen the man in the distance pulling the briefcase out of a pillar. Coupled with the dead body, Max could only assume it was someone from The Sixteen moving the device. They must have known Robert was in custody and that he could give up the location. They thought right. Max hurtled over the jackhammer and pieces of broken concrete pillar which had fallen to the ground, and sidestepped another worker's body.

Up ahead Max saw the man he was chasing spin and fire a burst of rounds in his direction. Max ducked in behind some scaffolding and old pillars. Bullets chipped big chunks out of the ancient bricks and pinged off the metal. Max gazed out from behind the pillar and saw the man running again, so he set off after him. A few seconds later, a second burst of gunfire rained out and as Max dived for cover, he saw the man kick the leg of a nearby scaffold. There was an almighty noise which echoed through the dark passageways. Max looked down the walkway in horror, the roof and walls had caved in, blocking his path.

"Flash," Max yelled into his comms unit. "He's closed in the tunnel. Turn around and get up top."

"Ack." Flash responded turning and running back the way he came as fast as his legs would carry him.

Max continued down to see if he could get through. It was no use, the tangle of metal and brick and soil made it impossible to pass. Max turned and ran back the way he had come, he knew the man would escape. Flash was fast, but he surely could not get topside in time.

"Prince, you there?" Blake asked. *"What's the sitrep?"*

"One man, mid-to-late forties, has the device in his possession," Max said puffing as he ran. "He must have weakened the scaffolding because he took it out with one kick. The roof caved in blocking the path. Flash is in pursuit, but he has a big lead."

"*It's Flash,*" Flash interrupted. "*Just got to the steps, going up now.*"

Max heard him speaking to Statton asking for a rear exit to the tunnels.

"*I have two dead workers at the rear exit,*" Flash said. "*No sign of our suspect.*"

"*Roger that,*" Blake noted. "*Come back when you are ready. I will see what I can find.*"

"On our way," Max said as he climbed the last stair up to the forecourt.

"Sorry, Max," Flash said joining Max near the car. "He was too fast. He's gone."

"Fuck!" Max yelled punching the back window of the car and shattering it, cutting his hand. "Son of a bitch!"

"Fuck, are you okay?" Flash asked moving in to take a look at Max's hand.

"I'll be fine," Max grumbled biting a piece of glass out of his hand and spitting it on the ground. "Let's get back to the embassy."

"Thank you, Mr Statton," Flash said as Max climbed into the passenger's seat. "We will be in touch."

"What about my guys?" Statton said. "And, my family, should I be worried?"

"No, sir. We will find him."

"Agent Shaw does not look like he shares your optimism."

"Oh, don't worry," Max said stonily. "I'm going to find every one of them and fucking kill them."

Flash got in the driver's seat and drove off, leaving a worried looking Statton kicking a few rocks about in thought.

"*Prince, Flash, do you copy?*" Blake asked.

"Yes, Hermes, we're here mate," Flash replied. "On route back to the embassy."

"Change of plan, check your messages. We found him on satellite and we are tracking him through the city."

"How?" Flash asked as Max pressed the screen of the car's entertainment system.

"MI6 repurposed a satellite and placed it over the area."

"I didn't think they had one which could be positioned in time," Max said as the navigation system opened with a message from Blake.

"They didn't, I used the city's CCTV network to find him and follow him until the satellite caught up."

"That's great mate," Flash said hitting the siren and following the marked route. "We will get him."

"Keep me posted."

"You got it."

"I feel like a bit of a dick for punching the window now," Max said starring out his window.

"Yeah, want to talk about that? Don't think I have ever seen you lose it like that. Are you sure you're okay?"

"It's just a cut, I'll be fine."

"You know that's not what I meant."

"I want to find these arseholes, Flash. I'm just frustrated. They killed Jonnie. They have to answer for that."

"He was a good kid."

"I got him killed, Flash. I can't forgive myself."

"You didn't kill him, Max. He signed up, like we all did. He knew what he was getting into."

"That may be true, but he was on my team. Like you, Kate, Blake and Hulk, you are all more than just colleagues and friends, you're my family now. Since Lachlan, you have all been there for me and if someone hurts my family, well, I will find them and put them to death. The sooner, the better."

"We will find them, Max, and you can put an end to this whole saga."

Max looked at Flash and for a moment was flush with emotion.

"I'm sorry, Max, I didn't mean that to sound trivial," Flash said weaving the car in and out of traffic. "You know I loved Lachlan like a brother. I just meant I think ending this will help you get closure."

"You're right," Max said choking up. "It's Lachlan. I haven't slept one night without seeing him dying in my arms, over and over. Every night since I found out it was Shadow and The Sixteen or whatever bullshit name they have for themselves, who killed him. It's like I'm repeating all those months of heartache I went through after he died, all over again. It was my fault, Flash. They killed him to get to me. I need to put an end to them once and for all, then maybe I can let him rest in peace."

"And I will be right beside you the whole way brother."

"Thanks, Jacob."

The pair sat in the speeding vehicle in silence for a few minutes gathering their thoughts. Max looked down at the blue line on the navigation system, they were getting closer.

"Hermes, you there, mate?" Max asked.

"Yes, Prince," Blake replied.

"We're gaining on him. What sort of vehicle are they in?"

"It's a Volkswagen Golf. White. Licence plate Alpha, Charlie, two, four, Romeo, Golf, Lima."

"Ack. Thanks mate."

A few blocks later, Flash pulled the big Chevy in behind a row of cars which were at a standstill, the intersection ahead was blocked. Max saw a white car in the line, four or five cars ahead of theirs.

"I've got them," Max said pointing to the white vehicle up ahead. "Stay here in case the traffic starts to move again."

"Got it," Flash said as Max climbed out.

Max stepped up onto the footpath and casually walked towards the white VW. When he was only one car length away, he locked eyes with the driver in the side mirror. The little VW revved hard as the man from the construction site accelerated and jumped his car up onto the opposite footpath. Max fired two shots into the back window shattering it and he gave chase on foot as the VW cruised down the footpath. He fired two more shots and he thought he saw one hit the driver, but the car kept going. Flash had pulled up onto the footpath too and Max jumped back in.

"I think I hit him," Max yelled over the rev of the engine. "Stay with him."

"Got it," Flash said hitting the accelerator.

By the time the VW had made it to the corner, Flash had gained on it and slammed into the boot. Max opened the sunroof and stood up on his seat exposing the top half of his body through the roof. He levelled his pistol at the rear window again and fired as the VW started to round the corner. It took off down the narrow street and Flash gave chase with Max still standing through the sunroof, he braced against the roof for the turn. Flash got close and Max fired two rounds into the roof of the VW, and it swerved into oncoming traffic sending cars erratically onto the footpath and into Flash's way. Flash braked hard to avoid an oncoming collision with a station wagon before hitting the gas again to try to catch the little VW.

"Get me alongside him," Max yelled down as Flash approach the VW.

The big Chevy cruised in beside the white VW. Max looked in to see the driver holding his right shoulder with his left hand which was covered in blood. Max had hit him previously and he was clearly in pain. The driver looked out the window and saw Max pointing the pistol at him. He hit the brakes and Max and Flash shot past him. Max spun around and found himself staring in through the windscreen of the VW. Just as he was about to fire, the driver pulled hard on the steering wheel and careened across the road to the opposite footpath. Max tried to line up a shot, but pedestrians and parked cars were blocking him. Each time he tried to take a shot someone was there or his view was lost.

"Hold on!" Flash yelled up through the sunroof.

Max wedged his elbows into the sunroof's edges as Flash slammed his foot down on the accelerator. They overtook the

VW and shot down the road. When they were several car lengths in front, Flash held the gap and waited for his opportunity. Less than five hundred metres later he got his chance, he pulled hard on the wheel and jumped the gutter, blasting his horn as a warning to pedestrians on the footpath, then he slowed the car slightly allowing the VW to catch up. Max saw his chance, he sighted the driver and took two shots. The bullets sliced through the windshield, the first slamming into the driver's head and the second his chest. The driver fell forward dead and slumped on the steering wheel. The VW lost control and smashed into the back of a parked truck, stopping it in its tracks. Flash hit the brakes then threw the car into reverse and stopped just short of the VW.

Max jumped out and ran to the VW. The whole front section had crumpled and fallen away, but the cabin was surprisingly intact. The front and side airbags had deployed blocking his view. He tried the driver's door, but it was jammed, so he moved to the rear door. It was grating, but it eventually opened. Max could not see the suitcase, so he crawled in and looked over to the passenger's side of the car, next to the dead driver and found it sitting comfortably on the seat. He opened the case and examined the device. The timer was running.

"Hermes, we've got the device," Max said dragging it over onto the backseat. "But, the timer is running. Thirty-one minutes."

"Okay, Prince," Blake said calmly. *"Can you describe it for me?"*

"It has a long silver canister running diagonally from corner to corner. Wires from the top end of the canister lead down to a black box which has a red digital timer display."

"In the bottom corner or perhaps on the bottom of the canister, can you see a serial number?"

"Nothing in the bottom corner, checking under the canister," Max said lifting the device. "Serial number Bravo, Foxtrot, Echo, one, seven, zero, India, November, nine, nine."

"Pulling up the schematic."

"Flash, can you bring me the kit?"

"Right behind you, mate," Flash said passing the small tool bag through the backdoor to Max.

"Thanks," Max said unzipping the little bag.

"Okay, Prince," Blake said. *"What colour wires do you have at the top?"*

"Green, yellow, red, white and black."

"Okay, I need you to use the cable cutters to strip back the protective coating on the yellow and green wires, but don't cut the actual wires."

"Ack." Max said taking out the cutters.

He gently cut the rubber coating on the yellow plastic coating and slid it apart exposing the copper wire. He did the same for the green wire.

"Done, mate," Max stated.

"Good, now I need you to attach your bypass cord to those two wires, it should be in your kit," Blake said trying to remain calm.

"Got it," Max said as he pulled out a short red wire with alligator clips on either end and attached them to the exposed wires. "Done."

"Okay, great. Now, you will need to do the next two steps in quick succession. You have to cut the white wire, that will send the timer into a fast countdown, but it will also open the timer box. You'll need to tell me very quickly what the four levers are on. They will be either on X or O for each lever. Got it?"

"I think so."

"Once I know what the levers are doing, you will need to get a small screwdriver and reverse a couple of the levers, changing them to X or O. Understood?"

"We will soon find out."

"Okay, Prince, let me know what you are ready to proceed."

"Ready. Cutting the white wire."

Max cut the white wire and the timer started rapidly counting down, but as it did the lid holding the timer popped up. Max opened the lid and looked in.

"I have cut the wire and opened the timer box, but there are only three levers I can see, Hermes, not four," Max said quickly as he started to sweat.

"Shit, they must have swapped the timers!" Blake exclaimed.

"I need to know what levers, Hermes, the timer is counting down in a real hurry."

"Fuck, fuck, okay. It has got to be the secondary configuration, X, O, X. Is that what you have in front of you?"

"No, it's X, X, O."

"That does not make sense."

"I'm just telling you what I see, mate."

"How long have we got?"

"It's hard to say, but I would guess only a couple of minutes."

"Okay, right, fuck. Okay, umm, digital display, Russian suitcase nuke, steel wires, steel canister."

"It hasn't got steel wires, they are copper."

"Copper wires?"

"Yes."

"Well, that changes things," Blake said rapidly tapping away at his computer.

"You need to move, Hermes," Flash said nervously behind Max. "This thing is getting closer and closer by the second."

"You've got this," Max reassured. "I trust you, Blake."

"Okay, I've got it," Blake said his voice cracking slightly. *"The levers should be positioned as X, O, X. You need to invert the last two in sequence."*

"Got it," Max said using the small, narrow tip of the screwdriver to flick the tiny levers into position.

As he flicked the second lever from X to O, a small beeping sound started.

"Can you hear that, Blake?" Max asked anxiously.

"Yes, it hasn't got anything to do with the lever," Blake said with panic in his voice. *"Flick the next one now, hurry!"*

The beeping was getting faster. Max flicked the lever from O to X. The beeping stopped. He closed the lid and the timer screen was black.

"The screen's black," Max said tensely. "Are we good?"

"Yes," Blake said breathing out in relief. *"Well done, Prince. You stopped it. Thank you."*

"No, thank you, mate. Could not have done it without you."

"Thanks."

"Just out of interest, what was the beeping noise?" Max inquired.

"It was the one-minute warning."

Chapter Twenty-Three

"Where's Max?" Hulk asked walking into the embassy's conference room.

"He's with the medic," Flash replied. "How was your flight?"

"Longest flight of my life. My team's in trouble and the whole place is going to shit. Talk about feeling trapped and helpless. Anyway, everything okay with Max, I didn't read an injury report?"

"He's got a cut on his hand from earlier, they are just throwing in a couple of stitches."

"Alright. Good job earlier, Flash, you and Max saved a lot of lives, including all of ours. Well done."

"Yes, sir. Max deserves most of the credit, and Blake, they disarmed the bomb."

"Well you got him there to do it, so you deserve credit too."

"Where's Kate?"

"She went back over to the conference venue to inspect the security arrangements. The Duchess of Cambridge is due to address the meeting when it resumes."

"The daughter?"

"Yeah, the Duchess is getting an expanded role as His Majesty takes on fewer official duties."

"And what about the Prince of Wales, wasn't he due to make an address?"

"He did the official opening. His sister is doing the keynote address on behalf of His Majesty."

"Okay, whatever. Has Kate indicated when the PM will be able to head back over?"

"She just called, they can head back over within the hour," Blake said walking into the room and taking a seat at the conference table.

"Thank fuck for that. He has been pacing in the halls and he keeps walking past my office and popping in for a chat. I have been here about an hour, but he's making it feel like three. It's hard to get anything done."

"We'll all be out of your hair soon," Flash said smiling acknowledging his boss's distain for politicians.

"Good, keep me posted," Hulk said marching out of the room.

"Did you see him?" Flash asked awkwardly.

"Yeah, I just came from the medical centre," Blake said confused by Flash's tone and the incident. "The cut isn't too bad. How did you say he did it again?"

"Between you and me?"

"Of course."

"He punched the back passenger window of the car and shattered it in frustration when the guy with the nuke got away."

"That's understandable, he was upset with himself. He was probably blaming himself for failing. It all turned out okay though."

"I think it's more than that, Blake. He told me after about how he was going to hunt them all down and kill them."

"That's what we are paid for."

"It was his tone, Blake. There is something different. A look in his eyes. A determination. It's personal for him. He was talking about Lachlan and how he hasn't slept since the incident with Shadow a few months ago. That whole event brought up some memories and feelings he was just starting to get over, if that's even possible."

"That's what Shadow wanted, to mentally scar him. He may never get over it. I'm not sure I could. He's tougher than me though, that's for sure."

"Something has changed, Blake. I have never seen him like that. I'm worried about him. After all he's been through, then the torture, his interrogation of Russo on the plane and losing

Jonnie. I'm afraid he's going to snap. I think it's starting to take a toll on him."

"And you're worried he will make a mistake?"

"Maybe. Mostly, I'm worried he is pushing himself too hard. I'm worried about him, as a friend. I don't want him to get hurt. He will do anything to bring these people to his justice and I'm afraid of what that could look like."

"What exactly do you think he would do? He just disarmed a nuclear weapon in the backseat of a car. I agree he has been through a lot, but I trust him to make the right calls and stay focused."

"Thank you, Blake," Max said walking into the room and looking between his two friends and colleagues. "I love you like a brother, Flash. If you've got issues with me, you should bring them up with me, not with people behind my back."

"I'm sorry, Max," Flash said standing and walking over to Max. "You have been through a lot. Maybe you should stay here for a few hours, get some rest and then come and find us later."

"You don't think I can do my job?"

"I think there is a lot on your mind and with everything you have been through in the last twenty-four hours, let alone the last few months, since, the incident, well, no one would blame you if you needed some time to get everything sorted."

"I'm fine, Jacob. I can do what needs to be done. I need to do what has to be done."

"You need to do it? That's what's worrying me, mate. You need to kill these people. It won't stop the pain and it won't bring him back."

Max grabbed Flash by the shirt and pushed him into the wall, holding him there. He moved in to within a few inches of his face to stare him in the eyes. Flash could see some anger, but mostly hurt in his best friend's eyes.

"I'm sorry, Max," Flash said looking Max in the eyes. "I'm just worried about you."

Max let go of Flash's shirt and stepped back. He stood there for a few seconds looking at his best friend, regretting his reaction. He wasn't sure what came over him. He went to speak, but Hulk walked into the room.

"What's going on in here?" Hulk asked looking around. "I feel some tension."

"Nothing," Blake covered. "We were just having a conversation. Everything's fine."

"Is that right?"

"Yes, Hulk," Max said turning to Flash. "Right, Flash?"

"Yeah," Flash agreed after a few seconds. "Yeah, everything is fine."

"Good," Hulk stated, "Kate just called. The conference centre is open again. You two need to escort the Prime Minister and his team back over."

"You got it," Max said walking to the door, ready to get away from what had just happened. "Let's go Flash."

Flash looked at Blake, but neither said anything, then he followed Max out the door.

Chapter Twenty-Four

There was a screech of tyres and horns blasted. Pedestrians stopped in their tracks and watched in horror as two trucks smashed through the line of traffic. Cars were pushed off the road up onto the footpath. Glass shattered and windows broke as some of the vehicles were thrown into nearby shopfronts. Anxious shoppers and pedestrians fled in fear as the trucks rolled on.

At the end of the street the first truck banked hard right, pinning itself against the wall of the corner pub. The second truck banked left, scraping the first as it moved into position against the flower boutique on the left. The trucks had sealed off the road.

The two drivers climbed out on the far side, raised their automatic weapons into the air and fired. People ran for their lives away from the men who were dressed from head to toe in black combat gear. The two men checked their watches then walked calmly towards their next target.

At intersections to their left and right, the two men could see their comrades exiting their trucks and walking in the same direction as tourists and locals fled in fear.

Chapter Twenty-Five

Max and the team had returned to the conference centre. They were standing watching the crowd from the side of the auditorium. The Australian Prime Minister was sitting in the front row listening to the Duchess of Cambridge's address. Max had only been partly listening to the third in line for the throne, his mind was elsewhere, thinking about what Flash had said. Maybe he was right, but Max was not going to rest until he found all the people responsible for Lachlan's death. Max watched as the short, round woman on the stage extolled the virtues of the Commonwealth on behalf of her father the King.

The King of England and his line of succession had ascended to the throne in a bizarre and historically unique fashion. The former Queen had passed away and her immediate successors had each abdicated following months of scandal. From tabloid sex scandals to inappropriate use of public money and embezzlement, the scandal tarnished the whole Royal Family. Leak after leak hit the papers, systematically over a period of months. The image of the Royal Family, as well as that of the Monarchy itself, was in unprecedented turmoil. For the good of the nation and the Commonwealth, the whole family relinquished their claims to the throne. In the months following the new King of England and his family had spent time resetting the public image of the Monarchy and growing into their roles. Finally, the tide was turning and the people where returning their support to the Monarchy.

"His Majesty the King and my brother, the Prince of Wales, both understand the importance of this incredible organisation," Her Royal Highness Princess Victoria said from the lectern on stage. "The Commonwealth has stood for decades as a symbol for democracy and freedom. Following the events which saw my father take on this humbling and momentous burden for the people, our family has endeavoured to return the trust and faith of the people in, not only this organisation, but the very Monarchy itself."

The Princess was interrupted by the applause of the room and a standing ovation.

"Thank you," she continued placing a hand over her heart in gratitude to the crowd. "Thank you all for your support. Together, we will continue to rebuild our strength on the world stage and together our nations will combine to fight for freedom and liberty, and for a world of peace."

Applause erupted and once more the Princess paused to allow the room to give her a standing ovation.

"But," she said changing her tone as the crowd resumed their seats, "this will not be an easy task. We have enemies without and within. They hide in plain sight seeking to bring us down, seeking to destroy our way of life and seeking to impose their extremist views on our nations. I wish to echo the statements made by Prime Minister Kirby from Australia today, to note, we will not sit by while terrorists try to destroy us. It is only through strength, unity and determination, can we defeat our enemies and give the people the nations and the world they deserve. Our defence and intelligence services must be properly equipped to serve our nations and protect the realm. We must seek new ways to uncover those who would hide behind women and children, the cowards that they are, seeking to do us harm and bring them to the light and to justice by any means necessary. And, we must encourage our neighbours to consider joining this auspicious and remarkable organisation as a bastion of hope and promoter of peace throughout the globe. While some internationals organisations and institutions have faltered and failed, the Commonwealth prevails and we must do what we can to ensure its ongoing strength and dominance – for the betterment of humankind."

The woman spoke for over half an hour, but it dragged into almost an hour as she was continuously interrupted by applause. Max noticed the highly inflammatory language she was using, including some sections of the speech which strayed into political comment, which he thought was unusual for the Royal Family. Given she would have been briefed on the earlier failed terrorist attack though, he presumed she was just being overly passionate.

Following the speech, Max and Flash escorted Kirby and the Australian delegation to a private dining room which had been set up within the conference centre upstairs. The delegation was meeting for a working dinner with the United Kingdom delegation, led by their Prime Minister, Stephen Morgan. Morgan walked into the room, followed by four of his Ministers and senior staff. They shook hands and then took their seats opposite Kirby, the Australian Trade Minister and their Chiefs of Staff. Kirby apologised that the Foreign Minister could not attend as she was unwell, but he had asked her Chief of Staff, Alistair Turner, to sit in in her place.

As the meeting commenced, Max had told Kate to head back to the embassy. Babysitting duty was bad enough from one or two of them, but three AIS agents seemed ridiculous. He asked her to help Blake research The Sixteen and any other names they may have had over the years. In particular, he wanted to know who the other members were, so he asked her to go back and question Russo and Robert again, and to look for anything connecting all the known players.

Max stood in the back of the room, hardly listening to the long conversations about trade relations between the countries, instead he was thinking, trying to piece it all together. His mind kept wandering back to Russo's codebook, the little leather diary he found on the plane. He knew it was important, but just could not figure out the symbols. He hoped the analysts at AIS were having more luck. Max's thoughts were abruptly interrupted by the crackle of his comms unit followed by numerous people shouting in his ear. His heart raced as his adrenaline kicked in. He watched as Flash and the Federal Police around the room, as well as agents from MI6 and MI5 pressed their ears trying to unjumble the sounds they were all also hearing. Then he heard them, two words of clarity, 'under attack', followed by gunfire. The attendees all stopped talking as if sensing something was wrong and look at the agents surrounding them, who were all wearing the same shocked expression.

"We have to move!" Max commanded. "Prime Minister, please come with me."

"What is it, Max?" Kirby asked stumbling up out of his seat.

"The centre is under attack," Max said helping Kirby up as the agents all moved into position. "We need to get all of you out of here now!"

Max dragged Kirby quickly around the table, as the lead MI6 agent pulled Morgan up out of his chair. The other Ministers and staff all scrambled up, knocking over some chairs in the process.

"Flash, hard and fast, rear exit," Max ordered and pointed for the door.

"Got it," Flash said turning and taking the lead.

Flash opened the door, took a left and raised his pistol to scan the hallway.

"Let's move, Max," Flash said starting down the hallway.

Max led Kirby out of the room, closely followed by Turner. The MI6 agent and Morgan were just behind them. Carrol and Stevenson had the rest of the Australian delegation in the middle of the pack, followed by the remaining UK delegation and agents. They were all moving together as one big unit, but Max knew if they were caught like this there would be a blood bath.

"Carrol," Max said into his comms unit. "Take the Ministers and remaining delegation to Evac B, we will head to Evac A with the Prime Ministers."

"Understood," Carrol said without question, breaking his group away from Max's and leading them across the centre to a side exit which they had workshopped earlier.

"Good luck," Max said without stopping.

"And same to you. See you on the other side," Carrol replied as he marched quickly down the side corridor.

Max and Flash led their smaller group to the top of the main staircase which climbed to their floor near the rear of the building. A wild spray of bullets flew up the stairs. Max grabbed Flash and dragged him back behind cover, and stopped the group in its tracks, as the bullets impacted. Max dived across the steps to the opposite side, as more bullets slammed into the roof and wall behind him. He was already across and behind cover when a third volley rang out. Max and Flash took it in turns of firing down the stairs, but it was no good, they were pinned down.

"We need to find another way out," Flash yelled across the gap.

"Agreed," Max shouted over the sound of gunfire below. "What about A, three?"

"Worth a shot, if we can check ahead to make sure it's clear."

"Hold them here, I'll check and call it in. The group should be out of the line of sight if they get low and hug that wall. Send them if I tell you it's clear."

"Got it."

"Here," Max said sliding Flash two more magazines for his pistol. "One minute."

"Roger."

Max turned and ran in the opposite direction from where they had come from, down a long corridor to the back of the building. He took a right and followed the wall around ten metres, where he found a set of louver windows. He pulled the metal lever and opened the louvers, below he could see the carpark and a swarm of activity. To the right, conference security and police were barricaded firing at what looked like an army of men all dressed in black tactical gear trying to take control of the centre. Max removed ten of the louvers from the floor to about waist height.

"Clear, Flash," Max said as he slid out the last three louvres. "Danger close, but we can make it."

"Ack." Flash acknowledged. *"Prime Minister, get as low as you can, head over to that wall and crawl past the gap. Once*

you are clear, stand and run. Max is down the far corridor on the right."

Max heard Kirby say something, but he was moving that was the main thing. Max watched as guards, police and members of the intruding force fell one by one, two storeys beneath him. Kirby arrived lipping as fast as he could, the young man from earlier was with him, Turner, followed by Morgan, his Chief of Staff and two MI6 agents.

"We're going down over the awning," Max explained to the two agents. "We will head right, one of our Landcruisers is parked in the second row. Do you have a vehicle you can get to?"

"Yes, white Jeep," the lead agent said pointing. "Fourth row."

"Good," Max said turning to Kirby and Alistair and handing Kirby his ring. "Follow me, as close as possible, we are heading for that car. If I don't make it, you get out of here. Use the ring to start the car, you remember how it works?"

"Yes, okay, Max. Yes, I remember the brief," Kirby nodded more than a bit flustered and shocked at what he was witnessing. "Thank you. You will be right behind us?"

"Yes, of course, I will be right with you," Max said before speaking into his comms unit. "Flash, you there?"

"Yes, mate," Flash answered.

"We are heading out, give us one minute, then move your arse."

"Got it. See you soon."

"Right, let's move," Max ordered jumping down to a metal awning a metre beneath the window.

Max helped the two Prime Ministers down as well as the two political staffers. One of the MI6 agents jumped down as Max heard gunfire in the hallway behind them. He was worried about Flash, but could not stop. He had to get the Prime Ministers to safety. Max ran along the awning to the right, towards the carpark. He could hear Kirby and the others closely behind him. The gunfire below was like a warzone.

"Max, I'm coming through the window, but I'm under heavy fire!" Flash yelled. *"The MI6 guys and I will hold them off as long as we can."*

"Thank you," Max said his heart sinking at the thought of losing his friend. "You take them down, then get to the car, you hear me?"

"I'll try to get there, but the important thing is getting the PM out."

"I know," Max reluctantly agreed as he finally reached the end of the awning. "Okay, Prime Minister, you need to climb down the lattice. It is going to be hard, but you need to move as fast as you can. Two of you can go at a time. Prime Minister Morgan, please go too. As soon as the PMs are down enough, you two climb over and head down too."

Max helped Kirby and Morgan over the edge. The two staffers were shifting nervously, waiting for their turns. They kept looking back to make sure they were not being followed. Bullets rang out on the metal awning and smashed the glass behind Max. The group had been spotted and several members of the intruding force from the ground were shooting up at them from the distance. The two staffers fell to the awning in fear. Alistair started crawling for the edge to climb down, while the other staffer, the UK Prime Minister's Chief of Staff, huddled up in a ball clutching his chest. Blood poured out onto the awning under him.

"Fuck," Max exclaimed as he dropped down and search the staff member trying to find the wound and put pressure on it.

As he rolled him onto his back, the colour drained from his face and he went still.

"Go now!" Max shouted at Alistair who did not need to be told twice.

Alistair threw his legs over the edge and quickly followed the Prime Ministers down the sharp metal lattice. Max looked over the edge and saw they were making very slow progress. Bullets were pinging off the lattice and support beams. Whenever a bullet hit the metal structure all three men froze in their places and clung to the lattice for their lives. This was taking too long. Max ran back along the awning looking for the source of the closest gunfire. He found his mark and opened fire. His pistol was no match for the automatic weapons firing up at him, but his aim was better. He found two of the intruders and dropped them with several bullets each. The main threat to the PMs was neutralised, but it would not take long for the attackers to work out who was on the lattice and start firing again.

"Flash, you still with me?" Max asked.

"Only just," Flash replied. *"One of the MI6 guys is down and we are holding back an onslaught."*

"The PMs are almost to the ground. Pull out now and we will follow them down."

"We are on our way."

Max watched as Flash and the remaining MI6 agent jumped out of the window through the opening Max had created in the louvers and started running towards him. They were several metres along the awning before any of the chasing force got to the window. Max fired at the window, shattering several louvers above the attackers, forcing them back into the building. The three agents ran for the edge and the lattice to begin their climb, as a couple of intruders jumped down onto the awning to give chase.

"You two go!" the MI6 agent ordered. "Protect the principals."

All three agents fired and killed the intruders on the awning.

"We can all make it," Flash said willing the agent to follow.

"No!" the agent said handing Flash his badge. "Call it in when you get clear, now move!"

"Thank you," Flash said passing the agent his gun and some spare magazines.

Max and Flash headed over the edge and down the lattice as the MI6 agent held off their pursuing force. In less than half the time it took Kirby to get down, Max and Flash were on the ground and running hard towards the AIS four-wheel drive.

Kirby and Morgan were already in the backseat when they arrived and Alistair was desperately pressing buttons on the navigation system. Flash looked back towards the awning to see the MI6 agent fall in a hailstorm of bullets. He got to the driver's door and told Alistair to move over into the passenger's seat. Max climbed into the rear of the car, into the luggage hold. He slammed the door shut as Flash hit the ignition button.

"Where does the ring go?" Alistair asked.

"It goes behind the volume knob," Flash said.

"You didn't put it in there though and the car started."

"There are sensors on the steering wheel too, throw that back to Max. Strap yourselves in, this could get hairy."

Alistair and the PMs did up their seatbelts as Flash pulled the big Landcruiser around in line with the driveway. Alistair tossed Max his ring and he replaced it on his finger to ensure his weapons would work.

"You ready, Max?" Flash asked revving the engine.

"Almost," Max said pulling a small carpet panel out of the cargo hold lining.

Max entered his pin into the small panel which had been hidden behind the carpet patch in the rear of the car. A false floor had rolled away revealing a secret arsenal under the floor. He pulled out an HK416 assault rifle with grenade launcher and loaded a fresh magazine. He also loaded four large cylindrical canisters into a second shotgun sized weapon.

"Locked and loaded," Max said handing Kirby the shotgun. "Can you please pass that up to Flash?"

"Umm, sure," Kirby said handling the weapon with care and passing it slowly to Flash. "What kind of gun is that?"

"The gate opening kind," Flash smiled lowering his window and slamming his foot on the accelerator.

The big car jumped off the spot and raced down the road towards the exit. Security guards and police had cleared a path, and the car powered through into the no man's land between the guards and the attacking force. The car was getting pounded by bullets, but they pinged off the hardened vehicle without a dent. A concrete barricade had been moved aside to allow the attacker's vehicles to enter. One was about to drive through as Flash accelerated towards the gap. The vehicle stopped to block their way.

Flash put the shotgun like weapon out the window and fired twice. With two deep sounding thunks, the projectiles burst out of the launcher and flew through the air followed by a soft white and grey trail, before slamming one after the other into the blocking vehicle. It erupted in a ball of flames. Flash put his window back up, just as the Landcruiser drove through the gap where the attacking car had been.

Smoke and flame engulfed the vehicle, and it bounced over some big divots left by the explosion, then smashed into what was left of the car, pushing it aside. Max raised an internal bulletproof glass wall between the luggage hold and the backseat, then lowered the rear window. As soon as the car was out of the smoke, he opened fire into the intruding force. Some fired back, while others dived for cover. Max took down several men, before four white Audi's spun around and gave chase. Max could hear and feel the thuds as the four-wheel drive hit several men firing at the car. He wondered whether Flash was deliberately swerving to hit them or if they were trying to block the vehicle's path, either way they were losing. Max fired shot after shot into the intruding forces taking them down, until they sped out from the barricades and into London's streets.

Max reloaded as the heavy vehicle turned the corner. The four Audi's were only seconds behind. The first was gaining on them. Max waited patiently. He sat with his legs spread into the back corners of the luggage space and with his back pressed against the backseat keeping him in place. The rear door was high, only his shoulders and head stood above in the open space. It had a narrow window at the top, slightly narrower than the standard build of this car. It was not an impossible shot for his pursuers through the window, but close enough, and it gave him a bulletproof cover for most of his body.

The first Audi gained ground with every passing second. Max breathed out, slighted his mark and took the shot. The bullet smashed through the first Audi's windscreen and hit the driver in the face. Blood sprayed on the windows as the car veered wildly to the left. The car crumpled like a soft drink can as it hit the back of a parked semitrailer.

"Max, we've got a problem!" Flash yelled not taking his eyes off the road.

"What is it?" Max asked as he fired off a burst of rounds at their chase cars.

"The roads are blocked off!" Flash shouted turning the big car down a sharp right-hand bend.

Max looked out the window to see two trucks blocking the road they had been on. They were wedged tightly in the gap, closing off the street and footpaths from shop to shop.

"Coincidence?" Flash asked swerving to avoid a parked car.

"Doubtful," Max said firing at the closest chase car. "See if you can find a hole. We need to get to the safehouse."

"Got it," Flash agreed as he took another sharp right to avoid two more trucks blocking the roads. "Definitely, not a coincidence."

Max steadied himself after the turn, finding the second chase car only metres from him. A man dressed all in black was sitting on the doorframe on the passenger's side door, readying to take a shot at Max. Max fired two shots, as a bullet from the man on the door narrowly rushed past Max and hit the bulletproof screen inside the car. His two bullets had hit the windscreen, but missed the driver and passenger. He would not miss again.

He pumped the grenade launcher hanging from the barrel of his rifle and it spat out a grenade with tremendous force. The driver tried to steer clear of the incoming projectile, but instead, he perfectly lined up the man sitting on the passenger door. The grenade hit him and exploded. His body was torn violently apart, blood and body parts painted the inside of the second Audi. The door he had been sitting on was ripped off and the explosion tipped the car onto two wheels. As it fell back onto all four wheels, Max saw the driver's hand wipe blood from the window. Just as the driver's head became visible on the other side of the glass Max fired sending a bullet through his hand and into his head. The Audi jumped the gutter and destroyed a letterbox and garbage bin sending mail and rubbish flying through the air, before it ploughed into a boutique and came to a sudden, abrupt stop. Flash turned hard right again, more trucks had blocked the roads, forming a massive square perimeter around the conference centre.

"They've boxed us in!" Flash exclaimed. "We are going to have to open one of the roads."

"Hold on," Max said lowering the bulletproof screen and turning to Kirby. "Pass these up to Flash."

Kirby took three more grenades for Flash's launcher and passed them to Alistair.

"You are going to have to load those in for me," Flash said to Alistair.

"I don't know how," Alistair said looking at the shotgun like grenade launcher.

"Here," Flash said passing the launcher to Alistair. "Pull back on the slide on the side there. It will expose an opening. Insert the grenades one by one, round end towards the front."

"Got it," Alistair said loading the launcher. "Only two fit."

"Close the slide and keep the third one close in case we need it," Flash said taking the launcher as Alistair put the third grenade in his suit pocket.

Flash steered the big vehicle through the narrow streets until he came within a block of the next truck barricade. He wound down his window, took aim and shot the two grenades from the launcher. One hit and exploded, followed by the second. Smoke and flames engulfed the trucks.

"Is it clear?" Alistair asked as Flash wound up his window. "I can't see because of the smoke and fire."

"Only one way to find out," Flash said tensing up, "hold on!"

The big four-wheel drive hit the gap where the grenades had exploded. With a great crunch it hit what was left of the trucks, the right wheels hitting the angled axle of one of the trucks and putting them up on two wheels for several nerve-wracking seconds. The big car was too heavy though, loaded up with all the bulletproof glass and metal. It bounced over and when he had it back under control, Flash hit the accelerator.

Max steadied himself again, feet locked into the far corners and back against the wall. *Wait,* he told himself, fighting the instinct to shoot. *Patience,* he told himself, *it will come.* He waited, breathed out, then fired. The first Audi hit the truck's axle and flipped onto it side, sending sparks flying across the bitumen. The underside of the car spun towards Max, just as the grenade he fired arrived.

The grenade hit the exposed petrol tank and turned the Audi into a flaming wreckage. It broke in two spraying oil and petrol, and fire over the final chase car. It drove between the two sections of its former comrade's car and continued the chase. Flames were licking up into the air from its bonnet and roof, even the doors and windows looked to be covered in flames as the petrol and oil ignited. As they gained on the four-wheel drive Max unleashed a whole clip into the windshield. It rolled on for several metres before slowing to a stop in the centre of the road. Engulfed in flames, it burned until its own oil and petrol lines caught fire. The final Audi exploded, shattering nearby windows and sending a pillar of thick black smoke into the atmosphere, as Flash weaved the big AIS Landcruiser around the corner and through the London traffic towards the safehouse.

Chapter Twenty-Six

Flash had driven around the London streets for almost an hour, doubling back and taking large circuitous routes through the city to make sure they were not followed. When both Max and Flash were satisfied, they headed to the AIS safehouse. Flash had waved his hand in front of a small sensor and the garage door rolled to the side. Flash had spent some time restocking the vehicle's weapons cache from a safe inside the garage as Max led the PMs and Alistair into the safehouse upstairs.

The safehouse was a large apartment with four bedrooms, two bathrooms and two living spaces with a kitchen and laundry. One of the bedrooms had been converted into a small armoury and secure communications room. Another bedroom was converted into a makeshift walk in wardrobe and it was full of clothing from combat uniforms to police uniforms through to formal tuxedos and everything in between, in a range of styles and sizes. The third bedroom was fitted with four bunk beds and the master bedroom had a king-sized bed with ensuite. On most occasions, safehouses were used by one agent, very rarely would they be used by more, but they were fitted out just in case. The kitchen was stocked with long-life products and ration packs, enough to get several agents through more than a month held up in the safehouse if necessary. Max hoped they would not be staying that long. The embassy AIS attaché had stocked the safehouse will fresh supplies as per the policy for when AIS agents were in town, in case the safehouse was needed. Max had shown the PM and Alistair through the apartment and told them to help themselves to whatever they wanted, but to stay off their phones.

"Hulk, it's Prince," Max said from the secure phone in the communications room.

"Go ahead, Prince," Hulk answered. *"Are you okay?"*

"Yes, we are fine. Flash and I have Prime Ministers Kirby and Morgan with us, as well as Mr Alistair Turner, the Foreign Minister's Chief of Staff."

"What is their condition?"

"Safe and well."

"And, you and Flash?"

"We're fine too."

"That's good kid. It was a real shit show down there."

"Tell me about it. Did Carrol get the other Minister's out?"

"Yes, they came straight to the High Commission. They are here safe. We have the building in lockdown."

"What about the conference centre, how many dead?"

"Unsure, at this point in time, but it's a lot. Couple of high-profile leaders, diplomats and staff among the dead, as well as a number of guards and police."

"Jesus."

"But that's not all, the Duchess of Cambridge is missing."

"What?"

"She was at an official dinner with the Canadian Prime Minister who's been shot dead, as were more than half of her delegation and several of the Princess's staff. The security services have thrown the city into lockdown, an immediate curfew across London, until she is found."

"Any clues to her whereabouts?"

"Not yet. Every agency from across the Commonwealth is trying to get access to the conference centre security camera footage. It's taking some time to sort through the bullshit."

"And, the rest of the Royal Family?"

"They are being moved to a secure facility, one of the bunkers, I presume."

"What about Alpha and Hermes, any progress?"

"They have questioned Russo and Robert again, but they are not cooperating. It seems now you have saved Robert's life he has shutdown again."

"And, Russo?"

"Much the same."

"Tell them to keep digging, we need to find out who else is involved in all this."

"They will."

"What about Alpha's research on The Sixteen?"

"I will get her to give you a call to discuss what she has found."

"Great. Thanks, Hulk. We will hold up here until further notice. You'll let the Brits know about Morgan?"

"Yes, I will tell them he is safe, but I won't tell them where he is."

"I think that's for the best, until we can find out who is involved, let's keep everything close."

"Agreed."

"One of the MI6 agents who helped us get out gave us his badge before he was shot down. His name was Mark St. John, badge number one, seven, zero, eight, one, three. He trusted us to get Prime Minister Morgan out. It might help calm the British when you don't tell them where he is."

"Great. That will help, I'm sure. Appreciate it, kid. Good luck and Godspeed."

"Thanks, Hulk," Max replied before ending the call.

Max walked into the lounge room to find Flash and the other three men watching the rolling news coverage.

"...to repeat, the Canadian Prime Minister, Jacinta Trembley, has been confirmed to be among the dead as well as the Canadian High Commissioner to the United Kingdom and their Assistant Trade Minister," Phelps said. *"While it is no doubt a dark day for our nation and a tragedy that this horror can take place on our soil, spare a thought for the Canadian Government and the Canadian people who have lost so much today."*

"How this unspeakable incident has been allowed to happen is an outrage," he fumed. *"Years of weakness and inaction from successive governments has left us near defenceless. Our arrogance, topped with our willingness to just*

throw open our borders to the worse of the worse has led us to this sad place today. To think that a world leader can be assassinated, murdered, on our soil is shocking in its pure horror and in its magnitude."

"This is what both the Australian Prime Minister, Edward Kirby, and Her Royal Highness, the Duchess of Cambridge, Princess Victoria, were alluding to in their speeches," Phelps raged. *"The Commonwealth is under attack, our nation is under attack and our very existence is threatened as extremists rise up and fulfil their supposedly Allah-directed duties. All while our leaders cower, obfuscate and procrastinate in a dereliction of their duty to protect us. The Prime Minister has been trying to take action, but the left, led by the insipid Leader of The Opposition blocks him at every turn, pandering to the left and the same protestors who were picketing outside CHOGM. Where are they now, I ask? Still waving their placards in the streets? Still worried about their civil liberties? Wait until the terrorists win and Sharia Law becomes the norm, then maybe, just maybe they will understand what it means to have their civil liberties crashed. We need a change in this country. We need leaders we can be proud of and who we know can defend and fight for us. We need a change."*

"There is no news yet on the safety or whereabouts of the Prime Minister Stephen Morgan and Number Ten has yet to comment on the incident. Our sister stations in Australia and New Zealand are also syndicating this broadcast and we want to let viewers know in those countries that comment has been sort from your governments on the incident and on the safety of your delegations too. I will continue to bring any new details to you, my viewers, as soon as we have them. In the meantime, stay safe. Pray for our nation and for the Commonwealth during this dark moment in our history."

"Oh God," Kirby lamented. "Jacinta, she was such a lovely person. How terrible."

"Yes, she was a great person," Morgan agreed. "She will be in my prayers."

"And, mine."

"He will not be though. God, I hate that man."

"Who, Phelps?

"Yes. To say he is biased would be an understatement likes of which have never been heard before. He a far-right, holier-than-thou, sanctimonious, melodramatic, fanatical, pompous, grandiose arsehole. He is what my mother would have called a magnificent prick."

"We have a few of them in our country too."

"The absurdity and outlandishness, let alone the lack of civility, it takes to lambast government and the parliament at a time like this is beyond compare."

"He sounds like he is in your corner."

"For every vote he wins me, I lose two on my left."

"Now, is not the time to be thinking about politics. Our countries need us to lead. They need to see strength. They need to know we can protect them."

"Can we though? Look what just happened on our watch. Maybe he is right, maybe we do need change."

"To what?" Kirby asked as Morgan stared blankly at the wall without replying.

They sat in silence for a few minutes until Max walked into the room.

"Max, what can you tell us?" Kirby asked eager to break the silence.

"Unfortunately, nothing good," Max lamented taking a seat. "Princess Victoria is missing and we've got too many dead on site to get an accurate figure at this point in time."

"The Duchess is missing?"

"Yes, every intel agency in the Commonwealth is rallying to find her and our allies are reaching our with offers of assistance."

"They think she was kidnapped?"

"Yes. She was dining with the Canadian Prime Minister. She may have been the target all along."

"Max," Morgan interrupted, "I need to talk to my government."

"I understand, sir. I will arrange a secure line in the comms room, but I need you to keep your mobile phones off. We cannot take the chance that someone could be monitoring the calls and locations of your phones. Hulk has informed the head of MI6 that you are alive and safe, but we have not shared your location. Until we know it is safe, we will bunker down here."

"Thank you, Max. I understand. I will keep the location secret, but I need to take control of the situation."

Yes, sir. I will set up the call."

Max stood to leave when the television broadcast was interrupted.

"We have breaking news from the site of the Commonwealth Heads of Government Meeting which was brutally attacked earlier today," Phelps said. *"Her Royal Highness the Duchess of Cambridge, Princess Victoria, is missing. Sky News has obtained this security footage from the venue of the Her Royal Highness being dragged from the conference centre to a waiting car. I warn the following footage is shocking."*

The screen cut to a CCTV camera overlooking the main entrance to the convention centre. A group of men in the black military gear ran out the doors and down the stairs, rifles pressed to their shoulders and firing at targets off screen. Two men followed with a shoulder each under the Princess's arms, dragging her towards the waiting vehicle at the bottom of the steps. The short, heavy set royal, was putting up a hell of a fight, but the two men were too powerful. They shoved her hard into the backseat and climbed in after her, then the car sped off out of shot.

"It is difficult to watch," Phelps said over a replay of the footage. *"Here is Princess Victoria being dragged to the waiting vehicle, but she is not going quietly. It looks like she is trying to fight off the two men, who look to be wearing police or military tactical clothing. I am sorry, it is hard to watch. Our thoughts are with the Princess and the Royal Family at*

"Who do they think they are, Sky News, showing that footage?" Kirby demanded pointing wildly at the television. "She looked in terrible distress and God knows where they are taking her. Shameful and horrific! I am outraged at their lack of decency, let alone the security risks of showing that footage."

"There is a bigger issue, Prime Minister," Max interrupted looking to the two world leaders. "I would like to know how they got the footage. Hulk told me it had been difficult for the agencies to coordinate, including giving out access to the CCTV footage from the centre, and now its live for the world to see on Sky."

"I'm sure he will look into it."

"I am glad I'm not on the end of those phone calls."

"I know what you mean. Hulk isn't known for keeping his cool."

"And, this is going to send him over the edge for sure. Prime Minister Morgan, please follow me, I will set up you call."

Max helped Morgan connect to his national security chiefs and council. True to his word he refused to give them the location, but assured them he was safe. Alistair excused himself and went to the kitchen to make everyone tea and coffee. Max sat in a comfy big leather lounge chair and took out Russo's codebook. He studied the first page of the last section. There was a list of numbers one through to sixty-four on the left-hand side of the page. In the second column there were eight letters A to H and in the third column where the numbers one to eight. There was a red circle around a number in the left-hand column. Max checked another page and found a red circle around a number in the left-hand column. There was a blue square around a number in the left-hand column. Again, he checked another page to find a similar marking. Each page had two yellow diamonds, one over a letter in the second column, one over a number in the third. Finally, each page had a green cross through a number in the left-hand column.

"A through H," Max said mostly to himself, focusing on the second two columns. "One to eight."

"What's that?" Kirby asked walking over.

"It's a codebook. I think it's significant for The Sixteen. I found it on one of our targets. She won't tell me how it works."

"May I see it?"

"Of course," Max said passing over the book. "See it has these letters A to H and the numbers one through eight on the right-hand side. Each page has two yellow diamonds one in each column."

"It could be a chess board."

"Sorry?"

"Chess boards use algebraic notation. Each letter and number correspond to a position on the board. A through H on the bottom axis of the board, one through eight going up the board."

"They use chess ranks to define their hierarchy, so it certainly could be that, but what are the moves. D, five. It doesn't tell me what the move means."

"Maybe that's what these other markings are for?"

"Wait a minute," Max said as he scanned the pages for a minute. "The red circles are only on the numbers one though thirty-one and the blue squares only on numbers one through twelve."

"Dates?"

"Maybe. Red for the day, blue for the month."

"There must be hundreds of pages in there," Kirby said watching Max turning the pages. "What do you think the dates mean?"

Max did not answer, he was flicking between pages, then he saw something he had not seen earlier. There was a small number on each page. Originally, he thought they were page numbers, they were in fine print, but now he realised they were years. Each phase of the book was another year, twenty-four years in the book. Max felt a chill run down his spin. He flicked to the phase he was looking for and started madly turning the pages, examining the red and blue markings. Then he found it, the date Lachlan was killed. His blood ran cold. He stared at the page in shock and wondered if it could be coincidence. He turned to a more recent phase and found a second date he was looking for, the day the Commonwealth Building in Sydney was attacked. Then another, the date the Australian Parliament was attacked.

"They are dates of attacks," Max stated looking up to Kirby. "This is The Sixteen's playbook."

Max ran to the communications room and told Morgan he urgently needed to use the phone, but before he could make the call an alarm sounded in the apartment. Something had triggered the proximity sensors.

Chapter Twenty-Seven

Max hit the keyboard in front of Morgan and the computer monitors all changed from views of the UK's cabinet ministers to CCTV footage of their building. The four screens on the left were external cameras, while the four on the right showed footage from inside the building. Max watched as armed men dressed in black combat gear surrounded their building and started for the doors.

"Flash!" Max yelled through the door. "Get in here!"

"What's going on, Max?" Morgan asked in a panic. "Is that this building?"

"Yes, sir, I'm afraid it is."

"What are we going to do?"

"The alarms would have signalled our High Commission security teams, they will send back up. We are going to need to hold these guys off as long as we can, until they get here."

"There is an army out there. How will we hold them off?"

"As best we can, until backup arrives."

"You are not filling me with confidence Agent Shaw. How do we even know you teams will turn up in time?"

"They will get here as fast as they can," Max said opening the weapons cabinets as Flash walked in. "Gear up, Flash, they're here."

"Got it," Flash said reaching for an MP5 and spare magazines. "How did they find us?"

"I don't know. Right now, we need to just hold them off."

Max loaded his MP5 and placed two spare magazines in his jacket pockets. He put his pistol and spare magazines in his underarm holster, and he clipped his hunting knife to his belt. Flash did the same, then they both loaded smoke and flashbang grenades in their belts and the two agents headed for the door.

"Do not open this door under any circumstances," Max commanded, looking each of the Prime Ministers and Alistair in the eyes. "We have the access keys, so we do not need to knock."

"What do we do?" Kirby asked nervously.

"Pray backup gets here in time," Max uttered opening the door and heading out into the hallway.

Flash closed the door behind them and they heard the metal locks slid back into place. Max raised his MP5 and headed down the hallway. The safehouse was on the fourth floor, but AIS had purchased the whole building so the remaining units were empty. Max led the way, scanning the hallway with his MP5, while Flash scanned behind. They moved in lock step with each other, years of practice and countless operations together meant they knew each other's every move. They moved down the corridor, then down the stairs, level by leave scanning and sweeping until they reached the stairs which led down to the first floor. Flash levelled his gun at the front door, while Max ducked into a nearby apartment. He moved quickly through the unit to a bedroom at the rear. Inside the built-in cupboard was a small safe. He waved his right hand, wielding his AIS ring, in front of the sensor then pressed his thumb to the scanner. The safe opened and Max pulled out a leather gym bag which he flung over his shoulder and ran back to Flash.

As Max arrived at the stairs, the front door exploded and seconds later three men stormed through. Flash took them down with two shots each. The third man fell back out into the street, stopping his remaining comrades from entering. Max took the brief reprieve to open the gym bag and remove two small devices. He clipped the first to the step just in front of Flash, then tapped him on the shoulder.

Bullets rang out in the small foyer as four men stormed the door, running through shooting wildly unsure of the agents' locations. Max and Flash returned fire as they ran back up the stairs.

On the second floor, Max planted the second device. Without stopping, Flash ran past Max, up to the third floor. Max took three stairs at a time up following Flash. When he was close to the top, an explosion rang out from beneath him as the first of his proximity mines went off on the stairs below. Max knew the explosion would have killed the man who stepped near it and possibly a few others, if they were close enough, but he also knew it would slow the intruders.

He reached the top of the steps to find Flash waiting. As he ran past, Flash hit a panel in the plaster of the wall and it broke free. He flicked the plasterboard onto the floor exposing a small electronic keypad. He waved his ring in front of the sensor and pressed his thumb to the biometric reader. Halfway down the stairs a series of metal barricades rose out of the steps blocking the path. One after the other, they locked into place creating a solid metal wall. Max and Flash ran up the stairs to the fourth floor and re-entered the apartment.

"What is happening?" Kirby demanded. "Have they gone?"

"No, we have put up a barricade and planted some explosives," Max explained reloading his weapon. "That should slow them down."

"Slow them, not stop them?"

"It will not stop them, sir, but it will hold them off for a while."

"How long?"

"Thirty-minutes, maybe."

"Will backup arrive in time?"

"I don't know," Max conceded sitting his MP5 on the table.

Max paced by the lounges in front of Alistair who was fidgeting nervously. Kirby and Morgan were standing at the dining table chatting quietly. Flash came out of the communications room.

"The AIS team is on route," Flash clarified sitting at the table and reloading his MP5. "It will be tight."

No one said anything.

"Max, did you hear me?" Flash asked.

"How did they find us?" Max asked, staring at the wall, deep in thought.

"Maybe they knew the location before we even got here?"

"It's unlikely, only a few people in the world know where this safehouse is."

"Maybe they somehow got into our comms?"

"The comms room is too secure and the messages are encrypted end to end. Unless."

"Unless what, Max?"

"I need to see everyone's phones."

"You told us to turn them off before we got here, Max."

"Did you all turn off your phones?" Max asked turning to Kirby and Morgan.

Kirby and Morgan both nodded and sat their mobile phones on the table. Max pressed the buttons looking for a response, but they sat dead on the table. Flash held his up too and Max nodded, before turning back to face Alistair.

"What about you?" Max insisted.

"I don't have my work phone," Alistair said nervously shuffling in his seat. "It's still sitting in the conference room back at the convention centre."

"What about your personal phone?"

"I, I don't have one."

"Bullshit," Max declared dragging Alistair up off the couch by the shirt. "You said work phone. Why clarify if you don't have another type? You would have just said my phone, not my work phone."

"I don't know why I said it, you, you just make me nervous," Alistair said clutching at Max's arm trying to free himself.

"You should be nervous. Do you know what I have been through to arrive here? I have been tortured, I have been shot at, I have lost friends and I lost the only person I have ever loved. These people are responsible for all of these things and now they are here to fucking kill us before I get the chance to rebalance the equation. So, I am only going to ask this one more fucking time, where is your personal phone?"

"I don't have one," Alistair said looking away and cowering trying to pull himself free.

Max started patting down Alistair's jacket and he began to squirm trying to break Max's grip.

"Let me go, please!" Alistair pleaded. "I don't have a personal phone."

"Max, let him go," Flash said walking over and placing a hand on his best friend's back. "You have been through a lot, mate, I know that better than anyone, but look at your actions today. You are letting them get to you."

"Yeah, listen to your friend," Alistair implored. "Attacking me isn't going to bring your boyfriend back."

Max punched Alistair hard in the face. He fell backwards, tripping on the mat and falling to the floor. Max turned and locked eyes with Flash. Flash recognised the pain in his friend's eyes, but he had never seen such anger.

"You need to calm down, Max," Flash said trying to soothe his friend's anger. "We need to get these three to safety. We have a mission to complete and this is not helping."

"That is what I am trying to do," Max said pointing to the two Prime Ministers before turning to Alistair. "Save them and complete the mission, but he is fucking hiding something."

Max tried to push past Flash to get to Alistair, but Flash moved in and blocked his path putting his hand on Max's chest to stop him.

"What do you think you are doing?" Max questioned with frustration and anger in his voice. "Get your hand off me and get out of my way."

"You're losing the plot, Max," Flash said sadly. "I can't take it anymore. I'm sorry, but I'm relieving you of your command and when this is all over, I will be recommending you be removed from active duty until you get your shit together."

"You can't be serious."

"I am, Max. You are my friend, my best friend, and I can't stand to see you like this. You have been slipping. Every day since Lachlan died you have been marching towards the cliff edge. What happened with Shadow and Sam just pushed you further, and I don't want you hurt anyone, especially yourself. You need help, Max."

Max stepped back, then threw a punch into Flash's stomach. He buckled over and Max pushed him to the side.

"Let me do my job," Max instructed walking past Flash. "You can recommend whatever the fuck you like when this is all done, but until then stay out of my way."

Flash tackled Max into the couch and the two agents wrestled to the ground. As they hit the carpet and rolled throwing punches at each other, Kirby ran over as fast as he could with his limp.

"Max!" Kirby yelled at the agents. "Flash! Stop, for one fucking minute, just stop! You both need to see this."

Max and Flash stopped wrestling and both looked up from the carpet to see Kirby pointing at something on the carpet. They followed the line of his arm and finger to the object on the carpet. Alistair's personal mobile phone sat on the carpet beside its unconscious owner. It had fallen out of his pants pocket when he hit the ground. The screen flashed with a new message, one of many sitting on the home screen. Max looked at Flash with indignation and without speaking stood and walked over to pick up the phone. Flash did not say a word, he just got to his feet and stood watching Max.

"Tie him to one of the dining room chairs, Flash," Max ordered retaking command. "Then wake him up."

Flash disappeared into the other room while Max read the various messages sitting on the little screen. Flash returned and dragged Alistair up onto the dining room chair, then flexicuffed him to the arms and legs. Max walked over and showed the two Prime Minister's the messages on the screen. Flash snapped an ammonia stick under Alistair's nose causing him to throw his head back to try to escape the smell. Max tossed Flash the phone as he walked over to Alistair, so he could read the messages.

"We need to have a conversation," Max said without emotion, dragging Alistair's chair into the centre of the room.

"What the fuck?" Alistair asked before his eyes widened as he realised he was tied to the chair. "Wait, please!"

Max backhanded him hard across the face. Alistair cowered, pulling his face down close to his shoulder, trying to hide from a second blow.

"What is your role in all of this?" Max inquired.

"I don't know what you are talking about," Alistair said insolently, but without looking Max in the eyes.

"Oh, let's skip the bullshit, I found your personal phone and I read several messages on the home screen. So, tell me now, save yourself some pain, what is your role in all this?"

"I want a lawyer."

"The Prime Minister is just over there, both of them are actually, why don't you ask them if you can have a lawyer?"

"No," Kirby stated. "Tell him what he needs to know, Alistair."

"What about you Mr Morgan?" Max asked turning to Morgan. "think he should get a lawyer or talk to me?"

"I, I don't think I should be in here for this," Morgan quivered, looking to Kirby.

"This is the reality of our work Prime Minister. We need information and he has it, and we haven't got long until his friends kick down that door and put a bullet in your head."

"Do what you need to do," Morgan finally stated before walking out of the room.

"Oh dear, Alistair," Max said mockingly turning back to his captive. "Guess that means no lawyer. So, tell me what I need to know."

"No," Alistair defied looking away.

Max walked out of the lounge room into the bathroom. He put the plug in the bath and turned the taps on full, then walked back into the lounge room. He grabbed the back of Alistair's chair and dragged it towards the bathroom. Alistair began thrashing about, but he could not break free of his restraints. Flash followed Max into the bathroom and the two agents lifted Alistair, still tied to the chair, into the bathtub.

"Last chance," Max said getting in Alistair's face. "Tell me how you are involved?"

"No, I can't," Alistair said starting to cry. "Please."

"Fine," Max said tipping the chair forward and dropping Alistair face first into the shallow water, the chair pinning his neck to the bottom of the tub. "You have less than a minute before the water is over your nose and mouth, then we will see how long you can hold your breath. If you change your mind, just shout or maybe blow some big bubbles or something."

Max and Flash walked into the hallway, as Alistair started to spit and blow water from his mouth and nose.

"I'm sorry, Max," Flash conceded. "About before."

"Yeah, I know," Max said. "Me too."

"Are we good?"

"I need you to trust me, Jacob. You're my best friend, I would never put you or the team at risk, and I always act with the mission in mind. I would never jeopardise any of that for personal reasons, including retribution for Lachlan."

"I know, mate, but it's not us I'm worried about. It's you. I want you to get some help. Can you promise me you will see someone when this is all over?"

"Let's just get this done," Max dismissed after a few seconds of silence, before walking back into the bathroom leaving Flash to stare at the wall.

Alistair was spitting water from his mouth and trying to drag in air through narrowing passageways. Water was splashing all over him and almost completely covering his nose and mouth. A few seconds later his nose and mouth went completely under and he started to buck and slide, but the chair had him pinned and the flexicuffs on his arms and legs meant he could not move. The flexicuffs had cut into his wrists and blood was starting to drip into the water turning it a light pink. Max starred at Alistair, locking eyes with him and refusing to blink. Panic was starting to creep into Alistair's eyes.

"Ready to talk yet?" Max said calmly.

Alistair was briefly defiant, but then nodded reluctantly.

"Sorry, I didn't get that?" Max feigned.

Alistair began to thrust about, panic gripping him as he fought the body's natural reflex to breathe. It would only be seconds before he involuntarily took in a lungful of cold bloody water. His eyes screamed and begged Max to save him. Max put his hand on the back of the chair and pushed down.

"Maybe I should just leave you here to die, one less arsehole in the world to deal with," Max said getting down closer to Alistair's ear as he began to convulse and gargle. "I will put you back in if you don't answer my questions."

Max pulled the chair up and dragged it back up into the sitting position. Alistair coughed and spluttered, he was crying uncontrollably and shaking in fear.

"How do you fit into all of this?" Max asked.

"I am a candidate to replace Shadow as a knight at The Sixteen's table," Alistair coughed.

"What do you know about The Sixteen?"

"They exist to keep order and promote peace."

"Through terrorism and war, and attacks like the one at the conference centre?"

"I don't always agree with their methods, but the cause is right."

"What does their membership look like?

"There is the king and queen, a bishop and a rook, plus twelve knights."

"How do they recruit people to these roles?

"There are two places for knights from each of the six regions around the world, Africa, Asia, America and the Caribbean, Europe, the United Kingdom and the Pacific. When a vacancy opens, they choose candidates who are then elected to take the chair by the group."

"Who is the king?"

"I don't know."

"Who is the queen?"

"I don't know that either."

"Who do you know?"

"I know the Bishop, Robert Hardy. His name is Robert Hardy."

"Do you know anyone else who is at the table, as you put it?"

"Yes, only one other person."

"Who?"

"Janelle."

"Janelle who?"

"Janelle Rhodes."

"How does she fit in?"

"She is one of the knights. She is the longest serving member, other than Robert, and since you took Robert and Gloria out of action, she has been calling the shots with the king."

"Where can I find her?"

"You haven't heard of her? She works for the Sky News. She's a major news anchor."

"I don't get to watch much tv. How did you get involved?"

"They approached me and asked if I believed in the monarchy and serving King and country, and if I believed in a world free from war. They asked if I would act to promote peace and liberty."

"What else aren't you telling me?"

"Nothing, I swear."

Max grabbed the chair and started to unbalance it.

"Wait, no, please!" Alistair begged trying to fight against Max. "Okay, okay. My dad. My dad was a member of The Sixteen. Harold Turner, he was a recruiter."

"A knight?" Max asked.

"No, a pawn."

"He must be so proud you are moving up the ranks."

"He's dead."

"How did he die?"

"Patrick Scott killed him."

"Hulk killed him?"

"Yes. Hulk found out he was stealing secrets from defence intelligence, so he shot him."

"Sounds like Hulk. So, why would you risk the same happening to you?"

"I wanted to destroy AIS and Hulk. If there is peace, there is no need for any of you. I thought it would break Hulk, to destroy his life's work and everything he has fought for. The man cares for nothing else."

"You mentioned peace, who would protect your peace once it is established?"

"The new laws the Commonwealth nations will roll out after all this will be just the beginning of a push for greater security and policing. People will beg for safety and security. And, once the attacks stop and peace is achieved, and we establish a world led by a leader of strength and courage, instead of the insipid leaders we have now, we won't need AIS. People will only know compliance and order."

"Control the population, it sounds like you and your friends want to takeaway liberty and choice."

"Liberty and choice must be minimised to ensure compliance. Only through strict laws and adherence to those laws can we have peace."

"It sounds like we would lose more in the long run."

"Think what you will, we will prevail."

"No, you are the real terrorists, you will fail."

"You mentioned a leader. A world leader, rather than multiple world leaders. Is that your play, create a world-wide dictatorship?"

"In the long term, yes. But in the interim will settle for power, closer to home."

"We've got a problem," Flash interrupted walking into the bathroom and handing Max Alistair's phone. "They are sending back up in too."

Max read the message. *Find a place to hide near the back of the apartment, we are coming in from the roof.*

"The roof?" Max frowned. "The only way they could do that is by helicopter."

The two agents ran to the communications room. Flash typed a command into the computer and one of the monitors changed to a radar screen. A small dot was moving fast in a direct line for the safehouse.

"Fuck!" Max said. "Call Hulk, we need backup ASAP."

Chapter Twenty-Eight

The helicopter came in low over the roof and hovered in place. Two ropes dropped from the side doors, followed by six heavily armed men. When the men were safely on the rooftop, the ropes dropped from the helicopter and it turned and flew off in the direction from which it came. The six men fanned out with their weapons pressed against their shoulders and started to make their way across the roof to the door. The lead intruder was fifteen metres from the door, when Max jumped up from behind a nearby air-conditioning unit and put a bullet in his head. Flash was on the far side and took down another unsuspecting attacker from cover behind a large brick chimney.

The remaining attackers scattered for cover, while firing at Max and Flash's positions. Bullets slammed into the air-conditioning unit, pounding the metal surface, forcing Max back behind it. Two of the attackers had set their sights on Max. One unloaded volley after volley of bullets into the unit pinning Max in place, while the other circled to find a shot. Max scanned to his left waiting for the circling intruder he guessed was coming. Three air-conditioning units to his left, the attacker's head peered around to find Max, but instead it found a bullet from Max's gun. The attacker dropped to the ground and rolled to the side, Max fired another bullet into the back of the attacker's head and he stopped rolling and laid still.

The bullets were still hitting the opposite side of the unit, but Max could hear them hitting different spots with every burst. The attacker was moving. Max moved slowly in the opposite direction. When the bullets stopped, he ducked around to the right of the unit and stuck his head around to check the side which had originally been getting hit by bullets, just as his attacker ran past, oblivious to Max's movements.

Max quickly dashed around the unit and followed the attacker. The attacker raised his gun and fired into the air-conditioning unit and the ground where Max had been hiding in cover when the helicopter landed. He was surprised when he found Max was not there. Before he got the chance to look around, Max kicked him hard in the back sending him flying off the roof and plunging him eight storeys to his death. Without stopping to look over the edge, Max spun on his heal and unloaded six shots taking down the remaining two attackers who were circling around to take out Flash. Their bodies hit the rooftop and did not budge. They were dead.

"Let's move, Flash!" Max yelled lowering his weapon. "All clear!"

"Thanks, Max," Flash said running over to join him. "You can be sure they were coming in from below at the same time. We need to get out of here."

"Couldn't agree more," Max agreed running for the door and the stairs back down to the safehouse.

"Wait," Flash shouted stopping in his tracks. "What's that?"

Max turned back to face the sound and he saw it, another helicopter coming in fast and low.

"Let's hustle," Max said holding the door open for Flash.

Flash ran as the helicopter turned ninety degrees and folded a mounted machine gun out through the door. A line of bullets tracked across the rooftop towards Flash. Max opened fire at the helicopter, but his bullets bounced harmlessly off the metal frame, until he found his mark. He fired a volley through the open door of the helicopter and the bullets bounced around the cabin. The helicopter's fire slowed, but did not stop.

Flash run past Max and down the first flight of steps. Max fired again, this time hitting the gunman. He saw movement of troops in the back of the helicopter and knew they were preparing to land and take a chance at a second assault. He turned and ran, following Flash down to the apartment.

Flash held the door open for Max and he ran through and into the bathroom. He cut the cuffs on Alistair's arms and legs, before flexicuffing his hands again and dragging him out of the bath.

"One wrong fucking move!" Max barked. "And, I will kill you."

Alistair just nodded and walked into the lounge room with Max's gun pointed at his back.

"We need to move," Max explained.

"Are you sure that's wise?" Kirby questioned. "I mean, shouldn't we wait for backup?"

"They are still a few minutes away," Flash noted returning from the communications room. "But, our attackers are nearly through the barricade. They've got the garage locked up and they are on the roof. We need to go."

"What's the plan, Max?" Kirby asked unsure of what to do.

"We are going out the front door," Max said. "No other option."

"Agreed," Flash said. "I'll get the bag. Let's go."

Flash led the small group down the stairs and asked them to hold their position. Max took up the rear, ready to hold off the men from the second helicopter. Flash ran down and planted another mine on the barricade before sprinting back up the stairs. He ducked around the corner for cover then fired two shots into the mine. It exploded with tremendous force, splintering the barricade throwing lethal shards of metal in every direction, but by far the bulk of it flew back down the stairs, in the opposite direction, clearing their path.

Flash moved onto the stairs as the smoke cleared, two men lay dead on the other side of the space where the barricade had been. A third man was crawling away clutching his chest and trailing blood. Flash shot him twice in the back then continued down the stairs, scanning and sweeping with his MP5. He fired three shots into a man on the second floor, killing him.

Max fired a volley of bullets into the wall behind them, forcing the attackers at their rear back behind the wall for cover, then he tossed a smoke grenade onto the landing between the stairs. It began spewing smoke before it had even landed, filling the hallway and slowing the rear attackers. Max fired some warning shots through the smoke to make them second guess their chase.

Flash took down another two men as he made it to the ground floor, as Max dropped another two smoke grenades then placed the final proximity mine on the stairs. Max ran down past the Prime Ministers and Alistair to Flash's position. Flash fired at anyone coming near the door, then Max threw two flashbang grenades out into the street. The white flashes were visible in the open doorway, giving Max and Flash the signal to move. They got to the door and both ducked their heads out, Flash on the left, Max on the right. They both opened fire, taking down several troops who were holding their eyes and ears. Max fired in both directions as Flash reloaded, then Flash did the same for Max, as more attackers approached.

"Get ready," Max ordered. "We need to move, location Echo."

"I'll get the Prime Ministers," Flash said.

"Roger, I'll clear a path. Can I have a couple of your smoke grenades."

Flash handed Max three smoke grenades and threw the fourth down the path to the left, before returning to the foyer to collect the Prime Ministers and Alistair. Max threw all three grenades in the same direction as Flash had, up to the left. As smoke began to fill the street and block the road. It was a still night, so the smoke hung in the air.

Max headed into the street to the right. He drew his pistol with his left hand and welded the MP5 with his right. A small group of men were running down the right-hand footpath and two were on the far side of the street. He squeezed the triggers. Three of the men on the right were hit and fell while the third jumped behind a parked car. One of the men on the far side was hit in the neck and fell to the ground clutching his wound as blood poured through his fingers. Max lined up the second guy who had stopped to look down at his friend and he fired with both guns, taking him down. The remaining guy shot in Max's direction from behind the car, forcing Max to dive into an open door recess.

Max waited patiently until he heard the gun run dry then he ran towards the car. When he was only a few metres from the back and preparing to jump onto the roof, four more men came running around the corner and started shooting at him. He dropped to the ground, dropping his MP5 and rolling hard into the gutter. He flattened himself down as low as he could, but he was still exposed.

"Prince, we are taking fire!" Flash yelled over the comms unit. *"I'm going to have to take them around the block."*

"I'm pinned down, Flash," Max replied. "At least five, could be more. Move if you can, exfil without me, if you can."

"Roger, Prince. Good luck."

"You too," Max said rolling onto his stomach as bullets hit the concrete all around him.

Max fired three shots towards his attackers. He could not be sure, but he thought he hit one. He checked his belt and found the last flashbang. He pulled the pin and rolled it as hard as he could down the road and under the car the attacker had been using for cover. It went off as it rolled out from under the boot next to the attackers. They stumbled about, holding their eyes and ears.

Max rolled hard over and over into the middle of the street and shot two of the men. Bullets ripped into the ground next to him, one crazing his leg and causing him to grit his teeth and flinch in pain. He rolled left again into the opposite gutter as bullets chipped into the stones beside him. When he hit the concrete of the gutter, he aimed and fired two shots which hit the attacker in the chest. He fell to the ground as Max's gun clicked empty.

The attacker got to his knees, he was not dead. He reached for his gun and started to aim for Max. Max fumbled for his pockets trying to get his spare magazine. His hand got stuck in his jacket pocket. Max looked at the attacker just as the barrel drew level with his eyes, then a shot rang out and Max's heart stopped.

The attacker's head exploded. Max looked around for the source of the shot, but before he could find it, more gunfire rang out from the direction of his attackers. He sprung up on all fours and flipped left up onto the footpath, scrambling to his knees and crab walked as fast as he could move in behind a parked vehicle. Another shot rang out from high up behind Max.

"You're clear, Prince," Jonnie said over the comms unit. *"He's down."*

"Bravo, is that you?" Max asked.

"Yes, Prince. I'm here. Alpha is on route to assist Flash."

"Me too, give me some cover."

"You got it, boss. Moving now."

"Good to have you back, kid," Max said getting to his feet and running towards Flash's location.

"You guys better hurry, we are pinned down," Flash explained. *"And, I am almost out of ammo."*

Max ran harder than he had ever run. Jonnie took down three men in his path. Max ran past as their bodies hit the ground. He loaded his spare magazine into the pistol as he ran. Jonnie dropped a man on the right, as Max took out two in front of him. Ahead he heard gunfire. He cleared the smoke and saw Flash one block ahead behind a car pinned down. The Prime Ministers and Alistair were with him huddled behind the car. Bullets were pinging off the vehicle and the concrete.

"It's Alpha," Kate said. *"I'm coming in from the far side. Hold on, Flash!"*

"I've only got one clip left," Flash said clicking it into his weapon.

Max saw two groups of gunmen firing on Flash and moving in. Max shot one gunman in the back, then another, as Jonnie took down three men. Some of the group of attackers turned back to fire at Max. He and Jonnie fired on them, but he had to duck for cover behind a van.

"I can't get through there's too many of them on this side," Kate explained. *"I'm going to have to shoot my way through these motherfuckers."*

Max heard the gunfire over the radio as Kate opened fire on her side.

"It's too late, guys," Flash said resolutely as the attackers started moving in towards the car. *"I need to slow them down. Get ready, on my mark."*

"No, Flash, hold position!" Max ordered. "We're coming! We're nearly there."

"You can't make it through in time. Finish the mission and remember what I said about after this is all over, Prince. You will always be my best man. Tell Jane I love her."

"Flash, no!" Max cried running out from behind cover firing wildly at the attackers.

Jonnie fired too, but there were so many of them. A bullet hit Max in the left arm, but he kept running and shot the man who had shot him straight between the eyes. Flash stepped out from behind the car and ran at the attackers firing his pistol, taking down two men on Kate's side of the car. When it clicked empty, he threw his knife at the closest attacker and pierced it through his neck killing him instantly. Then Max watched in horror as all the attackers turned their guns away from the car where Kirby and Morgan were in cover, to Flash and opened fire.

"No! Flash!" Max yelled still running as his best friend was cut down in a violent hail of bullets.

Max leapt off his left foot, drew his knife with his right hand and slammed it into the top of the skull of an attacker. As he landed, he ripped it out, spun and stabbed it down with all his might into the temple of a second attacker. The third man in the line was taken down by Jonnie, as Max pulled the dripping hunting knife free and threw it end over end into the remaining attacker on their side of the car. He snatched up the knife and one of the attacker's rifles, and ran for Flash whose body was lying still in the middle of the road. He dropped to his knees beside his fallen friend and opened fire, screaming at the line of attackers as he took them down. One after the other they fell, as Jonnie and Max took them out. The rifle clicked dry and Jonnie's shots stopped as the sole surviving attacker sighted Max over his rifle.

The attacker pulled the trigger, but the gun clicked empty. He looked at the weapon, then tossed it to the ground and started running for Max with flick knife. Max stood ready for the fight, but a shot rang out from behind the attacker and Max watched as his face exploded. He fell to the ground only metres from Max in a bloodied mess. Through the smoke, Max saw Kate lower her rifle and start jogging in his direction.

There was a commotion behind him. Max turned to see Alistair with his flexicuffed wrists pulling back hard on Kirby's throat and he had a pistol pointed at Kirby's head. He was dragging the Australian Prime Minister backwards down the street, away from Max, and he had found one of the attacker's weapons.

"What's the plan, Alistair?" Max asked looking Alistair in the eyes. "How far do you think you can get?"

"Just let me go!" Alistair yelled pulling Kirby back and using him as a shield. "I can't go to prison. Do you know what they would do to someone like me in there?"

"Let him go, Alistair. It's over. Look around you. You have nowhere to run."

"I want immunity and a pardon, and I want the RAAF VIP jet to take me to a non-extradition country."

"That's not going to happen, Alistair. Just put down the gun."

"Fuck you, Max. I'm not going to gaol. I just wanted peace."

"Look at this, Alistair. Look at the bodies piled in the street. Does this look like peace to you?"

Alistair looked around and loosened his grip slightly. Kirby took the chance, reached up and grabbed the gun pulling it forward. Alistair fired two shots, which Max dived clear off, before Kirby managed to free the gun. Alistair let go of Kirby and started to run back down the street away from Max. Kirby threw Max the pistol and as he caught it, he fired two shots. Alistair's leg buckled as the first bullet hit him behind the knees, then Alistair's body was blown to pieces as the second bullet, which had been intended to hit his hip to immobilise him and stop him from getting away, hit the spare grenade Flash had handed him in the vehicle during their getaway earlier in the evening. The blast smashed windows and rocked cars setting off more car alarms. Max looked at the pistol, then dropped it and walked back to where Flash was lying.

"You got him, mate," Max said dropping to the ground beside Flash. "Your grenade got him."

Max looked at his friend and felt the heartache of loss sweep over him. He was gone. Max broke down and cried in the middle of the cold London street cradling Jacob 'Flash' Gordon in his arms as he said goodbye.

Chapter Twenty-Nine

"I'm sorry, Max," Kate said softly walking over and placing her hand on Max's shoulder. "But, we have to go. We need to get the PMs out of here."

Max just continued to stare at Flash and hold him closely. They had been through so much together. Max felt overwhelming guilt that he had not been there for his friend, that he could not reach him in time to save him and that for the last two days they had fought for the first and only time in their whole friendship. Max felt defeated and utterly devastated. Flash had been there for him when Lachlan died and without his support, Max doubted he would have made it through.

"I'm sorry, boss," Jonnie puffed running down the street towards Max and Kate. *"But, we've got incoming on our position."*

"How far out?" Kate asked.

"One block," Jonnie said. *"Get to the car."*

"Ack. Max, we need to go."

"I'm not leaving him here," Max said.

"We have a team from AIS coming with the police, they will pick him up," Kate said grabbing Max by the back of the shirt. "Come on, kid. He would want you to finish the mission."

Max remembered Flash's last words about finishing the mission. He embraced his fallen colleague and friend one last time, then softly lowered him to the ground and stood up.

"Let's go," Max choked out.

"I'm sorry for your loss, Max," Kirby said.

"Me too, young man," Morgan said.

"Thank you, both," Max said holding back the tears and finding his resolve. "There will be time to grieve later, for now though, we need to get you to safety."

Max heard the loud crack of a sniper rifle and turned to see Jonnie running at full speed in their direction and holstering his rifle on his back after taking a warning shot in the opposite direction. Max grabbed one of the fallen attacker's rifles and a spare magazine.

"Get them to the car," Max ordered shouldering his rifle and aiming high past Jonnie. "We are right behind you."

Max fired several rounds high and wide in an arc around Jonnie to hold off the approaching attackers.

"Keep running, Alpha's getting the PMs to the car!" Max shouted as Jonnie reached him. "Glad you are okay, kid."

"Good to see you too, boss," Jonnie said turning and facing back down the street and shouldering his rifle. "Let's give them some time to get to the car."

Max smiled and the two agents started firing at the attackers peering out around the corners in the distance.

"Cover our tracks," Max directed.

"You got it," Jonnie said pulling the pins on several smoke grenades and throwing them into the street in front of them.

The attackers knew Max and his team were on the move, so they came out of cover and started to run towards them. Max and Jonnie opened fire through the thickening smoke, taking down a couple of attackers each. When the smoke was thick in the street, they both turned and ran towards Kate and the waiting vehicle.

Two blocks down they found Kate and the Prime Ministers in the AIS Landcruiser. The two agents climbed in and Kate drove off towards the Australian High Commission.

"We can't go to the embassy," Max said. "They found the safehouse and they attacked the convention centre. We need somewhere off the grid."

"Any thoughts?" Kate asked.

"Yeah, we need to check into a hotel for the night. The closer the better, the roads are in lock down, so we need to get in quickly, so we aren't spotted."

Kate drove for a few blocks to make sure they were not followed, then turned into the carpark under the hotel Max had suggested. She drove down into the basement and found a park.

"Jonnie, see if you can access the hotel's security system," Max commanded. "Kate, pack some bags."

"Ack," Jonnie said reaching for his tablet computer.

"You got it, boss," Kate agreed climbing out and walking to the back of the vehicle to load up weapons from the car's cache.

"Accessing the network," Jonnie relayed. "Okay, I've got cameras and elevators, and the full electrical grid, and every computer hooked up to the hotel's system. What would you like me to do?"

"You need to get us a room," Max said. "Then as soon as Kate is ready, I want you to give us a rolling camera outage to the lifts then to the room. I picked the hotel because of the keypad entrance to the room, so we don't need to go to reception."

"Roger that. Logging into their booking system now, suite twelve, thirty-two booked. Accessing the cameras and lift system now, calling elevator B to our floor. Thirty seconds out."

"Ready, Kate?"

"Yep, boss," Kate said shouldering the bags. "Got a few little toys here to play with in case we need 'em."

"Good. Drop the cameras, Jonnie. Prime Ministers follow me, please."

Jonnie hit enter on his tablet as Max and his team climbed out of the Landcruiser with the Prime Ministers. Max led them towards the elevators. He found elevator B as the doors opened and he escorted his team and the Prime Ministers inside. Jonnie had blanked out the cameras in the lift and as soon as they were inside, he pressed a command and the elevator rose to the twelfth floor without stopping.

"I have changed the code to five, four, three, two, one," Jonnie explained as the door to the lift opened.

Max walked out first checking the hallway. It was clear. He walked across the hall, found their suite and punched in the code. A small green light flashed and an electronic mechanism clicked. He pushed open the door then signalled for his team to follow. Once they were all through and in the room, Max again checked the hallway, before clicking the door closed.

The suite was a large opulent space with marble and gold fixtures. It felt regal and old-worldly. It had a large kitchen and bar, and a sunken lounge area. A separate dining room and four bedrooms and three bathrooms.

"Back from the fucking dead with expensive taste, kid," Kate said dropping the two duffle bags on the dining room table and looking around the room.

"It was one of the last rooms they had left," Jonnie noted sitting the tablet on the table.

Max had walked over and was standing near the bar, looking down at the floor. His hands were gripping the back of a large wooden bar stool so tight his hands were turning white and shaking.

"Fuck!" Max roared slamming the chair into the tiles over and over until it broke to pieces then he tossed a hunk of wood, that used to be the chair back, into the row of expensive glasses above the bar shattering them.

Max stood breathing deeply trying to calm down. He was shaking from anger and grief. The four others in the room stood perfectly still watching him, unsure how to respond. Max ripped an expensive looking artwork off the wall and smashed it across the bar, sending glass and broken frame flying into the air around him. He stood staring out the window next to the bar and caught a glimpse of his own reflection. He hardly recognised the person staring back. His long hair had unravelled from his makeshift bun and his beard looked scruffy. His eyes were red from crying and the bag underneath were partly black from his torture and partly from exhaustion, and his suit was wet with sweat and blood. *Who is that man?* Max asked himself. *What would Lachlan think of him now?* He took a moment to calm himself, before he turned to look at the terrified Prime Ministers and his concerned teammates.

"I'm sorry," Max conceded getting control of his emotions.

He walked over to the group leaving the partly destroyed bar behind him.

"It's good to have you back, Jonnie," Max said shaking his young team member's hand and embracing him. "You saved my arse once again."

"Thanks, boss," Jonnie said softly. "I'm sorry about Flash."

"Thanks, kid. Rooting out every last one of these motherfuckers will be a lasting legacy to him. What do you say, want to help me find them?"

"You know I do."

"What about you?" Max asked turning to Kate. "Want to find these arseholes and put them down?"

"Fucking oath, boss," Kate said cracking her knuckles. "Just point me at them."

"Good, thank you both," Max said looking at each person in the room. "Why don't you all take some time to rest, then we will regroup to figure out a way forward?"

The two Prime Ministers nodded, both in some shock from what they had seen and experienced during the day.

"No phones!" Max yelled after them as both world leaders nodded again and headed for a bedroom each.

"I will get the weapons set up first, in case we need to shoot any more arseholes," Kate said heading into the dining room.

"I'm not tired, Max," Jonnie said eager to please as always. "What can I do to help?"

"I need you to find out everything you can on Janelle Rhodes. She's got a seat at the table."

"The table?"

"Yes, it is the place The Sixteen, as they call themselves, give to their senior members. A place at the table. They have a king who calls the shots, a queen as their second-in-command. A bishop who seems to run things like a CEO. The rook who manages their finances and twelve knights, two from each region, Asia, Africa, the Pacific, the UK, Europe and the Americas. Janelle is one of the knights, but apparently is the longest serving. Since we have Russo and Robert, their rook and bishop in custody, it's likely Janelle is taking on the bishop's role and pulling the strings."

"What's their endgame?"

"Allegedly, they stand for peace."

"Through terrorism."

"I know, right? Fucking lunatics."

"Fucking lunatics is right," Kate said walking back into the room. "I had been looking into it back at the embassy, before we got the call out to come help you. The Sixteen was apparently a group of advisers to the King at certain points in history. It was made up of a bunch of so-called important people. You know noblemen, aristocrats, lords, church leaders, royalty and military leaders. I found scattered references that said they operated as advisers helping run the government on the King's behalf.

"So, do we think this mob are linked to the ancient The Sixteen?" Max asked.

"It's unlikely. Throughout history there are examples of councils or courts, advising the monarch, but they were replaced by modern day formal institutions like parliaments and executive councils."

"So, what do you think?"

"Hermes and I think these guys started calling themselves The Sixteen and started using their symbols and terms to give themselves some structure and unity. Plus, I reckon they probably think it's cool to use codenames, since that's how we work too."

"I have to say, they are pretty good at keeping a low profile. There isn't much on them. Most of the evidence mentioning The Sixteen comes from human intelligence, as in, it was tortured out of the suspects or someone overheard something here or there and reported it."

"They picked a name which represents an almost mythical group of advisers to the king," Jonnie pondered. "You mentioned before they have a king who is pulling the strings.

Maybe these people picked the name to continue to play at the idea that they were serving and advising their king?"

"Right on the money," Kate nodded. "That's what Blake and I reckon too."

"What about this?" Max said pulling out Russo's codebook.

"The symbol is mixture of British royal symbols, the lion, the roses and the diamond to symbolise power and domination everywhere, north, east, south and west are the points of the diamond. And, obviously it has sixteen flowers and sixteen thorns."

"We started to decode some of it before the safehouse was attacked," Max explained opening the book and pointing to the symbols. "We think these represent years and dates, and the PM thought the letter and number combinations could represent chess moves."

"It makes sense," Jonnie said. "Using chess ranks and chess moves, but what about the other numbers?"

"It has to be the location of the attacks, but I'm still not sure how to decode it. We know the dates of some of the attacks and therefore we could figure out the locations, but there is still something missing. Why don't you two start from some of the dates of attacks we know and see how many of the codes we can figure out, maybe it will reveal a pattern and we can see where they plan to attack next?"

"You got it, boss," Kate said as the two agents moved to the lounge room to work.

"I've got to make some calls," Max said walking to one of the bedrooms.

Max walked into a spare bedroom and sat on the end of the bed. He looked out the floor to ceiling windows over the London skyline. The streets were eerily quiet given the lockdown.

He took out his mobile and scrolled through his phone book until he found her number. He sat staring at Jane's number the pain was almost unbearable, tears welled in his eyes and he felt choked up. As he went to press the call button, the phone rang. An incoming encrypted call.

"Prince," Max said his voice breaking silently.

"It's Hermes," Blake said. *"Are you clear? Did you manage to get the PMs out?"*

"Yes, they are safe. We have moved to an alternate location. I've got Bravo and Alpha with me, plus Mr Morgan and Mr Kirby."

"That's great, Prince. The AIS crew are moving in now to secure the safehouse. They tell me it looks like a warzone. I'm glad you all made it out."

"We didn't," Max sniffed, his voice cracking again. "Flash. Flash, didn't make it."

"My God, Max, I'm so sorry."

"Me too. I know you were close too."

"Want to talk about what happened?"

"We had to get out of the safehouse. I tried to clear a path, but I got pinned down. Jonnie saved me. Flash headed for an alternate route, but he got wedged between two attacking forces. He knew we were coming, but wouldn't get there in time. To buy us some time he sacrificed himself to distract the attackers and draw fire away from the Prime Ministers."

"It sounds like he died a hero, Max."

"He did."

The pair were silent for a moment.

"He's still in the street," Max said trying to hold back the tears. "You need to pick him up."

"I will get him back to the High Commission," Blake said choking up himself from the loss of his friend, but also hearing the pain Max was going through and wishing he could be there for him. *"And I will make the arrangements for his return with us to Australia."*

"Thank you."

"I am really sorry, Max. How are you holding up?"

"I'm not really holding up at all, Blake."

"I understand."

"No, you don't. I'm going to hunt down every last member of The Sixteen and kill them."

"We need to play this by the book, Prince. I want you to stay safe. You need to watch your back."

"No, Blake, they need to watch theirs'," Max said feeling the anger rising again.

"Just promise me you will be careful."

"I can't promise that, but I will do my job."

"I know you will. Just be careful, please. I don't want to lose you."

Max sat in silence for a moment thinking about what Blake had said.

"Thank you, Blake," Max said. "I'll try my best."

"I know. I'm sorry to move us back to work, but what is the plan?"

"We need to arrange safe passage for Prime Minister Kirby back to Australia and we need to get Prime Minister Morgan back to Number Ten."

"Hulk is working on a plan right now for Kirby and he has spoken to MI6. They are obviously keen to have their PM back under their protection."

"I bet, I'm sure they love their little cousins doing their job for them."

"About as much as we would."

"Fair enough. Listen, I've got to make a call."

"Jane?"

"Yeah."

"Okay, please pass on my thoughts and tell her if there is anything she needs, she only needs to ask."

"I will. Let me know when you have plans from Hulk."

"Will do. I'm sorry again, Max."

"Thanks, Blake," Max said ending the call.

Max starred at the phone, breathed in and out deeply, then pressed the button for one of the hardest calls he would ever have to make.

Chapter Thirty

It had been over an hour since Max had spoken to Jane. He had showered and changed into some combat gear Kate had brought up from the car. He sat on the end of the bed thinking about the call. Jane was understandably upset, but Max noticed the almost calm tone in her voice, like she had prepared herself for this news since the day she found out about Flash's real job. Max promised to get his body back to Australia and to not rest until he found every least person involved in Flash's death. Jane knew he meant it. She ended the call with a warning. She told Max that Flash had been worried about him, concerned by his actions and brutality, and upset because he felt like he was losing his friend. Max felt his heart break. His friend had been trying to help him, trying to get him back to some sort of normal life after Lachlan's death.

Max had been slipping, he had felt it, but he ignored it. He pushed it aside to continue his hunt for Lachlan's killers, to do his job and save innocents. He had let himself go in many ways, including his scruffy appearance. But, now Flash was gone too and the same people were responsible. He knew if he was going to have any sort of normal life he needed to walk away. But, he couldn't. Not now, not ever. And, Jane knew it too. She told him that Flash would not want him to fuss over him, but she knew it would not help deter him. She had seen the passion in his eyes when he and Lachlan were together. She had seen the pure love and joy on his face when they announced they were engaged. The same love and happiness missing since the day Lachlan had been taken from him. Jane knew Flash's death would only add fuel to the raging fire burning inside Max. Her warning was simple 'don't let it consume you'.

Max sat staring at Russo's codebook, but the numbers were blurred. His mind was racing, a mix of sadness and seething anger. Jane was right. He was trying to fight the anger, but it was winning. His mind turned to Lachlan and the happiness they had shared. From the day they had met until the day he died in his arms, Max knew Lachlan was the love of his life. Max's guilt over his death was crippling and the constant loop of his murder played in his mind whenever he closed his eyes.

A tear rolled down his cheek. He thought about Sam and how Shadow had tried to kill him in the same way as Lachlan had died. He thought about how Sam had showed him that he could feel again, but he knew it was not forever. Jane knew too. She told Max to call Sam and let him know. It was only fair. She promised she would look after him and that even with the timing, it was the right thing to do. Max agreed and called Sam. They both agreed it had been coming and ended it with both men happy for the time they had been together and agreed to be friends.

Max's focus shifted back to the codebook. The numbers and dates. He found the date of Lachlan's death and starred at the page. The love of his life had been reduced to a handful of dusty of photos in a house he hardly spent any time in anymore and a page in a terrorist's codebook as a permanent marker of their history. Lachlan had been killed by The Sixteen to break Max. Well, they succeeded, he was broken. No longer was he the man full of love, seeking a long life full of happiness with his partner, surrounded by friends. Lachlan and Flash were dead, and all that remained was hate. His mind cleared and a solitary purpose moved front and centre – Russo, Robert, the king, the queen, every last member of The Sixteen and their supporters – he was going to take them down or die trying.

"I'm sorry, boss," Jonnie said knocking then walking into the room. "But, Kate's got AIS on the line. They think they have worked out the codebook."

"Thanks," Max said clearing his throat and following Jonnie from the room.

Kate was at the dining table, it was covered in paper and a couple of tablets and phones. Her secure mobile was on the table connected to AIS. The Australian Prime Minister was pacing nearby with a cup of coffee, listening in to the call.

"He's here, Hermes," Kate said as Max entered the makeshift conference room. "Go ahead."

"Prince, you were right about the codebook," Blake explained, *"all of the pages are dates which line up with attacks across the world."*

"Do we know what's coming next?" Max asked.

"No. We have dates, but the location data can't be deciphered. It's two numbers, the best we can come up with is we think one is the page of a reference book of some sort and the other is a grid reference like a chess board. We think you need a map or some other reference sheet which you then overlay with the chess board. The numbers one to sixty-four then pinpoint the position on the board and location of the attack on the map or reference material underneath."

"So, do we have the reference book?"

"No, we are scanning all possible books, but there are billions of pages to scan through and, even then, it could take considerable time."

"We don't have time."

"We are going as fast as we can."

"Well, move faster."

"We will do what we can."

"What about MI6?"

"They are getting ready for Morgan's transfer."

"When?"

"They are on their way. I will keep you posted."

There was a commotion on Blake's end of the line.

"Hermes?" Max asked. "What's going on?"

"Just a second," Blake said as an aide passed him a note. *"The scanners at Perth Airport have picked up a signature."*

"A signature?"

"Weapons grade plutonium."

"In what?"

"They are not sure yet."

"What?"

"The signature is shielded."

"You mean, they have detected it, but they haven't found the device yet? What's the hold up? Isn't the airport under increased security?"

"Yes, it is. We have a few people on camera and we are tracking them through the airport. We think one of them has the device."

"Jesus, Blake. We need to tighten the noose."

"Standby, we've got the feed coming in on the secure link. You will be able to access it on your tablets."

Kate spun the tablet around and Kirby moved in behind Max to get a look. Multiple camera footage screens divided the tablet screen. The images were being captured from the vests of border security agents in the terminal.

"Zoom in on four," Max ordered after a few seconds monitoring each screen.

"What is it, Prince?" Blake asked as the fourth image filled the screen.

"The stickers on the briefcase. They are diplomatic stickers. We used to use them when I worked at Parliament House. When we would travel overseas and needed to get documents in past customs. The stickers cover the box or case, extending diplomatic immunity to the item, meaning customs can't open it."

"Why would they be in Perth?"

"Exactly. Canberra yes, but anywhere else is a bit of a stretch."

"It would be a good way to get something into the country."

"Tell the team to move in."

"Are you sure?"

"Tell them to get close and use the Geiger counter."

"Border force team Juliet, this is AIS. Get close to your subject and take a reading."

"Roger AIS," the Juliet team leader said.

Max watched as the Juliet team leader pulled out a Geiger counter and moved in closer to the target with the diplomatic briefcase. Within a metre of the target, the counter spiked the needle flicking to the right and a series of clicking beeps sounded.

"Take him down!" Max ordered.

"Juliet one," Blake said. *"Cleared to proceed, take him into custody. Extreme caution on the briefcase."*

"Roger AIS," the team leader said.

The footage showed the team leader dropping his Geiger counter and drawing his pistol.

"Freeze! Get down on the ground!"

The man holding the briefcase stopped in his tracks and turned to face the Juliet team. He started protesting about being a diplomat and having immunity. The Juliet leader repeated his command and the man, after a few seconds, gently sat the briefcase down. As he was standing back up, he pulled a small device from his pocket and pressed the button. A blinding white light flashed across the space and the Juliet team leader's camera moved about as he shifted on his feet. Max could hear the screams from the crowd and the groans from the border force team. As the camera refocused, Max saw the supposed diplomat running for a nearby door.

"Juliet one," Max yelled into the phone. "He's on the move. On your nine."

"Roger, AIS," the leader said trying to focus. *"Fucker used some sort of flash device. Vision is slowly coming back. Juliet team, nine o'clock. Weapons ready. Lockdown the terminal. You two, secure the device."*

The footage focused on the doorway the diplomat had fled through. The team's boots were squeaking on the tiled floor as they ran. One of the men ran ahead and on the leader's signal opened the door. The four team members moved through into a side corridor. As they passed each doorway, one of the team would check for the diplomat. They cleared four rooms, then came to a hallway which led off to the right. The team leader ordered two of his team down the corridor and he continued on with his remaining teammate.

They swept and scanned until they reached the far doors. A security panel had been smashed and wires were hanging loosely from the socket. The team leader tried the door and it opened. His team member was through first and Max watched in horror as a fire axe slammed into his face without warning, sending him flying back into the corridor. The leader cursed and yelled for the diplomat to freeze, as the camera slowly came around the corner of the door. They were in a large hanger with conveyor belts flying past carrying luggage from around the terminal to the arrivals lounge.

The diplomat was running at full speed away from the border force leader who started to give chase. Max was impressed at the officer's speed as he tore through the hanger after the target. The diplomat dodged left, between some conveyors and was out of sight. As the Juliet team leader approached the turn, he slowed, then stopped, Max knew he would be checking around the bend. Then there were three shots and the footage started moving again. The border force officer had shot the diplomat as he was kneeling in the walkway between the luggage belts. The Juliet leader ran closer as the diplomat hunched over grasping and hugging his stomach. There was blood all over his suit and pooling on the ground.

"Get on the floor," the Juliet leader said.

"First you have to break it," the diplomat said coughing blood out onto the concrete. *"Then it can be rebuilt."*

"What?"

"Our mission, to change society and the world, like a forest, it starts with a cleansing fire which encourages new growth and life," the diplomat said straightening his back and looking up at the Juliet team leader.

"Juliet one!" Max yelled into the phone. "Take the shot!"

"Repeat, AIS," the Juliet leader said.

"Shoot that arsehole, he has his phone in his hand. It's one of the triggers, take him down!"

"Today, I start the fire," the diplomat said smiling and pressing his phone screen.

There was no time to see the bullet hit the diplomat in the forehead, before the screen went black losing the feed. The feds from the other unit's cameras were also instantly cut. The screens were all black with white writing reading *Signal Lost* and there was silence on the line.

"Hermes?" Max asked nervously. "Please tell me we just lost the feed."

"It went off," Blake said sadly through his shock. *"The device detonated. All units are down."*

"We failed."

Silence hung in the air. Kirby's eyes filled with tears and he fell into a nearby chair and stared blankly at the wall. Max was still hunched over the tablet as if willing the screen to change, while Kate and Jonnie sat in silence.

"What's the blast radius?" Max asked after a full minute of silence.

"We had a satellite overhead," Blake explained. *"It took out the airport and about a block leading up to the terminal. For a small tactical nuke, the radiation zone will be a couple of kilometres in all directions, but should be just short of the city. Hulk is ordering the military to take command. They will start by evacuating people in the direct line of the fallout cloud which is moving east as per our scenarios we have war gamed, we will start broadcasts advising residents of what to do."*

"How many people?"

"Unclear. Several hundred at the airport and surrounding instantly killed by the blast. Could be that again in longer term casualties from radiation, maybe more."

There was silence in the room again as the team contemplated the horror of what had just happen.

"What do we do now, Max?" Jonnie finally asked cutting the silence.

"We push on," Max choked out. "We have to stop them."

"How are we going to do that? They've got nuclear bombs."

"And, they are willing to use them. We must find them and stop them. We can't give up."

"A nuclear bomb just blew up part of one of our major cities, Max. You said it yourself, we failed."

"Yes, we did," Max said standing and looking Jonnie in the eyes. "But, we won't fail again. Are you ready to help me end this?"

"Yes, of course, Max."

"Good. Hermes, where is Morgan's car?"

"They should be arriving any minute."

"Good. We are on our way back to the High Commission as soon as he is in the car. I need to have a word with Robert."

Morgan walked back into the room as there was a rap on the door.

"My security team is here," Morgan said walking into the room and moving for the door.

"Wait," Max said but Morgan flung it open.

Four men dressed in heavy combat gear stormed into the room and surrounded Morgan.

"How did you know they were here?" Max asked.

"They called me," Morgan said holding up his phone. "You surely did not think I would go without talking to my people?"

"I said no phones."

"I know Agent Shaw, but I do not work for you. These men however, they do."

All four guards raised their weapons and aimed at Max and his team.

"It really was a shame about Perth," Morgan said smugly. "It was a beautiful city."

"What are you doing, Stephen?" Kirby asked standing up. "What's going on?"

"I am sorry old boy. I thought about recruiting you to our cause, given how you threw yourself at that new legislative agenda of yours. You are so very good at inciting the right-wing masses against our enemies. It is just a pity you could not see that the people you were focusing all your energy and hate on were the wrong people. The Arabs and the Russians, the North Koreans, they could never achieve what we have and what we will. We will break society, tear it back to its roots, then rebuild it to ensure human beings can finally live in peace.”

“Under your rules?”

“Well, I will certainly play a large roll if the king so desires.”

“If you’re not the king, then who is?” Max asked.

“I hold the rank of queen in our little game, but who knows the king may yet fall and if she does, then the people will need someone to turn to. A strong decisive leader, ready to lead our world into a new age.”

“You will never get the chance.”

“Oh, Agent Shaw, you embarrass yourself. Your threats mean nothing. My men here are going to put bullets in each one of you, then we will finish our plan.”

There was a loud crack as a bullet slammed into the head of one of Morgan’s guards. It exploded showering the UK Prime Minister in blood. One of the rear agents grabbed Morgan.

“Shoot him!” Morgan yelled pointing at Kirby before he was dragged out of the room by his guard.

The remaining two guards opened fire. Max and his team scattered. Max dived to the ground and scrambled along the floor towards the dining room table. Jonnie ran and jumped over the couch, slamming into Kirby and knocking the big armchair over. Kirby and Jonnie tumbled over, and Jonnie dragged Kirby into cover behind the chair. As Max got to the table, Kate slid a pistol under it. It stopped in front of Max on the carpet. He grabbed the weapon, clicked off the safety, and rolled in behind the lounge. He nodded to Kate, who had taken cover behind the table, and the two agents sprung to their feet and offloaded multiple shots into each guard. The two guards fell in a bleeding, awful mess.

“Clear,” Max said.

"Clear," Kate said.

"I've got a situation here," Jonnie panicked. "Help!"

Max leapt over the lounge and moved around the armchair to see Jonnie holding a bleeding wound in Kirby's stomach.

"Kate, first-aid kit," Max ordered.

"We've got it, Max," Kate said rushing over with the kit. "Go get that son-of-a-bitch!"

Max looked at his two teammates and to Kirby.

"You heard them, Max," Kirby said through bloodied, gritted teeth. "Don't worry about me, I'll be fine. Go get that arsehole."

Chapter Thirty-One

Max grabbed an MP5 and holstered his pistol, then took off as fast as he could after Morgan. He ran down the corridor and found the fire stairs. He kicked open the door and jumped down four and five steps at a time. On each landing, he checked the path was clear, then started moving again. One the third floor, the fire exit door opened. A pistol wielding hand came through. Max leapt from the landing down the remaining stairs and slammed hard into the door. He heard a sickening crack as the man's arm broke. His attacker's pistol fell to the floor, so he picked it up, before dragging open the door. Two other attackers were standing there, so Max shot both of them, before putting the guy with the broken arm out of his misery with a bullet to the head.

"It's Prince, Alpha, Bravo, do you copy?" Max asked into his comms unit as he ran.

"Here, Prince," Kate replied. *"Go ahead."*

"Get Kirby out now, there are other attackers in the building. On route to you."

"Ack. Moving now."

"You take the AIS car, get him back in the embassy."

"Roger that."

Max bounded down the stairs, finally reaching the carpark exit. He gently opened the door to see Morgan being rushed out to a waiting Jaguar which was flanked by two black GMC four-wheel drives with blackened windows.

Three of Morgan's men were running for his door. He kicked it open and fired six shots, two for each approaching guard, taking them down. The guards with Morgan in the distance glanced quickly at Max, then lifted Morgan and ran him towards the rear of the Jaguar.

Two guards climbed out of the rear four-wheel drive and started firing at Max, but Max had been expecting that. He dropped the first attacker with a single bullet through the neck.

He fell clutching his throat. The second guard had moved to the rear of the GMC. Max threw the empty pistol at the guard. As he ducked to dodge the incoming pistol, Max ran, leapt off his left foot, drew back his right fist and slammed it into the guard's head sending it backwards into the rear window of the four-wheel drive, cracking the glass. Max grabbed the guard's head and smashed it into the rear window, twice in quick succession, shattering it, as the big vehicle started to move.

Max let the guard's unconscious body drop to the concrete and he stepped onto the tow ball of the fleeing GMC. He clung desperately to the tailgate through the shattered glass window. With each bump, the glass would cut his arm. He grabbed his pistol and used the butt to smash out the remaining glass, then hurled himself into the rear luggage space.

There was a guard climbing over in the backseat from the passenger's seat. The driver slammed on the brakes, throwing Max over into the backseat and causing his comrade to fall back into the front of the cabin. The driver hit the accelerator again, following Morgan's car out of the carpark. Max had fallen face first onto the backseat and was rolling over as the big security guard jumped through the little gap onto him and started punching, kneeing and trying to headbutt him. Max raised his arms and blocked what he could. The guard was massive, his weighty frame alone was pinning Max down.

The car sped up the ramp and out of the carpark. As it left the ramp, it jumped and bounced on the road, before turning and following Morgan. The bounce was enough to lift the big guard off Max for a second. Max took the moment, raised his knee and as the car bounced back down, he slammed his knee into the guard's groin. He groaned in pain. Max grabbed his hunting knife and stabbed the guard in between the ribs.

The guard bellowed as Max ripped the knife out and tried to stab him again, but the big guard grabbed his hand. He got to his knees pinning Max down again, before dragging Max's knife wielding hand in between them. The big guard was trying to turn the knife on Max and it was taking all of his strength to hold him off. The car made a sharp turn and the guard fell backwards. Max took the opening and slammed the knife into the guard's chest. The guard punched Max in the face then threw several punches which Max managed to block. He dragged his legs out from under the guard and elbowed him in face, three times. One the third, the guard fell back and Max used his legs to kick the guard back against the door as Max got to his knees.

The guard was getting weaker, but was still angry, he gritted his teeth as if begging Max to engage. Max pressed his feet hard against the door behind him, then sprang forward pressing the knife deeper into the guard's chest with one arm. As the guard tried to fight back, Max flicked the door handle with his free arm. The door flung open and the guard tumbled backwards, half out the door. He was desperate to keep his head from hitting the rushing bitumen, but Max's knife was still lodged in his chest ripping into him with every bounce or sit up attempt. Max wrapped his left foot in the seat belt behind him and tucked his right foot behind the driver's seat, not wanting to be dragged out by the big guard who was clinging onto Max's vest.

Max reached out, grabbed the knife handle as the guard tried to pull him from the car. Max ripped the knife out and slammed in down twice into the guard's abdominals making it impossible for the guard to hold his weight up off the bitumen. The guard's head bounced on the ground, once, twice, three times, and roared in pain and fear. The guard's shoulder hit the gravel, then his upper back caught the road surface and ripped him from the car. The massive rear tyre ran straight over him and his lifeless body lay dead in the London street.

Exhausted and in pain, Max dragged himself up, got to his knees and moved for the driver. The driver slammed on the brakes and Max fell between the front seats. The driver started punching him with his free hand as he hit the accelerator. Max blocked the punches, waiting for his opening. The driver made a quick, sharp turn, and Max plunged the knife up into the driver's armpit. Max struggled to move his big frame around, but managed to get to a seated position on the centre console.

"Two choices," Max yelled over the revving engine. "Keep following the Prime Minister or get out."

"Fuck you," the driver said speeding up.

Max checked the road ahead and saw a row of trees nearby. The driver was deliberately going to crash the car. It jumped the gutter and ripped out a street sign, as Max bounced wildly around in the little cabin, before the car made a beeline for the park.

"Wrong answer," Max said reefing out the knife and stabbing it into the driver's neck.

The driver went rigid, planting his foot on the accelerator. Max opened the driver's door and tried to push him out, but the seat belt caught him. He fumbled around until he found the buckle. It clicked and released, Max threw his shoulder into the dead driver's body shoving it out the door, then grabbed the wheel, steering it back over the footpath and onto the road. As the GMC four-wheel drive bounced back onto the bitumen, Max climbed into the driver's seat and hit the accelerator chasing Morgan.

The roads were clear thanks to the curfew, so it was not hard to follow Morgan. The convoy had wound its way through the London streets and was heading out of town. Max gave an update to Blake as he pursued the luxury getaway car.

As they entered the freeway, the Jaguar sped passed the lead four-wheel drive, which had slowed. Max raced in beside the matching vehicle in no time and was confronted by three guards with weapons aimed right at him. He slammed on the brakes and ducked down behind the doorframe, as bullets ripped into the car in a violent hailstorm. The windscreen and windows all shattered, showering Max with glass.

He hit the accelerator and fell into line behind them after a few seconds, taking away their clear shots. He sat forward and pulled his MP5 over his shoulder. Taking the wheel with his left hand, he aimed the MP5 right through the now glassless front window. He opened fire at the guards' four-wheel-drive, shattering the back window.

He saw two of the guards trying to get into position to fire back. He accelerated and smashed into the back of the car. The guards inside all fell. Max fired a burst through the open windshield, hitting the front passenger and one of the rear guards. The second rear guard looked down at his fallen comrade, before opening fire at Max.

Bullets slammed into the front of Max's car. He swerved trying to avoid them getting a clear shot at him. Smoke started to rise from beneath his bonnet and Max swore to himself. He could not let them get away. He planted his foot, pulled into the left lane and opened fire as his car overtook his attackers. He fired three shots into the back-passenger window killing the rear guard.

As he pulled in beside the other four-wheel-drive, he could see the front passenger he hit earlier holding his shoulder and shouting at the driver. The driver saw Max out the window and started pointing and yelling. The wounded passenger turned and opened fire, shattering his window. Bullets slammed into the side of Max's car. Max yanked hard on the wheel, smashing his car into the side of the attackers' car. The passenger lent away from the crash instinctively and braced himself. Max fired one shot through the open windows. The bullet hit the passenger at the base of the skull before exploding out his face, followed by a spray of blood and bone which covered the windscreen and the driver. The other car swerved as the driver struggled to see.

Max accelerated forward passed the other four-wheel drive, opened his door then hit the brakes. The attacker's car raced past, ripping the door from its hinges. Max hit the accelerator again, but as he started gaining on the other car, he jammed his MP5 down on the accelerator and wedged the butt into the seat. He steered his car towards the other and waited, then he jumped.

Max's car pulled left before flames erupted from the engine. The driver of the second vehicle turned covered in blood to see Max jumping through the air. The exploding car trailing off to the left. He smiled and steered away, but Max caught one foot on the sidestep and one hand wrapped through the doorframe. His other foot bounced on the road as he tried to pull himself up onto the sidestep. The driver lent over and was crawling wildly at Max's fingers trying to dislodge him as the car sped down the freeway. He punched wildly at the stitches on Max's hand and Max groaned in pain.

Max grabbed his knife and slid it down into the recess in the door, just as the driver manage to break his grip. Max fell, but the knife held his weight with his other hand. He steadied himself, then managed to get his other foot on the sidestep. His old car exploded as it hit a barricade, sending a thick plume of smoke into the sky.

He pulled himself up and moved back towards the passenger window. Max felt the driver accelerate. They were gaining on the Jaguar. Max struggled to pull himself into the vehicle. The driver was fighting him off and the wind racing by was pushing him around with tremendous force. He looked around to see the Jaguar coming in behind him. The driver was going to slam Max between the two cars. He sprung off the sidestep and threw himself through the window on top of the dead passenger as the Jaguar and GMC cars collided. Max looked back through the shattered window to see Morgan screaming at his driver and guards, and pointing furiously at Max.

The guards from the Prime Minister's car wound down their windows and started firing at Max and the guard. The driver in Max's car was hit. Like his comrade before him, his foot slammed down on the accelerator. Max was taking cover under the doorframe as bullets ricocheted through his car. He grabbed the wheel and tried to keep the car straight, not that it mattered he could not see where he was going anyway.

He dragged at the fallen driver's foot trying to pull it from the accelerator. Bullets continued to hit the car, as the driver's leg finally came free with one last pull on his trousers. Max heard the Jaguar continue on and the bullets stopped. Max opened the driver's door, pushed dead guard's body out and climbed into the driver's seat. Max hit the accelerator and gave chase.

Several kilometres later, Max finally was gaining on the Jaguar. He had his foot pressed to the floor and the engine was roaring in the big car. He pulled in beside the Jaguar and yanked hard on the wheel, slamming into the side of the luxury sedan. He could see Morgan yelling again. The guards raised their weapons, but Max slammed into the them again. Pushing the Jaguar against the metal barricade of the freeway. A terrible screeching sound of metal on metal rang out with a shower of orange sparks. Max yanked right, then hard left again bouncing the big car into the side of the smaller Jaguar. Sparks and screeches again filled the air. Up ahead, Max saw his opportunity.

Max yanked hard on the wheel pulling the big car free of the Jaguar. He waited for a split second, then threw the car left into the Jaguar, just as the metal barricade finished. The Jaguar pushed out, off the road, then violently crumpled in a sudden, nauseating crash as hit collided with the start of the new barricade. The driver and front passenger were thrown through the windshield.

The driver hit the barricade several metres away and fell in a tangled mess of limbs. The passenger slid along the roadway, tumbling like a rag doll, before lying dead on the side of the road. The Jaguar flipped onto its roof, after ripping out several metres of barricade, and slid along the freeway. Sparks flew and pieces of metal and glass and plastic left a trail back to the barricade. It came to rest on its roof and what was left of its bonnet in the centre of the freeway.

Max stopped his car and reversed back to the Jaguar. He climbed out and drew his pistol. Max looked in through the back windows. Morgan was hanging loosely from his seatbelt and looked unconscious. His face was covered in blood. The final guard was lying on the roof, he was obviously not wearing his seatbelt, but somehow, he was still alive. He was trying to drag himself out of the vehicle. Max put a bullet in the back of his head.

He walked around to Morgan's side of the car and smashed out the window. He reached in and cut the PM's seatbelt. Morgan fell hard onto the roof of the Jaguar. Max dragged him free of the wreckage and checked his vital signs. He had a pulse, but was in bad shape.

"Hermes," Max said into his comms unit as he starred at Morgan. "You on comm?"

"Yes, Prince," Blake replied. "I'm here. Are you okay?"

"Yes, I've got Morgan. He's, well, I'm not sure he's going to make it."

"What happened?"

"He had a car accident."

"Okay, where are you? Do you need someone to come and collect you?"

"Did Alpha and Bravo get Kirby out?"

"Yes, he is with the High Commission's doctor, they are preparing him for surgery."

"Will he pull through?"

"The doctor says he's got good odds considering were the wound is. The bullet missed his organs."

"Good," Max said looking back at the upside-down Jaguar. "Son-of-a-bitch."

"What?"

"He's got one too," Max noted walking over and pulling a leather-bound book from the rear of the Jaguar. "I found Morgan's codebook."

Max saw the familiar logo on the cover. He undid the lock and started leafing through it. It was the same as Russo's in every way, but one.

"He wrote notes in his," Max said smiling. "Stupid fucking prick, wrote notes in a codebook."

"Does it say what's coming?" Blake asked.

Max flicked to the final section. Morgan had written on every page. He found the pages with today's date.

"Ground attack Commonwealth Heads of Government Meeting, London," Max read aloud. "Tactical nuke, London, target HRH."

"HRH?"

"His Royal Highness. They wanted to kill the King, not just their stupid pretend king, the actual King."

"Jesus."

"There's more. Tactical nuke, Perth, is on another page. This one's got 'Plan B' scribbled on it like a maniac wrote it and capture HRH, the Duchess of Cambridge, London."

"They still have the Princess, Max. Does it say where?"

"No, it just says London, but there are references to maps and books. Here I will send you a photo of it."

Max took a photo of the page and references, and sent them to Blake.

"Jesus, you were right about the handwriting," Blake said. *"Clearly a lunatic wrote that."*

"Fuck me," Max said staring at the next page. "Blake, get the Americans on the phone right now."

Chapter Thirty-Two

"Roger AIS, our detectors are on and we have started screening every item of luggage, including diplomatic briefcases," the Federal Bureau of Investigation field agent said. *"We have a backlog of planes circling the city and both arrivals and departures are hours behind. The President is anxious that these delays will cause a public backlash."*

"We have credible intelligence that the same group behind the tactical nuclear explosion in Perth are planning an attack on San Francisco," Blake said as calmly as possible. *"We believe an attack is imminent."*

"Roger that AIS, we will keep the channel open. Thank you for the tip."

"Good hunting," Blake said. *"Did you hear all that, Prince?"*

"Yes, I did," Max said accelerating hard down the freeway back towards London. "He's just feeling the pressure, but the codebook is very clear. Morgan wrote San Francisco on the fucking page."

"Where is he?"

"He's duct-taped in the back of the car."

"He's the Prime Minister, Max. I don't think you can just tie him up in the boot."

"He's a fucking terrorist, Blake. He killed Flash and he's responsible for Perth, and..."

"And, Lachlan."

"Yes. He killed Lachlan and thousands of others like him."

"We can't let this get personal, Max."

"They made it personal. I didn't."

"I know, Max, but you are better than this. I have seen you rise above pain and suffering like no one else. I know you can put it aside to get the job done."

"I know my job, Blake, but I am going to make them suffer."

"I know, Max, but please, just don't do anything rash. These people are connected and well-funded. They aren't the sort of people we can just torture or kill."

"We are on route to the High Commission. We will figure out what to do when we get there."

"Thank you, Max."

Max drove through the London streets towards the Australian Embassy. As he approached, the guards moved the barricades and waved him through. He drove down into the underground carpark and shut off the engine. Blake was waiting for him by the elevator, holding the door open. Max dragged Morgan out of the car and over to the lift. Blake saw the blood and bruises on Morgan from the crash. He was in bad shape.

They rode the elevator down to the holding cells and Max stripped Morgan down to his underwear before tying him to a steel chair. He was unconscious and slumped over as Hulk walked into the room. Blake's phone rang and he left the room.

"Hi, kid," Hulk greeted Max shaking his hand. "Looks like you've been through it."

"You could say that, boss," Max agreed.

"I'm sorry about Flash, he was a great agent and I know how close you two were."

"Thank you."

"We will find a way to make it right."

"Finding every one of these arseholes and putting them in the ground is the only thing I can think of that will make it even close."

"I understand."

"So, you approve?"

"I didn't say that."

"But, you won't stop me?"

Blake walked back into the room and put his phone on the table.

"Sir, you need to hear this," Blake said pressing the speaker button.

"Place the briefcase on the ground and put your hands in the air!" the FBI agent demanded.

"San Francisco?" Hulk asked looking to Blake.

"Yes," Blake nodded.

"Now, slowly get down on your knees and remove your jacket. Lay down and place your arms behind your back. Okay, take him."

There was a commotion on the other end of the line as the agents moved in to arrest the diplomat. A few seconds later the agent was talking to the AIS team who had taken custody of the London weapon after Max defused it. Max listened as the AIS team talked them through the process to disarm the bomb. He heard them cut the final wire and defuse the weapon, and everyone on the line breathed a sign of relief.

"AIS, this is FBI One," the FBI lead agent said. *"The weapon has been successfully defused. Thank you for the assist."*

"It is our pleasure FBI One," Blake acknowledged. "We will be in touch."

"How very exciting," Morgan coughed smugly from behind the three agents. "Pity you did not quite get there in Perth."

Max, Hulk and Blake turned to face the British Prime Minister as he spat blood onto the concrete floor. Max started for Morgan, but Hulk grabbed his arm and walked in front of him, taking the lead.

"Mr Morgan," Hulk said calmly. "You are in the custody of the Australian Intelligence Service. Nobody knows where you are. You have been linked to terrorist activities around the world, including a tactical nuclear device which was detonated on Australian soil today. You should know the law gives me a significant amount of power to question, detain and arrest you."

"I am the Prime Minister of the United Kingdom," Morgan bellowed arrogantly. "You know nothing about power. You should release me while you still can."

"I'm just going to stop you right there. Our Prime Minister is at this moment in time speaking with your Attorney-General and Deputy Prime Minister, and the Supreme Court Chief Justice. In a few minutes, all three will be speaking to His Majesty to remove you from office. You, Mr Morgan, have no power, no rights and no chance of escape. You will answer for your crimes. Every single one of them."

"I would like to make a deal."

"That was quick."

"I am a realist, General, if what you say is true, I would like to make a deal to avoid prison."

"Tell me who the king is in your little game?"

"I will not say a word, until I have immunity."

"You son of a bitch!" Max yelled losing his patience. "I should put a bullet in your head right now!"

Hulk turned back to Max and raised his hand. Max stopped and starred at his boss, then he nodded to Hulk. Hulk turned back to Morgan.

"That's very good," Morgan said smiling cockily at Max. "Can you get him to sit and rollover too?"

"Mr Morgan," Hulk said with more respect than was granted, "this man is the best field agent I have ever worked with. He can outshoot, out run and out class every solider I ever had under my command. He is also the most gifted person I have met at extracting information from suspects. Trust me when I tell you, it would be better for you to cooperate with me, than have him ask you the questions. So, why don't you tell me what I need to know?"

"She's one too, you know."

"What?"

"Like your super-agent there, the king is a homosexual," Morgan said with pure distain and vitriol dripping from his words.

"I take it from your tone, you don't approve?"

"It is a sin against God, General Scott. They should have killed you in Rome, Agent Shaw. I ordered those jets to force you down and hand deliver you to the church. The same church you desecrated years ago when you killed Archbishop Benjamin Wright."

"It was you?"

"The Archbishop was a good friend of mine and we were working together to spread Catholicism."

"Is that part of The Sixteen's plans?" Hulk asked.

"Yes, in part. God is but one part of the plan. The world has lost its way and the church is part of the solution. Only through the word of God and with the right people in control, can people truly be safe and secure."

"The right people in control, that's the second part of your plan?"

"It is."

"You were the Prime Minister, what more power could you want?"

"We need a more thorough change than the parliament can provide, especially with the unpredictability of the election cycle."

"Sounds an awful lot like a dictatorship."

"If that is what is needed to secure peace, then so be it."

"So, who is it, the person you trust to become dictator?"

"Me."

"But, you are the queen, not the king."

"For now, her reign is nearly over."

"So, you planned to take over?"

"I still plan to."

"How do you think that is possible from in here?"

"I told you I want to make a deal."

"You are delusional, Mr Morgan. There are no deals to be made."

"I will tell you where to find both kings, if you let me go."

"You will tell us, but we won't let you go. Wait, both kings?"

"A little slow to catch that, General, maybe you are slipping a bit in your old age. Yes, both kings."

"Your supposed king is the only one we are looking for."

"What if I told you she has captured the Royal Family?"

"What? That's not possible."

"The Royal Family didn't make it to the bunker. She intercepted them."

"You are lying."

"Our reach is far and our hands never idle," Morgan said self-righteously and laughing to himself as Hulk, Blake and Max left the room.

"You can't be seriously considering letting him go?" Max asked as the door closed behind them.

"Take it easy, Max," Hulk pleaded. "We don't even know if he is telling the truth."

"Let's assume he is," Blake said, "I agree with Max. He admitted his role and that he has other ambitions. He is clearly dangerous, we cannot let him go."

"I will speak to the Attorneys-General and Prime Minister Kirby. Blake find out what you can about the Royals and Max see what you can find out from Morgan before we make any decisions, but take it easy in there. He is still a world leader, we need to do this by the book."

"I can't promise that," Max dismissed.

"Then maybe you should think about not going in there."

"I'll be fine, just find out what you can."

Hulk and Blake headed for the elevator. Max took a couple of minutes to calm himself, pacing in the hallway, then headed into Morgan's holding cell.

"Ah, Agent Shaw," Morgan said almost gleefully. "Back to release me, already? I should probably get a few years in gaol for all the crimes I am apparently responsible for. Weapons of mass destruction, fraud, mass murder, corruption, I have done it all, allegedly. But, here you are to let me go.”

Max just starred blankly at Morgan.

“I hope she does not kill them before you realise me, I am telling you the truth,” Morgan said with a self-satisfied smile on his face. “I can help you stop her. We can save the Royal Family.”

Max starred at Morgan, but again did not move or reply.

“I really do look forward to getting out of here,” Morgan said looking to the door then to Max. “So much to do. It is a pity our illustrious leader will have to die, she has been a competent leader, but I just cannot have a gay running the world. And, that is what our leader will be you know, not a world leader, but the leader of the world. We are going to change the course of human history for the better, Agent Shaw. Sure, I am happy to use you people to get things done. You can be quite good at what you do, but it is just not right, the way you live your lives and we certainly cannot have one of you as our highest leader. In fact, I think society would be better off without you. The Archbishop and I discussed it at length, the scourge of homosexuality. I must say, gay rights will be removed across the world when I become leader. It is the only thing the Muslims get right as far as I am concerned.”

Max watched the smug and satisfied look spreading across Morgan’s face, but he did not move or respond, he just stood there staring, thinking.

“You know, I despise the idea of gay marriage,” Morgan rambled on, “when Shadow ran that blade through Lachlan’s stomach, he did the world a favour, one less gay marriage breaking God’s laws. One less gay even.”

Max turned away from Morgan, the pain and hate rising, as Blake walked back into the room.

“They have agreed to release him,” Blake said starring in contempt at Morgan who was smiling broadly. “If his information leads to the capture of the leader of The Sixteen and the safe return of the Royal Family.”

"I've got a better idea," Max said coldly.

With ice-cold determination, Max swung around on his heel and took two steps towards Morgan, drew his pistol and shot him in the head.

"Jesus Christ, Max," Blake whispered with an uneasy calm in his voice. "What have you done?"

"What I needed to, to get their attention," Max said.

"You can't assassinate world leaders, even the guilty ones. And, he was tied up, you broke the rules of engagement."

"Sure I can. I just did. Fuck the rules. They don't play by them, so why should I?"

"You know why, Max. We need to rise above them and be better than they are."

"That hasn't worked, Blake. They use our own rules against us. I won't let them keep killing innocent people. We knew this man was guilty and now I know he will no longer be able to hurt anyone."

"Max," Blake pleaded taking Max's hand and locking eyes with him. "Don't lose yourself to win."

"Maybe I'm already lost, Blake."

"I don't believe that," Blake said squeezing Max's hand. "I do not believe that."

They stood there for a minute holding each other's gaze, before Max broke the silence.

"Can you please get the door?" Max asked walking behind Morgan's slumped body and dragging the chair across the room.

Blake opened the door and Max dragged the chair with Morgan's body still tapped to it into the hallway.

"Open Robert's door," Max said.

Blake reluctantly unlocked the holding cell and pushed open the door. Robert looked up and watched Blake walk into the room, then his eyes narrowed trying to focus on what the Max was doing. He was dragging a steel chair backwards across the concrete, screeching it on the concrete. When he got within two metres of Robert, he swung the chair around. Morgan's lifeless body slumped in the chair, straining against the tape.

Robert's eyes widened in fear and horror as he saw Morgan's bruised and battered body, and the bullet hole which said perfectly centred in his forehead. Max left Robert to stare for a few moments and watched the shock and realisation spreading.

"I am going to ask you a series of questions, Robert," Max stated with an unnerving calm, cold tone as he drew his pistol and chambered a round. "If at any stage I think you are lying to me, I am going to shoot you. The now former Prime Minister was very inciteful, but as you can see, he tested my limits. I'm sure you, like the others in your little cabal, have read my file and you know what I am capable of. Mr Morgan here is surely proof of that alone. Am I understood?"

Robert was in shock, he did not move or speak. Max walked over and slapped him, hard across the face.

"Am I fucking understood?!" Max screamed getting down in Robert's face breaking his line of sight with Morgan.

"Yes," Robert said hesitantly, his voice cracking.

"Where have they taken the Royal Family?"

"The bunker."

"Which bunker?"

"The Royal bunker in Guildford."

"That is where they were taken for safety, but I know your organisation has taken them hostage. So, why don't you tell me where The Sixteen took the Royal Family?"

"The Guildford bunker. They are still there! Where better than a government funded nuclear bunker?"

"How did your people get in?"

"Our reach is far and our hands never idle."

"I'm so sick of hearing that. What is the plan?"

"They will be assassinated."

"Why?"

"To make room for the new world order."

"Who is the king? Who is your new world leader?"

"I won't say," Robert dismissed looking down at the floor. "I believe in her cause."

"Which is?"

"Peace."

"Through dictatorship."

"It won't be a total dictatorship. We aim only for the removal of a few institutions and processes, and to encourage nations of the world to come together, to unite under her leadership. So, at last humankind can know and enjoy lives of peace, free from war and hunger, free from pain. A perfect new world."

"That's not what Morgan said. He was aiming for full dictatorship, with one change, he was going to be the King."

"That son of a bitch."

"Power is corrupting, Robert. There will always be someone angling to take charge and who knows what they are capable of. Look what your organisation has done. The deaths, the weapons, the unspeakable damage to our society. But, how will you control the individual without your structures? How will they behave when they have no limitations on their power? How can you trust they will live up to your ideals?"

"Morgan was an idiot. Too obsessive, too conservative, too extreme. A fascist in hiding."

"And he was your number two, who had eyes on the top job. He spoke as if it was easily within reach. You may think your king is a rightful ruler, who will promote peace, but what about the next one or the one after that? Democracy may be flawed in many ways, but autocracy is worse, especially if you lose control to someone like Morgan."

"We won't."

"You almost did," Max snapped in Robert's face. "Who is in the king and where can I find her?"

"I cannot tell you," Robert said looking Max in the eyes. "I believe in her."

Max drew his pistol and shot Robert in the knee.

"Max!" Hulk said bursting into the room. "Get out here now!"

Max followed Blake and Hulk out into the hallway leaving Robert sobbing and writhing in pain.

"What the fuck did you do?" Hulk asked.

"I shot him in the knee," Max said confused. "He knows more than he is letting on."

"I meant with Morgan."

"He pushed me over the line and I needed to make a point to Robert. Russo is next."

"What point?"

"That I am not fucking around. They detonated a nuclear bomb on Australian soil and tried to do the same here and in America. They killed thousands of people all so they could take over the world or at least parts of it by building terror and fear. The same terror and fear they are seeking to use to get rid of annoyances like government and democracy. It is all so they could take power for themselves and impose their will on the people. And, they killed my fiancé and best friend. I will do whatever it takes to find every last one of them and put them in the ground."

"You can't kill someone who is tied to a chair, Max, especially when that person is a world leader."

"He's not a world leader, he was a terrorist."

Hulk paused for a moment at the thought.

"This is what you trained me to do, Hulk, and it is exactly what I am going to do," Max said. "You needed someone who could think like them, someone who could get in their heads and act like them. Someone willing to do whatever it took to achieve the mission. They need to know I am capable of it and they need to believe it. Everyone needs to believe it. And, with this they can. They seek to damage the world, we seek to preserve it. Every terrorist in the world needs to know if they fuck with us, we will kill them, regardless of who they are and what they are hiding behind. There is no place they can hide and I am going to show them."

Hulk just stared at Max.

"These people know nothing but strength," Hulk said mostly to himself in thought before turning to Max. "Do what you have to. I will deal with the fallout, but Max, this is not a blank cheque, there are limitations of what even I can get done. We need proof and we need to be sure."

"I understand, Hulk," Max agreed. "You know I will do what it takes to get the job done."

"You were right when you said this is why I hired you. Go do your job."

Max turned and walked back towards Robert's cell without another word.

"Hermes, drag Russo in here, will you?" Max called over his shoulder.

Robert looked up in horror as Max walked back into the holding cell.

"You see, Robert," Max said confidently walking over and placing a hand on Robert's mutilated knee. "I have just been given the go ahead to do whatever I like to you."

Max squeezed Robert's bleeding and damaged knee causing him to wildly thrash about and scream. Tears streamed down his reddening face as the agony took hold. Max slammed his head down on Robert's nose, breaking it and sending blood gushing from his nostrils and the large cut which had instantly split open on the bridge of the old man's nose. Robert groaned and his body ached as pain shot from his nose and knee flooding his brain.

"The pain stops when you give me names and locations," Max said as Blake dragged Russo into the room. "Who is the king?"

"Ask her!" Robert yelled looking to Russo. "She knows her much better than I do."

Russo looked at Robert with fear-filled eyes, her trust betrayed and dread washing over her. She looked to Morgan's slumped over body and saw for the first-time what Max was truly capable of, and now the burning anger in his eyes was focused on her. She tried to pull away, but she was tied tightly to the metal chair.

"Who is the king?" Max asked Russo while levelling his pistol at Robert's head. "I will give you ten seconds before I put a bullet in Robert's head, then turn my full attention on you. Ten. Nine."

"I cannot tell you who she is," Russo protested.

"Eight," Max said, "seven."

"It is her girlfriend!" Robert screamed.

"It is true," Russo conceded, "and, you of all people should understand why I will not say her name. You lost your fiancé, Agent Shaw. What would you have done to protect him?"

"Anything," Max accepted calmly before shouting, "but, you and your girlfriend killed him. So, give me a fucking name!"

Robert squirmed in his chair trying to get clear of the gun. Russo sat staring at Max cold as ice.

"Six," Max said, "five, four, three."

"It is Victoria!" Robert yelled. "Princess Victoria is the king!"

Max watched Russo's eyes change and he knew in that instant it was true.

"The Duchess of Cambridge wants to kill her own father and take power?" Max asked.

"Yes," Robert said defeated.

"You son of a bitch, Robert!" Russo screamed. "I hope he fucking kills you, because if he doesn't, I will."

"Get her out of here!" Max ordered.

Blake dragged Russo out, the metal chair scrapping on the concrete. She hurled abuse at Robert the whole way and with tears streaming down her face.

"Don't you touch her!" Russo yelled at Max. "I will find you and kill you too!"

Max heard the holding cell door slam shut and Russo's threats were silenced.

"You are going to tell me everything, start to finish, on Victoria and The Sixteen," Max said clicking the hammer back on his pistol and pointing it at Robert's head and placing his mobile on Robert's lap to record. "Start talking."

Chapter Thirty-Three

Television and radio stations around the world had been on a constant loop of broadcasts reporting on the terror events in London and the attack in Australia. Rumours of a failed attack in the United States were starting to spread between the networks and the first stories were starting to appear on global news sites. Countless commentators were speculating on the group responsible and what they could be planning next. International terror experts, former military chiefs and special advisers to presidents and world leaders were lining up for interviews.

Right-leaning political commentators, like Kevin Phelps, were praising Australia's tough new terror laws and the attack was emboldening their claims. They were preaching vast crackdowns and restrictions on immigration, more checks on foreigners and even some suggesting rounding up Arab Australians in concentration camps until they were cleared by the intelligence services.

More left-leaning pundits were arguing the exact opposite and blaming the right for inflaming tensions and even encouraging terror. They argued that the right-wing media was manufacturing or simply ignoring evidence to place the blame on Muslims and other minorities. Riots were breaking out in the streets of major cities in Australia and there were growing numbers of people filling the streets in London and throughout the United Kingdom, defying the curfew.

The Sixteen was winning. Fear was spreading and hate was rising.

The political commentators on all sides were in agreement on one thing though, a single question – where are our leaders? It had been several hours since the attacks on the convention centre and the detonation in Perth, but the world was yet to hear from either the British or Australian Prime Minister and people were starting to speculate on their fates.

Within a matter of seconds of each other, news site and stations began to broadcast a live feed coming in from an unknown source which showed the bound and bloodied British Royal Family. His Majesty the King was sitting bound to an ornate chair with blood dripping from his mouth. His shoulders were gently rising and falling with his shallow breaths. His son, the Prince of Wales, heir to the throne and future leader of the Commonwealth was bound next to him. It was clear he had also been beaten. His breathing looked strained. He was unconscious and his head was slumped forward with his chin resting on his chest.

Finally, in the third chair sat Princess Victoria, the Duchess of Cambridge, third in line to the throne behind her brother and niece. She too looked beaten, but she was conscious. Behind them hung a black flag with white Arabic writing.

"Today, we claim victory in the fight for our cause," a man said entering the shot dressed head to toe in black combat gear and balaclava which obscured his face. *"Allah, has seen fit to bless us with the presence of the British Royal Family and has asked me to be His weapon in the spread of His Will on earth. You have already seen the success we have had today in the death of hundreds, if not, thousands of Australian infidels in Perth from the detonation of a nuclear device on their soil. We have also attacked the Commonwealth Heads of Government Meeting killing many leaders and their infidel supporters and staff. The most protected people in your countries are not safe from us and your intelligence and defence agencies have failed to protect you. Our reach is far and our hands never idle. We will succeed in bringing on a global caliphate and as you can see your pathetic laws and institutions cannot stop us."*

"You will never win!" Princess Victoria mumbled defiantly. *"Our nation and the Commonwealth will never fail. We will hunt you down and show you how freedom and justice work."*

The man walked over and backhanded the Princess.

"Filthy, infidel whore!" he spat. *"You have no right to speak to me!"*

"Go fuck yourself!" Princess Victoria yelled. *"I am third in line to the throne and I know better than some Middle-Eastern terrorist how this country and the nations which support freedom work. You will never win and I have every right to say whatever I like, whenever I like, to whomever I like. You will never silence us!"*

"We will see if you remain so sure of that after I kill your father and brother on live television."

"My family serves the Commonwealth and if we are to die for our people, then so be it."

"What about Princess Scarlett?" the man said nodding to someone off screen.

The ten-year-old daughter of the Prince of Wales was dragged into the room by a man dressed all in black. The little girl was crying and tried to reach for her father, but was pulled back.

"You son of a bitch!" Princess Victoria said trashing about in her chair. *"Don't you touch her."*

The footage cut away and the anchors of the various channels came back on with shocked expressions, some were even in tears from what they had just witnessed. It took a while for some of the commentators to begin to speak, but not so, for Kevin Phelps, he launched into an explosive tirade within seconds.

"Our hearts go out to the Royal Family and to all our brothers and sisters across this great Commonwealth," Phelps said. *"It has already been a dark day, but it seems the darkness is continuing to spread. As I predicted, these devastating attacks are in fact the work of Arab fundamentalists. I have been criticised in recent hours for this prediction, but this footage shows my vindication. This is exactly what I have been saying. We need to bring in laws which weed these people out and remove them from society. They cannot be allowed to continue spreading their hate and their abhorrent views on the world. We have seen what they are capable of. What did the terrorist say, 'our reach is far and our hands never idle'. They will never stop. We need to fight fire with fire and we need to*

do so now. This is a fight we must take and it is a fight we must win. For God, for the Commonwealth and for the very survival of the world we know and love."

"As we reported earlier," Phelps continued. *"There was an attempted bomb attack in London. I have since heard from one of my trusted sources that the Australian Intelligence Service stopped the device from detonating in downtown London, only blocks from Buckingham Palace. It is clear from the events of today that the Royal Family, the very foundation stone of our democracy and the Commonwealth, has been a target from the beginning. And, how real is the threat? Well, other than the broadcast we just witnessed, I can confirm that a nuclear device, similar to that which was successfully disarmed here in London, has detonated in Perth. The death toll is unknown at this stage, but we do know it had wiped out the Perth airport and parts of the surrounding suburbs. The best guess is somewhere in the high-hundreds from the initial blast and the potential for thousands more from the fallout. This is a devastating day for the world and our prayers are with all Australians as they come to terms with the terrible event that has just taken place on their soil."*

"I have heard people are taking to the streets," Phelps bellowed slapping the table. *"And, I encourage you all to do so! We need to show our leaders, wherever they are hiding, that they cannot sit back and let these people win. It might not be popular or socially acceptable to all the little lefty latte sippers out there, but we should be rounding up Arabs and anyone who does not subscribe to our way of life and we should be forcing them to prove their allegiance to our nation or putting them back on a boat to where they came from. Terrorism in all its forms is a failure of humanity, failure of good in the fight over evil and a failure of government to act. I, for one, am sick of inaction and I call on Prime Minister Morgan and Prime Minister Kirby to stand up and address their nations and the world, and tell us exactly how they plan to put these terrorists out of action."*

"I hope for all our sakes that the Prime Ministers are working closely with our intelligence agencies to find the Royal Family and rescue them," Phelps said calming down slightly, before revving up again. *"His Majesty, by the Grace of God, of the United Kingdom of Great Britain and Northern Ireland, and of his other Realms and Territories, King, Head of the Commonwealth, Defender of the Faith. How is it possible this great man has been captured and beaten to within an inch of his life? And for his son, the charismatic and may I say personal friend of mine, the Prince of Wales, to suffer the same fate? Let alone the fact these animals also possess the King's only granddaughter, Princess Scarlett, who we saw at the end of that footage in tears – explain to me how this is possible!"*

"But, there is something else I would like to discuss from the footage we just witnessed," Phelps noted. *"Sadly, the terrorists have also captured and beaten the Duchess of Cambridge, Princess Victoria. This proud and strong woman, who gave a remarkable speech at the CHOGM meeting about the strength of the Commonwealth. Well, she just gave those terrorist arseholes a little bit of that trademarked strength, standing up to them, even though she was bound and bruised and bleeding. She said to these terrorist vultures, who have shone how manly they are by tying up a defenceless woman, she said exactly what we were all thinking – you will not win, the Commonwealth will prevail and the people will rise up against you. She also demonstrated the strength and leadership we have all come to respect and love from this Royal Family, and the dedication she and her family have for our nations, when she said they were willing to die for us. Talk about devotion to duty and to the people. Like her father and brother, Princess Victoria is a true Head of the Commonwealth and Defender of the Faith, and our thoughts and prayers are with her and her family in their hour of need."*

Chapter Thirty-Four

Max, Kate and Jonnie had parked their four-wheel drive in thick bushland a few blocks away from the Guildford Bunker. The bunker was buried under Guildford Castle. Under the security arrangements put in place during the crisis, the land was fenced off behind a large metal barricade and police had been roaming the grounds. Max and Kate could see some of the police officers' bodies strewn about the grasslands as they approached part of the fence near an overgrown section of bushes. In the police officers' place patrolling the scenic fields were guards from The Sixteen dressed in full combat uniforms and heavily armed.

"Bravo," Max whispered into his comms unit. "Are you in position?"

"Yes, Prince," Jonnie responded from his position on the roof of a nearby building. *"I count twenty in the fields. In your direct line there are five, plus two at the nearest door to the castle."*

"Roger that. Give us a few minutes. Let us know if there are any changes."

"Ack."

Max and Kate began snipping through the wire fence. They cut a slit low and parallel to the ground then down to the grass creating a narrow space to crawl under.

"We're ready," Max said putting the plyers back in his vest.

"Roger that," Jonnie acknowledged, *"no changes. They are all just holding their positions."*

"Got it," Max noted crawling under the fence. "We are moving."

"I see you. Target one, fifty metres, straight ahead, behind a small row of tulips. You will need to take down, the second target at the same time. He is sixty metres, at your one o'clock behind the same row of flowers."

"Ack," Max acknowledged army crawling fast beside Kate across the field to cover behind some concrete sculptures. "You get the guy on the left."

"With pleasure," Kate said flicking off her safety. "On your mark."

"Move, now," Max ordered sprinting out from behind the sculpture and running as hard and fast as he could.

He covered the green grass in his path in seconds and leapt the row of yellow flowers. As he landed, he spun to his right and fired two shots into the guard from his silenced pistol. He heard the sharp hisses of Kate's silenced pistol seconds before his own. The two agents pulled their respective dead targets in behind a row of hedges.

"One of the guards is looking in your direction," Jonnie explained. *"Do you want me to take him down?"*

"Not yet," Max said. "Your rifle is silenced, but it is not silent. Just tell me where."

"At your nine, about halfway to the castle. Near the fountain."

Max ducked his head around the hedge and saw the guard, he was standing and looking in their direction, but was not moving. Max holstered his pistol, the guard was beyond its range and dragged his MP5 over his shoulder. He rested the butt against his shoulder and sighted in the guard through the short scope. He fired two shots and the bullets spat from the silenced barrel. The guard fell backwards into the fountain.

"Move now," Jonnie directed. *"Two to go, beyond the fountain, one at your ten, the other at your two."*

"Got it, moving," Max said. "Take the one on the left, Alpha."

"Will do," Kate agreed running hard across the open space.

As Max and Kate got closer to the fountain, they saw the waters were starting to run red with the blood of the fallen guard. Unfortunately, they were not the only ones to see it. The guards near the castle door saw it too, as did the two remaining guards in the fields. Then they sighted Max and Kate running in their direction. Max and Kate fired at the two guards on the lawns, taking down their targets before they had a chance to reach for their weapons. As they turned for the door guards, they saw them raising their rifles. It would be close, but then Max heard two shots in quick succession ring out. He watched as the two door guards fell to the ground.

"Thanks, Bravo," Max said looking back to the building were Jonnie was hold up. "Any movement from the shots?"

"Yes, boss," Jonnie lamented. *"I'm sorry, I didn't think you would make it in time."*

"It's okay, you did the right thing. Thanks. Now, where are they?"

"Two coming in from the left at Alpha's ten and eight. Three from your right between your two and four."

"Roger that. Hold off unless we get stuck."

"Ack."

Max and Kate took cover behind sculptures on their respective sides of the field. Max fired his MP5 wounding one of the guards charging in his direction. He fell to the ground clutching his neck, even from a distance Max saw how much blood he was losing, he would die quickly. He turned his gun towards the closest guard who was covering the ground between them quickly. Max fired, but the guard was sidestepping and dodging. He flicked the small lever on his MP5 to fully automatic and unleashed a burst of fire in a line at the guard. Two bullets struck the guard in the chest as he tried to dodge the incoming fire. The second bullet hit a smoke grenade in the guard's vest sending a pillar of smoke up into his face as he fell to the ground.

Max took the chance while the final guard was distracted to run towards the door of the castle. He fired a burst at the third guard hitting him in the legs. As he fell, he fired wildly at Max, but Max was behind the cover of another sculpture which splintered and cracked from the bullet impacts. Max waited patiently for the weapon to run dry then he sprung out from cover and fired two shots into the fallen guard's face and ran for the door of the castle.

Meanwhile, Kate had successfully killed both her attackers. The first was a clean shot between his eyes and the second was hit in the shoulder and the neck. She was waiting for Max near the door. When he arrived, she opened it and stormed in moving to the left, while he moved to the right.

Inside the old castle, they found multiple guards leaning against walls, sitting on old antique furniture and generally milling about oblivious to the world outside. Max and Kate opened fire, mowing down guards left and right. The guards were startled at first, giving Max and Kate time to take several of them down, but they recovered quickly and began firing. The two agents dived for cover behind an old table which Kate kicked over with one hard kick. Bullets slammed into the solid wooden tabletop, they would not last long behind it at this rate of fire. Kate threw two flashbang grenades over their makeshift barricade. The grenades bounced and clanged on furniture and across the centuries old concrete floor, then bang, bang. Kate and Max flung their weapons up over the tabletop and opened fire taking down four more guards.

A small group of attackers came running down the stairs to Max's right. He grabbed Kate and dragged her in the opposite direction, behind the wall of a small room. There was only one door and they had just used it, and no windows. They took it in turns of firing and reloading for several minutes before they heard Jonnie's voice on their comms units.

"Prince, Alpha," Jonnie asked. *"Still with me?"*

"Yes, kid," Max replied. "What is it?"

"You've got movement all around you, the guards outside are making their way towards the castle. Should I open fire?"

"Fuck yes, take them down!"

"With pleasure, sir," Jonnie said firing his sniper rifle and taking down his first target.

"Prince," Blake said. *"It's Hermes. They have started the broadcast. Can you get to the bunker?"*

"We are pinned down at the moment, but we are trying to break through," Max explained. "What's happening on the broadcast?"

"The terrorists are threatening to kill the King and his family on live television. They say they are going to do it within minutes."

"Why the delay?"

"I guess they are hoping more sites and channels start broadcasting it."

"Why are the stations even broadcasting it? I thought there were rules against that?"

"Some have chosen not to and are giving updates, but there are a lot of online sites carrying it. I guess the terrorists are hoping for a big audience."

"Fuck, okay, well, we will do our best."

"I know you will."

"We have got to move!" Max said. "Any thoughts?"

"A couple," Kate said retrieving a grenade from her vest. "I brought these along in case we needed to break the vault door."

"Hermes, you still there?"

"Yes, Prince, go ahead," Blake said.

"Have you got the code to the vault door?"

"Yes, Juliet, Delta, Foxtrot, Whiskey, one, seven, one, eight."

"Thanks," Max smiled turning to Kate. "You know what to do."

Kate hurled the first grenade out into the large open room just as several guards stormed in from outside. There were screams and shouts and cursing as the guards tried to run from the grenade, but it was no use. It exploded ripping the furniture into lethal projectiles and tearing the guards apart. Three of the guards standing closest to the grenade lost limbs in the explosion.

"Let's move," Max ordered heading back into the main room.

The two agents killed a couple of guards who had not died in the blast as they ran for the stairwell down to the bunker. As they arrived at the stairs, Max started down as several guards came in through another door behind them. A bullet hit Kate in the shoulder.

"You fucking prick!" Kate roared turning around and unloading a magazine into the guards. "Go, Prince, I will hold these arseholes off."

"You sure?" Max asked.

"I'll be fine, get your arse down there and save the day."

Max gave Kate his MP5 and spare magazines, and she handed him the spare grenade, before he jumped down the stairs four at a time, stopping on each platform to check the way was clear with his pistol. He found the first guard on the second level down and shot him twice in the head. Max passed him before he hit the ground. He killed two more guards on the decent before his pistol clicked dry. He loaded his last magazine into the gun as he jumped down the final set of stairs. As he hit the last platform, he saw the vault door in his path. He ran forward and was entering the code when he was hit across the back with a metal bar.

Max dropped his pistol and it scattered along the ground. He fell forward in pain, catching himself on the bar which rose from the floor to hold the keypad. He moved to his left as the metal bar slammed down on the keypad, shattering it. Max fell to the floor and rolled to the left just as Bradley smashed the crowbar down on the concrete where Max had been moments before.

He rolled as the bar crashed down beside him again, but this time when it hit, he rolled back over it ripping it from Bradley's grasp. He kicked Bradley's legs sweeping them out from under him. Max scrambled, turning around and climbing on top of Bradley.

The two traded punches as they wrestled on the floor. Bradley found his way on top of Max and started rapidly throwing punches at him. Max blocked most, but the occasional one got through. Max groaned as the fists hit his face. He dodged left and Bradley punched the concrete next to his head. He screamed in pain as the shock ran up his arm and Max hoped he had broken a finger or knuckle. Max saw his opening and threw a sharp jab into Bradley's broken jaw sending him backwards writhing in pain, clutching his jaw. Max got to his feet as Bradley stood groggily shaking his head.

"That looks like it would be painful," Max laughed. "Should we see how tough you really are?"

"Fuck you," Bradley said through wired teeth and obvious pain. "I am going to kill you."

"We will see," Max said leaping forward and throwing several punches.

The two men dodged and ducked, throwing punches as they bounced around the small foyer in front of the bunker. They traded blows. Left hook, right jab, head, chest. Max threw an uppercut to Bradley's ribs winding him and forcing him to hunch over. Max took his chance and jumped off his left foot into the air and slammed his right fist down on Bradley's head. Bradley fell to the ground on all fours. Max moved in to punch Bradley in the back of the head to knock him out, but before he could Bradley grabbed his legs and pulled them out from under him. Max fell to the ground and was barely able to put an arm behind his head in time to break his fall.

He hit hard, but his forearm took most of the blow saving his head. Bradley crawled forward straddling Max and throwing savage blows into Max's ribs. Max pulled his arms forward trying to block the punches, but he was sure at least one of his ribs had broken. He winced in pain with every impact. Max got the briefest moment when Bradley stopped to adjust his position and Max took it, punching Bradley in the jaw again. Bradley screamed in pain. Max took the chance during the reprieve to draw his hunting knife and he stabbed it into Bradley's side. It pierced between two ribs and Max twisted it sending agonising pain through Bradley's body. Bradley threw his head forward violently smashing into Max's nose and breaking it. Blood spilt down his face and into his mouth. Bradley pulled the knife out and lowered himself onto its handle trying to stab Max, but Max grabbed his wrists and held him off. The knife tip pierced his shirt, before finally sliding into his shoulder. Max screamed in pain as he watched Bradley's pain turn to a smile.

"How tough am I now?" Bradley asked smugly through his clenched jaw. "How tough are you?"

Max headbutted Bradley then kneed him in the balls. He pulled out the knife as Bradley clutched his groin and got to his feet. His ribs ached and his shoulder throbbed in searing pain. He spat blood on the floor and walked towards Bradley who was getting to his feet. Max kicked him in the face dropping him back to the concrete then he dived on top of him. Bradley tried to fight back, but the wound in his side was bleeding heavily and he was losing his strength. Max clutched his knife above Bradley's chest and leaned his body on the heal. Bradley tried with all his remaining strength to stop the knife, but it was no use. Max drove the knife down into Bradley's chest, blood dribbled from both sides of Bradley's mouth before his eyes went wide and his heart stopped beating.

Max got back to his feet and walked to the keypad. Bradley had shattered it, he could not enter the code. He grabbed the grenade Kate had given him and looked for a place to rest it near the lock, but there was nothing. He looked around and saw Bradley's body. He dragged it towards the vault-like bunker door and propped it against the steel. He pulled the pin on the grenade wedged it behind Bradley and ran. He bounded up the stairs and rounded onto the second set before dropping to the ground and curling into a ball behind the concrete and blocking his ears. The grenade exploded and Max flew back down the stairs as fast as he could move with his injuries.

The bunker door was damaged and a section of the metal had fallen away exposing the mechanisms. Max found the first set of cogs and twisted them with his knife until they fell away. There was an electronic panel with a series of wires coming from it and eight dials. The first four had twenty-six groves and the second set had ten. Max used the tip of his knife to move the groves into place. He counted the clicks as they went.

Alpha, one, Bravo, two, Charlie, three. Until he got to ten, J, Juliet. He continued down the line until he had manually entered the code Blake had given him.

The electronic mechanisms kicked in and the bolts all slid back into the door. There was a hiss as air escaped around the door and it opened. Max sheathed his knife and picked up his pistol. He clicked off the safety and made his way into the bunker. He swept room by room, clearing as he moved. He took down four guards with headshots by the third room. A guard ran around the corner in front of him and he shot him three times. He stumbled, but kept moving forward, so Max shot him again. As Max made his way to the main room, he could hear the terrorist talking to the camera. He was sprouting hate and taking credit for The Sixteen's actions. Max knew he was only there to wear the blame. Middle Eastern terrorists would be blamed for everything they had done and this was live proof. It was all part of The Sixteen's plan.

Max rounded the corner, his arm hanging by his side from the shoulder wound. Blood was dripping from his fingertips. He shot two of the guards, one of them fell knocking over the camera and breaking a small piece off. Anyone watching the footage could now only see the King and Prince of Wales who were both still unconscious, but breathing and the terrorist who had been talking to the camera standing behind them. They would not have heard anything though, because the microphone was the piece which broke off.

Max holstered his pistol as the unarmed terrorist screamed abuse at him. He drew his knife and in one fluid movement he threw the knife. It flew end over end through the air until it hit the terrorist in the throat. For those watching at home, all they saw was the terrorist shouting at someone, before he dropped to the ground clutching his neck with a hunting knife sticking out of it and then he bled out on live television.

"Oh, thank God!" Princess Victoria exclaimed. "You have come to save us. How wonderful. Please, please untie my father and brother. They need urgent care. My niece, have you seen her?"

"You can cut the shit right now," Max dismissed. "I know you are in on it, Your Royal Highness. I know you are the one calling all the shots. You are the king, the leader of The Sixteen. You are responsible for the deaths of thousands of people, including my best friend only today and my fiancé, several long and painful years ago. You have lost."

"Well, Agent Shaw, it is nice to finally meet you in person," Victoria said her gaze and tone turning to ice. "You have caused me considerable trouble, unravelling my plans. Years I have spent working on this. From business takeovers and political uprisings, to orchestrating scandals in the previous Royal Family forcing them out of the palace, I have had a hand in it all. This was my day of triumph, but at every turn you have seen fit to get in my way. If I could do it all over again, I think the one change I would make is to not allow them to kill your boyfriend, Lincoln, was it?"

"His name was Lachlan."

"Lachlan. Well, Lachlan's death really was a fuck up on Shadow's behalf. It did not stop you like he claimed it would. I now know it drove you and gave you purpose. Not to worry though, you will be joining your little dead fiancé soon. Although that is hindsight, in reality now that I can see the look on your face and the pain in your eyes, and in light of all the trouble you have caused me, I am glad he is dead!"

Victoria stood up and swung her arms around. She had not been tied up at all. She had a pistol in her hand and as soon as it was level she fired at Max, hitting him in the leg. He dropped to one knee, drew his pistol and fired his last shot. The bullet found its mark, right between her eyes. She stood lifeless, a blank stare on her face, then she collapsed on the floor. Anyone watching the footage would not have seen Max, but they would have seen Princess Victoria drop to the carpet in front of the camera with blood trickling down her forehead from the bullet hole.

Max fell to his knees, partly from blood loss, but mostly from his overwhelming emotions. Tears streamed down his cheeks, it was over, he finally had killed the person who was ultimately responsible for Lachlan's death. Years of heartache and torture and pain came rushing out. He pictured Lachlan lying dying in his arms and felt the distress all over again. He remembered the first time they met at college and their first kiss. And, he recalled the incredible happiness he felt when Lachlan had said yes after he proposed. He sobbed uncontrollably.

A short time later, his thoughts were interrupted by his comms unit.

"Prince, are you there?" Blake asked.

Max took a minute to compose himself before he answered.

"Yeah, mate, I'm here," Max replied.

"You need to get back here right away. The footage is already going viral. Phones are running off the hook and Hulk's angrier than I have ever seen him."

"Why?"

"You just killed the third in line to the throne on live television."

"She pulled a gun on me and she's a fucking terrorist! Let alone the fact she admitted to being involved."

"We could not hear the conversation, something happened to the sound. All we saw was the camera fall, the terrorist get hit in the neck with your knife, then finally the Princess hit the floor out of nowhere with a bullet hole in her head."

"I'm telling you the truth, Hermes."

"I am sure you are, but after Morgan and the Princess we need you back to be debriefed. MI6 is ready to tear the High Commission to the ground to get our evidence and to speak to you. They are pissed we acted without them and the Ministers in both countries are already starting to ask questions about due process and legal procedure."

"That didn't take long."

"You need to come in, Max."

"Roger that."

"See you soon."

Kate walked in behind Max and patted him on the back.

"How you going, kid?" Kate asked helping Max to his feet. "You look fucked."

"I have been better," Max laughed. "But, I will pull through."

"You are not going back, are you?"

"No."

"What are you going to do?"

"I am going to find the rest of them."

"And, kill them?"

"Yes."

"As far as I'm concerned, you are a fucking hero! Fuck due process! This bitch needed a bullet and so do the rest of them. Get out of here, kid. I will get the King and Prince of Wales back to the palace with Jonnie."

"Thanks, Kate."

"Will we see you again?"

"I'm not sure yet. I am going away for a while."

"Okay, kid. Happy hunting. Take some time, but come back when you are ready, we need you."

"Thanks, Kate," Max said hugging Kate with his good arm.

Max limped out of the bunker and up the stairs. His body was aching, each step felt like an impossible challenge. As he got to the top of the stairs, Jonnie walked in. There were bodies strewn everywhere.

"Jesus, looks like a warzone in here," Jonnie exclaimed before running over to help Max. "Fuck, are you okay, boss?"

"I'll be fine, kid," Max said smiling through the pain.

"Here let me help you," Jonnie said clutching Max's arm.

"I'm okay, Jonnie. Head down to the bunker and help Kate secure the Royals."

"Are you sure? You don't look so good."

"I'm sure, kid. I will meet you in the car."

"Okay, boss, sing out if you need anything," Jonnie said eagerly running off down the stairs.

Max walked out of the castle into the morning sunshine and closed his eyes letting the warmth soak into his skin. He breathed out, opened his eyes and headed for the closest car.

Epilogue

Max sat in a quiet little café sipping his coffee and finishing his breakfast. His wounds had healed and his skin was darker from months in the sun. He had continued to grow his beard, but trimmed and maintained it. His hair was longer too and was tied in a knot at the top of his head. He had lost weight and he felt fitter than he had been in years. He was wearing black skinny leg jeans and a tight-fitting dark purple t-shirt, and his reflective Oakley's sat on his forehead.

He was reading the London Times. Even with the passage of several months, the paper was still reporting on the incidents which had taken place. The AIS public relations team had been working in overdrive to get relevant and approved information out to the public. Prime Minister Kirby had given statements and evidence on the record proving Morgan was involved. The press was having a field day with the story, but there were more than a few journalists and civil rights activists calling for the spy who shot the former Prime Minister to be arrested for breaching his rights to trial. Others were calling the assassin a hero. Regardless of their point of view, they were united by one thing, they were calling for the assassin to come forward and provide statements to the public and to the courts.

When he left the castle, Max had thrown his guns, knife and phone into the river. He made his way to his own secret safehouse which he kept in London in case he ever needed to go on the run. He stitched his cuts then showered. He let the hot water run over his injured body, it ran pink from his blood, staining the white tiles. He cried again as the pain of Lachlan's loss washed over him. His tears fell down his cheeks and washed away with the bloodied water.

The following day, he bandaged his wounds as best as he could and dressed in a new suit. He met up with the manager of a local bank who had agreed to let him access his safe deposit box even though the bank, with the rest of London, was still closed as the city tried to clean up and come to grips with what had happened. Max kept deposit boxes exactly like this in many cities around the world in case operations went south. He collected two fake passports and some cash, as well as credit cards linked to those identities. He also pulled out a clean phone and international sim card.

Max fled to Greece and spent the next few months recovering and laying low. His only regret was missing Flash's funeral. He called Jane and apologised. He explained vaguely why he was not there, but she said she did not need an explanation. She said if he was chasing those responsible for Flash's death, he had her forgiveness and blessing. She told him to look after himself because it is what she wanted as his friend and she knew it is what Flash would want as his best friend.

Max had made his way back to London, once his body had healed and he had rehabilitated his shoulder. He had spent the long months in relative isolation gathering all the information he needed. He had not spoken to anyone from AIS since he walked out of the castle, but he did not need to, he had enough contacts and experience to find what he was looking for.

He finished his coffee and put his daggy leather bag over his shoulder. He walked through the streets blending in with the London hipster crowd until he arrived at a side alley which he entered. He followed the alley past a row of dumpsters until he found the door he was looking for. He checked over his shoulder and down the alley, then picked the lock. He moved into the building and clicked the door shut behind him. He made his way across the parking garage and found the elevator which he took to the third floor.

Max casually walked through the busy hallway as if he had all the time in the world and like he owned the building, so no one would take a second look at him. He slipped into the security room and quickly knocked out the two on-duty guards. He watched the little security monitor showing footage from the room where is target was located for a minute and listened to the conversation. Satisfied, he shut off the building's closed-circuit security cameras and uploaded a virus to lock the system for thirty minutes, giving himself enough time to get in and out. He took one of the guard's security access cards then headed back to the elevator.

When the elevator reached the thirty-first floor, Max walked out into the hallway and dialled a pre-set number on his phone. When it connected it triggered the second stage of the virus he had uploaded, shutting down the lights, air-conditioning and all power outlets in the building. He ducked into a small room and retrieved a balaclava from his bag. He put it on, pulled out his pistol then headed into a nearby room.

Inside the room, people were shouting and rushing about guided by the dim emergency lighting. A row of men and women sat in front of a bank of dead computers and monitors, and no matter which button they pushed the system would not respond. Max snuck into the room unnoticed and stood at the back. He looked beyond the computers and monitors through the glass to the television studio. The woman he had been watching on the security monitor had walked into the studio. She was irate, sitting at the desk demanding answers to why she was not going on air and the producers and staff could not answer, which was making her even more frustrated.

Max walked into the studio, following the shadows around the wall and found a position in the darkness. He waited until the aides and producers were clear then lined up his shot. He squeezed the trigger twice in quick succession. The bullets cut through the air and lodged in Janelle Rhodes' head and neck.

There was a moment of pause in the studio as her lifeless body wavered a few seconds, before falling out of the chair and onto the cold concrete floor. Screams echoed out and people ran from the room, while some searched for the source, the rest just ran in panic. Max used the chaos to dial another number and within seconds his uploaded virus had set off the fire alarms. People ran from the building and Max put the gun back in his bag. When the studio was cleared, he walked over and sat a small voice recorder next to her body.

The door to the studio opened and Kevin Phelps walked in. He saw Janelle's body lying on the floor and saw Max in his balaclava, and he froze.

"I heard you thanking Janelle a few minutes ago for all the tips she has been able to give you over the pass few months," Max said walking towards Phelps. "You have been nominated for a British Journalism Award for your coverage of the events surrounding CHOGM, am I right?"

"Yes," Phelps stammered.

"Did she give you all the background information and tip-offs during those events too?"

"Yes."

"Well, you should know, if you have not figured it out already, that she was involved in all of it. She was part of the same group as the Princess and Prime Minister, and they were terrorists."

"No, she, she was a friend."

"That maybe so, but she was also a terrorist. Maybe you should find some new friends and some new leads. Although, I've left a present for you over there with her. It's a recording proving her role in these events."

"Umm, yes. Umm, okay."

"Have a listen and do with it what you will. You know, come to think of it, this is the quietest I have ever seen you. I like you better this way. So much better than the hate and bullshit you are normally sprouting."

"Wait, just a minute," Phelps said regaining some courage. "I report facts."

"No, Mr Phelps, you spread hate and lies to serve yourself. You are no better than her, but you're not a terrorist, so I can't shoot you."

Max punched Phelps in the face, dropping him to the floor unconscious.

"A punch will have to do," Max said smiling," but when you wake up, I hope you change some of your world views."

Max stepped over Phelps and dialled a number he had not used for a while and hit call.

"It's me," Max said.

"Prince, where are you?" Blake asked. *"Are you okay? Alpha said you were pretty badly injured."*

"I'm fine, Hermes. How are you?"

"Well, we have been struggling to hold back the pressure that is piling up on us to explain everything, but the tide is turning. I'm sure you have seen the press."

"I saw it. It doesn't matter what they think."

"We know what you did was right and we have the proof, but politicians are swayed by public opinion and some of these guys are not letting up yet. They are calling for your head."

"Which is why I left."

"That did not help us much, I will be honest, but I understand your reasons."

"And, Hulk?"

"He is pretty angry at everyone really. He wanted you to at least call in."

"I wanted to give him some plausible deniability."

"We found the Princess's fingerprints on the gun, but some are still questioning her role in all this, especially the family."

"What does that mean?"

"It means you are not safe and clear yet."

"I understand that, they won't find me. We planned for this remember. I disappeared for months and I can and will do it again."

"I know, Prince. What are you going to do?"

"I told you I was going to do my job and that you would know when I had."

"You did."

"Well, that is what I am doing."

"What are you talking about?"

"I am sending you a recording and I have left a copy with the body."

"Whose body?"

"One of the members of The Sixteen."

"Who was it?"

"You will know soon enough. The recording will prove her involvement and guilt."

"What is the recording of?"

"Robert and I had a long chat when you dragged Russo out of the interrogation room that day, before we went to Guilford. He confessed to everything and gave me all the names of The Sixteen's members, including a list of people angling for membership, and their roles within the group. As I said, I left a copy of the relevant section of that recording with the body and I am sending you a copy now."

"It's not the full recording?"

"No. You get the next segment with the next body."

"I'm not sure about this, Prince, maybe we should be arresting these people."

"They had their chance and killed thousands of people. They don't get a second chance, they just die."

"Hulk's already fighting off inquiries and parliamentary committees. Leaving a trail of bodies is not going to help anything."

"Which is why I called you, Blake. He can't know. If he has to appear before the committees he can't lie, this way he doesn't have to."

"Your mind is already made up?"

"Yes. The first one already has a bullet in her brain. No going back now."

"And, if the committees or the Minister or the Hague wants to talk to you or worse someone else involved finds out what you are doing and tries to stop you?"

"They can try to find me if they like. I am doing this, not AIS. The trail stops with me."

"You will be hunted."

"Then let them come after me, if that is what it takes. We can't risk The Sixteen or any offshoots of it rising from the ashes. We need to end them all."

"So, why are you telling me all of this now?"

"Because you are the only person in the world I trust. It was you, Blake, that got me through all of this."

"How do you mean?"

"Remember that night on at the Wool Shed when you came into the shed to check on me?"

"Yes, I remember."

"You placed your hand on top of mine and told me I would make it. Ever since, whenever times were bad and the shit hit the fan, and well let's face it, that's been a lot in the last few years, I think of that moment and you help me through. You helped me when Lachlan was killed and you have always had my back. But, more than any of that, you looked into my eyes in the basement of the embassy when I was at my lowest point and you told me you believed in me. Your faith in me, got me through these last few months and saved me."

"I don't know what to say."

"You don't have to say anything. Just know that if we ever get through all of this and find ourselves together in the same city again, I would like to buy you a drink."

"It's a date."

"I hope so, Blake."

"Well, in that case, you better make the drink a double."

"You got it," Max laughed. "Thank you, Blake. I've got to go now. I will be in touch."

"Max wait, there is something I have wanted to say, but I have never found the right moment to say it…" Blake said but all he heard was silence.

Max had not heard Blake's last comment. He had ended the call and placed the phone back in his pocket. He took off the balaclava and threw it in his bag. He straightened his hair and left the studio.

He took the stairs, finally catching up to some stragglers who were having a hard time navigating their way down without the lifts. He moved past the last of them into the middle of the group and held their pace. When they finally made it to the lobby, Max was simply another member of the crowd exiting the building as the fire brigade arrived with their blaring sirens.

Max used the chaos outside to disappear.

The End.

Max Shaw will return in *Shaw Intervention*.

www.jwpublishing.com.au